Prai...

DAMNATION FALLS

'Wright has a strong sense of place ... Written in a deceptively relaxed style, this is a dark and compelling tale'
Guardian

'Strong characters and Wilkes's laconic narration make *Damnation Falls* a compelling ... saga of family deceit'
Financial Times Magazine

'Wright is a gifted storyteller, with a relaxed style which makes his narrative flow and brings his characters vividly to life'
Sunday Telegraph

'Complex, layered, but never labored, *Damnation Falls* weaves between fact and fiction, the past and the present, truth and lies, without ever missing a beat'
Sydney Morning Herald

RED SKY LAMENT

'Dark, gripping ... One of the joys of Wright's novels is the way he recreates the glamour and fragility of Hollywood in the post-war years'
Sunday Times

'His best and most important political and social statement ... The kind of art that stirs up old memories and pierces the soul'
Chicago Tribune

An intelligent and exciting web of violence and conspiracy ... Excellent writing'
The Guardian

CLEA'S MOON

'Wright's insights into masculinity, vulnerability and the limitations of self-awareness combine to make *Clea's Moon* a truly memorable debut'
Sunday Times

'Excellent, exciting first novel, packed with period details, written from the heart and suffused with rare feeling'
Literary Review

Edward Wright grew up in Arkansas and was a naval officer and a newspaperman before discovering the greater satisfaction of writing fiction. Although transplanted to California, he remains partial to barbecue and bluegrass music. He and his wife, Cathy, live in the Los Angeles area. Visit his website at www.edwardwrightbooks.com.

By Edward Wright

Damnation Falls
Red Sky Lament
The Silver Face
Clea's Moon

DAMNATION FALLS

Edward Wright

An Orion paperback

First published in Great Britain in 2007
by Orion
This paperback edition published in 2008
by Orion Books Ltd,
Orion House, 5 Upper Saint Martin's Lane,
London WC2H 9EA

An Hachette Livre UK company

1 3 5 7 9 10 8 6 4 2

A CIP catalogue record for this book
is available from the British Library.

ISBN 978-0-7528-8184-3

Typeset by Deltatype Ltd, Birkenhead, Merseyside

Printed and bound in Great Britain by
Clays Ltd, St Ives plc

The Orion Publishing Group's policy is to use papers that
are natural, renewable and recyclable products and
made from wood grown in sustainable forests. The logging
and manufacturing processes are expected to conform to
the environmental regulations of the country of origin.

www.orionbooks.co.uk

For my father

ACKNOWLEDGMENTS

This book is fiction, but its locales are real, and most of the sites described here, such as the falls and the bluff-side Colony, have counterparts somewhere in Tennessee – although I may have moved them around. As I looked into the past, Mary Boykin Chesnut's flavorful chronicle of the Civil War years, 'A Diary From Dixie,' was one of the things I found especially helpful. In my travels through present-day Tennessee, Rick and Rosie Fassnacht, of Chattanooga and Beersheba Springs, were gracious hosts, generous with their knowledge of local history. My friend Alan Kessler, M.D., helped me avoid numerous medical errors. Sara O'Keeffe and Jane Wood of Orion have been the editors every writer wants. And the Crime Writers' Association of Great Britain has once again shown me the kind of encouragement every writer needs. My agent, Jane Conway-Gordon, enthusiastically keeps me going on this strange journey, while my wife, Cathy, is the voice that says, 'You can do it better' – and is usually right.

Finally, I want to thank the ex-Army chopper pilot named Tom, who gave me only his first name. He had no direct role in the book, but by sharing his air with me during a life-changing moment about eighty feet underwater off Lahaina Harbor, he allowed me more time to do the things I wanted to do.

ONE

All through my growing-up, my father and I would often tramp through the woods around our small Tennessee town. Once, when I was eleven, I turned up a brass button. It was badly worn and tarnished, but I could make out the faint CSA on it.

My father held it in his hand and looked at it for a long time. Being of the South, and steeped in its history, I didn't need to be told that the letters stood for Confederate States of America and that the button had come from a Southern soldier's uniform. I knew that no battles had been fought there, in our part of the Cumberland Plateau, during that long-ago war, but I had heard other stories.

'Is this from the Burning?' I asked him.

'What do you know about that?' he replied, not taking his eyes off the object.

'Just what people say.'

'Nobody knows if that story is true,' he said deliberately. 'You shouldn't repeat it.'

'I won't,' I said, because I admired my father and wanted him to respect me. 'But where do you guess this comes from?'

'I wouldn't know,' he said, finally looking at me. 'But all kinds of things are buried around us. And whatever's here, one day the earth will give it up.'

You may have heard of me. If you have, you may not want to keep reading, because the word on me is that I have a little trouble with the truth. Well, yes – I have been known to twist things. I've had my fifteen minutes of fame, and when they were over I was tagged with a label that says, *Don't trust this one – he lies*.

So stop reading if you think I'm still playing fast and loose with the facts. But what follows is the straight dope. I've taken the liar's pledge and I want to be believed, more than I want anything else. And besides, if you stop reading, you'll miss out on a good yarn, full of love and lust, friendship and betrayal, trust, deceit, and the taking of lives. All those things, in short, which, for better or worse, make us human.

But let me back up and start, like a good reporter, where things began ...

As he crossed the Capitol Grille dining room, Sonny McMahan exuded power like a sharp cologne.

Diners at nearby tables turned to look at him, lifting their faces as if toward the sun. He flashed his teeth, waved, shook a quick hand here and there. He was a study in sheer alpha male presence, and, watching the spectacle, it was easy to forget for a fleeting moment that he had come to see me.

But then he spotted me, and the wattage of his smile turned even brighter. Eyes fixed on mine, he covered the rest of the distance across the carpeted room in long strides, reaching out a big hand even before he got to me. I found it immensely flattering. I think I was supposed to.

'Hey, bud.' Grabbing my hand in his and my elbow in his other, he squeezed hard. 'Damn.' Moving easily for a large man, he slid into his chair even as the maitre d', catching up, held it for him with a murmured 'Governor.'

'Damn,' he said again, shaking his head. 'Good to see you.'

I was flattered, as I mentioned, but not overwhelmed, and I wanted him to know it. 'So is "Governor" one of those titles you carry with you to the grave?' I asked him. 'Long after you've left office?'

'I imagine so,' Sonny said, flicking his napkin sideways and settling it with a practiced flutter into his lap. 'Governor, Senator, General, chairman of the homecoming committee ...' He cocked his head and squinted – an old Sonny gesture denoting playfulness. 'You're gray, you know that? And you're wounded.'

'I know,' I said, touching the spot in the center of my forehead where four butterfly tapes held together a recent gash. 'This was just a dumb accident. As for the gray, it started in my early thirties. At first it bothered me, then I tried to capitalize on it – you know, the man of the world, the columnist who looks like he's been around. One of my girlfriends called me the Silver Fox for a while, back when the nicknames she gave me were the printable kind.'

We talked for a while about unimportant things, just catching up the way friends do after a long separation, when you want to see how much of your old friend remains and how much has been washed away by time.

As we spoke, I studied him surreptitiously. I had kept up with his career over the years and had even spoken to him on the phone once, when he was governor and I was doing an article for the *Examiner*'s Sunday magazine on the nation's new breed of politicians. But it had been almost twenty years since I had seen him in the flesh.

He was bigger and beefier now, and there were lines at the corners of his eyes and in the gap between his brows. His clothes looked expensive, certainly a change from the Sonny I remembered. So what remained? The same square, well-structured face, a face you might call open were it not for the heavy eyelids that always seemed to be hiding secrets behind them; the big McMahan jaw, which a certain Knoxville hood had broken a knuckle against during one of our high school field trips. And the voice, a husky baritone I would have known anywhere. He had always used it to charm and bluff and bullshit his way around people. In the midst of all his tomfoolery, Sonny's voice was one of the reasons it was hard to dislike him.

Tish, he told me, had a commitment she couldn't escape but would try to join us when she could get away. 'She wanted to see you as much as I did.'

A waiter hovered and took our lunch orders. 'I've heard about this place,' I said to Sonny when the man had left. 'Somebody said that if you want to see Tennessee politicos and all the people who hang around them, the Capitol Grille is ground zero.'

He shrugged. 'I suppose so. There are other places too, more relaxed. But the food here's fine. Fine as frog's hair.'

'That's one of those expressions I haven't heard in Chicago much.' I looked around the room, with its arched ceiling, columns, oak paneling, and well-groomed diners. 'You know all these people?'

'Most of them,' he replied. 'Some staff people from the state-house. Assembly's not in session right now, so no senators or representatives. Some lobbyists, though. A lot of them live here year-round, and they can afford to eat at this place on a regular basis.'

He peered into the distance. 'He's railroads,' he said, pointing to a tall man in a well-cut suit sitting with a good-looking woman. 'I don't know that lovely thing with him, but I know she's not his wife.'

'Do you miss politics?'

He laughed so loudly that some of the nearby diners glanced our way, and I saw a woman roll her eyes and grin at her companion as if to say, *That's Sonny, all right.*

'I'm not out of politics. I'm just out of the kind where you have to get elected. But let's talk about you.' He began buttering a fat roll, and his look turned serious.

'I'm not going to beat around the bush. Damn shame, what happened to you. Tish and me, we've been talking about it. You'd think they'd give you more than one—'

'More than one chance? I guess it works that way in politics,' I said, remembering Sonny's first, unsuccessful, run at statewide office years ago. 'But not in journalism. We get held to a higher standard. Mass murderers and newspapermen. One strike and you're out.'

Sonny looked uncomfortable, silently admitting the truth of what I'd said, but he brightened quickly. 'So what?' he said as the waiter slid his poached eggs and buffalo brisket hash in front of him and a big shrimp salad in front of me. 'Fuck 'em and their higher standard. I want to offer you something to do.'

4

I nodded politely, waiting. He'd hinted at some kind of job offer when he called a few days earlier. And when he sent me a round-trip ticket, curiosity made me get on the plane. I was bored with Chicago, bored with being the former Randall Wilkes, the guy who still drew stares and whispers in bars and restaurants. And so I came to Nashville, to see what my old friend had for me.

'Could you use some work?'

'Maybe.' No sense in sounding desperate.

'Well, how about this? I want to write my memoirs.' He gave the last word an exaggerated pronunciation, as if to say, Listen to me being all French and pretentious. 'And I want you to help.'

I fiddled with my salad. During the flight down, I'd had an idea it would be something like this. Flackerie, as my old pals in the *Examiner* newsroom would call it. Writing for hire. Public relations. Image-shaping. All those things held in scorn by real journalists. The kind I used to be.

'Here it is,' Sonny went on. 'We think it's a good time for a book. Tish even has a title: *McMahan: A Son of the New South*. What do you think?'

'I like it.'

'So now that we've got the title, the rest should be easy,' he said playfully. 'Will you do it?'

I speared another forkful, playing for time. 'What exactly do you see me doing?'

'We want you to write it! I've got a ton of raw material put together by my staff – my whole career, from the day I first put out my shingle through my election to the Assembly and on into the governorship. We'll dump it into your lap, and you write it up in that style of yours. Oh, we've read your column for years. We got it off the *Examiner* website.'

'I'm flattered.' A small red flag fluttered somewhere in my brain cavity. 'Is this a summing-up kind of book or a curtain-raising kind of book?'

'Huh?' Now it was his turn to be coy. He knew exactly what I meant.

'I picked up a copy of the *Tennessean* at the airport when I landed last night. The op-ed page had a column wondering whether you're planning to run for office again, especially after …' I decided not to finish that thought.

He finished it for me. 'After the mess I made of it last time.' There seemed to be no resentment in his grin. A politician must have the hide of a rhino, I reflected.

'Well, they don't know dick,' he said around a mouthful of buffalo hash. 'That piece quoted two unnamed sources in the statehouse, and I know their names. They're both piss-ants. Look—' He paused to wipe his mouth. 'I won't close the door on anything, all right? But I've really enjoyed this last year, being out of the rat race. I'm just a country lawyer—' He caught my amused look. 'All right, a Nashville lawyer. And I'm finding out there's more to life than getting elected.'

'There's making money, for one thing,' I said. 'I read that some of your political friends have steered you into some very nice investments.'

A cloud passed over his face, and I sensed I'd gone too far. He was, after all, still one of the most influential men in the state, governor or not, and he was offering me a job.

The look dissolved. 'Maybe they have,' he grunted. 'No crime in that. But to get back to your question: I can honestly say to you that at this point I have no political ambitions. What's that the Marine says to St. Peter after Guadalcanal? "I've served my time in Hell." You want coffee?' He signaled to the waiter, who was at his side in a second.

'So this isn't a campaign biography,' I said.

'Nope.'

'But it isn't warts-and-all either.'

'Well …' He spread his palms wide, as if to show me he was holding no weapons. 'I did some hell-raising when I was growing up. You were usually there, remember? I don't mind folks knowing about the good times, but if I wanted all my warts to show, what's the point of hiring somebody? What I mean is …' His look turned almost devilish. 'If you want to tell a few lies about me, the good kind, I won't mind.'

'Is that why you picked me? Because I'm good at telling lies?'

I immediately regretted that, and his grim look made it even worse.

'No,' he said patiently. 'Because you're one of the best writers around. *Editor & Publisher* quoted somebody saying that once. And because you're my oldest friend, even if you've had some bad times lately and turned into a prickly son of a bitch.'

'Thank you for your honesty.'

'Don't mention it.' Our coffees arrived, and we began doctoring them. 'So anyway, you can start plowing through all that research stuff any time you want,' he said. 'If there's anything you need—'

'Not so fast,' I interrupted.

He stopped, eyebrows up.

'I don't want to write a puff piece,' I said. 'I want—'

He glanced up, looking across the room for a second. 'Hold that thought,' he said, reaching for my arm. 'You can come over and have dinner with us tonight and tell me exactly what you want. And we'll see if it fits with what I want.'

I started to speak, but he held up his hand. 'I've got to leave you now, I'm afraid. Got to put on my public relations hat, meet with some rich folks, and try to pry some money out of them. But here comes the prettiest former first lady in all of Tennessee. You can say the rest of your speech to her.'

I swivelled around in time to catch a woodsy scent and found my neck enveloped in cashmere. 'Hey, you,' somebody whispered.

There are Tennessee twangs that will take the varnish off your furniture, and there are twangs that come coated in honey and go down like your mother's milk. This was one of the latter. And one that I knew.

I struggled to my feet. Leticia McMahan and I hugged while Sonny looked on approvingly. 'He's making demands already,' he said to her. 'I thought it was time to call up my reserves. Knock some sense into him, will you?'

He turned to me. 'You don't want to say no to her. She's a deadly shot with that little 20-gauge of hers. She bagged more quail on our last hunting trip than I did.' He made a big fist, and tapped my shoulder with it. 'See you tonight. Come hungry.'

As he left, Tish slid into his seat. Two waiters materialized and swiftly cleared away the remains of our lunch, refilled my coffee cup and then, without being asked, brought her a pot of tea and a plate of small scones.

She looked at me for a long time, and her expression – unconcealed warm affection – hit me like a drug. I guess I hadn't been on the receiving end of any looks like that one for a long time, and I needed it.

'Sorry I'm late,' she said, 'but I had to talk to a business group. I skedaddled as soon as it was over.' She poured her tea precisely. Her hands were tanned and strong. Then she looked up at me again. 'How are you, Randall?'

I started to give her the stock answer, or maybe the sarcastic one. But, unlike her husband, Tish had always been one of those known for straight talk.

'I've seen better days.'

She nodded. 'You've gone gray. But I think it looks very distinguished.' She looked at me more closely. 'And you've been hurt.'

I touched the spot on my forehead lightly. 'Just a war wound.'

'Was it connected with what happened to you? At work, I mean.'

She's going to be hard to fool. 'I suppose so. But it's not worth talking about.'

We made small talk for a while, and I studied her, just as I had Sonny. I'd say her husband showed his age. Early forties and still vigorous, although a kid no longer. But Tish ... although she was the same age, it had not withered her one damn bit. She was still ahead on points. The lines edging her eyes were finer than his, and that wonderful jawline looked as if it could cut glass. The only real change I could see was her hair. Once a straightforward brown, it was now streaked with dark gold, all brushed and blown and pouffed. It looked just right for a Nashville woman of affairs and former first lady of the great state of Tennessee.

8

I had no trouble stripping away the years and envisioning the young woman I'd first glimpsed, back on the Vanderbilt campus, as she rushed past me headed for class with an armload of books. I asked a friend about her and was told that the long-legged sprinter with the flyaway hair was named Tish Alcott and that she was vice-president of the Thetas.

I was intrigued enough to find out more about her, which eventually led to … But that's another story.

I tuned back in to the conversation. Tish was talking about Sonny's mother, Faye. 'She's not doing so well. She still lives back home. We tried many times to move her up here, but she wouldn't have it. Now I'm afraid her … well, her mind is slipping. She's as sweet as ever, but she goes in and out. Sometimes she imagines things, like she's having a conversation with Blue. Other times, she's just not there at all.'

'I was sorry to hear about Blue,' I said. 'I saw the story on the wires a few weeks ago. Didn't get many details.'

'Not many of us were sorry.' A look of distaste passed over her face. 'One of his low-life traveling companions said Blue got drunk, fell off a dock, and drowned in the Mississippi a few miles north of Memphis. Newspapers ran it for a day or so and then forgot. Sonny didn't know whether to be happy or sad. Anyway, Blue never was much of a father to him, so …' She let the thought trail off.

I could have risen to his defense, maybe should have. But I let the moment pass.

'Faye's the one we're concerned about,' she went on. 'Sonny worships her. He says he never would have made it to governor if she hadn't pushed him every step of the way.'

'The way I hear it, he owes you a lot for that too. Some people say you're the brains.'

'I know.' She made a sour face. 'I'm the brains behind Sonny. Well, that's crazy. They just say that because he grew up poor and my folks had money. I'm supposed to be some kind of Henry Higgins who took this dumb country boy and molded him into something. Listen, Sonny McMahan just happens to be a natural-born politician, one of the best this state ever saw.'

9

It was easy to talk to her, so I decided to stray into sensitive territory.

'How did he let the governor's office slip through his hands?'

She was ready for that. 'Because we were stupid enough to let him get involved in friendships with some people who were doing business with the state, and the opposition jumped all over it. Although none of it was illegal, it was ethically wrong, and Sonny admitted as much. But the damage was done. It became the big issue of the campaign, and it brought him down.'

She stared into her glass. 'I blame myself as much as I blame him. He usually listens to me, and I should have warned him off. I didn't see it coming.'

'Sonny told me he doesn't have any more political ambitions.'

My expression must have given me away. 'You don't believe him?' she asked.

'I'm a newspaperman,' I said. 'Or was. I like Sonny, but I haven't believed anything a politician told me in years.'

She regarded me for what seemed a long time with a half-smile, as if pondering how much to tell me. Finally she said, 'Sonny's keeping all his options open. He may run for office someday. Then again, he's becoming quite the business investor, and right now he's enjoying the feel of making some real money – the kind of thing that's frowned on while you're governor.'

'I've heard about some of that. Real estate, right?'

She nodded. 'He's partners with some people who are looking at developing the Cumberland Plateau. To hear them talk about it, that area is Tennessee's next big thing. Money's heading in that direction, and Sonny wants some of it to be his.'

'Don't tell me he's going to turn Pilgrim's Rest into a strip mall.'

'I sure hope not,' she said with an exaggerated look of shock. 'I love your old hometown, and he does too. We bought a summer place up in the Colony. Did you know that?'

I shook my head.

'We've got Faye close by, and it's also not far from where your father lives. If you visit him, you could …' She stopped, sensing something in my look.

'My dad and I haven't been on very good terms lately, ever since I got fired. It's hard for him to understand.'

'I'm sorry,' she said, reaching over to pat my hand. 'If your mother were still alive, she'd understand.'

'After kicking my butt, maybe she would.'

'You know you've lost your accent?' she went on, adding a lopsided grin to take the sting out of it. 'All that time up there with the damn Yanks, and you're starting to sound like them.'

'Ouch.'

'You should come home, Randall, at least for a little while. This book could give you the excuse to do that. Maybe you don't get along with your father; that's your business. But Pilgrim's Rest is your hometown too, just like Sonny's. You must have some good memories there.'

'Let's say I'm interested,' I said slowly. 'I wouldn't want my name within a mile of the book.'

She looked ill at ease. 'He doesn't want your name on it,' she said. 'And you know why. He can't afford to—'

'Have any of my dirt rub off on him,' I finished for her. 'I sympathize. I guess we agree on that point, then.'

Her expression relaxed. 'Just do the work, and let Sonny get the credit. It's the kind of thing you do well, anyway – research and writing and bringing a subject to life.'

She wrote something on a pad of paper, tore the sheet off, and passed it to me. It was a dollar sign followed by a number, a fairly large one. She put her palms down on the table, finished with her pitch.

I was impressed. Somewhere between the appeal to come home and the subject of money, she had managed to sway me. 'All right, Tish,' I said. 'I'll do it.'

'Wonderful!' She reached across the table and squeezed my hand hard.

'What do you think about this?' she asked. 'You can work here in Nashville for a week or two, talking to people. Then, when you're ready, you can drive down to Pilgrim's Rest and move into our place in the Colony. We've been thinking of closing it down in the next few weeks, what with winter on the way, but we'll keep it open as long as you want to stay. It'll be your base of operations. You shouldn't have any problems.' She stopped, chewing on her lower lip. The Tish Alcott lips, I recalled, had been one of her more spectacular features.

'Something wrong?'

'No. It's just that we've had a few prowlers around the place, probably just kids from town. You remember the old divide between the town people and the cottage people? Nothing's changed. Anyway, when you move in, just let the police know you're there.'

'Maybe I'll take your little 20-gauge shotgun.'

'It's already on the premises.'

We stepped out into the overcast skies of an early fall day. Downtown Nashville was no Chicago, but it had its own style. The grand Hermitage Hotel, which housed the Capitol Grille, was dwarfed by gleaming high-rises that seemed to have sprouted up from the concrete since I was last here. Up the hill to the north, on Nashville's highest ground, stood the pale limestone bulk of the capitol building, scene of Sonny's triumphs and his last defeat.

Tish's ride, an SUV the color of butterscotch, was delivered, and she drove off after repeating Sonny's dinner invitation and giving me directions. As I stood there, wondering how to spend the intervening hours, I heard a voice.

'Excuse me.' I glanced to my left and saw a man standing at the curb, cell phone at his ear, looking my way. 'Are you Mr. Wilkes?'

He was a little below my height and somewhat younger, with round cheeks, a buzz cut, and a loud off-the-rack sport coat. As strange as it might sound, something about him said cop. I've spent hundreds of hours in the presence of police men and women, from desk sergeants to rookies, plainclothes types to division commanders, and I've learned to pick up the clues they give off.

'That's me,' I said to him.

He held out his cell phone. 'Call for you, sir.'

All right, I was curious. As I moved toward him, I got my feet tangled up – or appeared to – and stepped a little closer than necessary. Then, as I regained my balance, my hand holding the phone swept wide, parting his jacket just enough to give me a glimpse of what nestled beneath his arm.

Hardware.

'Sorry,' I muttered to him. Then, curiosity satisfied, I said hello.

'Hey, bud. I'm still in that meeting, but I just wanted you to know how happy I am you said yes.'

'How the hell did you know I said yes?'

'I got my ways. Randall, boy, I am pleased. I am *well pleased*.'

As he spoke, the sun came out, bouncing off the glass of one of the new buildings across the street. When Sonny McMahan is pleased, I thought, the natural world must resonate like a tuning fork.

TWO

The land is on the western fringe of Appalachia, and for hundreds of years it was too rugged, too remote to attract settlers. But in the 1830s a peculiar band of people driven by faith made the trek up to the southern Cumberland Plateau. Seeking a place away from the corruption of the cities, they founded a village near the site of a spring thought to have healing powers. They called it Redemption Spring, and they delighted in the waterfall that came from it and plunged over a steep bluff to the valley below. They named their town Pilgrim's Rest and vowed that it would be a place of peace.

Forrest Wilkes, *The People of the Southern Cumberland Plateau*

If you want to get to Pilgrim's Rest in a hurry nowadays, you just take Interstate 24 out of Nashville, point yourself southeast, and floor it. In an hour or so you'll find yourself climbing up toward the plateau. That's where you swap I-24 for a more quirky two-lane road, and after a stretch of slower and more careful driving, you'll be there.

I didn't want the shortest distance between two points, however. Tennessee's interstates are like those anywhere – straight and smooth, insulated from the land, punctuated by gleaming places to feed yourself and water your car. It had been a long time since I'd been where I was going, and I wanted to take it easy, test the bath water slowly, let the memories return one at a time.

So I decided to take the long way. I steered my rented Toyota out of Nashville in a vaguely easterly direction along a succession of 'blue highways'. They got their name, as I recalled, from some of the earlier maps, on which the older, unimproved roads were depicted in blue lines. I was headed on a blue highway tour of east and south Tennessee, acting as if I had all the time in the world. And in a sense, I did. I was on Sonny McMahan's dime.

In today's world, Tennessee's blue highways are like a trip straight back in time, meandering through places with lyrical names like Hurricane and Pleasant Shade. Middle Tennessee is still lush and green and pastoral at the onset of fall, its fields of harvested corn edged by low, wooded hills. It was late morning and I had the windows rolled down to let in the smells of rich earth.

Every now and then I'd slow down for a county seat, because those towns often included an old square with a county court-house in brick or stone, its clock tower overlooking a statue of a Confederate soldier, standing at easy parade rest, musket at his side. Some of the squares reflected the bigger world outside, with neon and chain stores lining the perimeter, which meant the soldier might be directing his gaze not at a rank of advancing Bluebellies but toward a Big 'n' Juicy burger joint or the local Piggly Wiggly market. Other squares managed to retain the old-time feel, with family-owned hardware and feed stores and cafes that functioned both as short-order diners and pool halls.

On the seat beside me rested a small pile of notebooks and tape cassettes, the fruits of a week of interviews in Nashville. I'd return to the capital for more later. Now, though, it was time to head to a quieter place, one where the memories of Sonny McMahan would not be so recent. How would the folks of Pilgrim's Rest, I wondered, recall their hometown boy who'd made good?

More important to me, what kind of book would I wind up writing? Would I nail down some useful truths about the man, or would this be just another vanity memoir? And did it matter? I'd already tried my hand at writing down the truth and failed miserably. At the very least, this new gig shouldn't strain my skills too much, and I'd see a nice payday at the end.

By early afternoon I had gradually made my way out of middle Tennessee and climbed to the Cumberland Plateau, the strip of high ground that runs southwest to northeast all the way from Georgia to Kentucky and separates the mid-state region from the Tennessee Valley to the east. My destination was still miles away – half the width of the state – but the geography was already familiar to me. And so my mind, naturally, found things to do. I thought of Sonny and Tish and went over some of the interviews. The wound on my brow itched, and I leaned sideways to inspect it in the Toyota's rear-view mirror. The four butterfly tapes were lined up across my forehead like shiny little tombstones. As I rubbed the spot carefully, I was dragged back to that night in Chicago, just two weeks earlier.

It had not been one of my better days. In the morning I was canned by the *Examiner*. I spent the first part of the afternoon sulking in my townhouse, reflecting on where I was and how I'd gotten there. I drank some.

Around four I went for a long walk, first over to Lincoln Park and then through the park to the lake. I turned south and kept walking, along that thin stretch of beach with the hard, flat blue of Lake Michigan to my left and the high-rise glitz of the Gold Coast arrayed to my right, just beyond noisy Lake Shore Drive. I was distracted by anger and hurt, and when I finally took note of my surroundings, I'd almost reached the Chicago River and I was tired and hungry and thirsty. The *Examiner* was not far away, but I wasn't welcome there. So I cut over toward Navy Pier, looking for a place where I wasn't likely to run into any of my old colleagues. Eventually I settled for one of those New World Irish pubs, with the wood paneling and the brass rail at the bar. It was not far from the NBC tower and was known as more of a TV than a newspaper hangout.

I got a draft beer and played a few games of pinball. Then I took a seat at the bar, ordered one of their towering cheeseburgers along with another draft, and watched the Bears play the Vikings in Minneapolis. The game was not going well. After I polished off the cheeseburger and beer, I switched to Glenfiddich, neat. Three shots later, the game was going even worse.

Then McGowan walked in.

Dennis McGowan, metro editor of the *Examiner*. My boss. The man who had hired me and, to round things off with a symmetrical flourish, fired me. He and his wife were passing through the bar on their way from the adjacent dining room toward the exit.

I spotted him. I turned my back. He spotted me. He came over.

'Randall.' He leaned over to study me. Even in my stupor, I could see the concern on his face. He spoke a few words that I mostly missed, but I caught the tone. I was having no part of it. When I found that ignoring him wasn't working, I swivelled around on my stool and suggested to him in my most reasonable tone that he take his wife outside and stuff her in the car and drive away. I believe that's the word I used. I was pleased at the connotation.

Anger crossed his face, and that was the only excuse I needed. As I saw his wife pull at his arm, I took a swing at him. I must have telegraphed it like Marconi, because he simply stepped back, allowing me to follow through by landing heavily on an adjacent stool, cracking my forehead on the rim of the bar.

The rest was a blur. I vaguely remember blood on my shirt, a disorganized ride with me in the backseat, and McGowan helping me into the hospital emergency room. The attendant who wrote down my particulars gave me an incurious look and said, 'You that newspaper guy, huh?'

And, because I was beginning to sober up, I clearly recall the look of pity on McGowan's face and of contempt on his wife's as they left me there.

'I wish you could see yourself,' he said to me.

The memory came to a sour end. I stole another look in the mirror, noted that the small wound was healing nicely, and picked off the tapes one by one, revealing my own tidy one-inch mark of Cain.

It was just dark when I pulled into Pilgrim's Rest. Shiny new businesses had sprung up on the outskirts – a family-style restaurant, a home-supply store, a small medical clinic, and a DVD rental place – but the downtown looked mostly intact. All the buildings were either one or two-story and faced with weathered brick. The hardware store, the drug store with its soda fountain, a dress shop, a café, the weekly newspaper, all looked familiar to me. The old movie theater was shuttered, though, and its marquee now proclaimed it to be the home of a church, with services every Sunday morning. The only lights on the main street came from the café, which was doing good business at the counter, and the newspaper, the *Cumberland Call*, where I saw a young woman sitting at a desk, bent over her work.

Funny thing: This town of eight or nine thousand people, where I had spent the first seventeen years of my life, had once been all the world I'd known, and it seemed plenty big to hold me and everything I knew. Tonight, I rolled through it in two minutes, and it felt to me like Lilliput.

Soon, without stopping, I was back on the dark highway, the heavy forest crowding up against the road, a dark tunnel on the fringe of my headlights. Two miles later I found the turnoff, unmarked as before, and I steered the car up and along the narrow and roughly blacktopped road that wound through woods to the Colony.

From the glimpses my headlights picked out, this place too was unchanged, as if stuck in its late nineteenth-century origins, when life moved at a slower pace, before radio and telephones and paved roads. There they were, back in the trees – the Drummond house, the Turner place, another whose name I'd forgotten, and many more, a couple of dozen altogether. All of them old and tall and very worn but still proud. Cottages, the owners called them, but they were much grander than that. I had grown up in one, and I'd no idea how special a house it was until I left the plateau and sampled the world outside.

The house I'd once called home was up the next left turn about a hundred yards. The Historian, the man who fathered me, still lived in that house, but I wasn't headed there. I kept going, turning onto the bluff road and rolling slowly until I came to one of the biggest of the so-called cottages, the summer home of Stuart and Leticia McMahan. It sat right on the bluff overlooking blackness that I knew to be a deep valley and a range of mountains several miles beyond.

The sign on the mailbox read Longstaff House, a name the place had carried for generations. That was one of the Colony's idiosyncracies. No matter who the present owner might be, the house would always be known by the name of its builder. Like most of the Colony homes, Longstaff House was imposing and vaguely Victorian. It stood three stories high, with white clapboard siding, striped canvas awnings over tall windows, and a screened-in wraparound porch. Shade trees taller than the house sprawled around the yard. The air was cool, verging on cold, and I could smell wood smoke from some of the neighbors' chimneys and, behind that, rain on the way.

Tish had given me a key and described the general layout. I pulled into the gravel driveway, parked by a side door, got out, and moving carefully in the dark began to unload my bags. I let myself in and went through the house quickly, turning on lights, locating the things I would need.

Coming from an average-size Chicago townhouse, I found the place enormous, a relic of an age when space was plentiful and the size of a rich man's house was limited only by his imagination. Longstaff House was drafty. Since it was intended only as a summer residence, the construction was not as precise or finished as one of the mansions of, say, Memphis – or as well insulated. But it had character, generations of it.

Tish had mentioned that she and Sonny sometimes held weekend house parties, and I found plenty of bedding in the closets and chests. The fridge and freezer were well stocked, as was the liquor cabinet. No Scotch, but then I was in bourbon country.

An hour and a half later, after overcooking a frozen dinner in their little microwave oven, I was comfortably ensconced in a rattan lounge chair on the section of the sprawling porch that overlooked the valley. I'd turned out the porch lights, and all was dark. The only sounds were the faint hum of the refrigerator and, through the porch screen, the hiss of breeze and the first patter of raindrops among the leaves. That, and the far-off, muted roar of the waterfall not much more than a hundred yards along the bluff from where I sat.

The ice tinkled agreeably as I raised my glass for another sip of bourbon. As easily as that sip, my mind swung back a small eternity to a particular day when I was strolling across campus hand in hand with Leticia Alcott, both of us lost in some inconsequential exchange – and in each other. In the present tense of that memory, I look up, see Sonny approaching, wave to him.

I've been wanting to introduce the two of you, I say. Sonny McMahan, Tish Alcott.

And they look at each other almost gravely, each weighing the other. The rough-cut scholarship student from my hometown, the sorority princess from old-money Nashville. Something passes between them in that instant, the expression of a need instantly and forever filled by the other, and I can't even see it.

Sonny makes a joke. She laughs. And I hurry off to class, leaving the two of them there, hoping they will become friends. Within days I see what has happened. It takes a long time for me to understand, but eventually I do. Tish has gotten a quick glimpse of something that she is later to discern with greater clarity, the diamond-like core in him that needs only a touch of polish to make it gleam. And the humor, and maybe a little of the ruthlessness too. And the strength and driving ambition that will someday turn him into ... what? She can't have known at the time. She only knows that she wants this raw energy in her life, and wants to add what she can to it.

I could have hated Sonny for taking her from me so casually, could have hated her for going. But both were easy to love and hard to hate. Unlike Sonny, I made friends slowly. I didn't want to lose them. So I never said anything. I kept them in my life. And to this day, I'm glad I did.

A sound intruded softly on the memory, a soft, rolling swell in the darkness out beyond the porch, announcing the real arrival of the rain and making me glad that I had beat the weather inside. Then I heard another sound, a sharper one.

Tapping. Someone at the kitchen door.

I made my way through the half-lit house to the back door, where I found the switch for the outside light and threw it. I almost gasped at the sight. A woman, her white hair soaked, stood there, tapping with her fingernails on the glass.

I swung open the door.

'Have you seen my husband?'

I saw that she was wearing only a nightdress, and it was plastered to her gaunt frame. Furry slippers were on her feet. Her mouth hung open slackly, and she looked both pathetic and frightening.

She repeated the question in a thin and querulous voice, and I realized I had been staring at her as if I'd lost the power of speech. As I opened the door wider, intending to get her inside out of the rain, I suddenly saw past twenty years' worth of changes and recognized her.

'Mrs. McMahan? It's you, isn't it? I'm Randall Wilkes.'

'Well, of course you are,' she said impatiently, brushing past me into the kitchen as a chill breeze tried to follow her inside.

Taking her damp elbow, I led her into the living room, where I turned on lights. 'You're going to freeze,' I told her. 'Please sit down.' I settled her on the sofa and wrapped an afghan around her shoulders and most of the rest of her, then turned to the fireplace, where someone had considerately laid three logs, kindling, and paper. In a minute I had it started.

'Can I offer you a glass of bourbon?' I asked her.

'I don't drink, you know that,' she replied rather primly. 'I've seen what it can do to those I love, and I wouldn't want it in the house. There are some can't handle it, and that's a fact.'

'Yes, ma'am.' Faye McMahan was one of the few adults I had always liked and admired, and I found myself slipping back into my respectful boyhood behavior toward her.

'My boy Sonny, now, he would never let alcohol get hold of him the way his daddy did,' she went on, gazing into the fire. 'Sonny was governor of this state, you know. And he's about to bring business up here to the plateau. No one's done that, but he can.'

'I'm sure he can,' I said. 'Mrs. McMahan, I'm working on a book about Sonny. May I talk to you sometime?'

'Leticia told me you're staying in the house,' she said abruptly. 'You'll be here until ...' Her voice faded and broke. Then her face became animated. 'You and Sonny are in trouble again, aren't you?'

'Why ...'

'Sam Dunham called. He said you were shooting at his cats with your BB guns.'

'Oh.' I understood. 'Yes, ma'am,' I said. 'But we won't do it again.'

She appeared not to have heard. 'Have you seen my husband?' she asked once more, and there was something pitiable in the way she asked.

'No, ma'am, I haven't.' What was I going to say? *He got dead drunk, fell into the Big Muddy, and drowned?*

'Well, he's supposed to come see me pretty soon. Now that the girl's gone to bed, you know,' she added conspiratorially. 'I got a call from Tulsa. So if you see him, you send him around. I'm right next door –' She indicated a direction over her shoulder, along the bluff.

'As soon as you get dry, I'm taking you back to your house,' I said. As I spoke the words, there came a frantic pounding on the back door, along with a young girl's voice.

'Is she in there?'

'Come on in,' I shouted.

She burst into the living room. 'Miz McMahan! Miz McMahan! Oh, Lord.' She was somewhere in her teens, with a chipmunk's face and unbrushed hair, and she wore an unzipped parka over what appeared to be pajamas.

'Oh, Lord,' she said again. Then: 'Miz McMahan, you scared the daylights out of me. I didn't know where you'd gone. I was afraid you'd ...' She let the rest go, unwilling to voice the possibilities. 'Let's go back to the house, all right?'

'This is Randall Wilkes,' the old woman said almost gaily in a hostess voice. 'One of my son's best friends. Randall, this is Opal Hicks. She looks after me. At least she does today. Some days, we have another girl looking after me. They're both very young and very nice, and they can even cook a little bit. And Opal plays gin rummy with me too.'

'Pleased to meet you,' Opal said distractedly.

'I went to high school with a Bobby Hicks,' I told her.

'My uncle.' She looked close to tears, distraught at having let

Faye slip out of the house. 'Miz McMahan, you're all wet. You could've gone and caught double pneumonia. Can we go back?' She turned to me. 'Thank you so much for taking her in and making her warm.'

'Well, I suppose I've visited long enough,' Faye McMahan said, standing up slowly.

'Please keep that to wrap yourself in,' I said.

'I believe I will.' She fingered the afghan for a long moment. 'I made this, you know,' she said. 'Back when my fingers could still do this kind of work. I knitted, I crocheted, I quilted. Blue used to laugh about it. "Everybody in this town sleeps under one of your quilts," he said. But I think he was proud.'

She stood up straighter. 'Thank you, Randall,' she said with a touch of formality. 'I hope you're comfortable in Longstaff House.' She turned to the girl. 'The Wilkses were always a nice family, Opal. I'm glad I let Sonny play with Randall here. Except for the BB guns.'

'Good night,' I said as they left.

But seconds later I heard rapid footsteps, and she was suddenly at my side again. 'Blue knows a secret,' she whispered. 'He's in trouble. Or Sonny. I can't remember. Dear Lord, I think one of them's in terrible trouble.' She gripped my arm, and her fingers felt surprisingly strong. 'Will you help him?' Her breath was warm and stale.

'I …'

'Please.'

The girl, exclaiming impatiently, took custody of her again. Faye's pale face turned back to me as she was led away. 'Please.'

What else could I say? 'All right.'

As they left a second time, her voice carried faintly from the kitchen.

'That's not a soldier's grave. Blue told me.'

The ice cascaded down the inside of the glass as I drained it, making that universal bar-closing sound. The fire, like the bourbon, should have provided a warm wrapper against the night.

But as I lay on the couch where my visitor had recently sat, and I felt the slight dampness in the fabric from the rain she brought in with her, I felt chilled. Every now and then I heard a thin, high keening sound, the wind working through a crevice in a door or window somewhere in the house. It was no lullaby. Chiming in with an occasional bass note was a far-off roll of thunder, like one of the mountain gods clearing his throat.

Faye had frightened me – her wild looks, her crazy talk. I could still feel the light imprint of her fingers on my arm. Compared to the kind, hard-working woman I'd known as a child, the sight of her now was devastating.

Poor Faye, I thought. If ever a woman deserved a medal for raising a son against adversity, it was she. The adversity's name was Blue McMahan. Rake, con man, absentee husband and father. Through all the trials of her marriage, though, Faye managed to keep Sonny on track. She fed him and patched his jeans and sent him off to school and, eventually, saw him sworn in at that big limestone monument atop Nashville's highest hill. And now Blue, who had been an embarrassment to Sonny throughout his governorship, was gone.

Faye had good reason not to miss him, but in her delusions she now talked almost fondly of him, expecting him to visit her like some gentleman caller of her youth.

Sam Dunham's cats. Sonny in trouble. Something about a soldier's grave. It sounded to me as if her mind was indeed slipping its gears, just as Tish had suggested. Poor Faye. Age is a bitch, isn't it?

I was getting sleepy. Tomorrow, I thought, I'd start making the rounds in Pilgrim's Rest, talking to those who remembered Sonny as a young man. Maybe I could glean a few tidbits from Faye, but it was doubtful. Anyone who went around planning a late-night rendezvous with her dead husband had only a loose connection with reality. My father was certainly one of those who could comment with some authority on Sonny, both as young man and as governor. His input would be valuable. But I wasn't ready to talk to him yet. Maybe later, when …

I sat up suddenly. My right hand held no glass. Looking down,

I saw it on the carpet, where my slack fingers had let it drop, and the ice cubes were now only puddles beside it. I had slept; time had passed.

And something had awakened me.

Then I remembered. Only seconds earlier, as the wind squealed faintly somewhere high up in the house, I had half-dreamed an accompanying sound, something louder, more urgent.

A human scream.

Crazy, I thought. You're letting the house and Faye's delirium get to you. But the half-dream was so recent, so vivid, I could still hear it in my mind's ear, still hear how it started on a note of anguish and then, suddenly, was cut off.

It was too real. My ears still rang with it.

My watch read a little after eleven. I scrambled off the couch and began turning on lights, went into the kitchen and found a big drawer that passed for a utility bin and, luckily, located a flashlight. It worked. I yanked on my jacket and stumbled out the door. My brain was still marinated in drink, but the shock of the outside air began to cut through the bleariness.

The rain had settled into a steady but not drenching shower, and I was heartened to see that every now and then the sky sizzled with lightning over there at the far end of the valley below the bluff, augmenting my feeble flashlight and ushering in another round of grumbling thunder.

Best I could make out, the nearest house was about thirty yards along the bluff to my right; I guessed it to be Faye's place. I covered the distance as quickly as I could, picking my way partly along a muddy path and partly through soggy grass.

The place showed no lights. It was a much smaller cousin to Longstaff House, almost identical even down to the wraparound porch – a guesthouse, maybe.

Approaching the side of the house away from the bluff, I opened the screen door and knocked on the inside door, once, then again, louder. Several seconds went by with no answer. I tried the door. It was unlocked.

'Hello?' Again, no answer, and I couldn't decide whether to take comfort in that or not. My wavering flashlight showed a corridor that led to the front. The house was warm. I called out again, feeling both foolish and on edge. The scream felt real to my memory, but I knew that there were plausible explanations. A toddler's cry. A woman's high-pitched, drunken laugh. I wasn't yet ready to assume the worst.

The main room, just off the porch, was fully furnished, but held no sigh of life. Ditto the kitchen and what seemed to be a guest bathroom off the corridor. I headed for the upstairs, which appeared to hold two bedrooms. In the first was a rumpled bed, an older woman's clothes in the closet, woman's things on the dresser, and an overall smell of the medicine cabinet. In the bathroom hung a damp nightdress. The room looked out on the upper level of a two-story porch, unscreened and empty of all save furniture. This was Faye's room. But where was she?

I moved down the hall to what I guessed was the second bedroom. The door was open, and when I shone the light inside, I saw something that made me catch my breath and sent my arm into a spasm that caused the light to jerk. I leaned against the wall and played the light carefully against the far wall, more steadily this time, and saw it again.

Young Opal Hicks knelt on the bed in her pajamas, head slumped forward almost prayerfully over her knees, her whole body canted slightly to the left against the wall, as if she had suddenly grown tired and needed the support. Her head, with hair splayed over her face, was turned toward me. But it was tilted at an unnatural angle, making her resemble a disheveled doll whose owner had played too rough with her and then cast her aside. Spit glistened in the corner of her mouth.

She seemed to be regarding my shoes. I took a step toward her and then saw her eyes and stopped. They were, in fact, like doll's eyes, like flat, shiny buttons with absolutely no life in them. And they were already losing their shine.

I've seen death. I've covered crime scenes as a young reporter and done ride-alongs with the Chicago PD as a quasi-celebrity columnist. I've seen your everyday gang shootings, of course, and witnessed a lethal injection at Stateville. I've seen the results of a large-caliber handgun inserted into the mouth and pressed up against the soft palate before the trigger is pulled. I've seen char-broiled adults and children carted out of a tenement fire. I've seen what five days of Chicago summer temperatures will do to the body of an obese man who strangled himself with three turns of electrical cord from an overhead pipe after his wife walked out on him. Through it all, I've prided myself on a strong stomach and the ability to take notes while holding my nose.

But I never liked it. Unlike some of the news boys who crave the adrenalin, I never became a death junkie. A Weegee. Death always scared me, repelled me. I never wanted to get too close to it.

After playing the light one more time around Opal's sad, crouching frame, I turned away and shouted Faye's name over and over, as loud as I could. No one answered.

Panic, I'm ashamed to say, began to take hold of me, and I tried to push it down. None of the violent deaths I'd seen ever involved anyone I knew. A simple, decent-seeming girl I'd just met was now dead, and the mother of my oldest friend was missing. I got moving.

Downstairs, my stomach in a knot, I stepped out onto the porch and shined my light around, still hoping I might find Faye huddled in a corner somewhere. Nothing, except for the usual assortment of weathered outdoor furniture. This porch, unlike the one at Longstaff House, was unscreened. I moved to the rail and looked out over deep blackness. Then the lightning flickered, and I saw the contours of the valley that rolled away for miles until it met a far range of mountains. Off to my left was the falls, unseen from the house next door but quite visible from here in daylight. Despite its ominous name, I'd loved Damnation Falls as a child. My mother had walked me there, and we had stood on the bridge that spanned the falling water, lost in the sound and magnificence of it.

Just as I turned to leave, another bolt fired up the sky, this one scarily bright. In an instant, I saw it all – the falls, the surrounding woods, the bridge that crossed the creek above the falls.

And something else, just below the bridge. Something white.

I took the steep porch steps two at a time, landed on the rough path that skirted the top of the bluff, and took off for the falls at a run, stumbling on rocks and gravel as my light shakily showed me the way. What seemed a long minute later, I reached the bridge but did not step out on it. The object, whatever it was, seemed suspended from the bridge railing on the waterfall side. It hung below.

Stepping carefully – a stumble could send me down the rocky slope and over the falls – I made my way down below the level of the bridge until I stood at the water's edge. Its roar filled my ears. I looked up, feeling the rain pelt my face. My flashlight followed my gaze.

But there was no need. The lightning hit again, flash-burning everything into sharp relief, and I saw her.

Faye. She hung by the neck from a rope that was knotted at the rail. Eyes half-open, her head tilted awkwardly, she looked up at the sky as if to say, *My goodness, will you look at this rain?*

Mesmerized, I played the light over her. She had changed into a fresh nightdress, but now it too was soaked. Rainwater ran in delicate rivulets from her fingertips and her toes.

Grabbing a sapling for support, I reached out to touch her foot. It was cold as a marble saint's.

THREE

The rest of the night passed in a series of jerky, disjointed images, like a scary silent movie run on a creaky projector. *The Cabinet of Dr. Caligari*, maybe, if the good doctor had hung up his shingle in East Tennessee.

First, I had to get away from the bridge and the death house, get back to Longstaff House to call the police. As I made my stumbling way over rock, grass, and dirt, my flashlight wavered wildly and I could hear the sound of my own constricted breathing. Somebody had snuffed the life out of two women in a house behind me, and he could be waiting in the dark anywhere ahead of me, behind any tree. By the time I made it to the house I was muttering to myself, arguing that no killer would stick around after he'd done his deeds. Nevertheless, I went through the house carefully, first locking the doors and turning on any lights that weren't already on before I felt safe enough to pick up the phone.

My breathless 911 call roused a sleepy police dispatcher who snapped awake at my mention of the McMahan name. After a half-hour wait, two Pilgrim's Rest PD cruisers rolled up, light bars flashing, one bearing the chief, the other carrying the two officers who made up the rest of his department. The next hour was spent in the rain and chill as we stood around under umbrellas out by the bridge. Since it took time to examine Faye's body before cutting her down, I did my best not to look at her again. I'd seen her dead and wanted to remember her alive.

Then we moved back to the guesthouse, where the police took

the rest of my statement while the cruisers' roof lights cast a wet ruby glow outside among the trees and the county medical examiner's people, who had showed up to handle the bodies of Faye McMahan and Opal Hicks.

Finally, near dawn, I headed back to Longstaff House and the toughest job: Sonny. The police chief had asked me if I wanted to notify him, and I said yes. I dialed the number in Nashville, woke him up and, speaking slowly, told him what had happened. After my first few words, I heard him lose all his air, as if he had been gut-punched. The next sounds were hardly human, just guttural gasps, a man trying hard to breathe. I heard Tish's voice in the background, its pitch and volume rising as she became aware of something horribly wrong.

Finally I finished, describing to him only what I considered necessary. The silence on the other end of the line lasted a small eternity. Then he cleared his throat once, twice. 'They know anything about who did it?' His voice sounded pinched.

'I'm not sure, Sonny. I don't think so.'

Another long silence. Then: 'Thank you for telling me. I'll be coming down.'

The day that followed passed in an equally disjointed way, not helped by my lack of sleep. The rain slacked off, leaving behind a lid of milky gray sky. Calls began coming in from the media, first the local paper, then the *Tennessean* in Nashville and the Associated Press' regional stringer in Chattanooga. In each case, I clammed up and told them to deal with the McMahan family and the police. Reporters are masters at getting the close-mouthed to talk, but not if the subject knows the game himself.

Then, midway through my third cup of coffee around ten, I heard tires crunching on the gravel. It was Sonny and Tish, in a black GMC sport-utility big enough to take Kabul. Behind them, at the wheel of another SUV only marginally smaller, was the character I had encountered on the sidewalk outside the Hermitage Hotel. All three were grim-faced. Sonny and I gripped, Tish and I hugged. They introduced their companion as Kenneth Lively. Acknowledging me with a nod and a quick, hard shake, he began smoothly transferring their luggage into the house.

Inside, I poured coffee for the McMahans and sat with them in front of the fire, where Faye had sat just hours before. 'Anything I can tell you?' I asked.

'Everything,' Sonny grunted. And so I did, as he and Tish listened with grim expressions. Whenever I was tempted to omit a detail, he pressed me for it. I was glad, in a way. Who wants to be the only one to carry around the memory of a bloody horror? Tell it, and others share the load.

Neither Sonny nor I ever wore a uniform, and I doubted that he had seen as much death as I had. But he showed his toughness as I recounted how I had found his mother. All through my story, he nodded over and over, looking off somewhere, those heavy lids hiding much of his emotion. When I had finished, he nodded one more time, then stood and went for the phone.

Before long the house had been turned into a kind of command post. The police chief, a man named Jerry Chitwood, came over to report that the bodies had been shipped to the county seat, thirty miles away, where the medical examiner would look at them.

'You know it's not for me to say, Chief,' Sonny said to him. 'You're in charge. But if it was me—'

'You'd call in the TBI,' Chitwood finished for him. The Tennessee Bureau of Investigation handled all statewide cases and often was called in when a small town's resources were taxed by a particular case. 'I've already done that, Governor.'

I watched the chief as he sat forward in his chair, holding his hard-billed cap in both hands. Jerry Chitwood, I suspected, had been a small-town cop most of his life. Growing up, I remembered him as a much younger deputy, known around town as a quiet and colorless but basically decent man. He had once collared me and Sonny – it was the notorious case of Sam Dunham's cats and the Daisy Red Ryder BB guns. He gave us a talking-to, made us apologize to Mr. Dunham, and notified our parents. My father and mother were upset, as was Faye

31

McMahan. But Blue, who happened to be in town at the time, was mostly just amused.

I came away with respect for Chitwood for the low-key way he'd handled the incident. Now, as chief and nearing retirement, he was noticeably thicker around the middle and thinner on the top, but he didn't appear to have changed much otherwise. Having a very visible murder dumped in his lap would have jarred him. Once it might have been said that my father was the most prominent citizen of Pilgrim's Rest. Now, without doubt, it was former Governor Stuart McMahan, whose mother had just been murdered. I had no doubt that calling in the Tennessee Bureau of Investigation was a very smart move for Jerry Chitwood.

The chief looked around the room, then back at Sonny. 'Governor, you'll be talking to the TBI boys soon, but I'm going to be involved with this too, and I feel like I should ask you: Did Mrs. McMahan have anybody who, uh …'

'Who didn't like her? Who would've wanted to hurt her?' Sonny's voice rose just a little. 'Not a single solitary soul in this world. And if anybody knows different, they should tell me.' He rubbed his eyes. 'Maybe you should be looking at who knew that girl. A boyfriend, maybe.'

'Opal Hicks.' Tish, who had just returned from a phone call with a *Tennessean* reporter, spoke up. 'Sonny, you should call her family.'

'I know,' he said wearily. 'I know.' A moment later he was on the phone, asking for the number, then making the call. As I heard him commiserate warmly with the dead girl's parents, I marveled at the man's skills. The dead woman's grieving son would find it almost impossible to make this call, I thought. But not the politician.

A discreet knock at the door, and the boys from the bureau had arrived. The lead agent, a man named Timms, offered his condolences, conferred briefly with Sonny and Chief Chitwood, and said he and his agents planned to go over the crime scene next door and would be in touch.

Then the chief left, and it was relatively quiet for a time. I fed the fire, and the three of us sat or lay in various positions around the living room as the afternoon wore on.

'Do you want me out of here?' I asked at one point.

'Of course not,' Tish said. 'You're in the main guest room. We're settled into our room upstairs, and Kenneth is next to us.'

'Who is he, this pistol-packing Kenneth?'

'You've got sharp eyes,' Sonny muttered, his own eyes half-closed. 'Ken used to be the head of my state police detail – the governor's bodyguard. We got along pretty well, and when I left the statehouse I offered him a job.'

'What does he do, exactly?'

'Whatever I need him to do,' Sonny said, closing the subject.

Kenneth Lively, with his round cheeks and restless eyes, had seemed too young to run a squad of state cops. Maybe he was older than he looked. I thought of asking why he would need to pack heat, as they like to say in Chicago. But I figured the question could wait.

Timms returned and asked to see me. It was clear that even though I had told Chief Chitwood a lot, the TBI agent wanted to confirm it and add some questions of his own. I sat with him out on the porch in the waning light for about half an hour while he went methodically down his list, noting my answers on a legal pad. His questions were precise, and I tried to answer truthfully. The only subject I held back was Faye's ravings, which I didn't consider particularly relevant.

Timms was casually but immaculately dressed in slacks and a light jacket, and he looked freshly shaved. Some might have thought him a bit of a dandy, but I find that a policeman who's spit-shined is likely to be equally serious about his job.

That favorable impression began to fade as his questions grew sharper. If I'd attended so many death scenes in the course of my work, he wondered, why had I behaved so irrationally at this one? In particular, why hadn't I acted more quickly to bring police to the scene, waiting until I returned to Longstaff House to call them?

'I don't know,' I said, showing my irritation a little. 'I suppose

I thought a smart killer would disable the phone in the house before he left. Maybe even before he killed them.'

'The phone works fine,' he said mildly.

'I didn't know that. And I had an even better reason for getting out of there,' I said. 'I thought there was a chance he might still be around.'

Timms moved on to my history with the McMahans and asked me how Tish and I had met. I was suddenly alert. Had he managed to do a quick check on me in the last few hours?

College, I told him.

'Were you going out with her?'

'Yes, I was, and I'll be damned if I know why you need this stuff.' My anger was showing, and I didn't care. I'd just realized that I was somewhere on his list of suspects.

We talked a little more, and damned if he didn't manage to touch on my job history in Chicago. Then he closed his notebook, stood up and left, and I rejoined Sonny and Tish – still simmering, but determined not to bother them with it. Kenneth Lively appeared to be off on some errand for Sonny. I took stock of the situation and discovered that the three of us were hungry. I volunteered to zap some frozen dinners in the microwave, but Tish shooed me out of the kitchen and took over. We ate almost silently at a small table in one corner of the living area.

Afterward, we all said goodnight, even though it wasn't yet eight o'clock. I headed for my room, where I got in bed and read for a while. One of the books on the night stand was one I knew well, a book the Historian had written years ago in a kind of throat-clearing before he got down to his real work, the Civil War. It was called *The People of the Southern Cumberland Plateau*. I thumbed through it until I found the chapter on Pilgrim's Rest, then the part I remembered best:

Except for their extreme religious beliefs, those who founded Pilgrim's Rest were typical of the people who settled the entire Appalachian chain. They were Scots-Irish who had originated in Scotland, migrated to northern Ireland, and then moved on to the American colonies in the early 1700s. They were a hard race, suspicious of crowned heads, and they had fought the English, in one way or another, from the battlefields of Scotland to the persecutions of Ulster to the American Revolution.

These new settlers from the lowlands of Tennessee were led by a gaunt unordained minister named John Crowder, known to most of his flock as Preacher John. He preached abstinence and hard work and believed in the imminence of the Second Coming, and he told his flock that withdrawal to the remote highlands would better prepare them to welcome their Savior. Several dozen people – men, women, and children, with their livestock and household goods – followed him there. In 1832 they reached the spot to be known as Pilgrim's Rest, not far from a clear-water source they called Redemption Spring, which fed a spectacular waterfall.

Rattling and banging from the kitchen downstairs. Too loud to be Tish. Sonny, I thought, looking for something to eat or drink and taking out his grief on the cabinetry.

Their journey, however, was troubled by exhaustion, disease and defections, and some of the group turned bitter and resentful toward the preacher who had brought them to that wilderness. Crowder answered their doubts with a fire-and-brimstone sermon at the edge of the bluff by the falls. He denounced the faithless among them and cast them out, telling them to make their way back to the cities. And in a warning to those who remained, he christened the waterfall with an ominous and frightening name: Damnation Falls …

Heavy treading on the stairs interrupted my reading. Sonny came in, wearing a thick robe over his pajamas. He carried a bottle and two glasses with ice in them.

'You want to get a little drunk?' he asked.

'If that'll help.'

'It'll help.' He poured me a slug and deposited my glass on the night table, then took the bottle and his glass over to the only chair in the room, a cracked-leather affair with a sprung bottom. He sat and sighed, looking at nothing in particular. His features sagged.

'To Faye McMahan,' I said, lifting my glass. 'Who took a no-count country boy named Stuart and singlehandedly turned him into the best governor this state ever had.' I didn't know if he was the best or not. I strongly doubted it. But that's called a white lie, and it's what you come up with when your friend needs to hear it.

His grin was part rueful and part appreciative of the lie, and he knocked back most of what was in his glass. 'Drink to that, by God.'

I followed suit. 'When Chitwood asked if she had any enemies, you said no,' I began tentatively.

'I meant it,' Sonny said quickly. 'She truly had no enemies. At least none I knew of. The only person who ever treated her bad was that son of a bitch she married. And being the woman she was, she never held it against him.'

'I told the chief and Timms pretty much everything about last night,' I said. 'All I left out was some of the things Faye said to me just before she left.'

He looked up at me questioningly from under those heavy lids.

'It was all over the place, so I didn't put much stock in any of it. She talked about Blue like he's still walking around among us – said he phoned her from Tulsa. Tish had told me she talked that way from time to time, so I wasn't surprised to hear it. She said Blue knew a secret, and she was afraid that you were in some kind of trouble. Or he was. She couldn't remember.'

'What kind of trouble?'

'She didn't say. But I have to wonder. Sonny … you know, every politician makes enemies.'

His head came up, and the look he shot me was hard. 'I've got political enemies,' he said. 'Not the kind of people who'd do anything like this. You can put that right out of your mind.'

'All right.'

'Did she say anything else?'

'Just something about a soldier's grave.'

'What about it?'

'I think she said "That's not a soldier's grave," and how she learned it from Blue.'

'Anything else?'

'No. Does any of it make sense?'

'Not to me. I'm glad you didn't mention any of this to the

others, though. It makes her sound crazy, and I don't want people to remember her that way.'

'I understand.' I drained the rest of my glass, and he rose to refill it. I didn't really want any more, but I saw that he had already freshened his own, and I couldn't say no. Just as in the case of the white lie, there are times when the friend needs you to match him drink for drink, and so that's what you do.

For an hour or so we sat and talked about Faye, about our growing-up, about some of the scrapes we got into. Sonny was on his third drink, and I had accepted mine but only sipped at it. His head sagged, and I could see how tired he was.

'Why don't you get to bed?' I asked him.

He nodded but made no move to get up.

'How long are you going to stay?'

A long breath in, then out. 'Through the funeral.'

'Sonny, this book feels a little irrelevant right now, don't you think? If you want me to drop it, or maybe pick it up sometime later, I wouldn't mind.'

'No,' he said forcefully. 'I want a book. And I want her to be in it. Especially now. Just remember to tell her story while you're telling mine.'

'All right, Governor,' I said. 'I'll do that.'

The next morning it appeared that Sonny and Tish would be busy with phone calls and visits and funeral arrangements. I decided it was a good time for me to pay a call on the Historian. Since nothing in the Colony is far away, I walked. On my way out of the yard, I glanced over toward the guesthouse, its back door and front balcony still draped in yellow police tape.

Once when Sonny and I were ten or so, I had bicycled from the Colony over to his place in town, a modest, almost ramshackle house that was largely held together by Faye McMahan's pride and hard work. It was winter. Blue, as was usually the case, was off somewhere. Sonny and I played soldier, or cowboy, or some such fool game until it was time for me to go home, and Faye noticed that I was getting hoarse and sniffly. She called my mother, reported my condition, and suggested that I stay the night so she could keep an eye on me.

I slept in Sonny's bed while, grumbling, he bunked on the couch where his mother had spread sheets and blankets for him. Sometime in the middle of the night I awoke to find Faye's cool hand resting on my brow. 'How you doing?' she whispered.

'Just fine,' I answered and drifted back to sleep. And the next morning, the crisis over, I cycled home. Funny, I thought. I'd forgotten that moment until now – the feel of her hand in the night, her quiet concern.

'Thank you, Miz McMahan,' I said in the direction of the house. And then, to myself: *If they find the psycho who did this, I hope they give your son a few minutes alone with him.*

The sky was low and leaden as I walked. The rain had mostly stopped, but a stiff breeze bore an occasional fat raindrop that struck my forehead or the back of my hand.

Ten minutes brought me to Wilkes Cottage. It was one of the few places in the Colony that bore the present resident's name, due to the fact that my great-grandfather had built it and various numbers of Wilkeses had always used it. Now it was down to one, quite possibly the last who would live there.

Wilkes Cottage was, along with Longstaff House, one of the largest in the Colony. It stood three stories high, finished in white wood siding, with an attic topped by a gabled, sharply angled roof. A two-story water tower was attached to the house at the back, a relic of the days before city water was piped in. Although the tower no longer had a function, it had been retained as a historical touch. Once, Wilkes Cottage may have been the grandest of the Colony homes, but today it had settled into a state that one might call 'shabby genteel.' Not that the Historian would mind. He was never one to be concerned about surface appearances.

I mounted the front steps, crossed the wide porch, its planks creaking underfoot, and knocked. I heard movement deep inside the house, and then he was at the door, showing no surprise to see me. His handshake was strong.

'I heard you were here,' he said. There was no particular

warmth in the tone, but no hostility either. 'Come on back. I'm having some tea. Would you like to join me?'

The sight of him gave me a small shock. He looked thinner and more stooped than I remembered, and for the first time he wore a full white beard. It gave him a patriarchal look that seemed to fit him.

'Sure.' I followed him through the large entryway, past the staircase and down the hall to his study, while he went to the kitchen. The room had not changed. Floor-to-ceiling book-shelves, the top shelves beyond reach unless you stood on a stool. His towering roll-top desk, piled high with more books and papers. Tables here and there, also piled high. Only one detail looked different – an artist's rendering that was displayed on a big upright piece of cork board where the Historian had always pinned articles, photos, and notes to himself. The drawing bore the title *Cumberland Memorial Park and Civil War Study Center*.

All through my childhood, Forrest Wilkes' study had been the most magical place I knew. Sometimes, as he worked at his desk, I would prowl the room, turning the pages of the books and examining the historical photographs, engravings, and reproductions of paintings that filled the few areas of wall not occupied by shelves. The burning of Atlanta. The siege of Lookout Mountain, 'the battle above the clouds.' Grant and Lee at Appomattox.

I looked around for a fancy framed document from the trustees of Columbia University but didn't see it. He'd won the Pulitzer for the second volume of his Civil War series, and learning of it way off in Chicago I'd been impressed. Any newspaperman who tells you he wouldn't kill for one of those things is a big fat fibber. Wouldn't have minded one to decorate my own wall. Fat chance of that now.

The room smelled to me like history, like stories told and yet to be told, and to this day the musty scent of old paper, whether in a private library or a used-book store, has the power to take me back to my father's study. During my times there as a child, I tried to be quiet but sometimes failed. If I turned pages with too much noise, he would say, 'This is a library, son. Read quietly.'

His study was the only place in the house – in my life, really – where I felt close to the Historian. But it was not to last. For, just as he was the kind of man more at ease with history than with life, so was he the kind of father made uncomfortable by having a growing, rambunctious boy around, a boy with skinned knees and a runny nose and a boy's loudness and impatience. Boys' pursuits were not his. He never took me hunting or taught me how to tie a lure or cast it just so, over there by the water-logged tree where the big bass should be. Once, at my insistence, he tried playing catch with me in the yard but gave up after bobbling the ball several times. My mother came outside to fill in for him.

For a few early years, I suppose, it was good being the son of the Historian, enjoying his stories and the musty smell of his books and papers. Then I became aware of all those things I wanted in a father and wasn't getting, and in that direct and selfish way of boys, I looked around until I found someone who could provide me with those things – a man named Blue, who had an easy grin and slightly dangerous ways. And my relationship with the Historian, always tentative at best, weakened, like a spider's filament stretched thin by the wind. By the time I left for college, it was at its thinnest.

Then, years later, came my mother's death. And then came my fall from grace in the world of the big-city newspapers, which caused him, for the first time, to express outright disgust with me. So for us, I supposed, that was that.

He brought me a cup of hot tea with lemon, the drink that fortified him throughout each day's study and writing, and another for himself. 'You could have stayed here, you know,' he said as he seated himself behind the big desk. He said it without reproach, just to get it out of the way.

'I know,' I said. 'It was easier for me just to stay over at the McMahans' place.'

'How long are you here?'

'I don't know for sure. I'm working on a book. It could be a while.'

'A book about Stuart McMahan.' In response to my look of

mild surprise, he went on: 'Pilgrim's Rest is a small town. And the Colony is an even smaller place. I don't think there are many secrets here.'

'Not many, maybe,' I said. 'But since last night, there's been one very big one.'

He nodded at me over the rim of his steaming cup. 'Faye,' he said quietly. 'I was shocked to hear. The police came by to ask if I'd seen or heard anything unusual during the night. I told them no.'

'Sonny's been hit very hard.'

'I'm sure. I've sent word that I'd like to be of help in any way I can.' He seemed about to add something but did not. I knew that his relationship with the McMahan family, and Sonny in particular, was complicated. He had been generous to Sonny years ago, largely because of my friendship. But I knew he did not approve of Sonny's record as governor.

'I saw Faye just before she was killed,' I told him. 'She was pretty far gone. Said Blue had been communicating with her, if you can believe that, and Sonny was in some kind of trouble. And she made another comment that might mean something to you.'

He waited.

'"That's not a soldier's grave," she said just before she left. Any idea what she meant?'

He thought for what seemed like a long time. 'Only one thing comes to mind,' he said finally. 'The two soldiers' graves in the town.'

'What graves?'

'Oh, that's right. Since you haven't been around here, you wouldn't know about them. Almost a year ago, some human remains, along with a few Civil War-era artifacts, turned up outside town. The bones were examined and found to be the proper age. Some experts were consulted, myself included, and it was determined that the remains were of two Confederate soldiers.'

'Confederate soldiers, up here in the middle of nowhere?' I'm sure my face showed my surprise. 'Does that mean there's some truth to—'

'To your favorite boyhood legend, the Burning?' He smiled patiently. 'It's too early to say with certainty. But they were soldiers nonetheless, possibly deserters. And they were buried with proper ceremony and a marker installed on the square in the town.'

'So what could Faye have meant?'

He shook his head. 'All I can say for sure is that those are most certainly soldiers' graves.' He paused for a moment, then added, 'And that may not be all. A few more human bones have been unearthed in the same general area, and they're undergoing tests. Who knows how many may eventually turn up, or what it all means? If nothing else, it'll give us historians a few things to think about.'

I looked around the bookshelves, spotting some familiar names on the multi-volume histories: Gibbon, Tacitus, Macaulay, Churchill, and many more. On the Civil War shelves, there were Freeman, Catton, Foote, McPherson and, of course, Wilkes.

I noted the three volumes bearing the Wilkes name. 'Will you have a fourth?' I asked him.

'God willing,' he replied. 'It will be called *Wilderness to Appomattox*. I'm hoping to finish it in the next year.'

'What's that?' I pointed to the artist's drawing.

'Oh … it's just an idea,' he said with a tone that bordered on gruffness. 'For a Civil War study center. It would be a park, like the battlefield parks, and also a place where scholars and historians could meet and talk about the war.'

I was mildly surprised. 'Too bad we had no battles fought in the neighborhood, then.'

He simply shrugged, clearly not inclined to discuss it further.

I felt uncomfortable making small talk with him and decided to get to the point. 'This book I'm working on … I'll be talking to anyone who knew Sonny while he was growing up here. Including you, of course. As you can imagine, I'm out of touch with people in the town. I'd appreciate it if you could help me draw up a list of interviews and maybe put me in touch with some of them.'

'If you like.' He said it with formality. 'What kind of book is it going to be?'

'Oh, you know. The typical politician's memoir.'

'Did he hire you to do it?'

'Is there anything wrong with that?'

'It depends on how you look at it,' he said mildly.

'Don't you get hired to write your histories?'

'Of course,' he said, giving me a hard and level look across the desk. 'But they're labeled as my work. And no one tells me how to write them.'

I felt myself getting angry. *Don't rise to the bait*, I told myself. But as soon as the thought passed, I struck at the bait just like a hungry bass.

'I suppose you're going to tell me that if I hadn't been a bad boy in Chicago, I wouldn't have to take such menial work.'

'When you express it with such precision, I don't have to,' he said.

'It's always been hard for you to cut me slack, hasn't it?'

'That's a vague generalization. If I had to express my feelings, I'd say I feel sad for you. Sad to know that you chased success and celebrity so hard you wound up destroying yourself.' I heard something approaching pity in his tone, and it made me furious.

I got up, bumping against the desk and almost toppling my mug of tea. 'I'm not destroyed yet,' I said, surprised at the heat in my voice. 'I'm just trying to move along. Looks like I won't be needing your help with this project after all.'

Full of righteous ire, I clomped down the front steps. I intended to go back to Longstaff House, but a memory plucked at my sleeve.

Soldiers' graves. For some reason they had been on Faye McMahan's mind in the last few hours of her long life. Maybe they were nothing. And they almost certainly had nothing to do with my book. But I suddenly wanted to see them.

FOUR

It was close to midday when I pulled into one of the parking spots ranged around the town square in Pilgrim's Rest. A light breeze was sweeping the plateau, clearing away much of the cloud cover, and the sun was threatening to break through. For a few seconds I watched the townspeople going about their business – after the pace of the Chicago Loop and the Outer Drive, my old home town seemed almost a relic, a quiet reminder of an earlier and simpler time. But the horrors of the world had a way of reaching down into even such a place as this, I reminded myself, and for a split second I unwillingly revisited the sight of Faye McMahan suspended by the neck, her dripping nightgown turned a harsh white by a blaze of lightning.

I saw no familiar faces around me, and I found myself comparing the compact downtown of today with the one I remembered. Not much had changed: I'd already noted the demise of the town theater when I whizzed through without stopping two nights earlier. Now I saw that a real estate broker's office had replaced the dusty dry-goods store where I'd once bought jeans. I wondered if, after decades of sleepiness, property was on the move.

Diagonally across the square, the *Cumberland Call* had a spiffed-up facade and a bold new sign. The square itself was an irregularly shaped patch of green, and the two buildings that stood on it, shaded by live oaks, looked the same. One was a tiny, rough cabin of logs and shingles dating from the early 1800s, the preserved home of an early settler. The other was a larger building of anonymous municipal brick construction that housed the town library on the ground floor and the local historical society upstairs. The society had not interested me much, and apart from one dutiful trip made with my tenth-grade history class, I hadn't spent any time inside.

It took me a moment to locate the square's only new feature. Made of stone and bearing a bronze plaque, the marker stood on a grassy spot between the two buildings, ringed by ornamental posts and chains. I stepped up to read it:

Two soldiers of the Army of the Confederacy, their names known but to God, met their end near our community during the great conflict of 1861–1865. They are interred here by the people of Pilgrim's Rest with our prayers that this country may never again be divided.

Interesting, I thought. What brought these two Johnny Rebs here, where no armies had passed? And what killed them? More to the point, I thought, recalling Faye's last words to me, are these really soldiers' graves? And why wouldn't they be?

My thoughts were interrupted by a far-off sound – eerie and unlike anything I'd ever heard. It was a kind of screech, long and drawn-out, followed by a series of yips in a high-pitched staccato. The noise seemed to come from somewhere inside the library. Needless to say, it was not one of those normal library sounds.

Curious, I climbed the uneven stone steps, went through the heavy doors, and stood looking around. Unlike the historical society, the library had been one of my favorite nooks. It looked largely unchanged, except for a computer terminal on the counter and a stack of shelves inhabited by books on audiotape. The wonderfully familiar musty book smell struck me full force – like my father's study, only more so.

Somewhere back among the stacks, I imagined, was the comfortable chair where I had first discovered the land of Oz, the chills of *The Illustrated Man* and, later, the more grown-up pleasures of *The Foxes of Harrow* and other bodice-rippers favored by the ladies of the town. Somewhere along the way, I also navigated the shoals and deeps of the Mississippi with Mark Twain and sailed around the horn with the crew of the

Bounty. Then came the day when I wandered into the history section and saw my father's name on several books and realized that he didn't just write for himself, he wrote for the world. I wondered if I could ever be like him. But that was then ...

I saw no readers this day. Back in the stacks I glimpsed the librarian replacing books on the shelves. Then came the sound again, even more shrill this time, a mindless squalling. It was from the upper level of the building, reached by the flight of stairs to my right. As I climbed them, I remembered the desperate scream that had awakened me at the cottage, the last sound uttered by Faye. But this wasn't a fearful sound, it was different, almost celebratory. What kind of creature ...?

At the top, I pushed through the door marked *Pilgrim's Rest Historical Society.* The upper floor was one big room taken up with exhibits everywhere. Near one of the windows was a desk, where I saw a man standing and working the controls of what looked like a tape player. One more howl, this one loud and clear, and the man switched the machine off. He noticed me.

'Hi there,' he said. 'Are you a visitor?'

'Kind of,' I answered.

'Interested in history? Look around all you like.'

'What was that sound?'

'Oh.' He grinned. 'That was a rebel yell. And you're one of the few people who've heard it.'

'You're kidding.' I walked over and gave him a look. He was somewhere around fifty, slightly under average height but solidly built, with a florid complexion and a thin cloud of sandy hair atop a full face. He wore rough khakis and scuffed boots, as if he were an archeologist just back from a dig. He was beaming at me for no apparent reason. He looked like a bright-eyed, barrel-chested cherub.

'Nobody knows exactly what a rebel yell sounded like,' I said to him. 'At least not for sure.' I had read my Civil War history.

'We do now,' he said proudly. He popped an audio cassette out of the machine. 'This was transcribed from an old acetate disc, recorded sometime in the late 1920s in a little town up in the Smoky Mountains.' Along with the smile, he had a fast and enthusiastic way of talking, as if his mouth could barely keep up with his brain.

'A music producer from the Lyrical Record Company in New York was traveling around the South collecting songs. You know, going right into people's homes, looking for authentic music. He found this old gentleman – a Civil War veteran – in the hills of Johnson County, a fellow who sang traditional songs. So he moved his equipment onto the man's front porch and recorded a bunch of songs.

'But before he began, he asked the man a few questions about the war, and the next thing he knew, the old guy was giving the rebel yell – "the way we whooped and hollered at Shiloh and Chancellorsville," he told the record man.'

'The rebel yell.' I shook my head slowly. The awful keening sound that chilled the bones of every Billy Yank lined up to receive a Confederate charge. Each student of the war had his own idea of what it might have sounded like – according to one description, it was a cross between an Indian war whoop and the cry of a fox hunter whose hounds are on the scent – but I'd always heard that the actual yell had been lost to history.

'How did this turn up?' I asked him.

He seemed pleased to tell the story. 'Well, Lyrical Records is long gone, so the disc sat on a shelf in a warehouse for a long time until a historian who'd heard rumors about it managed to track it down. His name's Forrest Wilkes. He lives right here, just outside town.'

'Oh,' I said. 'I happen to know him. He's my father.'

He looked at me for a long time. 'So you're Forrest's boy,' he said finally. That's one thing about the South. You may grow up and move through the greater world and even achieve something, but to the home folks you'll always be someone's boy.

He stuck out a hand. 'Olen Stringer.' The hand was strong and work-hardened, the accent Southern but hard to pin down. 'I run this place.'

'Randall Wilkes.'

His face took on a look of pained concern. 'I hear you've been

47

staying at the McMahans' place out in the Colony, and you were the one who, uh …'

'I found Mrs. McMahan,' I said.

'Must have been a terrible experience,' he said, shaking his head over and over. 'I'll be going by their place later this afternoon to offer my condolences. I have a lot of respect for the Governor. Do they know anything about who did it?'

'I imagine you know as much as I do,' I said. 'But no, I don't think they do. Yet.'

His expression eased, and he hefted the tape cassette. 'Your father tells me he's going to include something about this in his new book,' he said. 'It'll cause a little bit of a stir, finally tracking down the rebel yell. He's quite a historian, your father.'

'He sure is.' I was ready to change the subject. 'What can you tell me about the two soldiers buried outside?'

I may have imagined a brief hesitation before he answered. But his smile appeared genuine. 'What would you like to know?'

'Where were they found?'

'In the valley below the falls. You know the place?'

'Sure.' Damnation Falls swept over the bluff at the edge of the Colony and dropped more than a hundred feet down into a basin circled by dense, old-growth trees. Farther out, I recalled, the valley was farmland, but the area around the falls had remained largely untouched. The only route from atop the bluff was by way of a steep and twisting path. The falls had been a popular trysting place when I was in high school, and the perilous pathway down to the basin had only added to the allure.

'Well, that land was owned by a man named Burch at the time. He used it mostly for corn, and a little alfalfa. I was out there with a metal detector one day—'

'What? You found them?'

'I had that honor,' he said with a strange formality. The phrase sounded rehearsed. 'I'd done some reading about this area, and I became interested in a piece of old folklore—'

'The Burning?' He looked mildly irritated, and I realized I'd interrupted him again. 'Was that it?'

48

'Yes. It was just a story, but to me it had the ring of truth, and I thought I'd look into it. With Mr. Burch's permission, I spent almost six months looking around with a metal detector. I concentrated on an area where Mr. Burch had located a stone foundation of what may have been an old barn. And one day' – At this point his chest seemed to swell, and he stood a little straighter – 'I got a reading and dug down a few feet and turned up this.' He led me to a display case nearby, where he pointed out a flat, corroded hunk of metal, rectangular in shape and bearing the letters CSA. It was a Confederate soldier's belt buckle.

'That gave me some hope, so I kept digging – but very slowly, because I wanted to be careful. Two days later, I found what looked like a human bone. A rib. Then more bones. Some of them had scorch marks. I notified the police, and the medical people were called in, and the whole process of authentication … Anyway, the remains were eventually identified as those of two young males, and they were from the Civil War era. And the town reburied them, with honors.'

'So what does this say about the Burning?'

'Well, we have to be very careful here, since this is the first evidence to turn up. The story had a very vague beginning—'

'Strictly word of mouth, my father told me. No documents to back it up.'

'Well, yes,' he said a trifle resentfully. 'The origins were a little shaky. But since then, a journal has turned up that contains some hints.'

That was news to me. 'What journal?'

'The one your father found less than a year ago. Mary Hightower's diary. We keep it here at the society. He never mentioned it?'

'No, but then I haven't visited in quite a while.'

His look was full of questions, and I couldn't blame him.

After a pause, he picked up the thread. 'We may never have definitive proof, but the story has refused to die. And I think we can say that now, for the first time, we've given it some substance. And raised the visibility of our little town as a result.'

'How do you mean?'

He pointed at something in the center of the room and led me there. It was a display case on a table, about four feet square. Underneath the glass was a topographic scale model of several buildings arranged on an expanse of green, with a lake in the center. At first I thought I was looking at a plan for a country club. Then I saw the plaque that read: *Cumberland Memorial Park and Civil War Study Center*, and underneath, in smaller lettering: *Outerbridge Group*. It was the same thing I'd seen sketched in my father's study, but done here in three dimensions.

'This is a proposal for the biggest thing ever seen in this part of the state,' he said. 'A conference center that would attract writers and scholars and historians and archeologists from all over to live and study here, all of it arranged around the area where the discoveries were made. And it wouldn't be just for specialists. The center would include a Civil War museum full of exhibits, along with a luxury hotel. It could turn this town into a mecca for travelers.' He sounded as if he could barely contain his excitement.

'A kind of Disneyland of the Blue and the Gray,' I said. 'All because of a few bones.'

He laughed loudly. 'Oh, I've heard about you newspapermen,' he said. 'Especially you big-city boys. Well, you wait. As I say, it's just a proposal, but it may happen. And I'd make sure you get invited to the grand opening.'

'Would you be involved in this?'

'Who knows?' he said almost too quickly. 'It's all very tentative.'

'What's this Outerbridge Group?' I asked.

'A developer,' he said. 'I don't know a lot about them, but I hear they have vision. And one of their directors is Stuart McMahan, which is good enough for me.'

I took a moment to think about that. Tish had said there was money headed this way, and Sonny wanted some of it to be his. Looked like it would be.

'Maybe I'll come back some time and look at the rest of your exhibits.'

'Hope you do,' he said. 'This place has been spiffed up considerably since I became the director here a few years ago.'

'So you took over here after you found the soldiers' remains?' I asked. 'Was there any connection?'

'I suppose so,' he said quietly. 'The town saw that I was an enthusiastic amateur historian with a talent for making discoveries. The job opened up when the last director retired, and they offered it to me.'

'Where had you worked before?'

'I was with the National Park Service for almost twenty years,' he said. 'Park ranger.'

'Sounds like a good life.' I shook his hand and started for the door.

'Wait.' He caught up and handed me something. It looked like a brochure.

'Here's a little essay your father wrote on the Burning. It's our official position on the subject,' he said, sounding almost professorial. 'Remember, what's folklore today could be history tomorrow.'

'I suppose so,' I said. 'I hear you've turned up some new bones—'

'I had nothing to do with that,' he said quickly.

'Well, anyway, I guess they'll be joining the two boys down there on the square before long, won't they?'

His face lost all expression, and a few seconds went by before he spoke.

'Could be,' was all he said.

Outside, the overcast had burned off and the sun was bright, throwing everything into sharp relief and adding color to the faint golds and russets, the first turning leaves that speckled the trees in the grassy square. I settled into the driver's seat of my car, glanced over toward the old settler's cabin and the grave marker next to it, and remembered my surprise the day my father had first educated me about this region's dirty little open secret: During the Civil War, when the state voted to cast its lot with Jefferson Davis and the Confederacy, much of East

Tennessee's sympathies remained with the Union. Throughout that war, another war was fought by guerrillas and bushwhackers who roamed these hills spilling blood, acting out old hatreds and settling old scores. All of which explains why no Johnny Reb in bronze has ever stood gazing out over this particular town square. If any of this town's ancestors fought in that war, it was more likely under the Stars and Stripes, not the Stars and Bars.

I pulled out the brochure Stringer said my father had written and began to read. *A Legend of the War*, said the headline. There was no byline:

Over the years a story has been told in the town of Pilgrim's Rest. As with much folklore, this story could be a mixture of fact and fiction. We may never know the complete truth.

In the year 1863, so the story goes, two dozen Confederate soldiers captured during the battle for Chattanooga escaped from a train carrying them toward a northern prison camp. They roamed through the hills of the southern Cumberland Plateau until they came to the town of Pilgrim's Rest, where they asked for food. Unfortunately for them, the area was – although nominally controlled by the Confederacy – part of a pro-Union enclave. The soldiers fled the town and took refuge in a barn, but the place was surrounded by locals and burned to the ground. All the soldiers perished, and their bodies were buried on that spot.

The people of Pilgrim's Rest took an oath never to reveal what they had done. But little by little, the story emerged. The recent discovery outside town of human remains from the war era have lent new substance to the story referred to as The Burning. The great state of Tennessee, once divided like the nation, is now solidly part of the American South. And the people of Pilgrim's Rest, once shamed by the story of what their forebears may have done, are coming to accept it as part of their heritage.

We wish for all our ancestors a peaceful rest.

I recognized my father's writing style. He's done a pretty good sales job, I thought, folding up the brochure and putting it away. It absolves today's town of guilt and allows the residents to juice up the image of the place and cash in on a sensationalistic tale of blood and mayhem. If the conference center is ever built, I thought, maybe there'll be room out there in the meadow for a replica of the barn, complete with puppet figures waving their arms from inside, recorded screams played against the strains of *Dixie* ...

But my father's role in this puzzled me. He had always been strongly skeptical of the legend, cautioning me that it had no known basis in fact. Now his opinion seemed to have shifted in a dramatic way. The bones had turned up, for one thing. And what was that journal Stringer had mentioned?

I had once hoped the legend was true, for it appealed to the boy in me. Now, for the town's sake, I almost hoped it was not. How could you look at that faded tintype photo of Great-Great-Granddad up there on the mantle and imagine him throwing a torch inside a barn where a couple of dozen helpless young men crouched inside? Who would want that kind of stain on his ancestry? What kind of town—

'Hello.'

I looked up. A young woman stood by the car window. She held a disposable coffee cup, and the one detail I noticed at first was the pencil stuck in her tousled hair just over one ear. It gave her the look of someone in the middle of a job.

'Hi,' I said.

'You're Randall Wilkes, aren't you?'

'Uh-huh.' I looked at her expectantly.

'I thought I recognized you. I'd heard you were in town.'

I kept staring at her, waiting for something to click. She looked not the least bit familiar.

'I'm Charlene Singletary?' She said it in that Southern way that made it sound like a question, hoping to prod me into some kind of recognition.

That rang a faint bell, but it was not enough.

'I used to work at the *Tennessean*?'

'Oh.' Something finally clicked. But it was not a pleasant feeling, it was more the kind of thing that makes the stomach begin quietly churning.

I had never met her face to face, and I certainly had no reason to dislike her. But I always try to avoid people who remind me of certain things about myself.

Charlene Singletary was one of those.

FIVE

But there she stood. So I put on my polite face, got out, and took the hand she offered me. I noticed some of the finger-tips bore a gray-black smudge. It was just a detail, but it set off another small click in my head.

'You're at the paper,' I said slowly. 'The *Call*.'

'That's right,' she said. 'How did you—' She looked down at the hand I'd just given her back and grinned faintly. 'I've been reading proofs.' She rubbed the fingertips lightly together. 'I guess that's a giveaway, isn't it?'

'Well, it seems to be one of those things that never change,' I said. 'I imagine old Joe Pulitzer got ink on his fingers. But that wasn't the only tipoff. I caught a glimpse of you through the window of the paper when I drove into town the other night. I guess you were working late. So what are you doing in this town? Last I heard—'

'I know.' She paused for a moment, seemingly in no hurry. 'It's kind of a long story. I wouldn't mind telling you, if you have time for it. I'm on my lunch break. You want to have a bite, or a cup of coffee?'

Not particularly, I wanted to say. She saw me hesitate and added, 'I've been hoping I'd run into you, for a couple of reasons.'

Oh, well. She was friendly and not overly pushy, and I was hungry. 'Sure.'

A few minutes later we were seated at the counter in the busy Pilgrim's Rest fixture known, then and now, as Ida's. The place

55

was frozen in time, right down to the worn black-and-white checkerboard linoleum floor and the wire rack on the counter holding bags of potato chips and beef jerky. Only the staff looked unfamiliar to me. A big redhead with a heavy Appalachian accent took our orders.

'Do you still make slaw burgers here?' I asked her.

'We sure do, hon,' she said, eyeing me up and down. Everything about me, I'm sure, screamed, *Not from around here*.

After Charlene ordered a club sandwich and another coffee, I picked up the thread. 'Last I heard, you were covering politics at the *Tennessean*,' I said. 'So what brought you here?'

I heard the sudden sizzle of fatty meat being thrown on the griddle and caught its scent – one of those primal smells, no doubt about it. My stomach rumbled once, discreetly.

'Family,' she said simply, then added, 'My granddad.'

I vaguely remembered. All the time I was growing up, the *Call* had been edited by a gent named ... I searched my memory, then did a mental finger-snap: Walter Howard. She was his granddaughter.

'He's the reason I studied journalism at UT. Him and all those newspaper stories he used to tell me – interviewing Harry Truman and chasing Communists with Estes Kefauver for the AP, covering fires and police shootouts in Memphis for the *Commercial Appeal*.'

'So you studied journalism and aimed for the *Tennessean*,' I said.

She nodded. 'And that's where you came in. I always hoped I'd have a chance to say thank you in person.'

Over a dozen years ago, I'd received a note from her. Since she was several years younger, I barely remembered her. She was a recent college graduate about to test the waters of journalism and asking the big-city columnist and fellow product of our hometown for an open-ended letter of recommendation. I sent her one without thinking much about it and was surprised a few weeks later when she wrote to thank me and to say she'd landed a cub reporter's slot at the *Tennessean*, one of the state's two biggest papers. After that I'd sometimes see her byline and observed that she rose fast, eventually covering state politics for the paper.

'So,' she finished with a nice smile, 'thank you. In person.'

The unavoidable subtext here, of course, was my fall from journalistic grace. Charlene Singletary had once been an admirer of mine who was proud to use my name as an entree. Now she was an equal – more than an equal, really, since she still had a job. She'd watched my flame-out from a distance, possibly read about it in *Newsweek*. She had good reason to feel disappointed in me.

I was trying to think of something that might steer the conversation in another direction when Pearl set our sandwiches, drinks, and paper napkins in front of us. As soon as my companion took her first bite and courtesy had been satisfied, I dug in. The meat was juicy and slightly charred, the bun was yeasty and fresh, and the mustard-based slaw gave the whole thing just the right amount of tang and crunch. It took me right back to my teens, to rowdy gatherings at Ida's after pep rallies and football games. What was it Proust had said about the power of taste on memory?

The screen door flew open and a young woman bustled up to the counter next to Charlene. 'Hey, Pearl, she said, with a grin that took most of the edge off her impatient tone. 'Is it ready?'

Pearl ambled down to the far end of the cooking area to retrieve a takeout order in a paper bag. 'Here you go,' she said after her slow walk back to the cash register. 'Cheeseburger, extra pickles. Fries, extra crispy.' She said it in a bored singsong that sounded like part of a regular routine between these two.

'Thanks, hon.' The young woman, her small frame nearly lost in dirty white coveralls, dug into a pocket for money. Her gestures were quick and precise, and her long, dirty-blonde hair was tied in a tight ponytail. The fingers that counted out the change were stained here and there with grease or engine oil, an echo of Charlene's printer's ink. Two women not afraid to get their hands dirty.

'So how's the news business?' she asked, looking down at Charlene. 'Has anybody noticed this town's crawling with reporters? You know, I almost tripped over three of 'em on my way over here, one of 'em from TV. They all wanted to interview me. So far you're the only one that don't.' Her voice was both nasal and musical, typical of these parts.

'I'll interview you,' Charlene said. 'Tell me, ma'am, what's your opinion of all these reporters you've been tripping over?'

'Out-of-town trash, come here from the city to write up our murder story and make us sound like inbred hillbillies,' the young woman said almost gaily. 'And I'd like to tell you more, but I got to get back to work. Now you be sure and print that.' Gathering up her change and giving me a quick, curious look, she went out the door.

'Who was that?'

'Lita Ray Darnell,' Charlene replied with an amused look. 'She works at Dub's Garage, just off the square. Manages it, actually. Another born-and-bred, just like us, but the difference is she never left.'

'Did you say she's a Darnell?' I was thinking back a long way, trying to place her. I had a fuzzy image of a scrawny kid in her early teens, all knees and elbows, darting around in the background. But dominating the foreground was another image, another Darnell. I hadn't thought of her in a long time, but suddenly there she was, and the image was pure wide-screen Technicolor. I put down my sandwich. 'She had a big sister,' I said.

I tried to make it sound like a casual remark, but my voice gave me away, and Charlene shot me a quick look. 'She did? I know about a couple of brothers, but no sister.'

'Uh, yeah. Her name was Callie. She would have been older than you. And she moved away. I knew her in high school.' From deep down came a memory of a song on the car radio, a suntanned neck layered with damp curls, a laugh that caught in her throat, and a scent that ...

But I couldn't hold onto it. The Technicolor image faded to black and white and then went dark. I hauled myself back to the present, to our conversation. 'You still haven't told me—'

'How I wound up here? Pretty simple. My parents retired to

Florida. One day my granddad called and told me his health wasn't good, and he asked me if I wanted to run a small-town paper. I'd never thought about it, but it suddenly sounded very good to me. And I could tell it was important to him, so I said yes.'

I'd been studying her surreptitiously as she spoke. Charlene Singletary was over average height and on the angular side, with a face that was not beautiful but was not hard to take either. She wore slacks and a plain shirt, with a pocket full of pens, pencils and what looked like scraps of paper. Her hair was a light brown and was brushed in a casual way. Noting my look, she plucked the editing pencil out of the hair and made room for it in the pocket.

Mostly I was struck by the way she spoke. She had a rather low voice, and she used it with little inflection, almost apologetically. She had a quietly businesslike way about her, and it occurred to me that she was shy. Shyness was not an asset in journalism, and I wondered what it had cost her to bump heads with the big boys and girls as she tried to find her way in the hard-knocks world of state political reporting. Apparently she had done all right.

'You said you'd been hoping to run into me for a couple of reasons,' I prompted her.

She nodded. 'One was to thank you. The other ... Remember what I said about not much breaking news?'

'Uh-huh. That just changed, didn't it?' I said. 'Faye.'

She nodded. 'It's really turned the town upside down. Good for the paper, I suppose, but terrible for everybody else. I've talked to Chief Chitwood and the TBI agents. Governor McMahan was good enough to spend some time on the phone with me. The *Tennessean* has sent one of its best people here to look around, and the AP's staffing the story too. I'm working on an obit on Mrs. McMahan. I don't expect we'll scoop anybody on the investigation, but we're the local paper, and we're going to cover this story. I hear you haven't talked to any news people about the other night—'

'And you want me to talk to you.'

'Yes. Will you?'

I made a quick calculation. I no longer felt uneasy around her. If she was disappointed in me, she had the grace not to show it. Instead, she needed something from me. And I realized that, now that the Historian was no longer one of my resources, she might be able to help me.

'Okay.' I motioned for us to move into a nearby booth, away from Pearl's hearing, and there I talked for a while. I held off on some of the clinical details, since the cops would need to keep those under wraps, at least for a while. Cooperating with the police was not part of my genetic code, but Sonny wouldn't like it if I complicated things for them. Instead, I gave Charlene what we call color – the look and feel of the dark house that night, my emotional responses to what I'd found. I knew the kind of 'color quotes' that would add flavor to her story, and I provided plenty of them. Using a pocket notebook, the kind I'd often carried, she took notes in a quick and precise hand.

I watched her almost jealously. They say newspapermen have printer's ink in their veins and they never really leave the business. Maybe so. All I know is that as her pen flew over the notebook's pages, my own fingers itched to be taking notes again, for a real article, a real column. This vanity book project for Sonny was no substitute and I knew it. I imagined myself interviewing Charlene for a personality profile of a small-town editor. I looked around at Ida's and imagined what a good, textured column I could put together on this place, with its comfortable cast of regulars, its scent of frying grease, and its sense of time having stopped somewhere during the Roosevelt Administration. I wondered if I'd ever do my old kind of work again, and the feeling that swept over me was something like homesickness.

When I was finished, we got up to leave. She insisted on paying for lunch, to which I put up only token resistance. Out on the sidewalk, she offered me her hand. 'Thanks,' she said. 'I need to get back to work.'

'I'm working on something for the Governor,' I said quickly. 'Doing research for a book.'

Her look of puzzlement was so obvious – *With your reputation, what are you doing writing a book?* – I felt compelled to add, 'Just research. It's going to be a kind of memoir.'

'Oh.' I couldn't read the expression that followed. But I was pretty sure it wasn't admiration.

'You mind if I drop in sometime? You might be able to steer me toward some interviews.'

'Anytime.' She made a small wave and turned to go.

'Do they call you Charlie?'

'Not really,' she said over her shoulder.

That went well, I thought.

As I crossed the street toward my car, my gaze swept the square, once again reacquainting myself with the old and taking note of the new. Down a side street I saw Dub's Garage, its facade topped by the familiar neon sign with its 1930s-style lettering. A white pickup was parked near the entrance, and a white-clad figure sat on the fender.

Without breaking stride, I changed direction and headed toward the garage. It seemed illogical and natural all at once. If you'd asked me why, I might have said, she's Callie's little sister and let it go at that. But if you'd pressed me, I would have said I was doing something to revive the memory of Callie, to get close to her again in some way.

She watched me come with no expression, her jaw busily working. Her hands held the wax paper-wrapped remnants of her lunch, and the paper bag, now fully stained with grease from the french fries, sat in her lap.

'Sorry to interrupt you,' I said.

She shook her head, mouth full, but clearly in no hurry to finish. I gave her a minute. She polished off the last bite of the cheeseburger, dipped her hand into the bag, fished around, and extracted two french fries, apparently the last. She offered them to me with a questioning look and, when I shook my head, made short work of them. Then she wiped her mouth with one of Ida's paper napkins, stuffed the remaining paper into the bag, squashed it between two hands, and did a one-handed push shot toward a trash bin about ten feet away. Basket.

'Crowd goes wild,' I said.

'I saw you over at Ida's.'

'Uh-huh. I knew Charlene from a while back. We were just catching up.'

She nodded without much interest. She was shorter than Charlene, also prettier. Up close, I could see some of Callie's beauty in her. But where Callie had been womanly, even at nineteen, her little sister seemed more the tomboy. Her fine features were marred slightly by an irregularity to the bridge of her nose, probably an old break that had healed badly. Swallowed in the coveralls, her figure was an unknown quantity. But her neck and wrists looked thin, almost scrawny.

'You're Lita Ray, right?'

She nodded again, this time with a slight smile. She struck me as someone who was comfortable around men and who had no trouble handling them. It's probably a trait with all the Darnell women, I thought.

'I'm Randall Wilkes.'

'I heard about you on the radio,' she said. 'You're from Chicago, and you found Opal and Mrs. McMahan.'

'That's right,' I said. 'I actually grew up around here.'

'You don't sound much like it.'

I let that pass. 'Charlene tells me you manage this place. I remember it well. Is Dub still around?'

'Yep, but he doesn't come in much any more.' From inside the garage came the ring of a tire iron on concrete. 'I've got a couple of young guys who do a lot of the work. Dub wants me to buy him out, and if I can swing it, that'll happen in a year or so.'

'You always eat your lunch on a truck fender?'

She shook her head. 'Yesterday it was a '99 Explorer, and the day before … I forget. I just like to watch the world go by while I eat, that's all.'

'I think I remember you when you were … I don't know, nine or ten.'

For the first time she gave me a good looking-over. 'Maybe

I remember you just a little too,' she said. 'But I think your hair was brown. You knew my sister, right?'

'I sure did,' I said. 'I liked her. Always wondered what happened to her after she left town.'

A moment passed, and she waved casually to someone in a passing car. I began trying to think of something else to say when she finally spoke.

'Everybody did.'

'What's that?'

'Everybody wondered what happened to her.'

'You never heard from her?'

'Only once.' Her legs were crossed at the ankles, and as she rested her hands on the hood, the heels of her sneakers thumped lightly and rhythmically on the truck's tire.

'She talked to me about going off to Memphis, or maybe Atlanta,' I said. 'Getting a job as a waitress at one of the big restaurants. She joked that she'd get a boyfriend—'

'A disk jockey,' she finished for me. 'Somebody who'd play a song on the radio for her every night. She told us the same stories. So one night she didn't show up at Grady's – that's where she was working – and about a week later I got a postcard from her, from Memphis. And nary a word since then.

'What did the postcard say?'

Her heels stopped their rhythm. 'Why do you need to know?'

That stopped me. There was no friendliness in the question.

'I don't know ...'

A man stepped out of the garage and stood looking at us, making small, fidgety movements as he wiped his hands on a rag. He was wirily built, with thinning hair, and he wore coveralls like hers but several sizes larger. I saw now that he was staring at Lita Ray, and his face had an unguarded look of worry and impatience.

Following my gaze, she turned and saw him. 'Don't worry, I'm coming back,' she shouted in exaggerated tones like those a mother might use to a child. Reassured, he went inside.

She shot back the oversize sleeve of her left arm and looked at her watch. 'Well, I've got to get back to work.'

'Wait. Just a minute. I guess the reason I'm asking about Callie is because, uh … she was important to me.'

She waited.

'It's hard to explain—'

'I bet you're one of the guys who used to make out with her,' she said. 'That's probably why she was important to you, huh?'

'You're a hard-nose, aren't you?'

She shrugged.

'I liked her, and thought she was made of better stuff than a lot of the people in this town,' I said. 'I told you I've wondered what happened to her, and that's the truth. I guess I walked over here hoping you'd tell me she married that disk jockey and raised a houseful of kids somewhere.'

This time the look she gave me was neither friendly nor unfriendly. 'Well, I wish I could tell you that,' she said. 'But Darnells never had much in the way of luck.' She hopped nimbly off the truck and headed into the garage.

SIX

As it grew, Pilgrim's Rest attracted more of the faithful, and by the time of the Civil War it was a thriving community of several hundred, a kind of theocracy led by Crowder. Redemption Spring, outside town, served as a place of baptism and worship.

The late 1800s brought an influx of a new kind of settler, drawn by reports that the spring held medicinal powers. Pilgrim's Rest gradually lost its religious character and became a kind of spa for visitors who summered there while taking the waters and enjoying the clean air and scenery. The wealthier among them built elegant homes in the woods on a mountain bluff near the spring, and the collection of Victorian houses became known as the Colony. Although no longer quite as elegant, the homes still stand today, an impressive collection of nineteenth-century architecture in the woods of southern Tennessee ...

They buried Faye McMahan two days later, in the late morning of a mild, overcast day. The little Burning Bush Baptist Church was packed for the service. It was a simple and straightforward place of worship, done in white siding with a steeple, and it stood in a pine grove just off the highway outside Pilgrim's Rest. The windows and doors were open, letting in an occasional breeze that carried with it the sweet, green scent of pine.

Most of the people present were locals, the women in simple Sunday dresses with hats, the men in their one good Sunday suit, necks sunburned and hands work-hardened. Sonny and Tish stood out in that crowd, along with a few of their close friends who had driven down from Nashville to help them say goodbye to Faye. Opal Hicks' parents had been pointed out to me. Dressed plainly, they stood next to the McMahans. To the right of Opal's mother was Lita Ray Darnell. I wondered if she was related to the family. Out of her coveralls and with her dark blonde hair washed and brushed, she looked a whole lot better.

I glimpsed my father in a pew at the far right, sharing a hymnal with Charlene Singletary. Friends? I wondered.

Except for professional reasons, I hadn't set foot in a church in years. Make that decades. But if you're raised in the South, churchgoing is part of your blood and you never really lose it. Walk in the door, listen to one of the old hymns, and it all comes back.

It was a good service. The minister, an old boy I remembered, his pompadour now silver, spoke lovingly of Faye and of the son she had raised right and then sent out to make his mark in the world. There was no mention of Blue, which didn't surprise me.

From my spot near the back, I studied Sonny's well-dressed, bulky frame. He had been raised a Baptist, but since marrying Tish had spent more time breathing the more rarefied air of the Episcopalians. I had listened in to my parents' dinner table conversations and knew something about the delicate hierarchy of Southern churches, a subject worthy of Burke's Peerage. The more genteel denominations looked down on the Baptists, one reason being that they baptized by dunking the subject all the way under. The Methodists, who didn't dunk, were considered more middle-class, the Presbyterians even more so. And resting atop the Protestant pyramid were the upper-crust Episcopalians, who cut a swathe in the cities but who weren't even represented in this little place.

Looking around the chapel, the turnout made me feel good. It wasn't just Faye McMahan's son who had made a mark in the world. She had too, in her own way. My next thought was of her killer. I wondered if he was in this room right now; wondered if I would ever meet him, ever see his face.

The preacher's benediction brought me back. The service was

66

over. I knew there was more to come – in the South, the best funerals take their time. But the graveyard service and church supper were for the near and dear, so after joining the slow and somber exit from the church, I prepared to head for my car. Over where the parking lot met the highway I saw a giant TV van bearing the logo of one of the Nashville stations, its fancy antennae ready to beam the news from Pilgrim's Rest all the way back to the state capital. At the bottom of the steps I spotted Chief Chitwood, who was having a private smoke by the side of the building. I walked over to him.

'How are you, Randall?' He was in uniform, leaning easily against the building, and he held the cigarette cupped in his palm as if mindful of his surroundings.

'Just fine, sir. Nice service.'

He nodded noncommittally, waiting.

'Hope you don't mind my asking if anything's turned up.'

'You asking as a newsman or a friend of the family?' His tone was relaxed. He didn't seem very concerned either way, just interested.

'A friend, mostly.'

'Uh-huh.' He took a drag and let his eyes roam over the crowd as they exited the church. I wondered if he was looking for the killer. 'The Governor, he asked me as a favor to keep you up to date, as much as I can without messing up the investigation. Said you're a friend, and it won't do any harm 'cause you're not a reporter anymore and you won't be printing anything.' He squinted at me through the smoke. 'That's right, isn't it?'

'Yes, sir,' I said.

'Well, I can tell you a little. The TBI's been busy. Had a forensic team go through that house, looking for prints and fibers and DNA and everything. It's all being examined now. DNA is a long shot and could take weeks anyway. First guess, they think it was one person, that he was strong, and that he used gloves, so they're not counting on picking up much.'

'And causes of death?'

'Um.' He carefully dropped the cigarette onto the grass and ground it out under his heel. 'Opal was ... her neck was broken.

Mrs. McMahan's too. Difference was, he broke Opal's neck with his hands.'

I let that sink in. The image sickened me. Of all the many ways we have devised to kill our fellow humans, snapping the life out of someone with your bare hands is definitely one of the more personal. It feels primitive, it smells of the swamp.

'Chief, does this sound like anyone—'

'Has anybody been killing people like that?' he cut in. 'No, sir. At least nowhere in the state of Tennessee. We've got ourselves a brand new killer here. And you can bet there's a whole bunch of people who'd like to get their hands on him. Mrs. McMahan had a lot of friends.'

'I know. I'm one of them. What about Opal?'

'Boyfriends, you mean? Enemies? Nothing we've turned up. Her folks are churchgoing and strict, and they hadn't let her start going out with boys yet. And we haven't turned up anybody who disliked her.'

'Well, thank you, Chief,' I said. 'I appreciate your time.' Then, looking for a different topic on which to end the conversation, I asked: 'What happened to the bones that were dug up down below the falls? The new ones, I mean. How long before they'll be buried alongside the others?'

He stared at me hard for a moment. 'Funny you'd ask that,' he said finally. 'Those bones ... there was only a handful of them, a thigh bone, some fingers. Critters had dug up the grave, apparently, and scattered everything before we even got to it. What we found got sent to the state crime lab, like the skeletons that got dug up before. The lab folks have got a backlog, like always, and they've just started working on them. Recent murders are at the top of their list, not old bones.'

I waited, and nothing came. I could have let it go, but I felt a tiny itch, and something told me to scratch it.

'Is there something, Chief?'

Another pause, and he looked out over the now-thinning crowd. 'Well,' he said finally. 'They've just started, like I said. But they called me yesterday and said they're not a soldier's bones.'

I must have stared, not really understanding. He went on.

'They can tell just by looking that the bones are not nearly old enough. No more 'n twenty to thirty years in the ground, they figure. They might learn more when they get 'em under an X-ray.'

I let out a breath. 'So ...'

'Could mean anything,' he said. 'People who live in the country sometimes bury their kinfolk nearby. It's illegal, but they do it.'

'Sure,' I said. 'But it could also mean homicide, couldn't it?'

'That's right. But I don't like to jump to conclusions. I'm too old to be jumping to anything. I'm looking into our records, trying to find if anybody was reported missing anywhere in the county back then. At least I know it wasn't anybody from the Burch family.' He pushed himself away from the wall. 'If you want to know any more, you can read it in the paper. I've got to go, Randall.'

I watched him walk toward his police cruiser. Well. How about that? This quiet little place was turning out to have more than its share of sinister stories. Two violent murders, and then bones emerging from earth, bringing with them the possibility – maybe even likelihood – of another murder. What were the odds?

'Randall.'

I looked up to see Tish motioning mc over. She stood at the bottom of the church steps, where she and Sonny had stationed themselves, shaking hands with the leave-takers. But now there were no hands left to shake, and Sonny was standing in the church door talking to the minister. I walked over to her.

'How are you holding up?' I asked, knowing how inadequate the question must sound.

'Better than he is.' Her voice sounded worn out. 'I think the visitation really got to him.'

The two of them had spent the previous day receiving visitors at Longstaff House. I had been there for a while, but had mostly made myself scarce.

'Did you see how many people came by?' she said wonder-ingly. 'Friends, neighbors, everybody who loved her. It was a real crowd. Everybody brought food. Casseroles, salads, cold cuts, biscuits ...' A small, tight laugh. 'Lord.'

'You know you're in the South,' I said, 'when you can't bury someone without lots of good, home-cooked food.'

She seemed not to have heard me. 'She was such a simple woman,' she said, almost to herself. 'We didn't always get along at first, but that was mostly my fault. I never would have said this out loud, but I suppose I thought she was just ... you know, *country*. Very plain, very simple. I don't think she ever left Tennessee, her whole life. And I was this Nashville sorority girl who had never met anyone quite like her. It took me a while, but I finally saw how strong and straight she was, and what she'd done for Sonny. And I came around. I really loved her.'

'I'm sure you did.'

'Recently, when her mind started to go, it was so awful. You could see her slipping away. Sonny couldn't bear to think about it. He thought it would be a gradual thing, and how terrible it would be to lose her by inches. And now ... look how it happened. Even more awful.'

'I'm sorry, Tish. I have good memories of her too. They'll find out who did it.'

'Will they?' She sounded doubtful. Then she went on. 'Some of her friends, the old folks, they wanted to have a real old-fashioned Baptist wake, with Faye laid out right there in the living room. Sonny just couldn't do it, and I don't blame him. This has almost been more than he could—'

I looked up to see Sonny coming down the steps. His face was grim. He didn't speak, he just stared, his eyes on me but focused on something else. His strong features seemed slack, and even the big McMahan jaw looked less imposing. Finally, to me, he said, 'You'll stick around, won't you?'

'Here in town? Sure,' I said. 'As long as there's work to do. Will I see you back at the house?'

'Uh-uh.' He shook his head as Tish slipped her arm through his. 'We're packed and ready to roll. As soon as the supper's over, we'll head back to Nashville. I'm, uh, leaving Ken here. He won't bother you. He'll find another place to stay.'

I was instantly curious. But then it hit me, and I felt stupid for even wondering. Kenneth Lively was an ex-cop, and he did Sonny's bidding. What more urgent matter than to find out who killed his employer's mother?

So I just nodded, and Sonny nodded back at me, and the message got passed very economically, no words needed. I had a job to do, and so did Mr. Lively. I wished him good hunting.

Longstaff House seemed empty and drafty after all the comings and goings, but I appreciated the privacy. The days leading up to Faye's funeral had not seemed a good time to begin asking the people of Pilgrim's Rest what they remembered about Sonny McMahan, so I'd put off the interviewing. Now it was time to get productive.

A big parcel sat on the dining table, addressed to me in a familiar spidery script. Before driving here, I'd called my cleaning woman in Chicago and asked her to pack up a few things for me. I carried the box up to my room, dug into it, and extracted several changes of comfortable clothes until I got to the most important thing, my laptop computer. I'd cased the main room downstairs and satisfied myself that I could hook up the computer with one of the phone jacks for Internet access. Now I could work.

I opened the laptop on the bed and spread out around it all the notes and tape recordings I'd made in Nashville. Then, aided by the local phone book and my memory, I began making a list of people who had known Sonny as a boy – friends, relatives, neighbors, teachers, local businessmen. Tomorrow I'd start checking off names. Today, I could make other calls. The Governor knew people all over the place. I had a charged-up cell phone and a whole state to go roaming through.

For the next three hours I called numbers in Nashville, checking in again with people I'd first made contact with before driving here. True to his word, Sonny had had his office turn over to me a pile of raw material on his years as governor – legislative documents, speech transcripts, correspondence, news clippings. I'd noticed that while most of the material was filtered through the Governor's political prism, not all of it was. Parts of it, in fact, especially among the news clippings, reflected the views of his political opponents. Some of it was downright unkind toward him. Reading it, I gave my old friend points for candor.

The facts of his governorship could be had from the documents, so I'd spent much of my energy while in Nashville setting up face-to-face talks with both his friends and enemies. What I was after was a sense of the man as perceived by others, and my fresh round of phone calls helped add to the portrait of Sonny that was beginning to take shape in my notebooks. Like a lot of politicians, he was seen as both saint and devil. His supporters admired him for his service to the state, for bringing in industry, creating jobs and trying to turn around the public schools. His enemies criticized him for his coziness with big business, his free-spending ways, and what they called his 'cult of personality.'

Toward the end of my calls I spun off on a detour. It came out of my talk with Olen Stringer over at the historical society about the plans for the Civil War study center. The developer was something called the Outerbridge Group, and Sonny was one of the directors, Stringer had said. The group's plans sounded very ambitious, and something about the project had interested my father enough to cause him to put up that big rendering in his study.

Curious, I carried my laptop down to the main room, hooked it up to the phone jack and began surfing the Net. I found a few passing references to the Outerbridge Group, most of them in the *Tennessean* and centering on the announcement a few months earlier of plans for the project. One article quoted Sonny as saying it would 'revitalize the southern Cumberland Plateau, a place I love, and bring in visitors who may never have tasted its beauty before.'

The company's website consisted of a home page only and was mostly decorative. Its motto: 'Developing Tennessee for the 21st Century.' It touted the Civil War study center as being on its drawing boards but mentioned no other previous or current projects. Its address was an office in downtown Nashville, and Stuart McMahan was named as the company's executive director. Sonny wanted to put some investment money into the Cumberland Plateau. It looked like Outerbridge, staffed with some of his investor friends, was the vehicle.

The list of company officers included a half-dozen other names, only one of which sounded familiar. Lem Coldsmith. During my round of interviews in Nashville, Coldsmith was a name I kept running into. People described him as a friend of Sonny. He wasn't a politician, and he had never held a government job, but he seemed to play some kind of role in Sonny's life.

'If you want to know what makes Sonny tick, you should talk to Lem,' one of the statehouse regulars told me. ''Course,' he added with a chuckle, 'Lem won't tell you anything important.'

I asked around and found that Coldsmith was a businessman and a kind of minor celebrity, one whose face was on countless TV and newspaper ads promoting his chain of furniture stores. I phoned his office to ask for an interview and was surprised to be connected with him in seconds.

'What do you want with me?' he asked with hearty belligerence. 'I'm just a furniture salesman.'

'I'm told you're close to the Governor, and I'm helping him with this book project.'

'Did you clear this with him?' he asked. 'Talking to me, I mean?'

'He said I could talk to anybody I wanted to.'

'Call me back in a coupla weeks, and we'll see,' he said. 'You have a great day, hear?'

The light was fading outside, and my eyes were getting tired. I got in my rented car and drove out the highway toward an old dinner hangout called Grady's, a place where Callie had once waited tables. When I got to the location, Grady's was gone, replaced by something bigger and more impressive called the Hunting Lodge. It was decorated in ersatz rustic, with lots of varnished beams, and a neon sign that advertised home cooking. Inside it was spacious and pleasant-looking, noticeably more uptown-looking than Grady's or just about anything else around Pilgrim's Rest. I had a drink and dinner. The cooking wasn't home, by a mile, but it's hard to find really bad food in the South. At least since Reconstruction.

Back at the house, I sat for a while on the screened-in porch. In the few days I'd been there – had it only been four? – it seemed that the temperature had dropped a few degrees. It was shaping up as a chilly fall. The air was very still, and the distant roar of Damnation Falls sounded closer than it was. The sound worked on me like a lullaby. I was getting—

I sat up quickly, listening. A sound from below the porch, a rock being dislodged. The mountains, I knew, were full of deer and other critters. I hadn't seen a deer up close in a long time. I stood up, went to the screen, and looked down.

Just below the property line of homes standing on the bluff ran a public path. I had walked it myself many times. I couldn't see much because of the trees, but one clear patch stood out, washed in the faintest light of the moon. I stared at it for a few seconds, and then I saw the man. He was walking slowly, head down, from the direction of the guesthouse. When he entered the moonlit space, he paused, and looked up. If I hadn't been standing in darkness, I'd say he looked into my eyes.

When I saw his face, I pressed my hands against the screen and heard my breath spill out in a gasp. Lean figure, mop of still-black hair, features carved out of wood, with a wide mouth and deep valleys under the cheekbones. Dark clothing, and even though I couldn't make out the details, I somehow knew he had on a well-worn suit with a white shirt and tie.

I almost called out his name. But that would have been foolish. Blue McMahan, after all, was sleeping with the catfish at the bottom of the Big Muddy. Unless … unless he was here on the plateau, had come back to the place he'd once called home, to pay a promised visit to his wife. The woman who now lay in the ground.

As I stood there with his name stuck in my throat, he lowered his head and passed out of my sight.

SEVEN

I don't remember making the decision to go after him. I just know that a few seconds later, I had grabbed my jacket from where I'd tossed it on the living room sofa and the flashlight out of the kitchen drawer and was making my way down the steep stone steps that led from the base of the porch to the pathway below.

I kept the flashlight near my pants leg, pointing downward, so as not to give myself away. Here I was again, scurrying around in the dark with a flashlight, chasing ... who? If I was wrong, if my eyes and sleepy brain had deceived me and the figure up ahead was not my old friend but Faye's killer, then I was truly a fool. My steps faltered as I tested that idea.

No, I thought. I'd know that lean, hound-dog face anywhere. It was Blue, walking the Earth, and I thought of the line from the old song about Joe Hill: *Alive as you and me.* And so on I went, creeping after him like a footpad in pursuit of a stroller with a fat wallet.

Why all the stealth? After all, I knew him, had fished Tanner's Lake with him, had hunted squirrel with him up on Flat Top, had sat entranced while he spun his tales of life on the midway. Why not just call out his name?

Because I knew him. And the thing that always defined Blue McMahan was his secrets. What was it Faye had said? *Blue knows a secret.* No kidding. The man's life was a web of lies and subterfuge, of long, unexplained absences from home. Blue was a con man, and the only thing you know for sure about a con man is that the truth is not in him.

So, whatever had brought him back to Pilgrim's Rest and the Colony, he was not moving around openly, this so-called dead man. He may not be happy to know I'd seen him. If I called his name, how would I know he wouldn't skedaddle? And so I skulked after him.

It was surely no coincidence, seeing him here just days after his wife was savagely killed. As I walked, my mind went over all the possible reasons for his being here, and you can be sure I considered the theory that he might have killed her. Blue was many things, most of them bad, but was he the man who knotted a rope around Faye's neck and flung her over the railing of the bridge at Damnation Falls? My steps faltered again, and I grew angry at my own indecision.

I'd never been afraid of Blue, but I could imagine being afraid of him.

I knew he was somewhere up ahead. What I didn't know was how I would handle him when I caught up with him.

Watching the tight little circle of light cast just in front of me, I trudged along, careful for rocks, listening to the rhythm of my breathing and alert for any sound from up ahead.

Why even bother to chase him down, this old reprobate who had abandoned his wife and son and then tried to fool the world into thinking he was dead? Sonny hated his guts. I should have too, I supposed. Why didn't I?

Now that was a tricky one. Maybe it was partly because Faye had said he needed help, but I think it came down to this: Blue had given me something a long time ago, and I'd never had a chance to repay him. For a while there I'd thought it was too late. Now, maybe not.

I took my time, and I didn't catch sight of him on the path. He had less light than I, and he'd be stepping carefully. Only a few dozen yards later, the path rose gradually until it joined the bluff road I'd driven earlier that evening. There were no streetlights in the Colony, but in this open moonlit space visibility was better. I spotted him about forty yards ahead of me on the road, walking at a steady pace.

Then I saw him turn onto the road that led to the highway,

and it looked like he might be on his way out. I was beginning to recast my plan when I saw twin brake lights flash once, then again on the road ahead of him. A car, parked at the verge. Waiting for him? It looked that way. In another minute, he could be gone.

Again, no time to reflect. Trying not to make too much noise, I turned and ran back down the road, my sneakers making soft slapping sounds that I hoped would not carry to him. In a minute I was at Longstaff House and my car. Keys still in my pocket. I started up the Toyota, backed it out of the drive, and, with no lights on, headed after him. Taking the turn onto the road where I'd last spotted him, I saw nothing up ahead. I hit the headlights and stepped on the gas, tearing along the hundred yards or so until I reached the highway. I pulled out, looked frantically to the right. Nothing. Then left, and saw a pair of tail-lights just disappearing around a bend.

I took off and soon spotted him. Headlights were all right here, I reasoned. I was just another car on the road. But I held back, giving him a comfortable lead. This was a state road, reasonably well traveled. I passed modest homes by the road-side, dirt turnoffs that led straight into the woods, an occasional cluster of eateries and other small businesses, always trying to keep the other car just in view. After close to ten miles, I saw brake lights ahead, and he turned to the right into some kind of lighted area. I eased off the gas and rolled forward until I saw a tall neon sign and a motel, then stopped, killing my lights. I remembered the place and its winking red and blue sign. It was a no-frills establishment, just an office and fewer than twenty rooms laid out strip-fashion parallel to the road, and it had sat here all these years, aging quietly. The car in question parked in front of one of the rooms, and two men got out and went inside. Lights came on behind the curtained window.

I pulled onto the turnoff and parked near the highway but out of sight of the office. For about a minute I sat there deciding what to do. My choices were few: come back in the light of day, when he might well be gone, or follow through now. I got out and walked over to the other car. It was a beat-up Chevy with a Tennessee plate and a Knoxville dealer's name on the plate holder. The door of the room stood slightly ajar, and I could hear voices within. I drew a deep breath and knocked. No one answered. I knocked again, louder. A faint sound came from the other side of the door.

'Who's that?' I had hoped to hear Blue's voice and take it from there. But this voice was not his, so I put Plan B into effect.

'I'm in the room next door,' I said. 'Your car's got some kind of a leak. You ought to take a look.'

'Thanks,' the voice said. 'I'll take care of it later.'

'Fine.' I leaned up against the wall beside the door and waited quietly. Minutes went by, and I fidgeted, wondering if I should knock again. Then the door opened wider, and a thin man in dungarees and a checked shirt stepped out and headed toward the car. He saw me and stopped.

His eyes narrowed. He was thin, built along the same lines as Blue, and had some years on him, but looked like he could handle himself.

Time for the direct approach. 'I'm here to talk to Blue,' I said, putting on a friendly smile. 'Can you ask him to come out?'

'Never heard of him,' the man said, and this time the look was openly hostile. He turned to go inside.

'Just tell him it's Randall Wilkes,' I said, more loudly this time. 'And I'm still waiting for a chance to try that trick he showed me with the Phillips head and the ignition switch. I want to make sure—'

And suddenly there he was, framed in the doorway.

'Well, if it ain't Little Bit.'

He had on suit pants, a white shirt and tie, just as I had guessed. He also wore a wry, lopsided grin, which was about all the grin you ever got from him. He was twenty years older, and he hadn't really changed all that much. His features were still craggy, as if carved with a rough chisel before the carpenter got around to the smooth planing. If Sonny was beef, Blue was gristle. The only changes I noticed were a few more lines in the face and a little gray in the sideburns, which I couldn't have spotted during my earlier glimpse.

'Don't give me that Little Bit,' I said, repeating the name he'd hung on me when I was about ten. 'I'm bigger than you now.'

'I reckon you are.' He looked me up and down, unhurriedly, behaving not at all like somebody who'd just been smoked out of a motel room like a raccoon out of a hollow tree. Then he reached out a hand and shook mine. His grip was light and tentative, befitting a man who, all through my youth, had always seemed poised to catch the next bus out of town. 'You want to come in and sit a spell?' He opened the door all the way, and I entered. 'This here's Dewey Tackett.' He indicated his companion, who still regarded me with suspicion.

Dewey Tackett and I exchanged nods. His name sounded vaguely familiar, but I couldn't connect it with anything. The room smelled strongly of a combination of alcohol, cigarette smoke, and recently consumed fast food. A deck of cards lay neatly on the far bedspread, suggesting that they had been about to start a game.

'Damn fan's not working,' Blue said, leaving the door slightly ajar as before. He indicated that I should take the only comfortable chair in the room, and he and Dewey half-lay, half-sat on the two beds. Although Dewey was not quite as tall as Blue, both men appeared cut from the same rough bolt of cloth. Country cousins. Dewey picked up the deck and began idly cutting the cards, his movements fluid.

Blue, lounging on his rumpled bed, reached for a pack of Luckies on the bedside table. He shook one out, lit it, and laid it to rest on an ashtray, where it added its plume to the already murky air. All his moves were slow and deliberate, just as I remembered them. His hands, like Dewey's, were long-boned and graceful, card shark's hands.

None of my questions felt easy. I've interviewed hundreds of people – rogues and saints, politicians and condemned murderers – and I should have been able to handle a broken-down con man. But I had too much history with him.

Finally I just blurted it out. 'Faye's dead.'

He nodded. 'I know that, Lit—' He stopped. 'Randall.'

'Is that why you're here?'

He gave me a surprised look. "Course it is.'

'But you weren't at the funeral.'

'Well ...' He rubbed lightly under one eye with a long forefinger. 'I don't suppose I was. But I was out there at the cemetery when they buried her. Close enough to see. Just a little distance away, that's all.'

'Blue ... a lot of people think you're dead, you know that?'

Another lopsided grin.

'Including your own son.'

The grin faded. 'I imagine so.'

'Why?'

He pursed his lips and glanced over in Dewey's direction, and said, 'Maybe we can talk about that some other time.' His sleepy eyelids concealed what he might have been thinking. It struck me that he and Sonny, who did not much resemble each other in other respects, shared those eyelids, just as both men were masters at concealment – Sonny the politician, Blue the confidence man.

'You two traveling together?' I asked, indicating his friend.

'Nope,' he said. 'Dewey met me here, just to chew the fat. We used to work the Morrissey Shows together.' I wondered if Dewey had driven all the way from Knoxville, and in response to my curious look, Blue muttered, 'Dewey told his missus he was just going to see an old friend. She, uh ...'

'She thinks you're dead, like everybody else?'

Dewey pointedly cleared his throat without looking our way. 'He's all right,' Blue said to him. 'Randall and me, we're old buddies. He's a big-time newspaperman up in Chicago.' He reached for the cigarette. 'Or was.'

I felt surprised until I remembered one of Blue's attributes. He was a self-taught reader who devoured books and newspapers. He would have read about me.

I was starting to frame my first serious question when Blue, gesturing toward his friend, said, 'Him and me, we go way back. I told you a few carny stories, but he knows even more.' He turned to Dewey. 'Tell him how you got started.'

Dewey looked reluctant at first, but after one more appraising look at me, he settled back onto his pillow, the cards still cradled on his chest.

'It was the late fifties when I joined the show,' he began. 'They were getting rid of the freaks – you know, the bearded lady and the armless man, all those acts – because people were starting to feel sorry for 'em, said they didn't belong in a tent with people staring at 'em all day. So most of the shows went over to games to make their money. I got started in the games, and a few years later Blue came along, and I broke him in. I was working the flat store on the midway when he asked if he could join up, and I got him started as a ride boy. A year later, he was my outside man, and then he took over the Football game next to me.'

I searched my memory. A lot of years ago, when Blue was spending part of one winter in Pilgrim's Rest, he had introduced me to the carny's vocabulary. A ride boy, I knew, was one of the young roughnecks who assembled and disassembled the carnival rides. They occupied the lowest rung of the carny hierarchy. The flat store was a trailer that held the most elaborate games on the midway, the ones that took in the most money. And the outside man helped the game operator by making sure that when he was fleecing a mark in the game, no crowd would gather to watch the fleecing. The number of ways of discouraging lookie-loos was infinite, limited only by the outside man's imagination. Some of them used physical intimidation, others showed more finesse.

'Old Blue was a natural at Football,' Dewey said, speaking in an amused drawl. 'He had this patter where he'd call out to folks walking by, and he could pick out the perfect mark and call out just the right thing to make him want to come in. Say it was some youngster with his girlfriend, Blue'd have something racy to say, make the boy laugh. Say it was a man and his wife, dressed good, Blue would say something funny but respectful. He just knew how to play it.'

Dewey, as you can tell by now, was not nearly as dour as I'd guessed from our initial encounter. He turned out to be a real raconteur – funny and wry and self-effacing in the way of many country people. But underneath I sensed the hard edge of the carny. As Blue had told me once, carnies look at all of non-carnival humanity as a flock of sheep ripe for fleecing.

Dewey went on, with occasional asides from Blue, to describe the Football game, a time-honored way of separating carnival visitors from their cash. To the mark it looked simple – a board with painted one-inch squares and a cup holding six marbles that would be tossed onto the board and settle onto the squares, each of which had a numerical value between one and six. The objective was to throw the marbles enough times to gain a hundred yards and 'score.' Only trouble was, the game was rigged in such a way that the operator could let the mark make it almost to the goal line and then put on the brakes, making it impossible for him to get that final yard. And all the while doubling the cost of throwing the marbles with each bet.

'One time I saw Blue start this old boy and his wife out at fifty cents a bet and work them up to sixty-four bucks on the ninety-nine yard line. When they left, he had over four hundred dollars of their money.' He was cutting the deck one-handed now, and I found myself staring at the cards as he talked.

'Didn't people ever get mad?' I asked.

'Sure,' Blue said, chuckling. 'But every carny knows the way you stay out of a fight is to just keep talking. Talk fast, talk friendly, let 'em know you're damn sorry they ran out of luck. Give 'em a teddy bear to walk away with. It makes 'em feel better. And here's something else to remember: No guy wants to admit to his wife or girlfriend that he's been taken.'

These two were a fascinating pair, and I could have listened to them all night. But that, I surmised, was the problem. The longer they talked, the longer it kept me away from asking Blue anything substantive. And maybe that was the point. I had the feeling that these two old carnies were waltzing me around.

'How about you and I go for a ride?' I asked Blue abruptly.

'Just when I'm getting comfortable?' I could barely see his eyes under those heavy lids.

'Blue, I'm just going to pester you until you talk to me.'

A long sigh. 'All righty.' He got up, picked up his suit coat from the back of a chair and turned to Dewey. 'You about to head home?'

'Yep,' the other man said. 'The missus is going to be wondering about me. I think I'll stay here a while and watch some of the Titans game first, though.'

'See you, buddy.' They shook hands, and we left as Dewey turned on the TV set and began flipping channels.

Outside, I studied Blue in the harsh motel lighting. In his sober clothing, he looked like a small-town undertaker who needed a shave and a haircut. He wore a Rotary button in his lapel, but Blue was no more Rotarian than I. He'd told me once that he liked to travel with an assortment of such buttons in his pocket. When he got to a town that seemed ripe for picking, he studied the signs out at the city limits that listed the service organizations, and he pulled out an appropriate lapel button to make sure he fit in. 'Sometimes I'm a Lion, sometimes I'm an Elk,' he told me. 'Sometimes I wear my Masonic ring.'

'So Dewey's going home,' I said. 'I figure that's his car. What about you?'

'Oh, mine's in the back,' he said, shrugging into his suit coat. 'I don't like to advertise myself. I'll stay here tonight and get going early in the morning.'

'Get going to where? Where do you live?'

'You ask a lot of questions, Little Bit.'

'I told you to stop with that name.'

'Then easy on the questions.' He said it in a friendly drawl, but he was clearly pulling rank on me, and I was once again the little boy and he the grown-up.

I took him to my car and we started back toward town. 'Can I assume you're not driving around with your own license, in a car registered in your name?' I asked him.

'Why don't we see if Buster's is still open?' Blue said by way of an answer. 'Get us a pork sandwich.'

We were in luck. A mile or so down the road sat the shack called Buster's, a combination gas station and eatery, and the 'Bar-B-Q' sign topped with a jolly pink neon pig was still lit up. Inside was a short-order counter and six tables. Blue made me go in first and look around. I came back to report that except for the counter girl the place was empty, so he went in with me. Atop the counter stood a fragrant, steaming pot of pulled pork smelling like meat-eater's heaven. Blue and I each had a mess of pork on a hamburger bun and an RC Cola and settled in at one of the rickety tables.

'Chicago, huh?' he said. 'You went Yankee on us.'

'I suppose so.'

'Until you got fired. For making stuff up.'

Bluntly put, but I nodded my head without hesitation. If I'd had H.L. Mencken sitting across from me, or A.J. Liebling or I.F. Stone or any of the other giants of American journalism, I'm sure I would have tried to squirm my way out of that one, offer up a rational-sounding excuse. But why bother with Blue? This was the man who had taught me how to hot-wire a car and deal from the bottom of the deck. He had always made me feel like a fellow miscreant, always acted like he was no better than me. I had no good reason to lie to him.

'So how'd you find me, anyway?' He said it as softly as an afterthought, but I wasn't fooled. Men like him don't like to be found until they're ready.

'I saw you walking along the bluff just below Longstaff House. You were dead, so naturally I wondered what you were doing there.' I felt it was time to quit making conversation and get some answers. 'Look, Blue, this is all very strange. You turn up just after Faye is killed. And right before she died, she told me she thought either you or Sonny were in trouble.'

His eyes lost some of their sleepiness. 'She did?' He chewed over his pork for a while, thinking. 'What kind?'

'She didn't say. But I don't have to tell you that if they spot you, the police are going to wonder what brought you to town.'

He washed down a mouthful of pork with a swallow of RC. 'Why don't you go ahead and ask me if I killed her?'

'Oh, hell ...'

'If I said no, would you believe me?'

I let out a long breath. 'Blue, I swear I don't know. But I'd try.'

'Well, I didn't.'

I was glad to hear it, but suddenly the irony of all this struck me. Blue, an inveterate liar, being interrogated by an ex-journalist whose career crashed and burned over the same issue – mendacity. H.L. Mencken, the truth-telling sage of Baltimore, would have had something to say about that. Somewhere on Parnassus, he and the other boys were enjoying a cigar and a good laugh.

I tried another question. 'Have you ever spent any time in jail?'

He looked surprised. 'No, 'course not.'

'Are you wanted for anything?'

He shrugged. 'Nothing important. Nothing to worry about.'

I didn't totally believe him. 'Are you in any trouble?' When he hesitated to answer, I plowed ahead.

'Why'd you set up that drowning? What—' I stopped. 'Wait a minute. When they ran that story about you, they quoted a friend who said he saw you fall into the river. I just remembered why Dewey's name sounded familiar. He was the friend.'

Blue barely shrugged, intent on his sandwich. A trickle of sauce started from the corner of his mouth, but he caught it with a paper napkin before it reached his chin. 'Just an old buddy of mine doing me a favor,' he said, mouth full. 'I don't want to get him in trouble.'

'You're the one most likely to be in trouble,' I said, leaning across the table, trying to get his attention. 'Don't you get that?'

'Not going to tattle-tale on me, are you?' He looked at me, unblinking.

'No,' I said, wondering if I could keep my word.

'Why not?'

That stopped me for a moment. It required an honest answer, a moment of candor, and Blue and I had not shared many of those. Irony was more his game.

'I guess it's got something to do with all the time you spent with me when I was a kid,' I said a little breathlessly, in a hurry to get it out. 'Talking to me, showing me things, how to do things.

My, uh …' This wasn't easy. 'My father didn't make much time for me. You did. I appreciated that.'

He looked up at me for just a second, then reached for his RC and drained most of what was left. 'You were pretty good company,' he said finally. 'For a kid.'

I started to respond, but he had more to say. 'I would have spent more time with Sonny,' he said in a voice I had to strain to hear. 'But he didn't seem to like me much. It was probably Faye bad-mouthing me. Can't say as how I blame him. Or her, either. I didn't make any better a father than my own daddy did.'

I started to say something encouraging, but it hit me that he was right. Blue was a terrible father. He was probably better suited to the role of the rascally uncle, the wild older brother, the role he played with me.

'Why did you want people to think you were dead?'

He kept chewing, eyes down again. I waited impatiently.

'That ain't really none of your business.'

'I'm trying to help you,' I said, feeling the anger build in me. 'If you don't appreciate that, you can—'

'I came to town because I heard about Faye,' he broke in. 'I wanted to be here. That's all. Now I can leave.'

'Not so fast.' I felt as I had some leverage with him, and I wanted to use it. 'Do you know who might have killed her?'

He looked almost stricken. Blue McMahan, a master at hiding his feelings, had let his mask slip. 'Damn,' I said. 'You do. Don't you?'

His face went expressionless again. I felt as if the questions were about to spill out of me now, uncontrolled, like spring water out of a bucket when you start to run with it. *She said you know some kind of secret. What is it? Did it get her killed? And why have you been hiding all this time?*

But before I could get any of them out, Blue surprised me. He began to talk in a low voice, so low I had to lean across the table to hear him.

'Maybe I know something,' he began. 'And maybe I got my reasons for not showing my face around these parts. I could tell you about it, but if I did, your ass'd be in a sling just like mine.

I'm too smart to do that, and you should be too smart to ask any more questions.'

No more questions? You don't tantalize a reporter like that and then tell him he can't ask any more questions. Would you tell Man o' War he can't run, Astaire he can't dance?

I had some leverage. But if you don't apply it carefully, you could damage the thing you're trying to move. So I took the mental crowbar in my hands and slipped it into the chink between the bricks, where the mortar was beginning to crumble. And, very steadily, I pushed.

'Blue, you've got to come into town with me,' I said in a low but urgent voice. 'Talk to Jerry Chitwood. He's all right. You've known him for years. Tell him what you know. Faye didn't deserve this. If you can help him catch whoever did it ...' I let the thought trail off, but I kept a firm grip on the crowbar, ready to put my weight on it again.

He looked doubtful. I knew my words sounded feeble. He had spent weeks in hiding, for reasons we hadn't even gotten around to discussing. He said he wasn't wanted by the police for anything important, but a man doesn't go underground for unpaid parking tickets. Why would he want to surface now?

Then he nodded slowly for what seemed like a long time. 'Tell you what,' he said finally. 'I'll think about it. Sleep on it. All right?'

I knew his stubbornness, and I could tell I wasn't going to get any more out of him for now. I settled up and drove him back to the motel. Dewey's car was still parked in front of the room. 'That game must be a good 'un,' Blue said.

As he got out of the car, I wrote down my cell phone number and handed it to him. 'Call me,' I said, knowing as I spoke just how unlikely that was.

As I pulled out onto the highway, I glanced in the rear view mirror. Blue was standing by the now-open door, motionless, with his back to the wall. Something about his posture didn't look right. I backed up and twisted the wheel to get a better look at him.

'Blue?'

It was then I saw his face in the harsh fluorescent light of the entryway. It looked drained of blood, eyes focused on something far away.

I got out and approached him. He looked stricken. I started to reach out a hand to him, but then I got a look inside the room and stopped.

The room was lit only by the flicker of the tube, and the noise told me that TV was still tuned to the Titans game. Tennessee was on the Cowboys' forty-two, fourth down, two yards to go. The Coliseum crowd sounded like a rolling wave of static.

Dewey lay face-up on the far bed, where he'd been during my visit. His posture was not relaxed. All his limbs seemed to be slightly bent and twisted out of position, like those of a man just roused from a sweaty nightmare. But he wasn't awake.

I smelled it then. It was like the odor of metal shavings left by a drill, like the taste of a copper penny on the tongue. And, of course, like death.

Breathing through my mouth, I walked carefully into the room. Dewey was fully dressed, as before. His face reflected not shock or horror but a look that was more a mixture of mild surprise and indignation. I couldn't make out the exact nature of his wounds; there was too much blood. It soaked his clothing from his neck to his groin, and much of the bedspread as well.

'He's dead, ain't he?' Blue asked from the doorway.

Feeling the pork sandwich stir in my stomach, I picked up the phone on the bedside table, dialed an outside line, then 911. As I waited for the voice, the words *I did this before* passed through my head. Once again I had found someone whose life had been murderously interrupted, and once again it was my duty to pick up a telephone and tell the world.

'His wife said we looked enough alike to be brothers.'

'What?' I tried to focus on my call, still waiting for someone to answer. I heard Blue's footsteps receding and wondered vaguely if he was going for the office manager. I stared at the carpet, knowing somehow that whoever had killed Faye McMahan and Opal Hicks had been in this room tonight. But not knowing why.

I heard an engine turn over and start somewhere behind the building. 'Blue?' I dropped the phone and headed for the door just in time to see a car, its engine straining, round the end of the motel and peel out of the lot, throwing gravel in all directions as it fish-tailed out toward the highway. Then it reached the concrete, laid a patch of rubber with a screech, and roared down the road, away from town.

EIGHT

'You got to admit, this looks real odd, don't you think?'

Chief Jerry Chitwood sat sideways behind the wheel of his official cruiser, a trim sport-utility. Behind me sat Timms, the TBI agent, whose first name I had just learned was Allard.

I had that hemmed-in feeling, as no doubt was intended. The chief had his arm over the back of my seat, friendly-like. Turning my head to respond to Timms' frequent questions was starting to give me a crick in the neck. And to top it off, the vehicle reeked of nicotine, a product of Chitwood's chain-smoking. It was like sitting in a warm, cozy ashtray with company you didn't really want.

'I know it looks odd, Chief,' I said. 'I can't help that. It happens to be the truth.'

We had been over it, and both men naturally had commented on the gigantic coincidence of my stumbling onto first one, then another grisly murder scene in a town where a burglary would be front-page news.

'I'm wondering how much I should believe you,' Timms said mildly. 'What I hear, you've had some trouble in the truth-telling department.'

I felt a lingering resentment from my earlier talk with him. Being the stranger in town, I no doubt had a place on his list of suspects. I was nervous but determined not to show it. The power of truth was on my side, hallelujah, and I was reasonably sure that the physical evidence in the murder room would turn up nothing damning against me. But let's face it, I was turning into a magnet for murder scenes. Any smart law-dog would suspect me a little, and it didn't surprise me that Timms had checked my resume.

So I was ready for his comment, and I didn't even bother to turn my head this time. 'That's right,' I said. 'I've had some trouble. It didn't involve murder. Everything I told you about this—' my gesture took in the door to the motel room, just a few yards away. '—can be checked out.'

'And you're absolutely sure Blue McMahan was here to-night?' This from Chitwood, as he lit up again. Glancing into the overflowing receptacle on the console, I didn't see how it could handle one more butt.

'Absolutely,' I said. 'Just as sure as I am that he didn't have anything to do with it.'

'How do you like that?' Chitwood muttered. 'Blue McMahan. Alive. But then he was always full of surprises, wasn't he?'

Although it should have been an easy decision for me, I had agonized over bringing Blue into this. But he was already in it. I didn't owe him a cover-up, and I wasn't about to risk my own neck for him. A simple check of Dewey's background would turn up his relationship with Blue, and for all I knew, the desk clerk had gotten a look at him. For better or worse, Blue had been resurrected from the Big Muddy and was walking among us. And besides, I knew his alibi was solid tonight – I was it. All I could do was pray that he had spoken the truth when he said he was innocent of Faye's death.

'Why did he run, then?' Timms, in spite of the late hour, was as sharply dressed as the first time I'd met him. I also guessed that he'd had a recent haircut, because he gave off the flowery scent of Lilac Vegetal. I thought that stuff had disappeared from the planet, but apparently there was a barber in Pilgrim's Rest who still used it.

'I think it's obvious,' I said. I tried to sound patient, but the draining of adrenalin from my system had left me feeling list-less, almost rubbery. 'He and Dewey looked a lot alike. I noticed it when I first saw them tonight, and Dewey's wife appar-ently commented on it too. Someone – the same person who killed Faye and Opal – came here looking for Blue. He walked in—'

'How did he just walk in?' Timms asked. He said it casually, but it was ground we'd already covered, and I had no doubt he was trying to trip me up, make me contradict myself.

'Like I said, the fan doesn't work in the room. They had the door open while I was there.'

'And when you left?'

'I honestly didn't notice. But Blue probably didn't close it all the way. Someone could have just walked in, taken Dewey for Blue, and killed him.'

A long silence, and I could hear the faint sound of Timms' pen moving across paper as he took notes behind me.

Chitwood spoke. 'I think we'll just leave Blue's name out of this for the time being,' he said. 'Until we get things sorted out. No point spreading it around that he's alive. In fact, let's leave your name out of this too. For now, this is just a murder in a motel.' He gave me a significant look. 'You understand?'

'Yes, sir.'

There was some more talk, more cigarette smoke, more doubtful responses to whatever I had to say. Finally they turned me loose around two in the morning. I drove back to Longstaff House and fell into bed, where I dreamed of Blue and Faye swimming in the Mississippi River, she in her nightgown, he fully clothed, both in their prime, the way I remembered them. She was smiling, and both of them waved to me. I wanted to join them.

The banging awakened me. It may have started as knocking, but by the time I grew aware, it had graduated to full-on, hard-knuckled banging on the kitchen door downstairs. I got up, made my way downstairs in my skivvies, and opened the door to find Kenneth Lively standing there. His usual bright-eyed, boyish look had been replaced by something harder, more judgmental. He looked like an angry chipmunk.

Since *What do you want?* seemed superfluous, I just stared at him.

'You not answering your phone?' His tone fit the look on his face.

'I turned it off.'

'The Governor wants to talk to you.'

'Fine. I want to talk to him too.'

'Why don't you call him now?'

I didn't need to be rude, but I guess you could say I wanted to be. I was set off by his tone, which resembled that of the head butler instructing one of his chambermaids. 'No,' I said. 'First I'm going to brush my teeth. Then I'm going to make some coffee—'

'You work for him, don't forget,' he said, turning away and heading for his car.

Once inside, I skipped the brushing and the coffee and went straight to the call, dialing Sonny's office number in Nashville. His receptionist put me right through.

'Randall, what the hell?' he said, skipping pleasantries.

'You've heard about Blue.'

'Damn right. He's *alive*?' This last word came loaded with astonishment.

'Alive as you and me. I sat with him last night, looked at him up close. It's him.'

'Well, I'll be ...' His tone was neither happy nor sad, just wondering. 'That means he rigged it, then, didn't he? The drowning.'

'I think so. But I don't know why.'

'Well, I guess nothing about him surprises me any more.'

He was quiet for a while, and I thought I could hear him closing his office door. 'Another killing there, I hear.'

I started to ask him how he was so well-informed, but the answer seemed clear. Kenneth Lively, the ex-trooper, was on the job. His first priority, I imagined, had been to set up a pipeline with Jerry Chitwood and maybe with the TBI as well. The chief had wanted to keep certain things from the public, but that obviously didn't apply to the Governor.

'That's right. One of Blue's old friends from the carnival. Blue and I had the bad luck to walk in on it just after—'

'And he ran.'

'Hmm?'

'Blue. He ran.'

'Right.' Something had gone chilly in Sonny's voice, and I wanted to be sure he understood. 'He had good reason. He thought the killer had come for him, and he took off.'

'Do you know where to?'

'No.' I felt the need to say this quickly. 'Sonny, I'm sure he didn't have anything to do with Faye's death.'

'What makes you so sure about that?' The tone was still there.

'Well, he was with me when—'

'All that proves is he didn't kill his old buddy. The kind of crowd he runs with, anybody could have done that one. No, I'm talking about how he turned up just around the time my mother ... after somebody ...' I heard his throat seize up with emotion. I also heard what sounded like a man hungry for vengeance.

'He told me he didn't kill her. I believe him.'

'You would. Considering what good buddies you are.' There it was. Years and years later, his first acknowledgment that Blue had been close to me in a way that he had never been with his own boy.

'Come on, Sonny.' It was all I could think of to say. It wasn't enough.

'Do you know how to find him?'

'No. I don't think he's even wanted for anything. But I figure if the police need to question him bad enough, they'll find him.'

'Maybe not fast enough.'

A long silence followed. I could almost read his thoughts over the line. Was he going after his father, sending someone to find the old man and bring him in? Or worse?

'I'm not sure where you're going with this.'

'It's my business.' It sounded like a dismissal. Then his voice softened a little. 'You've got plenty to keep you busy there. Just stick with it.'

'Sonny ...'

'I'll be in touch.' He hung up.

Wide awake now and stirred up, I put on some sweats and went for a short run to put myself back on an even keel. I ran through most of the twisting roads of the Colony, which followed no pattern and felt more like the work of Nature than of man. After twenty minutes I ended up at the old hotel.

According to local folklore, the hotel was the first real structure put up hereabouts. In the early days the pilgrims, drawn by the healing spring, would assemble in tents. After a few years they built the hotel, which they called Redemption House, to handle all the faithful who would flock here for their summertime revival meetings. They'd sing hymns in the open-air arena back in the woods and hold baptisms in Redemption Spring. Later, when the rich folks built their imposing homes nearby, the Colony took on a more secular air. But some of the church groups kept coming, and Redemption House – known by most of the locals simply as the old hotel – still stood out on the bluff overlooking the valley.

Full disclosure: Sonny and I, in the flower of our teen-age mischief-making, broke into the hotel one off-season just to have a look around. We were disappointed at the Spartan nature, the near-dowdiness of the place. There wasn't a real lobby, just a small check-in room, and next to it a sprawling, high-ceilinged dining room with a fireplace off to the side. The rooms, two stories of them, were in the building's two wings – unbroken vistas of long, uncarpeted corridors and small rooms with monk-like furnishings, bedding stripped and mattresses rolled up. Bored, we soon left.

The front was mostly one long veranda, just off the dining room, where guests could sit and drink in the breathtaking view. Now, with summer gone, the hotel's windows were boarded up, but a few cane-bottom chairs still stood on the veranda. I climbed the steps and took a seat on one. The veranda faced roughly west, and over the top of the hotel the climbing sun began to pour pale autumn light all over the green valley below. The eye of God, I reflected, can't have a view much better than this. No wonder the early settlers looked into their Bibles to find a suitable name for this structure and for the spring that watered this valley.

The falls, way off to my left, were not visible from where I sat. In the light breeze of the morning, their sound was so muted as to almost be part of the wind. I tried not to think of what I'd found there the other night and mostly succeeded, but I knew the image would remain inside of me until my last day.

Somewhere near the base of the falls, on Farmer Burch's land, things had emerged from the earth. First the skeletons of two young men who apparently died during the war that defined this country, the war my father had spent his life studying. Next, more bones, fragments of a skeleton barely two decades old. Another violent death, or just a quiet country burial?

Jerry Chitwood was digging into his records to determine who might have disappeared from these parts twenty or thirty years ago. Well, to stretch the meaning of the word, I suppose I was one of those. So was Callie Darnell, who had gotten her fill of Pilgrim's Rest around the same time I did and, in the words of Huck Finn, lit out for the territory. But the kind of missing persons the chief had in mind don't send postcards from Memphis.

As for me, here I was, once one of the town's wandering boys, now back for a visit. Blue McMahan too. Looks like the prodigals, the wastrels, the scalawags are coming home to Pilgrim's Rest. There's a country song in there somewhere.

Some of Faye's last words were beginning to come into focus. *That's not a soldier's grave*, she said. I'd assumed she'd meant the one under the stone-and-bronze marker down on the town square, and according to people who should know – my father and the town historian – she was wrong. But what if she'd meant the other grave, the newer one? People around here had figured these were more Civil War remains, but Faye knew better. And now, according to good old Jerry Chitwood, she turned out to be right. But how had she known, long before anyone else?

I thought back to that night, once again felt the clutch of her hand on my arm, the old-lady medicinal smell of her breath. How had she known?

Blue told me.

I felt as if I'd passed through a dark thicket and caught a glimmer of sunlight. Blue McMahan knew something – a secret, Faye called it. Something about the bones just given up by the earth. Did he know whose they were? Did he know how they got there? Did Blue know something about a murder? If that were so – and I know it was reaching, but I used to get paid to do that sort of thing – if that were so, then it made perfectly good sense that someone might be out to silence Blue. His quiet words to me at the barbecue joint had suggested something like that.

But why Faye? Maybe Blue had hinted at the answer to that too. He had returned, he said, for Faye's funeral; that was all. Maybe Blue had gone into hiding because of the awful secret he carried, and maybe the killer had gone to this horrendous extreme just to lure him back.

It was a theory, that was all. But it made a kind of goofy sense. And if it proved out, then it meant that there was a direct connection between those decades-old bones and the three recent murders.

Newspapermen love these connections. In the midst of all the randomness we write about, we desperately want to believe there are patterns to this life, patterns that help us make sense of it, that it's not all just about the collision of molecules.

Finally, I reflected on Sonny's enmity toward his father. Almost against my will, I played with a new idea. What if the attempt to kill Blue had been revenge for Faye's death? It was an ugly thought, because it led straight to Sonny, and it caused me to look at the boyish image of Kenneth Lively in an entirely new way. In the absence of anything solid to back it up, I decided to put the theory in the back of the drawer. I hoped I wouldn't have to pull it out again.

I made one final lap around the hotel, then walked back to Longstaff House, where I showered, shaved, made coffee, and scrambled some eggs. After breakfast, I poured a second cup, picked up the phone and, after a couple of tries, tracked down Chief Chitwood. He was 'mobile,' as the dispatcher put it, and I could hear the wind whizzing past the phone at his ear.

Our pleasantries were brief. I laid out my theory. He sounded preoccupied but listened politely, even asked a few questions, and promised to give it some thought.

'It's a little bit of a stretch,' he said. I could almost feel him calculating. The TBI had been riding point on the three murders, leaving him the quieter job of clearing up the identity of some old bones. Now some out-of-towner was telling him it may all be part of the same ugly ball of wax. The possibility was probably not welcome to him.

'I know, but it would explain a lot.'

'It would at that. Well, thanks, Randall.'

'Chief, are you looking for Blue?'

'Yes, I am. Timms has put out the word statewide. But right now it's just for questioning.'

'The Governor,' I said carefully, 'has a notion about his father.'

'I know, and he's entitled to it. I just want to talk to the man, that's all, and Timms feels the same way.'

I was relieved. At least the cops weren't going after old Blue with guns drawn. I'd no doubt it was some kind of crime to fake one's death, but that one, I suspected, would be very hard to prove. I just hoped Sonny's ex-bodyguard was not the trigger-happy sort.

'Anything new from the pathologist?'

'Oh, I nearly forgot. This'll surprise you, Randall. It surprised me. Turns out it was a young woman buried there.'

'What?' But I had heard him, all right. A young woman. I immediately thought of Callie. But that made no sense. She was long gone, out there somewhere looking for the DJ of her dreams. Wasn't she?

The chief's voice cut in on my thoughts. 'As soon as they got the thigh bone under an X-ray, they could tell the sex. But it was a natural mistake for us to make, you know? When it was first dug it up on Harry Burch's farm, we figured it could be one of the Civil War boys 'cause the men were smaller back then. You know the average soldier was only five-foot-eight and a hundred and forty-three pounds? I looked it up in one of your daddy's books. Anyway, if I turn up the names of any missing young women, we can try to run some DNA matches with family. If there's any around, that is.'

I remembered another question. 'Have you got word back on how Dewey Tackett died?'

More wind hissed past the mouthpiece. Finally he answered. 'Looks like it was a skinning knife.'

'What?'

'You know.'

'I know what that is. I've just never heard of ...'

'Anybody using one on a person. Right. Well, the crime lab's medical examiner said that's what it looked like. And he's a hunter, so he should know.'

I was trying to think of how to frame the next question, the clinical one. He anticipated it.

'The killer apparently cut his throat. That was the cause of death. And then used the gut hook to open him up.'

'Jesus.' I'd been deer hunting once. As a proper Southern boy, hunting game – squirrel, rabbit, possum, duck, deer – had naturally been part of my growing-up. I'm not the same as I was then, and looking back, it surprises me to admit how much I enjoyed it. Blood sports, stalking and killing other creatures, are part of the rite of passage for young men all over the South, and I found an undeniable excitement in it.

But, out in the woods one cold February morning, something shifted in me as I watched a man gut a deer. My reaction, a mixture of fascination and repulsion, told me that I would never be a dedicated, lifelong hunter. The process is called 'dressing' a deer, but the word is really a euphemism for gutting and skinning. It's messy and bloody, and it stinks.

The hunter's tool of choice is the skinning knife, often outfitted with a devilish-looking device opposite the blade called a gut hook. The gut hook, among other things, is used for precisely opening the body cavity without cutting into the intestines.

Thinking now of the last moments of Dewey Tackett, the image that took shape in my mind was a nightmarish one.

I shook my head to clear it away. 'Does this mean you're looking for a hunter now?'

'Could be. But you can get one of those things in any sporting goods store in Tennessee. I don't know yet who we're looking for, Randall. A bad man, for sure. Nobody wants a man like that coming after him.' He sounded tired.

'Thanks, Chief.' I hung up, not knowing if I'd accomplished anything, but at least I'd gotten him to listen to my idea.

Sonny wanted me back at work. And I was going to comply. But there was no reason I couldn't juggle two jobs at once.

Writing the saga of Sonny McMahan meant a paycheck. Uncovering the story of his father was more of an obligation.

NINE

The next week went quickly and felt good. I spent the time doing what I had done for years – talking to people, taking notes, sometimes running my little tape recorder. Every evening I would come back to Longstaff House, type up my notes on my laptop, and wait for the image of Sonny to sharpen. It wasn't what you'd call real journalism, I knew, but it was good to be playing reporter again.

Early one afternoon I went to the town bank and cashed Sonny's down-payment check to give myself a few weeks' worth of walking-around money. Then I headed over to the *Call* to see Charlene. I figured it was time to interview her about Sonny, his background, and his surroundings. Because of her time at the *Tennessean*, she would be well versed in his years as governor. And an even better source of hometown news. Next to the top cop, no one is likely to know as much about a place as the editor of the local paper. She had agreed to talk, although reluctantly. I sensed that, because of what she knew about me, she didn't totally trust me and would likely not part with anything sensitive, but there was that old favor I had done her, and that interview I had given her at Ida's. She owed me a little. And I was not too polite to collect. After all, I learned my trade in Chicago.

The newsroom of the *Call*, I found, was basically a couple of storefronts merged into one, with all reporters and editors rubbing elbows in one large room. The receptionist and the three reporters sat up front near the windows, the copy editors behind them. Charlene's desk was in the middle of the room, and the ad salesmen farther back. The pages were pasted up in the rear, and behind a set of big double doors was the pressroom.

I'd brought a bag of doughnuts from the local bakery to help ease my way. She thanked me and passed them around the room. Then she offered me coffee and sat back in her chair, neutral and a little cool.

'I appreciate your taking the time to talk to me,' I said.

'Don't mention it,' she said. 'Ask away.'

'I was going to start at the beginning and ask you how the town recalls Sonny's early days here,' I said. 'But lately I've gotten interested in his new business and his plans for developing the plateau, starting with this big project below the falls. Do you know who else is putting money into it?'

'Uh-huh,' she said. 'I've seen the list. They're mostly Nashville people, old boys he's been hooked up with for a while.'

'Wasn't it problems with friends that got him voted out of office?' I asked her.

She nodded. 'The wrong kind. He was getting campaign contributions from people who expected favors. Nobody ever proved a quid pro quo, but there were so many questions that I think the voters lost confidence in him. This shouldn't be as tricky for him, though. He's lined up a new set of friends who seem interested mostly in just getting a good return for their investment dollar, and they're willing to let the Governor pick their projects. Besides, he's out of politics now—'

'We don't know how long that'll last,' I broke in. 'What can you tell me about Lem Coldsmith?'

'He's the big dog of the pack,' she said with a grin. 'First among equals, since he's putting the most money into the company. He made the business pages regularly when I was with the *Tennessean*. All I really know about him is that he's self-made, a go-getter, and probably one of the most successful businessmen in the state.'

'I saw him on TV not long ago pushing his products,' I said. 'He was so cornpone it was embarrassing to watch. He has absolutely no shame.' I paused. 'Do you think he might be worth looking at?'

She waited a while before answering. 'Why?' She drew out the one syllable, making it sound as if it was something she'd thought about herself.

'Just for fun, maybe. Because he's colorful. But also because he sounds as if he's the key player here. Sonny wants this project real bad – wants it so much, I'm not sure he's using the best judgment. I just want to make sure he doesn't take another fall because of a friend.'

'What does this have to do with your book?'

'Well, look at it this way: If the project falls apart, I'm not sure Sonny will be as enthusiastic about getting a book done. But tell me the truth: Is this guy Coldsmith worth somebody's time or not?'

She just nodded, looking reflective. Finally she said, 'I'd been thinking the same thing, but I've been lazy, covering all the little things in this town. Maybe I'll put a reporter on him for a few days when I can spare one.'

'Good,' I said enthusiastically. 'If nothing else, you'll get a good personality sidebar. Now ...' I pulled out my notebook and set up my tape recorder. 'Let's get back to the hell-raising days of the Honorable Stuart McMahan.'

Just then, however, one of her reporters, a studious-looking young man, came over. Wiping the doughnut sugar from his fingers, he apologized for interrupting and leaned over to whisper something to her.

Whatever he said made her get up. 'Excuse me for a minute,' she said. She went over to the reporter's desk, picked up his telephone, and began talking in a low voice without sitting down. After a couple of minutes, she hit the switch, punched in a new number, and spoke for a while longer. When she hung up, she huddled with the reporter for a minute and then came back.

'Sorry,' she said. 'We're going to have to do this another time.'

'That's all right,' I said. 'Anything you can tell me?'

She hesitated, her lips compressed tightly, then shook her head.

'Is it about the killings?' She just stared. I got the feeling that she was trying very hard not to be rude.

'Come on, Charlene,' I said. 'I'm not your competition. If I learn anything, I've got no place to print it anyway. I'm just an old hometown boy. And I thought a lot of Faye.'

She seemed to reach a decision. 'It's not about Faye,' she said quietly. 'Chief Chitwood says they've got a DNA match on the bones. But he won't tell us a thing until the family's been notified, however long that takes. We're just going to have to wait around and make our phone calls.'

She smiled, and it looked like a genuine smile. 'So can we do this another time? Thank you for the doughnuts.'

That went well, too, I thought as I left.

Dinner came out of the freezer, and I had forgotten the taste of it as soon as I began clearing the table. Trying to plan my evening, I guessed that the choices came down to working on the book, reading more of my father's history of the town, or watching a little television. The ringing of the phone gave me a fourth – and much more interesting – choice. It was Jerry Chitwood.

'Hello, Chief.'

'Wonder if I could impose on you for something,' he said in his usual mumble. I could hear faint noises in the background that might have been music. 'I'm at the Hunting Lodge. You know the place?'

'Sure. I was over there the other night.'

'Think you could meet me here?'

'What's it about?'

He cleared his throat deliberately and began to explain. It took him a minute or so, and when he was finished, I wasn't sure I totally understood. But it was enough to make me curious. Barely fifteen minutes later I was pulling into the parking lot. As promised, he was waiting for me in the comfortable bar, sitting on a stool at the far end, where a mounted twelve-point buck's head looked accusingly down on all the drinkers. His attention was focused behind the bar, where the bartender and one of the waitresses were cleaning up some kind of mess. Bottles were missing from one spot on a shelf behind the bar, replaced by shards of glass. The shelf dripped. Peering over the bar, I saw the bartender sweeping up broken glass and the waitress mopping up liquid.

Chitwood saw me and got off his stool. 'She's out back,' he said. I followed him out a service door to the rear, where I saw his cruiser parked with lights blinking, one of his deputies behind the wheel.

In the back sat Lita Ray Darnell.

'What set her off?' I asked the chief.

'I could tell you, but that's for her to say.'

That made little sense to me.

'She under arrest?'

'No, unless the manager changes his mind,' Chitwood said. 'It's small stuff. I could make a drunk and disorderly thing out of it, but I don't want to. Main thing, I'd like to get her home. But she wanted me to call you first.'

'Can I talk to her?'

'Be my guest.'

I opened the door and slid in beside her. Lita Ray Darnell glanced at me sideways once, then reverted to eyes-front. She looked surly and mean, hardly in the mood for a conversation. Pretty as she was, the woman was no fashion plate. She wore rolled-up jeans, serviceable flat-heeled shoes, and a leather jacket embroidered over the left breast with a rampant guitar and the words *Grand Ole Opry*. She smelled drunk.

'Hi,' I said.

No answer.

'The chief said you wanted to talk to me.'

Nothing.

'He said you had a few drinks and broke some glass in there. Any particular reason?'

I waited a full minute this time. All she did was chew on her lower lip.

'Well,' I said, 'I've enjoyed our little chat. Next time you—'

She swung her head abruptly in my direction, her eyes boring into mine. 'You said she was important to you.'

It took me only a second to understand. 'That's right. She was.'

'You're the only one around here who's said anything like that.'

'Well ...'

'She's dead.'

'What?'

'They dug her up. Those bones. They're Callie's. She's dead.'

TEN

For long moments I was speechless. I wanted to argue with her, demand proof. But I'd heard her words, seen the certainty in her face, and knew it was pointless.

I saw Callie's face for just a moment, but I couldn't hold the image. My mind was too busy with what I'd just heard.

I waited to hear more from Lita Ray, the little sister. When nothing came, I tried questioning her as gently as I could, but she gave me no answers. After her one outburst, she seemed to have retreated into a place where no one could reach her. The look on her face now was one of unfocused rage.

I got out and spoke to Chief Chitwood. 'It was the DNA?'

He nodded. 'She's the only one who even gave a sample. I never came up with any names worth checking out anywhere in the county – anybody who'd dropped out of sight. Pretty much everybody was accounted for. Even Callie Darnell. We thought.'

'Then why—'

'One day Lita Ray stopped by my office to complain about some vandalism over at the garage. This was, I don't know, a few weeks ago, not long after the new set of bones got sent to the crime lab, long before they'd even identified 'em as female. We got to talking about it, and pretty soon, out of the blue, we decided to have her DNA tested, just to rule out Callie. I don't even remember which one of us had the idea first.'

'And the results came back today.'

'Uh-huh. Maybe she'd had a feeling. Who knows? But I can

tell you it hit her hard. She's a tough little gal, but this really ... Anyway, next thing I knew, I was getting a call from the manager of this place. He said she'd showed up already pretty well fried, sat down, ordered a couple of stiff ones, and started throwing things. He's used to handling drunks, but he said she was downright scary. Funny thing: I've known her for years, seen her drink a lot here and there, and she could always hold it, even better than the boys sometimes. But not tonight, I guess.'

He bent over to look in the window at her. 'She's in no shape to be left alone. I think I'll just drive her home—'

'I'll do it,' I said quickly. 'I don't mind.'

'Well ...' He shrugged, thought for a moment. 'Good of you to offer. I suppose she can send for her car tomorrow when she's feeling better.'

Moments later, we had bundled Lita Ray into my car. Except for offering an occasional slurred direction, she said little on the way.

Pilgrim's Rest is too small to have more than a few distinct neighborhoods. The way I remembered it, a lot of the folks with money lived out in the Colony, a few miles away, and everybody else lived in town, where some streets were considered nice and some were not. Lita Ray lived on a street of small one-story homes and yards that most Chicagoans would consider spacious, but the yards were not all well-kept. Some of them had sparse grass and rubber wading pools, with here and there a tricycle sitting around waiting for Junior to come outside and mount up. Near her front door sat two planters made from discarded truck tires. The flowers in them were not doing well.

I helped her inside. The small living room was something of a mess, just like its occupant. She headed straight for the kitchen, where she ran the faucet noisily and splashed her face, then dried off with a dish towel.

Part of one wall in the living room was a gun rack. I saw two older-model shotguns, a double-barreled 12-gauge and a 410, a .22 rifle, and a couple of handguns. All of them looked in good shape, with the shine of recent cleanings.

'You a hunter?' I asked her when she returned.

'Sometimes,' she said. 'I got all those from my daddy. He used to hunt anything that moved.'

'Usually it's the brothers who get their daddy's guns.'

'Is that right? Well, everybody knows my brothers got no business with guns.' She sounded bored. 'Can I offer you something to drink?' She was not wearing her hostess' face.

'No, thanks.'

She nodded, as if that settled it. 'Well, then ...'

When I didn't move, she leaned heavily against the door frame of what I took to be her bedroom. 'You waiting around 'cause you want to get in my pants?'

'Ah, no.' The words *I usually like my women sober and cleaned up* came to mind, but I decided she didn't need my sarcasm.

'Half this town does,' she said with no trace of smugness. 'Just like they did my big sister.'

'Congratulations,' I said.

'But if you're not interested—' She gave an exaggerated yawn. 'Then I'm gettin' to bed.'

Truth is, I might have counted myself right in there with half the town under different circumstances. She had an urgent and natural beauty, all sharp edges and quick moves, with caution signs posted here and there. I liked her Tennessee twang and how, in a certain light, I could sometimes see Callie there.

But no, I thought. It's only because she's the little sister. Can't you see she'd be trouble?

'Lita Ray, I'm sorry about Callie,' I said. 'If somebody killed her, I'm sure the chief—'

'You mean sad old broke-down Jerry Chitwood? He's going to find out who killed Callie?' She took a ragged breath. 'I don't think so. He's got new killings to worry about. And I don't think anybody else in this town gives much of a damn, either.'

'I do. I already told you that. I know you're drunk, but I want you to hear this. I care. Get it? I give a damn.'

I knew I sounded a little operatic, but subtlety wasn't working with her. Maybe drama would.

She appeared to reflect on that, still leaning heavily against the doorframe, her eyelids now half-shut. Then she nodded her head.

I didn't have to ask why no one gave a damn. Sure I'd been away twenty years, but I vividly remembered the small-town caste system here. Lita Ray, with her auto shop, was middle-class now, but she had scratched her way up from something altogether different. The Darnells, led by her daddy, Pike, were colorful examples of what the insensitive still like to call white trash. The mother and her two daughters, poor but basically decent, got along the best they could, while Pike Darnell drank and whored and sometimes spent the night in jail. The sons, I guessed, had not turned out any better.

'You want to tell me what was on that postcard?' I asked Lita Ray.

It took so long to sink in, I began to wish I hadn't asked the question. Drunks are never any good to talk to, especially if you need information from them. But she finally got it. Assuming a serious look, she raised a forefinger commanding me to wait and disappeared into the bedroom. In no time at all she was back, handing me the card. It was creased and worn, and it bore a garish photo of Memphis' Beale Street at night, all neon-lit, with throngs on the sidewalks and spilling into the street itself. I turned it over. The postmark was dated just shy of twenty years earlier, and the card was addressed to Lita Ray in careful block-letter printing. The message side bore nothing but a simple drawing.

I recognized it right away. It was a rocking horse, drawn in a stylized, almost abstract way. Just four quick strokes – a semicircle for the base, two straight, diverging lines for the struts, and a reverse S-shaped squiggle at the top representing head, mane, body, and tail all in one graceful swoop.

'She used to wear this, didn't she?' I asked Lita Ray. 'A pendant.'

She nodded. 'Some boy gave it to her, and she loved it. Wore it all the time.' Her words were heavily slurred. 'He told her it was gold, but it started to tarnish right away, so she knew it wasn't gold. But she didn't care, she liked it so much. She practiced drawing it, and after a while, she could do it real fast.'

She yawned hugely, not bothering to cover it up. 'Instead of signing her name, she'd just draw the horse.'

'What ever happened to the pendant?'

She shrugged. 'I don't know. Maybe she lost it. Maybe it got buried with her. Maybe the son of a bitch that killed her kept it for a little souvenir.'

I looked at Lita Ray's name and address on the card. It was done in crude block letters. 'Does this look like her handwriting?' I asked.

She shook her head. 'Not particularly. I never thought much about it.'

I started to ask another question, but she waved it away. 'I'm going to bed.' She went into the bedroom, and I left, closing the front door behind me.

I didn't leave right away but sat on the stoop for a while. It was pleasant out there in the dark – cool, and almost dead quiet, just me and the smell of wood smoke from a few fireplaces up and down the street. In the moonlight, the somewhat shabby neighborhood looked pearly white and pure. In the yard next door, a child's inflatable dinosaur toy had an eerie glow, its grin vaguely menacing.

Callie. Lord, she was something.

How to describe her? All right, start with her skin. She bragged that she had Cherokee blood in her, and indeed she seemed tanned year round. But it was in the summertime that you noticed it the most, when she wore light dresses with thin straps that showed off those golden arms and firm shoulders.

Then the face. It was roundish and high-cheekboned – again the trace of Indian. Eyes dark and long-lashed. She usually wore her hair cut short, and by the end of the summer the natural dark brown had been bleached to something the color of dark honey. A permanent half-grin, one that seemed to say *What are you looking at?* Followed by *D'you like what you see?*

Finally the body. Callie was curvy, with a little more meat on her than your typical nineteen-year-old. Strong calves. Average height, but everything distributed according to some kind of formula Pythagoras himself might have dreamed up. Or Vargas.

Put all this together, and you have a package that its owner must have been acutely aware of. But I'm not sure she was, not in the way you'd think. Oh, she knew how to flirt, all right. Her flirting skills should have been registered like a handgun. But most women endowed with her natural gifts would have hoarded them like treasure, or doled them out very carefully, the way John D. Rockefeller used to give pennies to ragamuffins. Instead, Callie shared hers.

I know what you're thinking. The town tramp. Well, maybe she was. But she never went with any man she didn't like. She never took money – at least as far as I knew – although she wouldn't turn down a present. She wasn't promiscuous by my definition. She just had a long succession of boyfriends, all of them blessed by her generosity of spirit and her preternatural sexual skills.

I was one of them. Surprised?

Now it looked as if one of those boyfriends might have killed her. Whoever it was, I wanted him found, as no doubt her little sister did as well. The joke here, the dirty joke, was that the list of suspects could be daunting, maybe overwhelming. And I wanted no one telling a joke at Callie Darnell's expense.

Even in the faint light I could see that weeds were encroaching on one side of the truck-tire garden to the right of the sidewalk. I leaned over and plucked at them for a minute, then sat back on the top step, satisfied that I'd prettified my little corner of the world.

I heard a sound behind me, the door opening. 'You still here?' she asked in a faint voice.

'Yes,' I said without turning. 'I'm about to go.'

'I got sick just now,' she said. 'Shouldn't have had so much to drink, I guess.'

'I guess,' I said. 'You be careful with that. You should get to bed now.' I got up. 'Maybe we can talk later.'

As I started down the sidewalk, I heard her say, even more faintly, 'She was the only one who ever looked after me.'

I kept going. It didn't sound like an invitation to chat. It sounded more like her way of saying good night.

Early the next morning, I awoke with the strong desire to see where Callie had been found. After a shave, a shower, and breakfast, I got in my car and drove along the narrow road toward the creek. A minute later I slowed the car to a crawl and crossed the wooden bridge that spanned the creek just above the falls, the bridge where I'd found Faye. The structure was only about twenty feet long, made of wooden beams with iron braces, old but sturdy. It creaked as I crossed it, and I could see rushing water beneath the planks. No more than a dozen yards downstream lay the falls, the water roaring and kicking up mist as it began its drop of more than a hundred feet.

Not far past the creek the road divided, the left fork heading back to the highway. I took the right, which soon took me over to the edge of the bluff and, in a series of hairpin turns, down toward the valley. In the old days the road had been dirt – gravel, barely graded – and scary, especially at night. I noted with surprise that it was now topped with asphalt and blessed with a guardrail. Someone was making improvements.

As the road bottomed out, I found myself in a familiar thick grove of trees that encircled the pool at the base of the falls. Various dirt turnouts had been flattened around the bases of the trees by generations of pimply-faced drivers and their dates. The ballpark, some of us called it – as in first base, second base, third base, home plate. Teenage humor.

A stream flowed out, headed vaguely westward. Then I was out of the trees and rolling along acres and acres of farmland, all of it devoted to corn. The harvest was past, and the tall stalks stood browning and useless in the autumn sun. This was the Burch farm.

I remembered the location of the farmhouse with little trouble and turned into the road. The house looked the same. Near the barn were a tractor and a pickup. When I pulled up in front of the house, two coon hounds came over to greet me, baying merrily.

Farmer Burch, it turned out, was not at home, nor was his wife. I found a teenage son, Jimmy, who seemed busy with something too important to be interrupted by an adult. But when I mentioned that I was a friend and houseguest of Stuart McMahan, one of the sponsors of the coming conference center that would one day transform this property, he roused himself and agreed to show me what I wanted to see. We got in the pickup, and he drove us down a narrow lane that bordered the farm on the north. After about a quarter-mile he stopped, we got out, and he led me into the rows of corn stalks a few dozen yards away. We soon came to a small open space, about fifty feet across, where the stalks had been cleared and the ground had been dug up.

'Right here,' he said, pointing to some spongy earth in the center of the space. There were no markers, no tools, no police tape. Just some soft earth.

'Who found the bones?'

'Dale,' he said. 'One of the dogs. We named him after Dale Earnhardt 'cause he's so fast. After Mr. Stringer found the two soldiers, a bunch of people from town came down here to dig. They dug all around, looking for more soldiers, and one day they noticed Dale sniffing this spot, and they dug here.'

'I heard there wasn't much of a body left,' I said.

'That's right. Just one big bone and some little ones. We figure animals dug it up first and scattered what they found.'

I nodded. It made sense. The animals had likely scattered the tattered remains of her clothes as well. But it was too bad. If they had found all of Callie's skeleton, it would have been obvious right away that they weren't looking at a man.

I stood there a while longer, looking down at the meaningless dirt, as if keeping vigil. Someone had killed Callie, had dug a hole here – not deeply, though, not going to too much trouble, probably in a hurry – and then laid her in it and covered her up. I wondered what she was wearing, if anything. One of those summer dresses with the thin shoulder straps and the flouncy skirts? Her rocking-horse pendant?

I wondered, too, how she had spent her last day on Earth and with whom. If she'd played the radio, flirted with anyone. I hoped she had not been buried face-down. I hoped her death had been quick. *Most of all, I hope I find you*, I said silently to her killer.

And then later, decades later, after the earth had done its work, animals had found what was left of her and began strewing her around. If it hadn't been for Olen Stringer's initial dig and old Dale's sharp nose, we'd never have known what the earth once held here.

'How about the other bones? Can you show me where they were found?'

'The soldiers? Sure.' He pointed toward the bluff. 'It's over thataway, not far. We can walk it.'

I looked where he pointed and saw a lone man in a broad-brimmed hat walking slowly, bent over, studying the ground.

Jimmy saw him too. 'These days a lot of folks come out here to look around,' he said. 'If they don't get in our way, mostly we just leave them alone.'

I recognized the man. 'Tell you what, Jimmy,' I said. 'You can leave me here. I'll walk around a while, and then come back to pick up my car. I appreciate your help.' I pulled a fiver out of my wallet and offered it to him.

'No, sir, you don't have to do that,' he said. 'Glad to help.' He got in the truck, turned it around, and drove away.

No, sir. How about that language? Jimmy was one of the polite, well-raised teenagers, a breed I'd almost forgotten during my Chicago years.

I walked over the uneven ground, headed for an area just short of the grove of trees, outside the farmed area. The Historian saw me coming, straightened up, and pushed his hat back on his head. It was straw, and some of the weave was coming loose.

'What brings you out here?' he asked. He looked wary, probably wondering if we were about to engage in another verbal donnybrook.

'I wanted to see the place where they found Callie Darnell,' I told him. 'It's right over there. Jimmy Burch showed me. You remember her, don't you?'

He nodded, still holding the wary look. 'Beautiful girl. It's tragic. After all these years, I hope they can find out what happened to her.'

'This where Olen Stringer did all his searching?' I asked.

'Yes,' he said.

'And I guess where he finally got lucky. Can you show me the spot?'

'Right here.' He pointed to the ground at his feet. He was standing in front of a grave-size excavation, the largest of several holes in the area.

'And all the rest of these—' My gesture took in the other digs.

'The police and some volunteers came out and dug around for several days, looking for more bodies. On the assumption that we had found some Civil War remains, we thought it might be a site of a mass grave.'

'Because of the Burning.'

'The story, yes.'

'But there were no other bodies?'

He shook his head. 'Which doesn't prove or disprove anything, of course. There could be a mass grave somewhere else. It all may turn out to be true.'

'Do you think it'll ever be proved?'

'No,' he said. 'I think it will stay on as a kind of legend, somewhere between truth and untruth. For some people, that's enough.'

'Stringer tells me you've turned up a little more evidence. Some kind of journal?'

'That's right. In my research I found a diary kept by a woman named Mary Hightower, who lived here during the war. She was a wonderful diarist and she described circumstances leading up to an event that sounds like the Burning. Unfortunately, the volume I found is only part of her diary, and it ends inconclusively. The other volumes, I learned, were destroyed in a fire in the Hightower home a long time ago. But you still might enjoy looking at it. Olen has it over at the Historical Society, and I'm sure he'd let you borrow it.'

'You always used to pooh-pooh the story. You called it bad history.'

His brow knotted, and as he hesitated in answering I sensed an argument on the way. Instead, he smiled faintly. 'Maybe I'm getting less rigid in my old age.'

'One thing's for sure,' I said. 'It's good for business, isn't it?'

'How do you mean?'

'Well, it's the only claim to Civil War history we have here. I'm pretty sure this conference center wouldn't be landing here if it weren't for the town's oh-so-colorful legend. Shiloh or Chickamauga or Lookout Mountain seem like much more logical choices.'

'Possibly.' He looked unhappy, as if I'd stirred up an unpleasant memory. For some reason I felt sorry. I'd last left him in a lather, all worked up over a perceived insult, and unsure if I wanted to see him again. Now here we were, once again having a civilized conversation. For all the ups and downs of our relationship over the years, some of my best memories were of our talks. I didn't want to spoil this one.

I thought of apologizing for the things I'd said, but I couldn't remember either one of us apologizing to the other. Instead I decided to just keep talking.

'What made him look here? Stringer, I mean? As I remember it, no one really knew where the Burning was supposed to have taken place.'

'That's true. I think there was a huge amount of luck involved. Originally, he was drawn to this spot because of this—' He pointed to something a few yards away, where knee-high weeds were growing. We walked over, and I saw the remnants of a stone foundation. Tracing it through the weeds with my eye, I estimated it to be about twenty by forty feet.

'I discovered this years ago,' my father said. 'The remnants of a barn, and it's old enough to date back to the Civil War. Good evidence, except for the fact that I can show you old stone foundations all over the Pilgrim's Rest area. So it's not conclusive. But it was enough to cause Olen to start looking here.'

'He sounds like an eager beaver.'

'He's an amateur historian,' he said with a shrug. 'Very serious about his work, but not much in the way of academic credentials.' I heard a hint of condescension in his tone, the superiority of the scholar, and I was glad to note that my father wasn't immune to normal human pettiness.

'But he found the bones anyway.'

He nodded. 'It's the sort of thing historians and archeologists dream about. But as I said ... *luck*.' He looked troubled once again, working on some kind of interior problem.

'So what brings you out here today?' I asked him.

'Oh, I don't know,' he said vaguely. 'Maybe I just wanted another look around before all this changes. The Burch family will be moving out soon, and the groundbreaking's a week from Friday.'

'Oh, that's right. I saw it in the paper. Where's everything going to be?'

For the next few minutes he described the conference center, pointed out locations of the various buildings – the main hall, the library, the museum, the audiovisual center, the living quarters.

'Look out,' I said. 'Here come the tourists.'

'Naturally we hope the tourists come,' he said. 'They'll be welcome. But it will be so much more than that. Most important, a new center for scholarship on the war, something this country's never had.' I could hear the pride in his voice, and for the first time I understood how important this thing was to him.

'Will you be involved?' I asked him.

'I think so,' he said. 'Your old friend Stuart has asked me to be the director. Nothing's official yet, but ...' He shrugged.

'Well, that's pretty impressive,' I said. I was tempted to ask him if he still disapproved of Sonny's politics but bit my tongue. It would have been a cheap shot.

He looked about ready to leave. 'Do you have a car here?' I asked him.

'No,' he said. 'I walked down from the Colony. I enjoy the exercise.'

'It's a hard slog back up, though,' I said. 'Let me give you a ride.'

'I don't want to put you to—'

'No trouble.'

On the drive back up the twisting road, I looked down on the valley, trying to imagine it transformed. My father said something.

'What was that?'

'I just said … an amazing find. Truly amazing.'

'Almost hard to believe, huh?'

He didn't answer.

ELEVEN

In light of the dire threat faced by our nation even as I write these words, my little journal seems a pitiable thing. But I take pen in hand nonetheless, emboldened by my husband's encouragement to write down all our family's concerns, all the events that threaten to shake the very foundation of this republic. And so I begin, with this first entry on the evening of April 19, 1861, full of shock and horror at the news from South Carolina. I feel – truly, all in our small town feel – as if a fire has been lit that will not cease to burn until it has consumed this country and those who live in it, north and south ...

The first and only surviving volume of Mary Hightower's diary was old and very worn, and one corner of the cover bore old scorch marks, but the binding was intact. The entries were made in a tight, economical, yet graceful script, the ink faded but still legible.

As my father had said, the book was kept at the Historical Society. 'This is mostly for scholarly research,' Olen Stringer had told me as he unlocked a display cabinet and slipped the diary into a protective plastic bag before handing it to me. 'But we can make an exception for you.' I thanked him, wondering why I found him so unlikable. Then remembering: His stuffiness, his false modesty, and his self-importance, for starters.

An hour later, after stopping in town for lunch, I sat out on the screened-in porch and began turning the yellowish-brown pages with care as I traveled back to another time. The Mary Hightower that emerged was a memorable character, an honest, God-fearing woman, a devoted wife, high-strung and intelligent. In other places and circumstances – upper-crust New England, perhaps – she might have run a salon, thrown parties for artists and politicians. But living in the small town of Pilgrim's Rest, childless and married to a hardware merchant, her world was much more circumscribed. All she had was her journal. And she poured herself into it.

The war, of course, was everything. As I leafed through the book, I saw the town's young men going off to fight. Because of the peculiar geopolitics of the time, many of them joined the Union Army, but some of their friends chose to enlist in the regiments of Tennessee, their native state.

And then the dying began. The lists of the dead were posted at the town's telegraph office, and Mary Hightower described the grief that greeted each local name. 'Clara Wilson's boy Bennett has fallen at Shiloh,' Mary wrote. 'She is inconsolable. I and others went to sit with her, but she can only weep. I find myself hating those who sought to divide this country of ours by seceding from it.'

As the fighting wore on, some of the divisions between blue and gray began to crop up in the town itself. Those few whose sons fought for Jefferson Davis' army found themselves ostracized. Some left town. The hatred that gripped the land settled over Pilgrim's Rest like a poisonous fog.

I turned the pages faster, knowing what I sought. Finally, just a few pages from the end, I found it: A group of young men, ragged and hungry, turned up in the town. Captured at the battle for Chattanooga, they had been put onto a train bound for a Union prison camp in the North but had escaped somewhere in East Tennessee and, after days of wandering, found themselves in Pilgrim's Rest. Begging for food, they were turned away at every door and soon understood that Confederates would find no sympathy in this town. They took to the road and, somewhere outside town, found an old, rotting barn where they took shelter. But someone spotted them, and a crowd from the town gathered. Mary's husband insisted that they go, and when they arrived at the place, she found a mob of men, women and even children there, yelling for blood:

Many bore torches, and they seemed to me like the fires of Hell, she wrote. *In the wavering light, the townspeople, our friends, took on a satanic look. The boys in the barn pleaded to be let alone – if not* to be fed and sheltered, then simply to be allowed to flee. But those in the crowd would not be moved. There were shouts of 'Shiloh!' and 'Lookout Mountain!' and the names of other places where parents had lost sons, sisters had lost brothers, wives had lost husbands.

Most forceful, most hateful of all was our mayor, a man I had long respected. This night he seemed transformed into an angel of vengeance. 'Come out and be hanged, you Johnny Rebs, or be burned out!' he shouted. My husband, may God forgive him, joined in the shouting, the cursing.

We heard a faint cry from within the barn: 'God bless Jefferson Davis and the Confederate States of America.'

I had reached the bottom of the last page. All that remained was a final parenthetical note: *I will continue this sad chronicle in my next volume – MH.*

I believe that's what you call a cliffhanger ending, I thought as I closed the book. But also pretty strong circumstantial evidence. This, coupled with the legend that refused to die, added up to a good case for the Burning. And wasn't it fitting that the rest of her words, which could have settled the story once and for all, perished in their own fire?

I headed for the dining table, where my laptop, notes, and audiotapes sat, a silent rebuke over my recent inattention to Sonny's book. I needed to talk to him, so I dialed his Nashville office. After parrying with his secretary for a while, I was able to track him down in a hotel room in Atlanta. He answered on the first ring.

'You there for a Falcons game?' I asked him.

'Just trying to get some business done,' he said. 'What's going on?' He sounded tired and irritable, so I decided not to waste his time with pleasantries.

'I'm not making much progress on the book, I'm afraid.'

'Don't worry about it. I know you creative geniuses need time.'

'I've been a little distracted by something else, and I need to talk to you about it. Did you hear about the bones they dug up on the Burch farm, the new ones?'

'Sure,' he said. 'They thought it was another soldier or two.'

'I know, but they were wrong. I thought Kenneth Lively might have told you—'

'I've had him working on other things,' he said abruptly. 'What's the story?'

'The crime lab came up with a DNA match. It's Callie Darnell. Do you remember her?'

A long silence, so long that I could hear the muted sound of voices and music on the TV set in his room. Then the clink of ice in a glass as he took a swig of something. He swallowed loudly and finally spoke.

'Callie Darnell.' Slowly, as if trying out the name. 'Hell, yes. Callie. Uh ... A year or two ahead of us. Worked at Grady's. Lot of guys had the hots for her.'

'Including you?'

'Sure. At least from a distance. But she liked older guys, mostly, and she looked like trouble. I never went out with her.'

'Anyway ...'

'But damn, I'm sorry to hear that. I thought she ran off to Memphis or someplace to work. What the hell happened?'

'Who knows? She had a lot of boyfriends. Including me. Maybe I was one of the few youngsters she took on, out of the goodness of her heart.'

'You dated her, huh?'

'More than that.'

'Damn, I'm sorry. I guess Jerry's working on it, then.'

'Uh-huh, although the trail's twenty years old, and who knows how far he'll get with it? The thing is ...'

'What?'

'I want to see what I can find out. I mean, I want to spend some time on this.'

He thought about that for a moment. 'Sounds like you're getting busy.'

'Uh-huh.'

'What about the book?'

'I don't know, Sonny.'

'I didn't hire you to do police work. If you want to ask around about Blue in your spare time, that's fine. I want him found too, for good reason. But this sounds like something else altogether. I hired you to help me out, not do your own projects.'

'I know.'

'What I heard, she was spreading her legs for half the horny toads in the county. I'm sorry somebody killed her, but—'

'You don't sound sorry.'

'I'm sorry when anybody loses her life,' he said a little loudly, and I wondered how much he'd had to drink. 'My mother just lost hers, remember?'

'I remember.'

'That's the kind of loss that matters to me, not Callie Darnell.' He paused. 'I need you on this book. You going to stick with it?'

I heard it in my mind right then, the double sound of one door closing and another opening. I suddenly knew that I was being faced with a very clear-cut choice. On the one hand, I could keep working toward that big payday, writing the book Sonny's way, fudging the truth here and there. It appealed to me. I liked the man, I wanted to stay friends with him, and I could use the money.

On the other hand, I felt the pull of a task that seemed much more important to me, one that could take me down darker roads, away from money, maybe even away from friendship. This road led ultimately toward the truth, which contrary to popular belief is not always a comfortable place to be. The truth can sting. How badly did I want it?

At the beginning of this saga, I had simply been Sonny's scribe-for-hire. Then his old man had come back like Lazarus and pulled me off on a detour. Now there was Callie, who was dead for real, but who was pulling me to her like a compass needle to iron.

Reporters have an expression: 'What's the lead?' – meaning, out of all the assorted facts making up this story, what do you lead off with? Sometimes it's a single fact, sometimes it's an amalgamation of several. But the lead paragraph is the essence of the story boiled down to one concise thought.

I had a lot of things on my mind. But Callie was my lead.

I took a breath. 'Sonny, I won't lie to you. There are some

things I need to find out. And right now Callie's at the top of my list. I shouldn't be taking your money if I—'

'Fine,' he said in a voice that said *Not fine at all*. I heard him finish his drink, the ice loud against the glass. Then: 'I guess I better find somebody else to do it, then.'

'If you like,' I said. 'You want me to move out of Longstaff House?'

His voice was dismissive. 'I think that'd be the polite thing to do.'

My face felt hot with anger. I had to strain to keep my voice down, my words restrained. 'All right, then. I'll get packed up and out of here, probably tomorrow.'

And that was it. I hung up, feeling surprised and drained. When I made the call, I'd no idea I was about to burn a bridge. Muttering to myself, I spent a while tidying up my files, notes, and tapes, figuring that at some point I'd be asked to hand them over to my successor. I'd already collected a down payment from Sonny, and I wanted my work, although incomplete, to prove worth something.

That done, I thawed a steak in the microwave, grilled it rarer than I usually like it, and washed it down with way too much sour mash. Then I fell into bed.

I lay awake for a long time, my head buzzing with the booze and the past twenty-four hours. Let the Honorable Stuart McMahan find some other hack to do his book. Someone who won't consider it beneath him. That's part of my problem, I thought. Not too proud to do hack work, but too proud to take pride in it.

I'd have stuck with it, gritting my teeth and taking the money – except for Callie.

Amazing, when you think about it. The town tramp. I can't even call her a girlfriend. We groped and grappled in the back seat of my beat-up Camaro a grand total of one time, and one time does not a girlfriend make. It was the summer after my senior year. I think she'd seen me mooning after her all summer and decided to send me off to college with something to remember her by. And did she ever.

It was my first time. She realized it midway through, and in the midst of my fumbling and self-conscious panic, she had the grace to giggle only once. Then she settled down to a gentle rhythm, smelling all the while like shampoo lightly flavored with sweat. She helped me over the rough spots, taking me up to that place where, for a few precious seconds, you can see a whole new universe.

Afterward she complimented me with what I now see as the whitest of lies, laughed throatily, re-arranged her dress, and said, 'Really nice, wasn't it?' We sat for the longest time, and she hummed a tune I didn't know. Much later, after she was gone, I learned that it was called *Wildwood Flower* and that it came from the legendary Carter family. It's a song that stretches way back into the collective memory of these mountains, about a cold-hearted man and a woman wronged. You'll often hear it up-tempo, but when Callie hummed it wordlessly that night, it sounded more like a lovely dirge.

And that was that. I drove her home and never saw her again. Two weeks later I left for college. But for a long time afterward, the odor of a certain kind of shampoo and the sound of *Wildwood Flower* acted on me like an aphrodisiac.

And of course I never forgot her. Because you never forget the first time, especially if it's presented to you as a gift from a generous woman.

So, when I had to choose between doing Sonny's work and finding out what happened to Callie, it was really no choice. Welcome to the new job, I said to myself, the one that don't pay beans. And don't come with no roof over your head.

Blue figured in this somewhere. Kenneth Lively had failed to find him, the cops didn't want him badly enough to expend time and manpower, and I suspected the time would come when I would have to hit the road in search of the elusive old con man. He knew Callie's resting place was no soldier's grave, and he told Faye. And she died, and someone came after him. It's all connected. Did this mean that whoever killed Callie – an old boyfriend? – also killed Faye, just to draw Blue out of hiding?

Could be. See the connections, I told myself. They're there.

Then I laughed out loud, lying in my bed, because strong drink always fools you into thinking you see things clearly. The next morning they revert to their old complicated selves.

For an instant I stood again in the doorway of young Opal Hicks' bedroom, staring at her sad and startled face. And I thought: There's someone else I should talk to.

But before I could come up with a name, I was asleep.

'Dammit, Randall, what did you say to him?' It was late afternoon. Tish stood outside the doorway looking windblown and frazzled, her butterscotch-colored SUV parked in the driveway.

'What did he tell you I said?' I opened the door to let her in. She wore a jogging suit and sneakers and, although tired from her long drive, she was wound up and ready for action.

'He's still in Atlanta,' she said angrily. 'He hardly told me anything, except that you quit the job.'

'Well, it felt more like he fired me, but why quibble? Won't you come in?'

'Dammit, Randall—'

'You already said that.'

She marched past me into the living area. 'He said you decided to work on something else. Some murder story, and it's not Faye. You acting like a policeman now, or are you trying to go back to newspapering?' Plunking herself down on the sofa, she glared at me.

'No, Tish, I'm not. It's complicated. I told Sonny I shouldn't take his money if I couldn't give the job my full attention, that's all.'

'Well, why can't you? I mean, you agreed.'

'I know.' I sat beside her. 'Things have happened. It would take almost too long to explain it to you.'

'Try me.' It sounded like a challenge.

I sighed. 'All right. But ...' I had a thought. 'You want to go for a walk?'

Minutes later, we were walking along the road that paralleled the bluff, toward the falls. The trees arched overhead, almost blotting out the sky. To our right, occasional gaps between the old houses afforded us a view of the valley, where the sun was making its descent.

When we got within view of the bridge over the creek, her step faltered. 'You want to go back?' I asked.

'No,' she said. 'It's a beautiful spot. Faye always loved it, and I do too. I'm not going to let some murdering son of a bitch spoil it for me.'

We walked on and reached the bridge. Damnation Falls roared, and some of its spray blew back and dampened us lightly. The valley lay spread out beyond, now more heavily speckled in the colors of fall. We stood on the bridge for a while, breathing in the mist. Then she said, 'Let's go up to the spring. I haven't been there for a while.'

After a fifteen-minute walk upstream along a deeply shaded path, we stood in a natural rock-lined bowl about eighty feet across, ringed by trees. The spring gushed out of the earth to fill the bowl, and the water was so crystalline that we could see the craggy shapes of the crevice that gave birth to it. Around the bowl, the early settlers had carved rough benches into the rocks, and they had donned billowing white robes and waded into the shallow end of the bowl to be baptized. Standing there, we could no longer hear the sound of the falls.

'Tell me what you've been doing,' she said.

It seemed a good place for storytelling, so I told her about Callie. I spoke falteringly, because until recently I hadn't even said her name aloud in twenty years and had never tried to express what she had meant to me, to my growing-up. Then I talked about her death and her stealthy, shameful burial. Tish, her anger now dissipated, made sympathetic sounds.

'And I want to see if I can help find out who killed her and why,' I finished. 'It looks like the kind of job that wouldn't leave much room for anything else.'

'I guess I understand,' Tish said, lightly touching my shoulder as we settled onto one of the stone benches. Then she began talking about Sonny. 'He's being pulled a dozen ways,' she said. 'Something about these new partners of his ... it's not working out.'

'Why not?'

'He won't tell me, which worries me, because he's always confided in me. I know he's afraid this project of his, the study center, may come apart. He's had his heart in it, and if it fails, it would just kill him.'

And maybe cripple his political future, I thought. But she didn't need to hear me say that; she already knew it.

The glade was darkening. She looked toward the falls. 'If we hurry, I bet we can make the sunset.'

When we reached the bridge, the sun was hanging over the farthest range of mountains like a drop of lava about to be extinguished.

'I need to know what's troubling him,' she said, looking out over the valley. 'There's a lot riding on the next few weeks and months.'

'Anything I can do?'

She shook her head. 'I wish there were, but you're not exactly his favorite person right now.'

'Tell me about it. We both said some things it would be hard to take back. But he made me choose.'

'And I can't make you choose differently?'

'I'm sorry, Tish.'

She saw me looking at her, and returned my look quizzically.

'I was just thinking how lucky he is to have you on his side,' I said.

'He is lucky, you know that?' she said with a grin. Then, after a pause, she turned serious. 'For as long as I can remember, what I wanted was just to get him what he wanted. I'd burn down the woods for him.'

'Lady, I do believe you would.'

'Look,' she said, pointing. The ball of lava was just a molten sliver, resting ever so delicately atop the black silhouette of the mountain. Then, as we held our breaths, it flamed out.

I took Tish to the Hunting Lodge for dinner. When we came back, she looked worn-out. We had a brief debate about the propriety of her spending the night in the same house with me.

Even though Sonny was no longer in office, Tish still had sensitive antennae regarding the way things looked.

'Caesar's wife, and all that,' she said with a yawn. 'Only trouble is, Caesar's wife is dead tired, so she's going to bed. If anybody asks, we'll tell them Sonny's on his way but got delayed. Ken's still here in town. We can say he slept here too, and he'll back us up.'

She said good night to me, then took her bag into the same bedroom where she and Sonny had slept. I got in bed and read for a while, then heard her rummaging around down in the kitchen. A minute later I heard soft footfalls on the stairs, and she stood in the doorway, a drink in her hand.

'I'm afraid I'm polishing off the last of this,' she said, lifting the glass. 'Do you mind?'

'Not at all,' I said, putting down my book. She was barefoot, her hair looked freshly brushed, and she wore what looked like very nice silk pajamas with her initials on the breast pocket.

'Sonny's going to kill me,' she said with a wry grin. 'I drive all this way down here, and when I get home, I'll tell him he's going to have to go out and find somebody else to do the book. Somebody who's not half the writer you are.'

She was making one last pitch at me, and I felt embarrassed for her. To cover up, I narrowed my eyes in an exaggerated squint.

'What are you looking at?' she asked.

'The vice-president of the Thetas,' I said solemnly. 'Who hasn't changed a hair. Except maybe the color of it.'

That made her smile. She leaned against the doorframe, just the way Lita Ray had the other night. For a long time she said nothing. Then: 'Last chance, Randall. Are you sure I can't change your mind?'

I didn't want to admit what I was thinking – that she was offering me some kind of trade. An almost irresistible, but also unimaginable, trade. In the next instant I rejected the thought. She was flirting with me, that was all. She knew she still had an effect on me, and she was using it. And the truth is, I didn't mind at all. In fact, I was flattered.

'I'm sure,' I said finally. 'Don't hate me, okay?'

She straightened up. Her look was almost sympathetic. 'I could never hate you. Good night.' Then she snapped her fingers. 'Oh, by the way. If it's all right with you, I'll just take your notes and things back with me in the morning.' Then she was gone, and I listened to her light footfalls on the stairs.

After turning out the light, I got to wondering: was that the reason she came down? To take possession of my notes and tapes? Nothing wrong with that, of course, since everything belonged to Sonny anyway. But I felt as if I'd been handled, managed. I could almost hear Sonny growling over the phone *Change his damn mind. And if you can't, then at least bring all his stuff back with you.* On that thought, I slowly found my way into sleep.

Then awoke – not jarred awake, as I had been the other night by the recent memory of a far-off scream, but troubled awake, naggingly, by something that was not quite right.

I lay there, listening, then heard it. A faint scuffling noise, quick and furtive, and very near.

Someone was in the room.

Tish. Damn it. What was she thinking? She had no business being in here. If she was determined to push this even further, I honestly didn't know what I'd—

No. Not Tish. The furtive movements were concentrated on my closet, and they were going on too long. It wasn't her. Then I caught the faintest whiff on the still air. Hard to define, but it wasn't a woman's scent.

I felt my diaphragm tighten even as I wanted to pull more air into my lungs. There were no weapons in the room. I remembered Tish mentioning her shotgun, but it hadn't occurred to me to look for it when I moved in.

The bedroom was almost pitch dark. Widening my eyes and peering past the foot of the bed toward the sounds, I still could see nothing of him, just the blackness of the open closet door. Then something – the glimmer of a small flashlight, held low.

I could lie still and hope he left. But Tish was in her room downstairs. Had he been there already? If not, was he headed there next? No choice: I had to do something.

I reached for the bedside lamp to turn it on. Startling him might make him run. If it didn't, I'd have to take my chances with him, and I was not optimistic. I'm not exactly one of those 97-pound weaklings Charles Atlas used to lecture America about; I've done some boxing at my club, and I try to stay in shape. But if I was about to face the man who hanged Faye McMahan, broke Opal Hicks' neck with his hands, and slit Dewey Tackett's throat with a diabolical hunter's tool, I knew I could be counting down the last few seconds of my life.

I reached for the switch on the lamp and swung my legs carefully out of the bed, feeling game but barely ready.

I never reached the switch. He heard me. And he came at me.

I grabbed the lamp and swung it at where I figured his head would be. It made solid contact, the bulb splintering, and he fell back to the floor.

'Tish!' I yelled as I got to my feet. 'Wake up! Get out and go for help!'

I tried to vault over the figure on the floor, make it out the door and down the stairs, but he grabbed an ankle. My legs tangled, and I went down in a heap.

As I tried to scramble back up, he drove at me, catching me chest-high, propelling me backward into the hall and, without pause, down the stairs. We hit the landing two-thirds of the way up, he on top. I was hurting from the impact, but the adrenalin now pumping through my system barely let me feel it.

'Randall!' It was Tish's scream.

I tried to yell out *Run!*, but all the breath had been driven out of me, and it sounded like a croak. Vague noises came from down below. Where was she?

Then I got my breath. 'Run!' I bellowed.

The figure came at me again. I feared a weapon, but could tell both his hands were empty. With great strength, he hauled me to my feet. I got in two left jabs, one of them a good one, feeling knuckles hit cheekbone, and drew back a right, ready to put all I had into it.

He was faster, though. He shoved powerfully with both hands, and I went over backward down the rest of the stairs, all the way to the ground floor, yelling painfully as I hit the flooring on my back, my head striking the wood an instant later. It took all the breath out of me, and for a few seconds I couldn't move at all.

I looked up as he started down the stairs unhurriedly, and in the murky light I saw his right hand go to his belt. My throat clutched. I tried to sit up ...

A deafening blast split the air. The figure on the stairs stopped, ducked, then vaulted over the railing. I heard two bodies collide, Tish scream wordlessly, and then running footsteps.

I don't know how much time went by, but I was aware of Tish kneeling beside me, touching me. 'You found your trusty 20-gauge,' I heard someone say. 'Good girl.' The voice was mine.

My head felt like a balloon loosed from its tether.

I passed out.

TWELVE

'*O*w.' Tish made an apologetic face, as if to suggest that someone of her station in life shouldn't admit to pain. The paramedic, a monosyllabic lad with a face straight out of the hills and hollers, was inspecting an ugly grapefruit-size bruise on her right shoulder, while she covered the rest of herself with one of those drafty paper robes.

We were in the emergency room of a small clinic, the closest thing to a hospital in Pilgrim's Rest. It was around midnight. Chief Jerry Chitwood was in attendance, along with one of his deputies. One of the clinic's two doctors, awakened at home twenty miles away, was on his way. Tish and I had arrived a half hour earlier, and had I not been so post-traumatic, it would have been amusing to watch the clinic stir itself with people and ringing telephones once it became known that the injured wife of Stuart McMahan was on the premises.

Tish and I were in miraculously good condition, considering. She had the bruise, a result of a hard kick from our night-time visitor as he vaulted the stair railing on his way to the back door. My front was virtually unmarked, but my back, from neck to waist, was a road map of scrapes and bruises where the stairs had pummeled me on my way down. And I had a slight concussion from hitting my head on the floor.

After the paramedic's exam, Tish stepped behind a curtain to dress. When she emerged in pants and a knit turtleneck, he produced a sling and expertly nestled her right arm in it. 'You'll want to keep this on for a day or so,' he told her.

'Thank you,' she said.

'Don't mention it, ma'am.' Another one of those boys they raised right.

We had told our story to the chief as he assiduously took notes. I stressed the point about two separate bedrooms, and he nodded without comment. Chitwood was not the sort to rush to judgment, I knew, although others might be. But it was too late to worry about that. Whatever the fallout, it couldn't hurt me, only my friends.

Agent Timms, who had been attached to the chief at the hip in recent days, was apparently out of town. After getting our statements, the chief had put in a call to Sonny in Atlanta, and I could hear the shock in Sonny's voice from across the room. Chitwood put Tish on with him, and she talked soothingly for several minutes, assuring him that she was all right and that I was too. He never asked to talk to me.

The doctor arrived and confirmed that there were no serious injuries, but he cautioned me to stay awake for several hours to make sure that the concussion did not mask something more ominous.

Finally all was quiet, and the deputy went outside to wait. The little examining room seemed a kind of haven, so we sat there with the chief for a while.

I noticed that my hand was shaking. 'We were very lucky tonight,' I said to him.

He nodded, averting his eyes as if he felt personally responsible for our close call. 'By the way,' he said, 'one of my boys went over there. Said the guy picked the lock on the back door. Wore gloves, too.'

'I don't care,' I said. 'We know by now he's a regular genius. And he's gutsy. And strong as a bull. We know all that. Dammit, Jerry, who is this guy, and how can he walk around town like this?'

'I don't know who he is,' Chitwood said evenly. 'I could almost swear to you he's not somebody I know. More than that I can't tell you. I don't think the TBI has learned anything useful either,' he added. His tone suggested a lack of patience with Timms and his boys.

'But it sure looks like somebody's got it in for either the Governor or his relatives,' he went on, speaking to Tish this time, 'and I promise you—'

'I wonder if that's true,' I broke in. 'I'll grant you, it seems to fit the first three killings. But tonight felt different.'

'How do you mean?' Chitwood asked. Tish was looking intently at me.

'He was in the house before we knew it,' I said. 'He could have killed us in our sleep. Instead he took his time. He seemed to be looking for something. Things didn't turn nasty until I woke up.'

'Right,' Tish said softly. 'Looking for what, do you suppose?'

'My notes, maybe.'

'And what could there be in—'

'Sonny's past,' I said. 'Politics, business, personal life. And a little about Blue, too.'

She shook her head slowly, acknowledging how much we still did not know.

At that moment Kenneth Lively rushed in, half-dressed and jumpy. 'The Governor called ...' he began. His eyes darted to Tish. 'Are you all right, ma'am?'

'I'm fine, Ken.'

'He wants me to drive you back to Nashville.' He shot me a look that can only be described as venomous. The former first lady had suffered injuries and indignities while in my care, and I was apparently being held responsible. Who knew what Sonny had told him?

'I'll just be a little while,' she said. She might have been addressing a store clerk, and it was pretty clear that she felt no special connection with him. 'Would you mind waiting outside?'

'Right now, ma'am,' he said in his state trooper's voice. 'I'm sorry, but he said right now. He thinks you're in danger here.'

'The danger's over, Ken, and I'm feeling very tired right now.'

'Give her a break,' I said to him.

'Don't give me orders, Chicago boy,' he said.

'Now wait a minute.' Sore as I was, I started up out of my chair when Tish's voice stopped me.

'Please! Both of you.' She turned to Lively. 'All right, Ken, if it's that important to my husband, I'll be right with you. Now please wait outside.'

He bumped my knee on his way out, and I could feel the challenge hanging in the air, like a playground taunt. Up until now he'd been coolly polite toward me, but now that I'd been fired, he could express his inner SOB.

Tish sighed loudly as she got up. 'We'll make a stop at Longstaff House to pick up a few things.' Favoring her shoulder, she stooped to kiss me on the cheek. 'You take care now,' she whispered.

'You're great to have around in an emergency,' I told her, squeezing her left hand. 'Say hello to Sonny. Tell him I'm sorry it didn't work out.'

Hardly had she made it out the door when Forrest Wilkes brushed the curtain aside, looking around distractedly, wearing a long coat over pajamas and slippers.

'I heard you'd been hurt,' he said.

I shot Chitwood a glance, and he responded with a guilty look.

'I'm all right,' I said. 'But we had a late-night visitor over at Longstaff House, and he stirred things up.'

'Are you going back there now?'

'Yes, but just to pick up my stuff. I've been evicted.'

'Then you'll come stay with me.'

'I'm not sure that's a good idea. It could be risky—'

'I insist.' He used his academic voice, and I knew there was no arguing with him.

Tish's SUV, with Lively at the wheel, was just pulling away from Longstaff House when we arrived. I waved to her, but her return wave was perfunctory, and she showed no expression, as if her mind was already on her next conversation with Sonny. She might be thinking she'd let him finish his night's sleep, or she might already be reaching for her cell phone. Sonny struck me as one of those people who wanted bad news delivered right away. And even though it wasn't nearly as startling as the news from the emergency room, it was still bad.

Inside, it took me only a couple of minutes to pack everything – two bags and my laptop. My notes and tapes, naturally, were gone. But she had left me something on the dining table. Her sweet little Remington 20-gauge semi-auto, the gun that had saved our lives this night, and a box of shells. The message was clear: You'll need this more than I will.

When I carried it out to the car, my father looked at it with distaste. He had a lifelong aversion to guns – another of those traits that made him anything but your average Southern daddy – and I had had to turn to Blue McMahan and other men to initiate me into that particular fraternity.

'Is that yours?' he asked.

'No, it's Leticia's,' I said. 'She asked me to hang onto it for safekeeping.' A small lie, told as much for his benefit as for mine.

'Well, I hope you'll hide it away where Mrs. Mullins won't see it.' Mrs. Mullins – I don't think I ever heard her first name – was my father's housekeeper, who washed his clothes and picked up after him and cooked his meals and, I suppose, darned his socks too. He had hired her not long after my mother died, and we had never met.

Minutes later we were at Wilkes Cottage, where I carried my things inside. 'You can stay in your old room if you like,' my father said. 'All we'll need is some bedding. But try to be quiet, so we don't wake up Mrs. Mullins.' We found what we needed in the camphor chest in the upstairs hall. He opened the door to what had been my room and turned on the light. It smelled musty but also strangely familiar.

'You don't have to help me make the bed,' I told him. 'I can manage.'

'I insist,' he said, then smiled almost imperceptibly as he realized he was repeating himself.

Together we laid out and tucked in the sheets, stuffed pillows into cases, and spread a blanket over the bed. Throughout this domestic task – something I'm sure we had never performed together before – we spoke not a word.

When we had finished, I said, 'I don't want to sound like a scaredy cat, but are all the doors and windows locked?'

'Yes,' he said. 'After Faye and Opal were murdered, I had a handyman go all over the place, checking everything. We have some extra locks now.' He dug into a pocket. 'Here are the two keys you'll need for the front door.'

I saw how exhausted he looked. The night must have taken a lot out of him.

'Good night, then,' I said. 'Thank you for letting me stay here.'

'It's still your room,' he said.

When he had gone, I loaded two shells in the shotgun's magazine and a third in the chamber, set the safety, and stood the gun in the closet just inside the door. Then I got undressed and fell into bed.

I was wired from the night's experience, but bone-tired too. Just before turning out the light, I looked around the room. It was almost bare, stripped of the accumulated junk of my teenage years. No pennants, no posters, no boyhood knickknacks.

But one thing remained. A set of books atop the dresser. Worn and dog-eared, read and re-read, all the familiar titles: *The Adventures of Tom Sawyer. The Boy Scout Handbook. The Martian Chronicles. All the President's Men. Gone With the Wind,* for crying out loud. And all the rest. Through all our ups and downs, he had chosen to keep my books right where I'd left them.

The next morning I slept late. When I came downstairs, breakfast was only a lingering scent of bacon and eggs, but the housekeeper served me coffee in the spacious, antiquated kitchen with its gas range that dated back to the Second World War. Mrs. Mullins, it turned out, was a country gal somewhere in her fifties. She had a plain but pleasant face, and she said little as she busied herself drying the last of the breakfast dishes.

My father, she told me, was already at work in his study. I decided not to bother him.

'Do you live here in the house?' I asked her. The question was out before I realized how abrupt it sounded.

'Yes, sir,' she said with what sounded like a touch of defensiveness. 'Mr. Wilkes, he give me the room upstairs at the end of the hall.' The room, I recalled, had been designed as a maid's quarters. Our family had used it as a guestroom.

I felt like the young lord of the manor, Hamlet home from the university. I started to ask her not to call me sir, but I thought I'd better leave things alone. She was more at home here than I was. If she wanted to call me sir, let her.

So I just said, 'Thank you for the coffee.'

'You're very welcome.'

The phone rang, and she answered it. To my surprise, it was for me.

'Are you all right?' Charlene Singletary asked me in a voice of quiet concern.

'I got a good scare last night, but honestly, I'm fine. You heard all about it?'

'Yes.'

'Of course you did. That's your job. And you probably want to nail down an exclusive with me before the *New York Times* beats you to it.'

'I'd be grateful for whatever you can tell me. And in return, I'll be glad to give you the background on the Governor and the town I promised you for that book you're working on. I believe we got interrupted.'

'Ah, well, my situation has changed a little since the last time I saw you, and our interruption has something to do with it. Sonny's decided to find himself another Boswell.'

'I thought you were friends.'

'We were. And are, I think. But it seems I've let him down. I won't bore you with it right now. Let me just say I'm not that interested in Sonny's background any more. I'm more interested in Callie Darnell's.'

'Really?' She was silent for a while. 'Maybe I can help you. The reason I called ... I wondered if you'd like to come over and have supper with me and Walter tonight.'

'Your grandfather? Sure. I doubt that he'd remember me, though.'

'Oh, he remembers you. He's got a better memory than both of us put together.'

After we hung up, I stood there in the front hallway, looking at my reflection in a mirrored coatrack that had once been my mother's. Walter Howard had been one of the town's stalwarts during my teenage years, a public man of character. During the civil rights years, they said, he made enemies by editorializing that the town and the state and the South needed to move forward, not backward. Time had proved him right.

He was one of those figures who added luster to the word *journalist*.

What, I wondered, would he think of me?

Charlene lived with her grandfather in a small, pleasant house on one of the oldest streets in Pilgrim's Rest. For about an hour before dinner, while he napped, she and I sat on their front porch, screened from the street by a thicket of wisteria and honeysuckle that blanketed the porch trellis. She sat on a cushioned wicker chair, I on the porch swing.

'You'd be more comfortable here,' she said, indicating a matching chair next to her.

'Are you kidding? I haven't sat in one of these things in years.' I gave a little kick and started the swing. The rusted chains squeaked softly. 'I know it's undignified,' I said, 'but I don't have any dignity left anyway.'

She laughed at that, a nice, relaxed laugh. I liked it. Charlene struck me as basically a serious person, with little time or inclination for play. I admire people who take life seriously, but I also took pleasure in making her laugh.

'I guess you've heard all about Callie Darnell,' I said.

She nodded. 'That was what interrupted us when you were at the paper the other day. We finally got the whole story. It's very sad. I never really knew her, but you did, didn't you?'

'Yes. In fact, she's the reason I'm not working for Sonny anymore.' Little by little, I told her about me and Callie, about my determination to find out what happened to her. The only thing I left out was Blue and the question of whether or not he knew anything about her death. Charlene stared at me throughout the story, transfixed.

When I had finished, she thought for a moment, then said, 'It looks like you have a new reason for staying here.'

We talked about the latest outrage to the peace of the town. I told her what I could remember about the last night's events. Again I was less than complete, holding back my conjecture as to what our visitor had been after.

As we spoke, I realized that the lid that Chief Chitwood had placed on Blue McMahan's involvement in the motel murder was holding tight. Charlene had apparently not heard anything about Blue's resurrection and subsequent visit to our town.

She took notes as I spoke, then excused herself to phone her notes to the reporter who was writing the story for this week's edition. *The Call* always circulated on Monday morning and printed the night before. This was Sunday night, and the edition should have been put to bed by now, but Charlene was holding a big piece of the front page for the story about the home invasion in the Colony that involved Leticia McMahan.

'Granddad is stirring, and the roast is done,' she said when she returned. 'You want to eat?'

Walter Howard reminded me of an old lion. He had a large head with an expansive brow and a mop of white hair that had not seen the barber's clippers in many a moon. He moved slowly, careful about his failing resources. Refreshingly plain-spoken, he ordered me to call him Walter. I liked him right away.

We sat down at the table. He had already heard about last night's events and pressed me quietly for some details. But the conversation soon turned to his favorite topic, newspapering.

'Chicago used to be one of the great newspaper towns,' Walter said. 'Competitive as hell. When Ben Hecht and Charlie MacArthur wrote *The Front Page*, it came right out of their experiences as Chicago reporters.'

'Yes, sir,' I said. 'It must have been fun. But those days are long gone. You don't see much of the old fast-talking, hard-drinking reporter. Still ...'

'What?'

'Oh, I was just remembering what it was like when I started at the *Examiner*. I was doing general assignment, and they had me running all over the place. I'd come back to the newsroom with a pocket full of notes, and I'd sit down and bang out something. And sometimes it was pretty good, even though I always wished I had more time. And then, right on deadline, I'd send it over to the night city editor, and I'd kick back for a while – get some coffee and a sandwich – and the city room would grow quiet, with just the night shift still around.

'Then, around eleven, we'd feel this rumble coming up through the floor, and we knew the presses were running. About a half-hour later, the copy boys would bring the papers up from the loading dock and hustle them around the room. I'd open the paper to look for my story, and the ink would still be damp, and it would give off this smell, this most wonderful ...'

I stopped, aware that they were staring at me. 'Sorry I'm so gabby,' I said.

'You miss it, don't you?' Charlene said.

'Maybe I do.'

'You didn't stay a lowly reporter forever,' Walter said to me. 'A while back, *Business Week* did a piece on the Chicago papers. There was a photo of some of the top editors of the *Examiner* standing in front of a delivery truck, and there you were – or your likeness – plastered all over the side of the truck.'

'I remember,' I said. I had been very proud of that poster. You could see me rolling all over the city, along with the slogan *Wilkes Gives It to You Straight*. Oh, the irony.

He let the subject drop, for which I was grateful. We dug into the meal Charlene had prepared – pork roast with green bean casserole. As a cook, she was a great editor, but I enjoyed myself nonetheless, and part of the enjoyment had to do with the obvious affection between the two of them. He spoke with pride of what she'd done with the *Call*, how circulation had kicked up a few hundred since she'd taken over.

I watched her out of the corner of my eye. She had a quiet integrity that, at this particular moment in my life, appealed enormously to me. I don't know if there was anything sexual in it – there probably was – but all I knew was I wanted her to like me.

An old quote swam to the surface of my brain, something from William Allen White, who for years had edited the *Gazette* in Emporia, Kansas: 'There are three things that no one can do to the entire satisfaction of anyone else: make love, poke the fire, and run a newspaper.'

I knew how she ran a newspaper. As for the other two, I wondered if I would ever find out.

When I tuned back in, Charlene was telling Walter about my interest in Callie Darnell.

He looked grim. 'This town's gone a generation or so without much in the way of violent crime. Now all of a sudden we have three killings and what looks like another attempt. It makes me sad. And angry. Now we find out about Callie. I remember her. She was a little wild, but sweet too.'

He turned to me. 'Some of this looks connected to the Governor or his family,' he said. 'You're his friend. What do you think?'

'I think it's possible,' I said carefully. 'Our friendship's a little rocky right now, but I hope that's just temporary. What do you think about Sonny?'

'I always liked him personally,' Walter said. 'I watched him grow up, but I didn't get to know him well until he was in office, and I began to write about his governorship. I disagreed with him on some things, but I was very encouraged when he began talking about developing the Cumberland Plateau, bringing in business. You know, for years all we had around here was coal and timber, and those industries weren't always kind to us. They took out more than they left. Now Stuart's talking about tourism, and that shows promise. But ...' He looked thoughtful.

'But what?'

'I'm just thinking, he and his partners have been buying up

a lot of property around here, planning for the day when it all pays off. I hope he's not overextending himself.'

'What are they buying?'

'Well, several of the downtown businesses, including the hardware store. You know the Hunting Lodge, that fancy new restaurant? They tore down Grady's and built that place. They've even made us an offer on the *Call*, but I'm not comfortable with the idea of a politician owning the local paper.'

'And there's this conference center,' Charlene said. 'Depending on who you talk to, it'll either save the town or turn the place into a big theme park.'

'It's shaping up as something enormous,' Walter said. 'In terms of Civil War history, it could eventually rival Shiloh as a magnet for visitors.'

'Really?' The battle of Shiloh had been one of the turning points of the war, and the Shiloh National Military Park, about 150 miles west of us, drew hordes of visitors every year.

'I believe it,' Walter continued. 'Speaking of which, Olen Stringer was once a park ranger at Shiloh. So he probably has some experience at handling crowds.'

'What's the *Call*'s position on the conference center?' I asked.

'I've editorialized in favor of it, and Granddad agrees with me. But I'm urging them to go slow, be careful, make sure only the best people are involved. People like your dad are a great start.'

'What about this guy Stringer?'

They looked at each other. 'He's been good for the Historical Society. Seems to be doing a good job. But there's something a little slick about him. The Governor clearly has selfish reasons for locating the conference center here, and it could very well be a good thing for the town. But until Olen Stringer turned up those Civil War remains, the town wasn't exactly the most appropriate choice, since there are a lot of places with more obvious connections to the war. His discovery just seems very convenient.'

'But he obviously found them. And they're the real thing.'

She nodded. 'That's true.'

'How much do you know about him?'

'Not enough. Walter thinks I should put a reporter on him and look into his background. I just don't have the people right now, especially with what's been happening lately. And also,' she added with the slightest smile, 'because I assigned somebody to a little project you suggested not long ago.'

Lem Coldsmith, I thought. Good. 'Well, thank you.'

'I know who you should talk to,' she said abruptly. 'Sis Lawlor. She knows everybody in town, and she might be able to help you with the Darnells as well as the McMahans.'

As I was about to respond, Walter cut in. 'Yes. Do talk to her. She's been around quite a while. You'd never know it, but in her day Sis Lawlor was one of the great beauties of the county. She had men hanging around her like flies around molasses. And she went and married some old boy who worked in the mines. No reflection on him, because I hear he was a good man, but she could have had just about anybody she wanted.'

I was intrigued enough to ask Charlene directions to Sis Lawlor's place, and she wrote them down for me. 'Before you send him out there,' Walter said, 'you should tell him about the key to her heart.'

Charlene looked slightly uncomfortable.

'What?' I asked.

'Sis' friends say she enjoys a swig of Southern Comfort every now and then,' she said finally.

'Hmm. All right. I'll go bearing gifts.'

We sat eating in silence for a while. They had been straight with me tonight, and I wanted to give them something in return. 'There's something I haven't told you,' I said to Charlene. 'I'd like to give it to you on background, if you agree. You won't print it or repeat it until I say it's all right. Agreed?'

She hesitated only briefly. 'Fine.'

For the next few minutes I told them about Blue McMahan, about how he had risen from the dead and then vanished again. About the secret he was supposed to know, and how I felt he was connected in some way to every violent act that had occurred.

When I had finished, Walter wiped his mouth with his napkin, looking thoughtful.

'Could he have done these things?' he asked.

'Not the Blue I know,' I replied. 'But I think he knows something. What's your opinion of him?'

'I think he's one of the least trustworthy men I ever knew,' Walter said evenly. 'I think he has very little in the way of morals, and he's capable of hurting people without even trying. The way he neglected his wife and son for years. But I also found him great company whenever he was around.' He shrugged. 'He's a paradox.'

'Are the police looking for him?' Charlene asked.

'Uh-huh. Just not very hard.'

Walter nodded several times. 'Then you may have to start looking for him yourself.'

The thought had been slowly taking shape in my head for days. Maybe all I needed was to hear it spoken aloud.

Walter looked sleepy, and the shadows under his eyes seemed to have deepened. I knew I had stayed long enough. 'I should go,' I said. 'Thank you for dinner.'

Charlene saw me to the door. 'He likes you,' she said.

'That's very nice. I want both of you to like me.'

She seemed about to add something, so I waited. 'You asked me about Charlie. The nickname.' She didn't meet my eyes. 'Some people do call me that. Some of my friends.'

'Thanks for telling me. Good night.'

That went well, I thought. This time I meant it.

THIRTEEN

I negotiated my way through the double-locked front door at Wilkes Cottage. The house was quiet except for the slow, throaty ticking of the antique Seth Thomas clock that had stood on a table in the front hall for as long as I could remember. Every Sunday my father had ritualistically wound it, slowly cranking the lead weights up to the top of the chamber. I had no doubt that the ritual continued.

In bed, I read for a while from my father's history of the town. I located the chapter on the Civil War and confirmed my memory that he had made no mention of the Burning, either as legend or as fact. Later, though, something had happened to lessen his skepticism. Mary Hightower's incomplete diary and the bones of a pair of Confederate soldiers, far from any known battlefield. Was that enough to change the mind of a careful scholar – or was there more?

I turned out the light. A parade of images swirled through my head as I lay there in the dark. Lost bones poking their way out of the ground. A frail old woman in a nightgown hanging from the bridge at Damnation Falls. Blue McMahan, eyes boring into mine as he wiped barbecue sauce from his chin and said, 'Not going to tattle-tale on me, are you?' A shadowy figure coming down the stairs toward me, reaching for something at his belt …

Enough of this, I thought. I felt like a kid scaring himself with bedtime stories. Reaching back in time for something more soothing, I found Callie. There she was, threading her way through the tables at Grady's, joshing the customers, her tray expertly balanced shoulder-high as she passed the table where Sonny and I sat. Sonny let out a soft whoop. 'Will you look at that?' he said, eyes following her.

I had yet to find the courage to ask her out, but I certainly didn't want Sonny to move first. 'You've got a girlfriend,' I pointed out.

An insolent grin. 'Who says?'

In an instant I was back in the present. A floorboard had creaked somewhere out in the hallway.

Seconds later I had the shotgun in hand, ready to disengage the safety. I crept to the door, listening. At first, nothing. I put my ear against the door and heard it – soft footsteps, from the direction of my father's room. As I strained my ears, the footsteps passed in front of my door, heading down the hallway.

Sick of being spooked, I put my hand on the doorknob and prepared to yank it open, then step into the hall and shout out a challenge. Then I heard another sound.

A light tapping on a door. Mrs. Mullins' door. Then the faint sound of the door opening and, after a few seconds, softly being closed.

Well, I'll be damned. This doesn't exactly compute, does it? On the other hand, why not?

I thought of what must have been my father's intense loneliness since my mother's death just a few years ago, and I tried to imagine what he might do to assuage that loneliness. But Mrs. Mullins, of the plain features and the country grammar? He could do better. On my mother's behalf, I felt a momentary flash of anger toward him. I tried to imagine these two discussing history or literature or antiques, and that didn't compute either.

I allowed various sarcastic thoughts take shape, then let go of them. I may be around for a while, I thought. Plenty of time for sarcasm.

The next morning I was just swinging my legs out of bed when my cell phone rang. 'Good morning,' Charlene said. 'I think I've turned up something.'

'On the furniture salesman?'

'Well, he's more of a furniture king, but yes.' Behind her voice I heard the usual newsroom music – the ringing of phones, the tapping of computer keys, the drone of voices. It wasn't nearly the level of racket. I remembered from the *Examiner*, but it still sounded like Gershwin to me.

When she didn't proceed right away, I asked, 'Is this going to make Sonny unhappy?'

'Randall, I don't know. But I think so.' Another pause. 'There's word going around that Coldsmith's having tax trouble.'

'Is that all?'

'No. Big trouble. Tax fraud.'

'Big enough to ...'

'Let's say that if the word turns out to be true, then it's big enough to put a big crimp in his business.'

I let out a soft whistle between my teeth. 'Is this common knowledge?'

'Are you kidding?' She sounded offended. 'Nobody knows about this, except for the IRS and a few people in the federal prosecutor's office. And one of the business reporters at the *Tennessean*. I'm sure Coldsmith knows they're sniffing around, but they wouldn't be ready to show all their cards yet.'

She had trusted me with a secret. Not many people had done that lately. I felt flattered and even a little humbled. 'Thanks for telling me this, Charlene.'

'Don't mention it. Because if you do, there'll be a price on your head.'

'Is it about to hit print?'

'Soon, I think. My friend has it first, naturally. After that, every paper in the state will want a piece of it. Coldsmith's a big name.'

'And now he's joined at the hip with the Honorable Stuart McMahan. I don't know Tennessee politics that well, but—'

'You're wondering if this could hurt him. Yes, it could. Because it's history repeating itself. Once again they'll call him the politician whose friends can't be trusted, and it'll be worse the second time around. And if Coldsmith gets involved in a long federal prosecution, even if they don't threaten him with jail, you know what happens to all that money he's sinking into the study center. The Governor would have to scramble for more cash.'

I had forgotten that for a moment. She was right. This could snowball, and the snowball could roll all the way from Nashville down to the Cumberland Plateau. The plateau is uphill, of course, but you get the metaphor.

We talked a bit more and then hung up. Tish had said Sonny was growing troubled about the project. Now I knew why. Coldsmith could feel them on his trail, and he had given off some kind of signal that Sonny was expert at reading. Sonny McMahan, who wanted to feel power in his hands again and who wanted to do something for his state, could lose everything he was after.

I wondered if it was too late for him to do anything about it.

'Help yourself. Don't be shy.'

Sis Lawlor sat rocking gently in a chair that had worn grooves in the floorboards of her porch. Her aproned lap was full of walnuts, and she worked intently at them, breaking them open with a nutcracker, then carefully picking the meat out of the shell and depositing it in a bowl that sat on a small table between us.

I took a taste. It was delicious.

'Now's the time to eat 'em, when they're fresh. They're full of oil, so if you don't eat 'em soon, they'll go rancid.'

Next to the bowl was a glass full of ice cubes and vaguely cranberry-colored liquid, and next to that was a tall open bottle of 100-proof Southern Comfort, which had gotten me the invitation to join her on the porch. I cradled my own glass in my lap.

'These are real good walnuts,' I said to her. 'You must grow a lot of your own food here.' I looked off to my right, past her Dodge pickup, where a half-acre or so of land had been devoted to vegetables.

She nodded, intent on the work in her lap. 'I don't need much,' she said. 'We didn't even get electricity or water out here until, oh, about thirty years ago. My husband, Will, rest his soul, he liked being independent, said we could get along fine on our own. But I wanted the electricity so we could have lights and a refrigerator and a radio. He finally gave in.' The radio was playing somewhere inside the house, a man's voice droning on about some kind of health remedy.

Sis Lawlor could have been an elder cousin to Mrs. Mullins, with the same rawboned country features. But she was a bigger woman, with the suggestion of physical strength in her aging frame.

'Is that an old spring house?' I asked, pointing in the other direction, where the forest grew closer to the house and a dry creek bed ran alongside the trees.

'That's right,' she said. 'Used to be, until the spring dried up. That was how we kept everything cold, milk and what have you. We'd just put it in jugs and sink it down in the spring.'

The house was small and made of stone. I'd heard of spring houses, but only as part of a vanished way of life. 'Can I see it?'

'Hon, it's all poison ivy back there, and cobwebs inside. I wouldn't go to the trouble, if I was you.' She dumped another small portion of nut meat into the bowl. 'So you want to know about the McMahans.'

'Yes, ma'am. Walter Howard told me you know everybody in town.'

'That means I'm old,' she said with a laugh that came out a guffaw. 'But he's right. This is for some kind of a book about the Governor?'

I nodded, reluctant to give her the particulars. The now-vanished book project was still a good excuse for talking to people. And eventually I'd try to steer her toward the subject of Callie.

'Terrible about Faye. And little Opal. We've never had nothing like that happen around this town, all the years I've lived here. Faye was a nice lady, even if she acted a little bit better than some of us, especially after her boy got elected governor.'

I just nodded, curious to hear someone express even a mildly negative opinion of Faye.

'Some of them McMahans was dirt poor, and some of 'em didn't mind how they made a living,' she said. 'Like that Blue. Who would have thought he'd wind up marrying somebody like Faye? Nothing in common, those two. She was a Hedgecock, you know, from up around McMinnville? Taught school for a while, before she married him. They were like oil and water. He was wild, and she mostly disapproved, but she kept quiet about it. There's an old song my people brought across the mountains a long time ago, called *Rake and a Rambling Boy*. Well, that song could've been written for Blue.

'I mentioned my husband, Will? Blue was his second cousin. Will worked in the mines and then in the timber business, but Blue, he never worked a day in his life.'

'He was a con man,' I said.

'Oh, he was that, all right. One of those silver-tongued devils. He could talk the men right out of their money, and the ladies ...' A mischievous look came over her. 'Let's just say he was a charmer, that old boy. A real charmer.' She shook her head, smiling. 'There was a time ...'

'A time?'

The smile vanished. 'Never you mind.'

'What do you remember about Sonny, Miz Lawlor?' I prompted her.

'Call me Sis, hon. Everybody does.' She flicked at a fly that tried to settle on a walnut. 'Nice enough boy. A little rambunctious, like a lot of boys. I have to tell you, I wasn't surprised the day he made governor. Always seemed there was something pushing that boy, you know?'

I know, I thought. I was too close to see it at the time. But Leticia Alcott, vice-president of the Thetas, saw it, didn't she?

I decided to shift gears. 'Sis, you heard about Callie Darnell?'

'Oh, my, yes.' Her eyes met mine for a second, and I saw shock and pity in them before she bent back to her work. 'That poor girl. Dead all these years, and who even knew?'

'Just the one who killed her, I imagine.'

'Well, God will punish that person,' she said in a matter-of-fact tone. 'And the one who murdered Faye. I feel it.'

'I hope you're right, ma'am, but I don't intend to wait for that to happen. Do you mind if I ask you what you know about Callie's family and friends?'

She looked at me sharply this time, and I doubted that I could get any lies past her. That was all right, since the truth should do just fine.

'I don't know what I can tell you, but you go ahead and ask.'

'How well do you remember Callie?'

'Oh, real well.' She smiled and nodded. 'She used to come and pay me visits, sit right there where you're sitting. I'd just lost Will, and I was lonely. And she was lonely too – not for boys, not for men, just for a chance to kick her shoes off and sit with another woman, let her hair down, talk about anything. I liked her a lot.

'She came from bad blood, you know, but she wasn't bad, just a little wild. Like Blue. You don't hate somebody for being wild if they have enough goodness to make up for it. And she did. There were folks in town that looked down on her, talked about all her boyfriends, her playing around. But she was nice to me, and I tried to be nice to her. Mostly I just remember how sweet she was. When she left – when we all thought she'd left – I just hoped she'd find someplace to be happy. And all the time—' She dug vigorously at the nut in her hand with the sharp little pick, her face grim. 'All the time, she was buried in the ground, right here.'

'What did you mean about the bad blood?'

She cackled. 'Hon, everybody knew about the Darnells. I try never to speak ill of folks, but the Darnells was trash, pure and simple. The daddy, Pike, he was trash, his boys was trash, and his wife – well, I suppose she was trash too, but he drove her into an early grave when the children was young.'

'I remember a couple of brothers, but they were older, and I didn't see much of them,' I said. 'What happened to them?'

'The older one, I forget his name – he hasn't been around for years. I heard he's in prison down in Georgia. The younger one's still around,' she said. 'Vern. He helps his sister out at the garage some, but mostly he lives out in the woods. People say he's simpleminded.' She shook her head. 'One look at him, you can tell something's wrong.'

'What about Lita Ray?' I asked. 'Would you say she's trash too?'

Sis looked reflective. 'Maybe not. At least she works for a living, so maybe she turned out all right. But if she did, it's a miracle. Her mama was dead, and there was nobody to look after her but Callie. And that father ...' Her face twisted into something ugly.

'What about him?'

'All I know is the talk, and I shouldn't repeat it. Except that I always believed it, and it's the lies you shouldn't repeat, not the truths. There was talk that the father did things to his girls, things no father should do.'

I felt the liquor turn to bile in my stomach. There'd been gossip in high school about the Darnells and their inbred ways. But it was mostly the snickering kind, and I didn't really believe it. At least, not then.

'What happened to him?'

'Oh, he's still around too,' she said, as if it were a kind of grim joke. 'But he's suffering God's punishment.'

'How do you mean?'

'The kind you find waiting for you when you practice the sins of the flesh all your life.'

She didn't seem inclined to elaborate, so I let it rest.

'Looking back, do you remember any of Callie's boyfriends who might have—'

'Been the killing kind? No, hon, I don't. But there was a lot of them, and that's sure the truth. Married men, single men, young men – boys, I suppose. There was all them college boys, you remember?'

I did. Tennessee Highlands College was about ten miles up the road from Pilgrim's Rest, and its surrounding town was too small to offer much in the way of entertainment, so students would come our way for a good time – dining, drinking, and sightseeing along the bluff. Over the years, Callie Darnell came to be known as one of the local sights, and she could often be seen riding through town in some college stud's convertible.

'She never told me the names of anybody she went with, but every now and then I could figure somebody out, put two and two together. I was able to guess a few of 'em.'

'Who were they?'

'I think I've rambled on enough,' she said. 'Jerry Chitwood, he asked me the same thing, and I told him I didn't know anything for sure, and that's the truth. If I knew for sure, I'd tell, because it would be the right thing. But everything else is just guessing, and not enough to hang your hat on. Or slander somebody's name.'

I was disappointed, but before I could try to change her mind, she gathered up the two lower corners of her apron in one hand as she stood up, cradling all the smashed walnut shells, and scooped up the bowl of nuts in her other hand.

'I've got a neighbor who's been ailing,' she said as she went inside. 'I'll save the rest of these for her.'

A moment later she was back with an ice tray, which she used to freshen the cubes in our glasses. She poured a generous slug into each.

'Now,' she said, settling herself. 'I've had enough sad stories about death and dying. Let's tell some good ones. You ever hear any of the Jack tales?'

'Just a few. A long time ago.'

'Who did you get 'em from?'

I told her. Back when I was in my early teens, Blue had taken me on a drive into the woods to look up a source of 'white lightning,' home-brewed sour mash whisky. When we got to the house – shack, really – he found that the expected new batch of sour mash had not materialized, and we had made the drive for nothing. But Blue was not one to waste a trip. He knew that his friend's grandfather was one of the region's great storytellers, and soon we were sitting on the steps of their front porch as the old man tuned up his voice and began telling one of his favorite Jack tales.

I was spellbound. When I got home that night, I snuck into

my father's library and dug through various books on Tennessee folklore until I found something on the history of the Jack tales. They were as old as the hills, brought over from England, Scotland and Ireland, and they always dealt with the fanciful adventures of a boy named Jack – just plain Jack – and how he uses native cunning to win out over a whole series of obstacles.

'That was Uncle Tim Tyrell who told you those stories,' Sis said. 'He's been dead years. He was one of the best. I learned a few from him. Here's one you maybe haven't heard.'

And she launched into a whiz of a Jack tale just for my benefit, a rousing fable involving a treasure, an enchanted girl, the most ferocious bear in the woods, and a Cherokee spirit that recognizes something kindred in Jack and agrees to help him finish his quest. Her voice took me back to my children's picture books, my mother's own storytelling voice, and all the magic that stories hold for us.

Toward the end, as Jack came down the mountain and saw the chimney smoke from his family's cabin, her voice slowed. The afternoon sun was in our faces now, and the Southern Comfort was doing its work.

'And when he took the gold out of his pocket, his father rejoiced, his little sister hugged him, and his mama cried,' Sis concluded. 'And that's the end of the story.'

'That was—'

'Now you tell one.'

'I'm afraid I don't know any.'

'Sure you do, hon.' Her voice was sleepy. 'Everybody's got at least one story in 'em.'

She was right. Of course I had a story. But was it something I wanted to speak aloud?

'Mine doesn't have a happy ending,' I told her.

'That's all right. Neither does life. You go ahead and tell yours, and I'll just rest.' She laid her head back and closed her eyes.

And so I told her my story.

FOURTEEN

I started by telling her about the Columnist and the world he lived in, the high-stakes, competitive world of big-city journalism. The Columnist, I told her, was hot stuff, with a thrice-weekly spot on page three of the *Chicago Examiner*, a platform for just about any subject that struck his fancy, a megaphone to send his thoughts out to the streets and suburbs. He wrote about the little guys and the fat cats, about the working stiffs and their bosses, about the people who ran Chicago and the people who didn't seem to count. He was responsible for the firing of a deputy mayor and the resignation of an alderman. He made people laugh and cry. They read him, they wrote letters to the paper, they argued about him in the bars. Some people called him the voice of the city. He had a job almost any other newspaperman would kill for.

I also told her about the Columnist's ambition, his drive to be not just good but the very best. He knew he wasn't the very best, because the Historian already had that title, along with a Pulitzer Prize to show for it. Now as you know, the Pulitzer goes to a whole grab-bag of writing types – novelists, biographers, poets, playwrights, historians, all kinds of scribblers. But old Joe Pulitzer, who dreamed up the prize, was a newspaperman, and it's still considered the gold standard for newspaper writing. The Columnist, naturally, wanted one to show to the Historian, for reasons we needn't go into but which are as deep as anything between father and son.

But his job wasn't easy. Three times a week he had to come

up with something that would stir people's anger or touch their humanity or just make them laugh at their own foibles. He ranged far and wide for his subjects. Sometimes he had to reach down inside himself for them. He liked to joke that his job was easy – he'd just sit down at the keyboard, open a vein, and bleed.

One night, when the Columnist was on his way from dinner to his car, he met the kid. The locale was a gritty stretch of street called Lower Michigan Avenue. Up above was the real Michigan Avenue, the Magnificent Mile, home of gleaming high-rises and high-end shopping. The lower level was dank and dirty, a place of loading docks and grimy dumpsters and rusty girders that held up the shiny street above. Tourists out after dark peeked under Michigan Avenue and decided that the lower level was not for them. It was not a place for a kid either.

The kid was filthy, with coveralls and sneakers without laces and a head of hair that might have been sandy-colored under all the dirt. He had a bloody nose, which caused the Columnist to stop and ask if he was all right. This met with a snappy and obscene response that would have caused most would-be good Samaritans to back off. But the columnist was the curious sort. He gave the kid a handkerchief to wipe his nose, and a minute later they were talking.

The kid's name was Rabbit. It wasn't his real name, naturally, but it was all he was going to give out. He said one of his mother's boyfriends had called him that because he seemed to be jumping around all the time. With his furtive look, the name seemed to fit.

Where do you live? the Columnist asked him. None of your business, the kid said. I been staying around here mostly anyway.

Where's here?

The kid pointed to one of the larger dumpsters, backed up against a loading dock. Over there.

You sleep there?

The Columnist's questions were making the kid suspicious. He had run into the kind of grown-ups who asked questions

– cops and social workers, mostly. They never did him any good. He looked about to take flight.

Here, the Columnist said, taking some money out of his pocket. Take this.

The kid took it, and an instant later, he was gone, darting between the pillars, heading toward the bridge that took the lower level across the river.

The Columnist went home, but he had trouble sleeping that night. He kept seeing the kid's dirty face, heard his little croak of a voice. He looked for him the next night, and the night after that, but there was no sign of him.

Then, on the third night, close to midnight, there he was, sitting in the deep shadows, his back against the concrete of a building's foundation, smoking a cigarette. The Columnist said hello and sat down beside him. True to his name, the kid still looked jumpy and gun-shy, but he didn't bolt. More money changed hands, and slowly the kid began to tell his story.

Nothing about it was pretty. Family moved to the city from West Virginia when the local coal mine played out. Father died of black lung their first year here. Mother tried to find work but was untrained for anything, so she began to rely on the kindness of men from the neighborhood, a poor white enclave full of refugees from the South.

A younger brother was rescued by his grandparents, who sent for him. But they didn't want the older boy, who was twitchy and rebellious. Mother brought a succession of boyfriends into their sad little apartment. One of them – the one who gave the kid his nickname – introduced her to dope. When he tried to do the same favor for the kid, the mom, in a rare act of courage, kicked the rat out. He was soon replaced by another, who stole from her, and another, who hit her.

By now the kid was living on the streets. He had discovered a knack for ingratiating himself with small-store merchants, offering to run errands for them, fetch lunch in exchange for a buck here, a buck there. Whenever business slowed, he snatched purses up on the Magnificent Mile and retreated to the shadows of the lower level. As he spoke, he showed the Columnist an emptied-out designer purse lying on the damp concrete next to him.

The Columnist was fascinated and appalled. Where does your mother live? he asked him. What's her name? Family Services, he thought, needs to get hold of this kid fast, before something happens to him.

But the more he asked, the more fidgety the kid became. Got to go, he said, springing up.

Wait, the Columnist said, holding out a handful of bills. Take this.

Thanks, the kid said, and was gone.

The Columnist called Family Services, and they sent someone over to look around but found no sign of the kid. They sent people into what they believed to be his neighborhood, asking around, with no luck. The Columnist went back to the lower level, walking in and out of its shadows, every night for a week after that. Nothing.

So he wrote the kid's story, what little he knew of it. He used him as an example of those who fall through the gaps in society's safety net. Rabbit just happens to be white, he wrote. A lot of these kids are darker-skinned. But they're all lost.

If you see this, Rabbit, he wrote, call me.

Rabbit didn't call, but others did, by the hundreds. Hundreds more wrote. Rabbit's story was quoted in the City Council chambers, and the head of Family Services went on television to say the city was making a special effort to find him and to help all children like him.

After a while, the story lost traction, as they say, and the Columnist moved on to other subjects. Then, a few months later, the Pulitzer Prize nominations were announced, and there was the Columnist's name under the category of feature writing.

Congratulations, people said. Wonderful work.

Thanks, he said. If they find the kid, it'll all be worth it.

And then the questions began, slowly at first, like a hum in the background, like the far-off sound of an elevated train headed our way. How come the cops and social workers never managed to locate the kid or his mother or anyone in their poor-white neighborhood who said they sounded familiar? How come none of the workers whose jobs took them down to the lower level, to load and unload freight and to empty dumpsters – how come none of them had ever seen him? And why, amid the wave of sympathetic letters, e-mails and phone calls, was there not a single one that contained the name or address of the kid or his mother?

Why, indeed?

You can see the answer coming, can't you?

The Columnist's boss, a man we've already met named McGowan, must have heard the far-off rumble, because he began to have quiet talks with the Columnist, just asking a few questions, probing a little. McGowan, you see, had been at this game a long time, and he knew something the Columnist only vaguely apprehended – that there was nothing so deadly to a newspaper as an untruth. If printed and allowed to stand, an untruth can fester and send out its poison to every corner of the institution. For a newspaper lives and dies by the truth.

So he asked his questions, and little by little he became convinced that a terrible lie had taken root there on page three, and the newspaper was growing sick from it. And one day he told the Columnist that.

And the Columnist, who by then was sick of the lie himself, almost physically sick from having to maintain it, confessed. The reason for it, he said, was simple. One day he had just dried up. He had no more stories to tell, no more thoughts to share with his readers. He had hauled up the last bucket of water from the well. All that was left was mud, and he couldn't write about mud.

He had a column due the next day and, knowing he was dry, had gone out to dinner and had too much to drink. The next morning, he would have to tell his boss, who was also his friend, that he was dry. And he imagined that his boss would look at him with a mixture of pity and scorn and tell him to take some time off, go recharge his batteries. And they would fill his spot on page three with a column by that young hotshot Gloria, who had lusted after page three ever since they had hired her away from the *Tribune*.

So he had left the restaurant, still tipsy, feeling immensely sorry for himself, when he passed under the lower level and saw this kid sitting against one of the girders. The boy was about sixteen, black, wearing hip-hop regalia. As the Columnist passed, the kid mumbled a request for some spare change, and the Columnist gave him some and went on his way.

That was it.

But by the time he had reached his townhouse, the Columnist had the kid fixed in his mind. White, not black. Instead of sixteen, closer to ten or eleven. He saw his whole history in a flash. So he brewed a pot of coffee and sat at the keyboard for the next three hours, telling the story of Rabbit.

Fiction, all of it. But it could have been true, couldn't it? And, more important, it could stand for a larger truth, couldn't it?

He told all this to McGowan, who listened patiently all the way to the end and then fired him. An hour later the Columnist was carrying his boxed belongings down to his car. He returned to his office, stood at the window, took a lingering look down at Michigan Avenue – the good one, the shiny one – and knew that he'd never hold down a newspaper job again. There were venal sins in journalism and mortal ones, and this sin was the kind that buried you.

One thing he hadn't told McGowan: The kid was not his first foray into fiction, just the most blatant. There had been other things, small deceptions, little hyperboles, the occasional made-up quote. Every now and then a composite character, one of those creatures who inhabit the shady world between fact and fiction, would saunter onto the page with just the right attitude, just the right quote to wrap up the whole column with a rhetorical flourish.

Tiny, insidious lies had been creeping onto page three for a long time. He could have told McGowan that. But he didn't have the guts.

Story finished, I looked over at Sis. She appeared asleep. I was half glad she had not heard what I'd had to say. I got up quietly and carried the empty ice tray out to the kitchen, thinking all the while about how Sis and I both came from a tradition of storytellers and how stories can be wonderful things, explaining to us who we are and where we come from. But I had forgotten one thing up there in Chicago: Stories are for front porches, not for the pages of a newspaper.

Back outside, I capped the bottle of Southern Comfort so the flies wouldn't be drawn to its sweetness. Then, as I prepared to tiptoe away, she spoke sleepily without opening her eyes.

'Is all that true or made up?'

'It's true.'

'Hard to tell the truth sometimes.'

'Yes, ma'am, it is.'

'But when you do it right, it's better than any old made-up story.'

She was quiet again, and I thought she might have dozed off. Then: 'I don't know if this is a hundred percent or not, but I'll tell you.'

'All right.'

She tilted her head lazily toward me and opened her eyes. 'Based on a few things she told me, I figure Callie spent some time with you not long before you went off to school.'

'Well, you'd be right.'

'And I knew she spent a weekend with Blue once. He drove her to Chattanooga, and they took that little train up to Lookout Mountain. She told me she loved it.'

I stared at her intently.

'You surprised?' she asked. 'You shouldn't be. Hon, Blue McMahan would chase anything in a skirt. He was just made that way.'

This took a little reflection. Blue had known Callie, sure. He had also taken a keen interest in my overdue sexual education. In fact, when Callie first showed an interest in me, I thought I saw Blue's hand moving somewhere in the background, arranging things. I wasn't resentful at his maneuvering on my behalf. I was grateful.

But he and Callie as a couple? As I said, I had to chew on that for a while.

'All right, maybe I'm not surprised,' I said finally. 'Do you remember any others?'

'Just one. Sonny.'

I was lifting my glass for one last sip, and it almost slipped out of my hand, splashing my shirt front with a few drops of peach-scented booze.

'This was before you went out with her,' she went on, seemingly oblivious to my surprise. 'It was, I forget, sometime in that year before she disappeared.'

'No,' I said. 'Sonny never went out with her.'

She gave me a sideways look. 'How do you know?'

'Well, he told me so, just the other day. And it made sense, because he was going with Ava Neal all through most of his senior year, right up until he left for college. She was the girl-friend he had the longest. And ...' I found I was fumbling for words.

She waited, a half-smile on her face.

'And Sonny was my best friend. I would have known.'

Or would I? I didn't know he was going to waltz away with the vice-president of the Thetas, did I? So if he'd had his eye on Callie, what makes me think I would have been sharp enough to see it? I felt anger beginning to stir, like something awakening. Some of it was directed at my old friend, but I reserved a good portion of it for myself.

'Maybe,' she said. 'Maybe you're right and I'm wrong. Like I said, she never told me names.' Then, in a softer voice, 'I bet you'll never guess what she wanted most in the world.'

'To move to Memphis, get a good job, and to have a disk jockey for a boyfriend,' I said.

She smiled sadly and shook her head. 'The thing she wanted most was to find herself a good man and get married. Knowing the kind of upbringing she had – that father of hers – it don't surprise me at all. Just fall in love and get married was all that girl wanted. She had her eye on somebody too. I tried to drag it out of her, but she wouldn't tell me.'

It was still light when I parked my car on the grass just off the road in front of Wilkes Cottage. To keep from disrupting the routine there, I had decided to stay out of the driveway. It was one of my favorite times of day – early evening, the sun about to go down over that far mountain hidden behind all the trees. The light was weak and silvery-gold, and the shadows were miles long as I walked up the brick pathway to the front door.

Just before I reached the steps, my eye caught sight of a figure under the magnolia tree twenty feet away, and I froze, ready to bolt. Then I recognized the smudged white coveralls, and I walked over to her.

'Hi,' I said.

She just nodded without much expression. She was sitting on the tangle of roots, her back against the tree. It did not look very comfortable there. Her right hand rested on the neck of an upright, half-empty bottle of Bud, holding it in a relaxed two-finger grip.

'You waiting for me?'

She nodded again. 'They told me you were out,' she said. 'I thought I'd just wait.'

'It's more comfortable up there on the porch.'

'I didn't want to bother anybody.' She looked haggard, with pronounced tension lines around her mouth. She seemed to have aged a few years since I first saw her bounce into Ida's to pick up her cheeseburger and fries.

'Where's your car?'

'Around the corner.'

'You want to come inside?'

'No, thanks.'

'You want to see me about something?'

'Yeah.' Still holding the beer, she leaned forward and hugged her knees. It was almost a little-girl pose, and it seemed to take years off her. 'I thought we might go get a bite to eat.'

She drove, and I hung on. I'd spotted her Mustang around town. It was a 390 cubic-inch V-8, one of the classics, and she had restored it lovingly. The dual exhaust made a nice, throaty growl as she zipped us through town and out on one of the country roads. Minutes later we pulled up in front of a grungy, dark-wood facade with a single blinking neon sign. *Possum's*, it said.

'I thought this place would've been torn down years ago, like Grady's,' I said.

'Every town needs a Possum's,' she said.

Inside, everything looked the same. A short bar to the right, a small eating area to the left dominated by a pool table. At the far end, behind swinging doors, a kitchen that emitted various fried smells. George Jones was on the jukebox milking *He Stopped Loving Her Today* for all it was worth. George's volume was cranked up to maximum, but he was still hard to hear over the noise of the crowd.

I started for a table, but she preferred the bar. We found seats and ordered two beers, plus some chicken wings and a salad. The beers arrived quickly.

'I've been looking for you the last few days,' I told her.

She took a healthy swig and wiped her mouth. 'I left town for a while, let the guys handle the garage.'

'Where'd you go?'

She shrugged. 'Oh, just around.'

A noisy, four-handed game of eight-ball was going on, and she watched the players for a while. Three of them were young, boisterous, and preppy-looking. 'College boys?' I asked.

She nodded. 'They discovered Possum's a while ago. It's like slumming to them. They come here, get drunk, try to pick up girls, and then go back to their homework, feeling like they've gotten down and dirty.'

The fourth player was older and quieter, his moves more awkward. While the college boys wore shorts and sweatshirts, he was more neatly dressed, with clean jeans and a pressed shirt. They seemed amused by everything he did.

'He usually plays with his friends,' Lita Ray said, almost to herself.

'Who?' I took another look and finally placed him. The mechanic at Lita Ray's garage, the one who came outside looking for her, the one she spoke to in reassuring tones.

'Is that Vern? Your brother?'

'Uh-huh. You know him?'

'No, I just guessed.'

Her food arrived, and she tore into a chicken wing and washed it down with the rest of her beer, then ordered another.

'I hear something's not right with Vern.'

She shot me a look. 'He just never finished growing up,' she said. 'He's like a big old boy.'

'Did you know he was coming here tonight?'

She nodded. 'I try to look after him, and I can see the table better from here.'

'The way Callie looked after you?'

'You're full of questions, aren't you?' She was clearly not comfortable with this. But she had asked for the talk, not me. Finally she answered.

'Yeah, something like that.'

Another swig. Remembering the incident at the Hunting Lodge, I wanted to get to our conversation before she had much more to drink. While I was trying to think of a way to encourage her, she beat me to it.

'Somebody tried to get at you the other night,' she said without looking at me.

'I guess you could say that, even though I'm not sure—'

'Whatever's going on around here, and whoever's doing it, you're right in the middle of things.'

'I seem to be.'

'The whole town's in a sweat, mostly because of Mrs. McMahan getting killed. I don't blame them. But all I care about is what happened to Callie. That was a long time ago, and people are already forgetting about her.'

I had no easy answer. She was right. The jukebox shifted gears, and Patsy Cline came on, a teardrop in every note.

Then she looked at me as she wiped her hands on her napkin. 'You said she was important to you.'

'She was. Still is.'

'You've been asking questions all over town. I can tell you're good at it.'

'No argument there. But I'm not the police.'

'I don't care. You're my best chance to find out who killed her. Will you do it?'

I'd seen it coming, and I had the answer ready. 'I'll try.'

'I want to help.'

'Good. I expect you to help. Two conditions, though: You have to answer all my questions. And ... I don't work with drunks.'

Her eyes narrowed for a second. 'Don't you ever take a drink?'

'I don't bust up bars.' *At least I think my bar-busting days are behind me. How does the old parental maxim go? 'Do as I say, not as I do.'*

She looked down at the beer. Then she slid the bottle away from her.

'No problem,' she said. 'I can take it or leave it.'

'Make that three conditions.'

She waited.

'I want to meet your father.'

Something crossed her face. It might have been fear or hatred or a combination of both. Then it was gone.

'No problem,' she said.

We heard a noise at the table and turned to look. One of the college boys had just scratched, and Vern had picked up the cue ball and was looking for a place to spot it. The boy, irritated at his own mistake, was putting on a show, waving his arms, leaning in toward Vern, mimicking his speech. The others howled. Vern turned away with a fixed half-grin, but the boy grabbed at his shirt.

Lita Ray saw it coming. 'Vern!' she yelled, jumping off the stool.

She was too late.

Vern's hand closed around the cue ball. With a punching motion almost too quick to follow, he rapped the boy in the forehead. The sound was surprisingly loud, even above the din. The boy's legs folded. Vern caught him. With no change of expression, he lifted the boy up and gently laid him out on the table among the brightly colored balls. The other boys stood frozen. I saw one of them mouth the words *Holy shit*.

Lita Ray reached him, grabbed him, turned him around, placed both hands on his face. I couldn't hear her words, but his grin faltered, and he dropped the cue ball, letting it bounce under the table.

She checked out the boy on the table, who was already trying to get up, then helped him onto his feet and handed him over to the others. Although I couldn't hear the words, her directions to them were clear, and moments later they were all out the door.

Taking her brother's hand, she brought him over to the crowded bar and sat him on her stool. The other drinkers looked at him uneasily. He sat facing out, heels propped on the rung of the stool, wearing a chastened expression, like a little boy sent to the corner. All that was missing was a dunce cap.

'What did I tell you about fighting?' she asked him, but not angrily.

'Only to defend myself,' he said. 'But he grabbed me.'

'But he didn't hit you,' she went on. 'You could've walked away. Isn't that right?'

'I suppose.'

'Well, next time walk away. And don't play with strangers.'

'Okay.' He was staring at me.

'I'd like you to meet Mr. Randall Wilkes. Randall, this is my brother Vern.'

'Pleased to meet you,' he said, offering a hand. It was calloused and strong. He wasn't extra large, but everything about him looked sinewy. He had lost most of his hair on top, with only a thinning fringe remaining on the back and sides. For some reason, it gave him a scholarly look.

My presence seemed to make him uncomfortable. I guessed that he didn't like to see his sister around men. I made a mental note not to make any sudden displays of affection toward her while he was around.

'Randall is a kind of investigator,' she told him.

'Uh-huh?'

'He's going to help us find out who killed Callie.'

Vern beamed at me. 'That's real good,' he said.

FIFTEEN

My cell phone jingled as I was brushing my teeth, getting ready for bed.

'How you doing?' It was Sonny.

'Oh, I'm all right,' I said, wiping the excess toothpaste off my chin with a towel and sitting down on the bed. 'How's Tish?'

'Still a little shaky, but okay. You know how tough she is.' I heard none of the earlier coldness in his tone. I was relieved, but it fit my memory of him. He had always been quick to anger, then just as quick to forget.

'Callie Darnell,' he said. 'Any luck?'

'No, I'm just getting started. But I had a good talk with Sis Lawlor this afternoon. You remember her?'

'Sure. She wrote me a nice note when I was elected. Sent me a jar of homemade strawberry preserves, too.'

He sounded absolutely guileless. Maybe she was wrong, I thought. But I had to ask him. As I began to frame the question, he broke in.

'Have you heard anything on the old man?'

'Blue? If you mean where the hell he might be, the answer's no. But I also—'

'Would you tell me? If you heard, I mean?'

'Sure I would. I'm not going to keep any secrets from you, Sonny, especially if it's about your father.'

'All right.' He sounded relieved.

'Considering your network of sources, I'd be surprised if you had to get the hot news flashes from me.'

'Jerry Chitwood promised to keep me in the loop,' Sonny said in a tired voice. 'But he's slow. And Ken ... well, Ken hasn't managed to turn up anything for me lately.'

'Sorry to hear that. And such a nice guy, too.'

'Security seems to be the only thing he's still good at,' Sonny continued. 'He's sleeping downstairs tonight, so I guess I can—'

'Where are you?'

'Right here at Longstaff House. I got in about an hour ago.'

'What are you doing here?'

'Lem's flying in early tomorrow. Before we have the ground-breaking for the conference center, he wants to see the site, have a look at the town, you know. So I'll be his tour guide tomorrow.'

'Hmm.' So many thoughts raced through my head, I couldn't think of a response. Sonny noticed my silence.

'You still there?'

'Yeah.' No point in putting this off, I thought. If it gets his hackles up, so be it. 'I need to talk to you.'

'Okay.'

'About Mr. Coldsmith.'

'Oh-kay.' More slowly.

'It's more of a question, actually. What if he had to pull out of your project?'

'I'd go someplace else for the money,' he said, his voice absolutely neutral.

'What if he got in financial trouble, and some of the damage rubbed off on you?'

'Who you been talking to?' His tone was less neutral now, more ominous.

'I can't say, Sonny. I'm just asking what if.'

'And what if I don't like your tone?'

'This is a friend talking to you,' I said. 'If you don't like my tone, well ...'

'Who else knows about this?'

'I'm sorry. I can't tell you.'

'Privileged information, huh? You've been a busy little ex-newspaperman, haven't you?'

'I guess I have.'

'Well, shit,' he said softly. Then he let out a sigh that rattled the phone.

'How much of this did you know?' I asked him.

'Some,' he said. 'I been hearing things, and I started asking around. Lem is a …' Another long exhalation. 'He's one of the smartest old boys I ever knew at making a dollar. Made himself out of nothing. But he always ran his company out of his back pocket, never had to answer to any board of directors, you know …'

A long pause. 'And he took chances. It was always with his own money, and it always paid off, because he was a lucky son of a bitch. But this tax thing …'

'The IRS doesn't mess around,' I said. 'And if he's prosecuted, you'll get dirt on you, just by association. You've already got the reputation—'

'Of being too cozy with the wrong people,' he finished for me.

'They say it lost you the last election,' I said. 'If you've got any idea of running for office again, this could finish you before you even declare.'

'I can tell you're about to give me some advice.' His tone was sour.

'You need to cut your ties with him. Today.'

'No.'

'He's poison.'

'Who asked you?' he said loudly. 'You're not working for me anymore.'

'Oh, that's right. I forgot.' When I sensed that sarcasm wasn't working on him, I plowed ahead. 'Sometimes you need a friend to tell you the truth.'

'Lem's a friend.'

'Not that kind. I talked to him on the phone, trying to line up an interview. He wouldn't see me, even when I used your name. He sounds like a type I've known from way back, the good old Southern-boy bullshitter who never walks a straight line. I've got a funny feeling that if he gets strapped for cash, he'll leave you high and dry, friend or no friend. You should start looking for other investors right now—'

'I can't,' he said, all the anger now gone out of his voice. 'Things are moving on the center, and it's too late to stop them.'

'Sonny ...'

'Look,' he said. 'When I was in office, I built a few roads and brought some business into the state, and I'm proud of all of it. But this is the biggest thing I've ever had my hand in. This center is going to wake up the plateau, it's going to shine a light on us. Tish wants this. Your dad wants it. It's something I want to be remembered for.'

'What if he pulls out?'

'Then he pulls out. But I'm not dumping him before he dumps me. Lem was the only one to come up with the kind of money we needed. I can't get it done without him. So I'll take my chances with him. Maybe he'll get lucky one more time.' He hesitated. 'I need this, buddy.'

I sat there gripping the phone. Sonny McMahan, who could be brutally direct and pragmatic, also had a vulnerable side. It was part of his charm. When he was governor, while his opponents hated him for his flaws, his supporters felt protective toward him. I was feeling that way now.

But I wasn't through offending him. There was still one more question to ask.

'I mentioned that I saw Sis Lawlor today,' I said as casually as I could. 'We got to talking about Callie Darnell and her many boyfriends. She told me you were one of them. I said I didn't think so, because you and I had already talked about it, and you'd said you never went out with her. But she seemed pretty sure.'

'Sis Lawlor,' he said disgustedly. 'Boy, oh boy.'

'What does that mean?'

'It means you aren't going to turn loose of this one, are you?' His voice was on a slow simmer, his tone deepening. I could feel the anger coming, the legendary McMahan temper, and I didn't want to be on the receiving end of it. But I couldn't stop now. The stakes were too high.

'No, I guess I'm not. I need to ask you again—'

'Oh, fuck it.'

'I need to ask you again, Sonny. Did you spend time with Callie?'

'Go to hell, Wilkes. All right? This is phony reporter bullshit. You don't do that for a living any more, remember? Give it a rest. I've got problems I'm trying to deal with, and I don't need you adding to 'em. Thought you were a friend of mine.'

'Friends don't lie to each other, Sonny.'

Long silence punctuated only by his breathing. I could feel so much tension travel along the wire, it almost made my hand tingle.

My right arm was stiffening up, so I shifted the phone to my other ear. Just as it got there, I heard him say, 'Yeah.'

'Yeah what?'

'Yeah, you know what. She was my girlfriend for about three minutes, toward the end of our senior year, all right?'

'Why didn't you tell me the truth?'

'Should be obvious,' he said, sounding bored. 'They're going to look at whoever she spent time with, and I don't need the grief.' I knew what he meant: If the ticking Len Coldsmith bomb went off in his face, then the public knowledge that Sonny had been cozy with a murder victim – no matter how innocently, no matter that the story was decades old – would certainly finish him off.

'Did you have sex with her?'

'No comment.'

'Sonny, tell me you didn't kill her.'

'I didn't kill her, buddy. I didn't. But you know how these things work. If my connection to her got out, it would not be good for me.'

'Yeah.'

'I didn't have to tell you the truth. I could have kept blowing smoke. I guess I trust you.'

'That's wonderful to hear, Sonny.' I think I hated him a little then. First for lying to me, then for admitting the truth and making me carry the burden of the lie along with him.

'I won't go public with this,' I said. 'But if it comes out from another direction, I won't lie to protect you.'

'All right, buddy. That's all I can ask.'

After a few more polite comments, we hung up, and I sat there on the edge of the bed, phone still in my hand, silently cursing him.

Good old Sonny. He still had the ability to make you want to look after him and slap him silly at the same time.

What was that he'd said, back when we first found out Callie had been murdered? *She was spreading her legs for half the horny toads in the county.* Colorfully put. Whatever had passed between the two of them, it had not left him feeling warm and tender toward her.

I hoped she wound up with a better epitaph.

'I think I'll stay here in the car.'

Lita Ray sat stiffly in the passenger seat, looking out at the house.

I was surprised. 'Are you sure?'

She nodded. 'I don't want to see him.'

'After we drove all this way—'

'I don't want to.' It came out a little above a whisper.

'All right.' I was irritated but tried not to show it. I had hoped she would ease my way into her father's company. Now I'd have to do it alone.

Or almost alone. I glanced in the rear-view mirror at Vern Darnell, who sat in the back seat with his usual half-smile.

We were about twenty minutes outside Pilgrim's Rest in the unincorporated area where it wasn't town but not country either. At her direction, I had driven off the highway to an area that looked fairly recently developed, with a sprinkling of cheaply built ranch-style homes on sprawling yards. This house, done in brownish-yellow shingles, looked reasonably well kept and bore a sign at the gate: Restful Acres. There wasn't a lot of acreage. Four cars in various stages of upkeep sat stacked up in the driveway or edged over onto the grass of the yard.

'Mr. and Mrs. Purdue take in boarders, mostly old folks, and collect their welfare or Social Security checks,' Lita Ray had told me on the way over. 'They'll stay there with her till they die.'

'This is for people who don't have family to take care of them,' I'd said to her. 'Your father—'

'He's better off there,' she had said, turning to look out the window at the passing countryside.

Mrs. Purdue, a bustling, stern-faced woman wearing a medical-looking green smock, answered my knock. I told her I was a friend of Vern and Lita Ray and had come along with the brother to visit their father. Looking vaguely annoyed, as if visitors disrupted her routine, she led us down a dark hallway to a large, under-lit room with comfortable chairs and a television set on a stand. Everything smelled of Lysol, with something sour underneath.

An old, bent man sat with his back to me facing the TV. The volume was turned off, and the screen showed a televangelist in the midst of an energetic sermon. Vern walked over to his father and lightly patted his head, the way you would an old dog. 'Hey, Daddy.' The old man turned his head slightly, then returned his attention to the TV.

Vern, it turned out, had come to spend the entire day with his father, something Lita Ray said he did once a month or so. On the drive over, I had told Vern it was important that I speak to his father in private, and he seemed to understand. Having greeted his father, he went over to a chair by the window, sat down, picked a magazine off the top of a nearby stack, and began leafing through it.

Mrs. Purdue looked at me curiously, obviously trying to figure out my relationship with this odd family. 'This here's one of his favorite shows,' she said. 'He says he don't need to hear it.'

'Why not?'

'I think they're reruns, mostly,' she said. 'Sometimes he says the words himself.'

'Do you have many other boarders here?'

'Just Mr. Simms, but he's bedridden. He don't ever come out of his room. And the new one, Mr. Briggs. Got disabled working for the timber company, but he can help out around here some. He's out back with my husband.'

Through glass doors behind the TV, I saw an older man in shorts and undershirt glumly pushing a lawnmower, and a younger man standing over a chopping block, splitting kindling with an axe. I watched him deftly split a piece into halves, then quarters. He was good with the axe, the way you'd expect an ex-lumberjack to be.

'Is it all right if I talk to Mr. Darnell?' I asked her.

'I suppose so,' she said. 'Sometimes he's not in the mood. Mr. Briggs is about the only one he gets along with all the time. Don't mind his language, all right?' She left.

I circled around and got my first look in twenty years at Pike Darnell. The tall, imposing patriarch of the Darnell clan was now shrunken and stoop-shouldered. His features were still craggy, but his neck looked too frail to support his head. His hair had been allowed to grow, and its lank gray locks curled on his bony shoulders. He wore Oshkosh bib overalls, faded to gray, with no shirt, and scuffed house slippers. Hair sprouted out from his armpits like dark weeds.

'Mr. Darnell?' I stepped in front of him, almost blocking his view of the screen. 'I'm Randall Wilkes. Do you remember me?'

His eyes came up to mine, and it was then I recognized him. They say you can sometimes catch a glimpse of the soul in someone's eyes. I don't know if I saw his soul, but I saw the Pike Darnell I remembered, and I remembered why I had once been afraid of him. I remembered the chilling sight of him driving his pickup through town, the hunting rifle mounted above his rear window, heavy eyebrows almost hiding his eyes. And I remembered the way we children would whisper about him, about the things people said he did back there in the woods where only Darnells lived.

'Mr. Darnell?'

He opened his mouth to reply, and out came a string of curses, slow and precise, aimed at no one in particular. They went on for quite a while. Some I had heard and some I had not. Some were from the gutter, and others sounded almost

Elizabethan. There was an earthy music to them, like song lyrics only he knew. Then, as if his throat were now properly cleared, he responded.

'You related to that Forrest? The one that writes them books?'

'I'm his son.'

'He's stuck-up.' The words came out slightly askew, as if his mouth was swollen or his teeth didn't fit.

He had not been shaved in several days, and his cheeks and chin were speckled gray. Having spoken, he bent over, pursed his lips, and spit out a gob of brown liquid into his lap, where I now saw his clawlike hands were cradling a Folger's coffee can. Then I saw the wad of tobacco he had nestled into his right cheek. He gave off an overpowering odor of the stuff. The Lysol appeared to have the edge, but just barely.

'I'm a friend of Lita Ray's, and I was a friend of Callie's,' I said, shifting over to the side so I could take the seat by him. The old man's eyes strayed back to the preacher, who now wielded a Bible aloft, pointing at it with his free hand, occasionally thumping it for emphasis.

'I was very sorry to hear about Callie,' I said. 'I'm trying to find out what happened to her, and I've been asking around about some of her boyfriends. I was hoping you could—'

'Boyfriends,' he muttered. 'Oh, she had 'em. She had 'em, all right. But she come home every night.'

'Do you remember any of them?'

'None of 'em counted, 'cause she come home to me every night.' I heard something start deep in his chest, something that could have been a cough. Or a sob.

'Dead, dead, dead,' he intoned, then let drop another gob. But he was careless, and some of it dribbled down his chin. He didn't bother to wipe it. 'My baby dead. Sweet, sweet girl.'

'Yes, she was.'

'Sweetest ass you ever saw, Callie. Tits too.' He let out a deep, rumbling belch. 'God almighty.'

Even though I thought I was ready for it, his words hit me like a blow.

He was still going. 'Little girl's pussy was mine,' he said with immense satisfaction. 'I had it first. Some others borrowed it sometimes. But I owned it.'

My bile rose. I almost forgot why I'd come, about trying to get useful information from him. I leaned toward him.

'I heard all about you,' I said, trying to keep it conversational. But my head was beginning to throb. 'I hear you screwed Lita Ray too.'

'Never touched Lita Ray,' he said almost primly.

'Just Callie, huh? You degenerate—' *Get ahold of yourself. Remember why you're here.* I leaned in closer. 'Did you kill her, Mr. Darnell? Did you kill your daughter?'

He was off somewhere else now, and I'm not sure he heard my words.

'My baby girl, Callie. Flesh of my flesh.' He was speaking in storyteller's cadences, like Sis Lawlor, but his words bore a different message. 'Loved to touch her, smell her. Rose of Sharon. Lily of the Valley.' His eyes had never left the preacher on the screen.

'You know, I'd kill you if I could,' I said.

'Hey, there, Pike.'

I looked up. The young man had come in silently. He took a seat on Darnell's other side.

'I been choppin' some wood,' he said, looking at me curiously. I couldn't tell if he'd heard my words. 'Thought I should help out 'stead of loafin' all day.' He touched his companion on the shoulder. 'How you doin'?' Then, to me: 'You a friend of his?'

'Not really.'

'He's a great old guy,' he said. 'Knows lots of stories. We look after each other here. Ain't supposed to drink—' He looked over his shoulder to see if Mrs. Purdue was around. 'But I sneak in a little liquor for him every now and then.' The fringe of a tattoo peeked out from under his shirt collar, and I wondered what kind of decorations lumberjacks favored.

'How come you're talking to him?' Darnell said, turning to Briggs, sounding agitated.

'It's all right, Pike,' the young man said, patting his shoulder.

'He's got no business here. Get him out of here.' He turned to me. 'My boy Vern's going to throw you out of here.'

'Now, you don't want Vern to get in trouble,' Briggs said soothingly. 'Don't you mind. The man's gonna leave. You want to play some cards?'

I wasn't quite ready to leave. 'Mrs. Purdue tells me you're disabled,' I said, leaning forward to see him better but careful to stay out of Darnell's spitting range.

'Well, you know how it is.' Briggs gave me a wink. 'I hurt myself on the job, but I'm trying to get back on my feet. I'm tired of outdoor work, though. Wouldn't mind some kind of office work. You know of anything?'

'No, sorry. I'm just visiting.'

'Uh-huh. Did Lita Ray come out with you?'

'You know her?'

'I've only been here a few weeks, but I seen her here once. Cute gal.' Another wink.

'She didn't want to come inside this time.' I got up. 'Good luck with finding a job. You might want to wipe his chin.'

On my way out, I saw Mrs. Purdue washing dishes in the kitchen. 'Thank you,' I said.

'Was he cussin'?'

'Yes.'

'I pray for him.'

'You heard about his daughter, Callie?'

'I did. Heard it from a neighbor. I told him, but he'd already heard.'

'From Lita Ray, I suppose.'

'I don't think so. She hasn't seen him in a while, and he doesn't like to use the phone.'

I stepped in closer and lowered my voice. 'Can you tell me what's wrong with him?'

'Besides old age?' She placed a dripping glass in the dish rack. 'Lita Ray didn't mention nothin'?'

'No, ma'am.'

'Syphilis,' she said, submerging both hands in the soapy water.

Which some people poetically refer to as God's punishment, I thought. The disease that begins its assault in the obvious place and ends by ravaging the organ that really caused all the trouble – the brain – slowly turning it to Swiss cheese.

I glanced in the room on my way out and saw a curious sight. Vern sat by his father now, holding one of his hands, head bent, looking like a son receiving his father's blessing. The old man's lips were moving.

Outside, I saw Briggs leaning against the passenger side of the car, talking animatedly to Lita Ray with a big grin on his face. His index finger was tracing a playful design on her shoulder. Everything about him said *small-timer, but thinks he's hot stuff.* As for her, she wore an expression that said she was putting up with him, but just barely.

I got in, and he gave me a just-between-us-boys look. 'Sure is a pretty lady you got here.'

'Sure is,' I said. 'See you around.'

As I pulled away, I asked her, 'New boyfriend?'

'Oh, yeah,' she said, laughing. 'The day I can't do better than the likes of him ...' Then she turned to look at me. 'Have fun in there?'

'Loads and loads.'

'Did you learn anything?'

'I'm not sure. But you can help me here. He all but admitted to me that he sexually molested Callie, but he said he never touched you. Is that true?'

I couldn't read her expression. She spoke almost calmly. 'Uh-huh.'

'Were you still at home when she disappeared?'

'Yeah. But I was smart. I moved out real quick.'

'But earlier ... Why did he leave you alone?'

'Because Callie said if he touched me, she'd kill him.'

SIXTEEN

On the way back, I wanted to talk to her, get her to open up some more, but for a while I couldn't speak. I felt almost sick. Having breathed the air of Pike Darnell, I felt infected with his toxins. Did he have a childhood, I wondered, full of running in the woods and playing with friends and watching the world unfold in front of his eyes? Maybe he did, but the face I beheld back there at Restful Acres had been aged in evil, the way bourbon is aged in oak.

'You don't look very happy,' Lita Ray said.

'I'm all right. Just thinking about your dear old dad. You mind if we talk about him?'

'I guess not.'

I knew there was a lot there below the surface – considering the kind of childhood she and Callie had had, it was inevitable. I was no shrink, but I knew how to do an interview.

'Your father talks like a hick,' I told her for openers. 'You talk better.'

'I finished high school,' she said. 'First one in my family. Callie dropped out in her junior year, but she made me promise I'd finish.'

'Your two brothers – did they do anything to Callie?'

'No.'

'Just your father?'

'That's right. Just him.'

I wondered about that. Maybe they didn't join in, but how could they not have known what was going on, and how could that not have had some kind of effect on them? Lying there in the darkness of the Darnell shack, hearing the sounds, half-knowing what they meant, the boys were being formed. Their father was teaching them his kind of manhood.

'I hear your other brother's in prison. What for?'

'What's he got to do with anything?' I could almost see her old defenses fly up. She gave up information the way Stonewall Jackson gave up ground.

'I'm just curious. Come on, humor me. What's his name?'

'Wingo.'

'That's a funny name.'

'It's Indian. The Darnells got—'

'Indian blood. That's right, I remember. Callie told me. How did you wind up with blonde hair?'

'My mama had blonde hair, and I took after her.'

She waved her hands vaguely in the air, as if trying to shape her words. 'Wingo. He's trash, if you want to know,' she said, with the same kind of venom she used to talk about her father. 'Him and my daddy, they had a big fight a long time ago, a few years after Callie disappeared, and Daddy, he kicked him out. Wingo wound up down in Atlanta, doing whatever white trash does, drugs and such. He killed a man, and they gave him twenty years to life. That's his story.'

I vaguely remembered him, a massive, brooding young man with a bushy beard, someone who rarely came into town, and when he did, people walked carefully around him. What a family, I thought.

'I need to ask you about Callie's boyfriends.'

'She didn't talk much about 'em.'

'I know, I know. She was the soul of discretion. I've already heard that from Sis Lawlor.'

'You don't sound like you believe it. Well, Callie wasn't the bragging kind.'

'But she must have dropped hints. There were a lot of boys hanging around her.' Like flies around honey, I could have added.

'That's right,' she said, laying on the sarcasm. 'She was giving it away to half the county.'

She had her window down all the way, letting in the chilly afternoon air and crisp scents of autumn. It was making a mess out of her hair, whipping her ponytail back and forth, but she didn't seem to mind.

I was already on the defensive. There was no way of digging into details of Callie's past without smearing her name, and Lita Ray sensed that I was reluctant to do that.

I already thought I knew a lot about what made Callie tick. As I said, I'm no shrink, but after years spent as a metaphorical fly on the wall, I know a few things about behavior. Once I wrote a column about a young woman who had racked up about a dozen arrests for prostitution in a hotel just off Chicago's Loop. One of the county social workers got to know and like her and suggested that I might want to do a column about her, without mentioning her real name. I found out that she came from a solid middle-class family out in Oak Park, that her mother was sweet but ineffectual, and that her father had molested her beginning at age six.

'Her father taught her early,' the social worker told me, shaking her head. 'To be loved, you have to give sex. She's still bartering for it.'

I turned back to Lita Ray for another try. 'Look, we know she had a lot of boyfriends.'

A sideways look, accompanied by a smirk. 'You know that firsthand, do you?'

'Yes, I do.'

'Well, good for you,' she said, her voice almost inaudible against the rush of the wind. 'I figure anybody who got to spend time with her was a lucky son of a gun.'

'No argument there. I know you looked up to her, and you must have been curious about who she was seeing.' My talk with Sis Lawlor was still fresh in my mind. 'I'm guessing Callie was closer to some of them than to others. If she was, she might have dropped some clues.'

She plopped her sneakers up on the dashboard. I waited for her to answer. We passed a roadside stand selling fresh sweet corn and pumpkins.

'I didn't know about you,' she said finally, 'but sometimes she'd talk about somebody she liked a lot, and I could see it in her face. She'd even talk about marrying him. "Who?" I'd say. And she'd just say, "Hush."'

'You must have an idea.'

'Oh, I do. I think it was Mr. McMahan.'

'Blue? I don't think that's a very realistic—'

'No. I mean the Governor.'

I chewed over that the rest of the way into town, rearranging the furniture inside my head to make room for the idea. Sonny and Callie. Sis Lawlor had planted the seed, and now Lita Ray had watered it. The son of a bitch had lied to me. He'd been quiet about it all these years, and now it was no longer just a secret about an old girlfriend. Murder had entered the picture. Could he have killed her?

Out of habit, I found myself jumping to his defense. Maybe he did sneak around with Callie. Maybe his father did too. So what? The list of suspects needn't be limited to those who'd known her most intimate favors. Someone who'd been denied a roll in the hay could have flown into a murderous rage, I supposed. Still, I believed that the most obvious suspects were those who'd made it all the way to home plate with Callie Darnell. I'd never be able to confirm all those names, but I had three:

Myself. Sonny McMahan. And quite possibly his father.

As we went around the town square on our way to Lita Ray's place, I spotted a familiar black GMC sport-ute parked in front of the Historical Society. And there was Sonny with a group of people over by the Confederate marker.

On an impulse, I braked and swerved my car into a nearby space. Twisting my head, I studied the group. Sonny, with his ever-present sidekick, Kenneth Lively. Also my father, Olen Stringer, a young, camera-toting woman I recognized from Charlene's paper – and Lem Coldsmith.

'You ever meet the Governor?' I asked Lita Ray. 'The ex, I mean? The hometown boy?'

'Uh-uh.'

'You want to?'

'Uh, I guess so.' She didn't sound so sure, but it didn't matter. This was all the excuse I needed.

I had no idea what the next few minutes would bring, but sometimes you just play a hunch. What was driving me, I think, was anger – at Sonny for letting himself be duped into yet another risky relationship and at Coldsmith for putting my old friend's reputation in jeopardy. Coldsmith wouldn't talk to me, and Sonny wouldn't listen to me. I'm not saying my behavior made sense. I was just tired of being ignored, and I needed to purge my system of the poison of Pike Darnell. With Lita Ray in tow, I headed toward the group.

Sonny saw me coming, and his first, unguarded expression told me he wasn't happy to see me. But then the politician took over.

'Randall,' he called out, motioning me over.

'Governor,' I said. 'Here's one of your constituents who'd like to meet you.' During the pleasantries, Coldsmith, to whom I was pointedly not introduced, gave me a wary look. He stood well over six feet, with a gangly frame, big hands and feet, and a long face that made me think of Ichabod Crane. He had the face of a country bumpkin and the eyes of a deadly poker player. I saw no sign of his joshing ol' boy TV persona. I wondered if he'd had a talk with Sonny. Or the federal government.

It was all very polite for a few seconds, and then I began talking.

'For those of you who don't know, Lita Ray is Callie Darnell's little sister,' I said to the group. 'There's been a lot of excitement around here lately, what with the death of the Governor's mother—' I glanced at Sonny, and his expression said, *Don't.* But I was already going down that road.

'And people understandably made a lot more fuss over that than they did over Callie. Now Lita Ray wants to find out who killed her sister and why. I'm going to try to help her.'

'That's a fine thing to do, Randall,' Sonny said quietly.

'I was working for the Governor for a while, on a book project,' I went on. 'But we've parted ways, and I'm sure he's unhappy with me—'

'Randall, you sound like you're making a speech,' Sonny said, treating it like a joke. I noticed my father staring at me. I should have felt awkward, but strangely I felt invigorated. Things needed to be said.

'I'll try to keep my speech short,' I said, going along with joke. I turned my attention to Olen Stringer, who was wearing a khaki bush jacket decorated with the emblem of the Historical Society. 'I guess we owe Olen a big debt, not only for finding these two soldiers, but also for indirectly leading us to Callie's body,' I said. 'It's pretty incredible when you think about it. I'm no archeologist – hell, I guess he's not either – but I understand the odds against this kind of discovery are pretty astronomical.'

The photographer backed away a few paces and began talking quietly into her cell phone.

Stringer, a smile frozen on his face, looked as if he was about to respond, but Sonny interrupted. 'We need to move on,' he said, making a show of looking at his watch. 'Mr. Coldsmith wants to have a look at the site.'

'Wait. Don't go yet.' I turned to the newcomer. 'Mr. Coldsmith, I'm sorry you didn't want to talk to me. I know you're investing a lot of money in our town, and we appreciate it.'

'I agree with the Governor. Sure sounds like a speech to me.' Without a smile to soften his features, Coldsmith's countenance was grave, even threatening. I reminded myself that the ability to make piles of money usually carried a certain hardness with it.

'He doesn't even live here,' Kenneth Lively said, speaking up for the first time. 'He used to be a newspaperman, but he got fired.'

'And you used to be a cop, but now you're a chauffeur,' I shot back. 'And I wasn't talking to you.' More schoolyard insults.

Coldsmith stepped up close and looked me up and down. After a moment, he said in a voice too low to be overheard by the others, 'Here's your private interview. I heard about you. Made a mess of yourself up north, and now you're poking around down here. Telling Sonny he could do better 'n me.' He was a couple of inches taller, and he seemed to tower over me as he spoke.

'I don't know why I'm wasting my time with a piss-ant like you. Why don't you go back to Chicago?' He turned away and said in a louder voice, 'We finished here, boys?'

I noticed a couple of things at the same time. Across the street Charlene came out the door of the paper and began to head in our direction. I also could see Lively surreptitiously working the kinks out of his fingers. If there's a brawl in the schoolyard, I thought, it will start with him.

'Here's a question I would've asked you if you'd given me a chance,' I said to Coldsmith. 'If you ran short of cash, would you dump this project? It's kind of important, because the Governor's counting on you, and so's the town.'

'We really have to leave,' Sonny said loudly. 'Everybody?'

At that point Lively seemed to pick up a wordless message from the ether, and he strode over to me, bouncing lightly on the balls of his feet. He looked like a middleweight warming up. I knew he was armed, but I wasn't concerned about being shot in a public place. Continuing the childhood metaphors, I felt like the little boy who knew the bully wouldn't pick on him as long as Teacher stood there in the doorway.

As he approached, I tried to take his measure. A few pounds lighter than I, an inch or so less reach. But physically fit, with years of law enforcement behind him, and despite his bright-eyed, boyish look, a tough character, no question.

When someone came for me that night at Longstaff House, I tried following the example of the Marquess of Queensberry, and I wound up getting bounced down the stairs. This time, I knew that if I didn't preempt things, I could get a beating.

He came up to me with both hands high, ready to handle me. 'Back away,' he said with a grin, looking prepared, even eager, as he reached for my lapels.

I raised my right foot and stomped down on his instep as hard as I could. I was wearing running shoes, but the impact registered on his face, and I followed up a second later with a left elbow aimed at his face. He saw it coming and ducked, but

I still connected with the skull, and it made a nice, meaty crack of a sound. Taken together, they were enough to send him down.

But I hadn't foreseen the other result: Sonny was standing directly behind him, and Lively's backward fall clipped him in the side, just enough to send him off balance. He fell heavily onto the granite marker, crying out as he landed.

Lively recovered nicely, catching himself on a hand and a knee. He quickly got up, his face twisted with anger and humiliation, and swept his jacket aside so that his right hand could reach the pistol holstered under his arm. I think it was the first time I had ever seen someone about to throw down on me, and it was a chilling sight.

'Are you getting this?' I shouted to the photographer, whose camera was indeed poised.

'Ken, don't!' Sonny cried out from his position on the ground. Lively froze, his face pale. As angry as he was, he was still cop enough to know that he wasn't going to shoot me. His right hand came slowly up to his head, and he lightly touched the spot where I'd hit him.

Charlene rushed past me to tend to Sonny, who was already scrambling up. I went over to him.

'I'm sorry that happened,' I said. 'Are you all right?'

'Oh, just fine,' he said, laying on the sarcasm. 'Everybody's just fine.' He brushed off his rear. Then, ignoring me, he said briskly to the others, 'If we hurry, we can show Lem the conference site before dinner.'

As the group headed for their car, leaving me with the three women, I watched my father go. I suppose I expected to see him direct a withering look back at me. But instead, his eyes were on Olen Stringer, and he looked concerned.

'Do you mind if I ask you what the hell you were up to?' Charlene said to me. She sounded both curious and exasperated, and I wondered if once again I'd lost some of her trust.

'It's hard to explain,' I said. 'I think I just wanted to stir things up a little and see what happened.' I rubbed my sore left elbow and took a deep breath, surprised at how good I felt. 'That tall, goofy-looking guy was Lem Coldsmith, our new benefactor.'

'I know who he is,' she said. 'I'm interviewing him later today.'

'Well, be sure to ask him how he likes our little town so far.'

On the way to Lita Ray's place, she was excited by the scene on the town square. It seemed to have confirmed to her that I was a good choice to play detective with.

'What do we do next?' she asked.

'I don't know.'

'Don't you have a plan?'

'I'm putting one together. Don't they need you at the garage?'

'This is more important.'

'All right, Nancy Drew. Stand by until I have further orders for you.'

'Don't talk down to me.'

'Sorry.'

As she got out of the car at her front door, she said, 'We need to make something happen, don't you think?'

I drove out to the Hunting Lodge for dinner. The smaller tables in the dining room were occupied, so I settled in at the bar and had the dinner special, chicken-fried steak, delivered to me. All the devastation of Hurricane Darnell had been cleaned up on the glass shelves behind the bar. As I ate, glancing only occasionally at the NASCAR race on the big screen, I thought about the day.

Sonny in a tight spot, but covering up like a true campaigner. The look and smell of Pike Darnell. The melodramatic dustup in front of the Historical Society. And the missing, elusive and mysterious Blue McMahan.

Lita Ray was right, of course: I needed to make something happen, but I couldn't tell her what it was: I needed to find a dead man, if only to determine exactly what he knew and why someone wanted him really dead. The answer to Callie's death – and quite possibly those of Faye, Opal, and the luckless Dewey Tackett – seemed to lead right to Sonny's scapegrace daddy. Finding him would be a tough job, maybe an impossible one, but no one else seemed to be tackling it right now.

I replayed my little monologue on the town square, a little surprised at myself. It was not like me to step into a situation like that on impulse, verbal guns blazing. What in the world was I thinking?

I knew, of course. In my awkward way, I was trying to save Sonny from himself, by separating him from someone who could bring him down. Had it worked? Probably not.

But I recalled Sis Lawlor's sleepy words on her front porch. They could have been addressed to the world at large, but they struck me like a fist.

Hard to tell the truth sometimes. But when you do it right, it's better than any old made-up story.

I think I was just ready for a dose of the truth. And I hoped others were too.

SEVENTEEN

I awoke with an idea. Even though it was barely daylight, I got up, dressed quickly, and quietly made my way downstairs and out the front door. Only one floorboard on the porch creaked a good morning to me, and I felt sure no one in the house had heard me leave.

Sunrise was still about twenty minutes away, and wisps of mist lay on the grassy yards. The soft slap of my sneakers on the asphalt was the only sound I heard as I walked down to the intersection with the bluff road, then turned left. One by one I passed them, the grand old cottages of the Colony, brittle with age but still proud.

I passed the big black SUV in front of Longstaff House and knew the Governor was still in residence. For all I knew, his guest of honor was staying there too, along with the pugnacious Ken. A few steps farther along I saw my destination through the trees, and I cut off the road.

The McMahans' guesthouse looked homely compared with the grander main residence. I was surprised to see that its back door was still swathed in yellow crime scene tape. The police had had plenty of time to go over the place, so I guessed that the tape would come down when Jerry Chitwood's understaffed force found the time to do it.

But whether they were finished or not, I had business there.

I dug into my pocket and extracted the one souvenir I'd brought with me when I was evicted from Longstaff House – a set of keys to the house next door. I'd found them, clearly labeled, in one of the kitchen drawers, and something told me I would need them someday.

I unlocked the back door, ducked under the tape, and went inside. It was shadowy there, but I touched no light switches, knowing the gathering daylight would help. Most of the kitchen surfaces bore the ghostly remnants of fingerprint dust. Just inside the back door I saw a discarded pair of evidence-technician booties and considered putting them on but decided against it. At this late date, neither my tracks nor my fingerprints would matter.

I went from room to room. Everything had the look of being gone over, with clothing and other articles moved and then replaced, but not always in the same spot. Upstairs, I paused to look in the small bedroom where Opal Hicks had died. It was absolutely bare – no bedding, no clothing, nothing. Young Opal had just been passing through this house, and she left no mark behind her.

Faye's bedroom, by contrast, had the look of a room whose owner had just stepped out for a while. It was full of a life-time's worth of accumulated things – shoes, clothing, bedding, souvenirs, and an assortment of the handmade quilts, afghans, sweaters, and other items Faye had made over the years. One day soon, Sonny and Tish would sadly clean all this out. I assumed the Tennessee Bureau of Investigation agents already would have removed anything that might qualify as evidence. But their idea of evidence and mine wouldn't necessarily coincide, and I wanted to see what they had left behind.

I started in the linen closet out in the hallway, then checked the bathroom. All the medicines appeared to have been swept up in the police search. Back in the bedroom, I made my way quickly through the clothes and the other bulky things. I went over the items on her dressing table and in its drawers – combs, brushes, make-up, a few pieces of jewelry.

Stuck into the frame of the dresser mirror were two snapshots. One showed Faye posing with Sonny and Tish by the overlook near the old hotel, all of them much younger, dressed up for some event – church, maybe – and looking very happy. In the other, Faye stood in the back yard, her arms around Opal Hicks and another young girl.

The shelf in the clothes closet was next. It was a jumble of shoe boxes, some holding shoes, some empty. One, though, was different, and when I opened the lid, I felt as if I were getting warm. It was a hodgepodge of memorabilia – postcards, more snapshots, small souvenirs of other times and places. In a decorative cardboard folder was a professionally done photo of Sonny posing with Faye in front of the statehouse. It bore the inscription *To Mama, who brought me all the way. Love, Sonny.*

There were older photos too, some of them dating back to Sonny's childhood. One showed him with me at around age ten, the two of us holding our BB guns at the port-arms position and looking ferocious.

Toward the bottom I found a shot of a young Faye with Blue. I couldn't tell if they were married or still courting, but they stood on a carnival midway, the background all lights and dazzle. Blue was rail-thin and darkly handsome. She wore a country-girl dress, her hair was slightly tousled, and her eyes gleamed with excitement. I wondered if she had any notion of what life with this man would bring her.

Intrigued, I looked for more carnival pictures. There were none, but I did find one more of a young Blue. He stood in front of a small country church along with two men and a woman, all of them dressed up. Blue stood next to the woman, who wore white and held a bouquet, and she was being kissed by the man on the far right. At far left in the photo stood a man who looked familiar. After a few seconds, I recognized Dewey Tackett. Across the bottom of the photo someone had scrawled in ink, *Minnie and the Okie tie the knot.*

I found nothing more of interest in the shoebox, so I pocketed the two pictures of Blue, replaced the box on the shelf, and left the room. On my way out, I noticed a monthly calendar on the kitchen wall with writing here and there. I removed it and paged backward. Some days carried pencilled notations about things to do or to expect, entered in two distinctly different handwritings. *Refill Rx* was a frequent reminder. *Call Your Son* appeared here and there. Every Monday bore the label *Prayer Group*. At the top of each page someone had written *Mon–Thurs*: *Junie;* and *Fri–Sun: Opal.*

Junie. Of course. When Faye had visited me that night, only hours before her death, she had mentioned that two girls were staying at the house overnight, fixing her meals, alternately looking after her. Junie must have been the other one, the second girl in the photo stuck in the bedroom mirror. The police no doubt had spoken with her, but I should have done so too, and the omission made me angry with myself. I was getting rusty.

One entry looked strange. About a month before Faye's death, someone had written in the Wednesday space, *Opal sick*, followed by the word *Who* and a question mark. It looked as if Junie had sought to find someone other than herself to fill in.

I took the calendar along with the two old photos and left, ducking under the tape and locking up carefully behind me. It was broad daylight, but still no one stirred on the road or in the nearby yards as I walked back to Wilkes Cottage.

I sat in the only unoccupied room at the Pilgrim's Rest Police Station, leafing intently through a small book on the table in front of me. The room, which I imagined could function as an interrogation room, held just the table and three chairs, and its walls were lightly soundproofed.

The morning had been productive. With the help of Chief Chitwood, I had run down the 'Junie' on Faye's calendar. She was the second of her care-givers, a high school girl named June Willets. I had called her at home and spoken briefly to her before her mother interrupted and made it known that she did not want me bothering her daughter. Before we were cut off, though, Junie had told me that she worked at the Big Scoop ice cream parlor on weekends.

More important, I had learned from the chief that Faye had had an address book and that it was now in police custody. If I tiptoed around the TBI agents, he hinted, I could get a look at it.

That was the book I was now studying. It was cheaply made,

with thin cardboard covers. The entries were in pencil, lightened with age, and there were not a lot of them. Most were simply local names and phone numbers, but there were some out-of-town addresses as well.

I was looking for anyone who might be an old friend of Blue. I didn't know how likely it was that Faye would have kept such a list herself, but I could hope. I was especially looking for any name that sounded like Minnie or the Okie.

No luck until I hit the letter 'T'. There it was – the name Tulsa, followed by a phone number.

I had two moments of slow-dawning clarity, one after the other. First, when Faye said she had gotten a call from Tulsa, she didn't mean Oklahoma. She meant a person. And second, isn't it likely that someone nicknamed Tulsa might also be known as the Okie? I would be willing to bet a modest amount that the old friend whose wedding Blue had attended carried around two nicknames. And that not long ago he had called Faye to let her know Blue was coming for a visit.

I've had moments like this as a reporter, when an important piece falls into place with a solid *click*, like a piece of precision machinery, and you know you have a good story. This time, though, it was different, even better, because this quest was infinitely more important to me.

I felt warm. A little tingly, even. But don't celebrate yet, I told myself. It's just a piece. It's not the final piece.

I wrote down the number and kept going until I reached the end. No Minnie. No other out-of-town numbers. But I had Tulsa.

'Thanks, Chief,' I said, returning the book to him on my way out. 'What's in the 901 area code?'

'Memphis, mostly. You find something?'

'I found a name.' I showed him my notes. 'I think this guy is an old friend of Blue, and I'm going to see if I can have a talk with him.'

'I think Timms already called him, and I don't think he got anything from him.'

'Well, I'm calling him too.'

'Remember what you said.'

'Anything I get, you get.'

I sat in my car and dialed the number. After a few rings, a woman answered, and I asked for Tulsa. She put the phone down and screeched, 'Mr. Jenkins!' Maybe a minute went by, and then I heard his voice.

'This is Randall Wilkes,' I said. 'I'm calling from Pilgrim's Rest, and I'm looking for Blue McMahan.'

'Don't know him.'

'Sir, I'm sorry to bother you,' I said, 'but this is important. I found your name in Faye McMahan's address book—'

'Well, hello, Mr. Po-liceman,' he said in an amused drawl.

'I'm not a policeman. I also found a picture of Blue that was taken at your wedding. To a woman named Minnie.'

'And how is everything down at the po-lice station?'

'Listen, dammit. Faye got a call from you not long before she died, telling her Blue was coming to see her.'

Silence.

'You're an old friend of his. He ever tell you about hanging out with a boy he called Little Bit?'

'Maybe.'

'Well, that's me.'

'Maybe it is, and maybe it ain't.'

'I was with him not long ago, just before Dewey Tackett was murdered. Dewey was in the wedding picture too. I think he was killed because someone mistook him for Blue.'

More silence. Then he said slyly, 'I hear Blue helped this Little Bit get his cherry popped.'

'That's right.' I was beginning to dislike him.

'What was her name?'

I let out a long breath. 'Callie. Her name was Callie.' It hurt to use her name that way, but I was desperate.

'Well, all right, then. I guess you're him. So what do you want?'

'I want to find Blue. I know he's on the run, but I'm trying to help him. Somebody wants to hurt him, and he needs help, whether he knows it or not.'

'He ain't here.'

'All right. I just want to ask you some questions.'

'You can ask 'em, but not on the phone.'

'What do you want me to do? Come there? You're in Memphis, aren't you?'

'Uh-huh. If you're serious about talkin' to me, you won't mind a little drive.'

I let out a sigh. 'Tell me how to find you.'

EIGHTEEN

I rolled away from Wilkes Cottage early the next morning. In twenty minutes, I was down off the plateau and making good time on the interstate headed northwest. Going through Nashville wasn't the shortest way to Memphis as the crow flew, but it was the fastest. This was not a blue highway trip.

The Toyota was topped off, my cell phone and laptop were recharged, and my tape recorder and fresh notebooks rode on the seat next to me. If Blue McMahan was somewhere out there, I was determined to find him. And, if possible, bring him back.

I'd run into my father at breakfast and mentioned to him that I was going to be away for a while, but I got little reaction. He seemed somewhere else – had seemed distracted, in fact, for some time.

I knew the big groundbreaking for the conference center was coming up in a few days. Politics and personalities aside, I knew how important it was to him, and I asked him if he was ready for it.

'I'm committed to it,' was all he said, pushing his scrambled eggs around on the plate. It seemed an odd answer.

The night before, I had phoned Lita Ray to tell her that I was leaving town for a while. I couldn't tell her the reason, of course, because like most of the world, she thought Blue McMahan was dead. But she suspected that it concerned Callie – and was right, in a sense – and demanded to go along. I said no, and she had some harsh words for me. To defuse her anger, I suggested that she search her memory and try to make a list of everyone she could remember Callie dating in the year or so before she disappeared. 'It will help,' I said. 'I'll talk to you when I get back.'

Two hours later I had lunch in Nashville, then picked up Interstate 40 southwest toward Memphis. I remembered Middle Tennessee as mostly farmland, but although the farms were there, increasingly I saw signs of industry in the countryside, urban sprawl radiating out from the state capital.

The highway cut through the less fertile uplands, then descended to the Tennessee River Valley. After that, it was lowlands all the way. I was in West Tennessee, where you begin to feel for the first time that you're in the Deep South, and I was headed for Memphis on the great, muddy Mississippi. Home of pork barbecue, the blues, and Elvis.

Not quite straight as an arrow, but straight enough, I-40 got me to Memphis in a little over three hours. Since I was unsure exactly what to expect from Tulsa Jenkins, alias the Okie, I first took the time to find and settle into a downtown hotel room. Then I got out my directions.

The address he'd given me was a few miles out Poplar Avenue, a street that had once cut through elegant neighborhoods but now looked tired. Along some stretches, modest churches sat next to convenience stores. I passed a faded but still showy Italianate mansion that now housed a drug rehab center.

Turning off Poplar, I drove two blocks, found the street name Tulsa had given me, and turned left. Mature oaks and magnolias overarched the street, their roots buckling the sidewalks. The address was a sturdy old two-story house surrounded by similar-looking neighbors.

Only the screen door was closed. When I rang the bell, a voice answered, 'Door's open.' I stepped into an entryway and saw a medium-size sitting room off to the right, where a black man in robe and house slippers sat reading a copy of the *Commercial Appeal.*

'Tulsa around?' I asked.

'Last bedroom on the left,' the man said, and went back to his paper. At the end of a narrow, dark hallway, I knocked on the door.

'C'mon in.'

Tulsa Jenkins sat on a recliner, feet up, facing me and the small TV set that sat atop a dresser against the wall to my right. Some kind of game show was on.

The room was stiflingly warm. Tulsa wore warm-up pants with gray socks and a pajama top. His left hand held the TV remote, his right held both a cigarette and a beer can, which he was setting down on a chair-side table as I came in.

'I'm Randall Wilkes.'

He nodded, muting the sound on the TV without turning the picture off.

'I appreciate your talking to me.'

Another nod.

'You mind if I sit?'

'No, 'course not.' He indicated the only other seat in the room, a straight-back chair against the wall to my left. I sat and looked around. Almost all the floor space was taken up by the bed, recliner, dresser, and a foot locker that functioned as a table. An old carnival poster from the Morrissey Shows was tacked up on the wall.

Tulsa Jenkins was big and jowly, with the look of a man gone to seed. I guessed him to be a few years younger than my father, but sitting in that rented room, surrounded by what were likely his only possessions, I had the feeling that I was looking at the end of a life. After his youth, the carnival, his wife Minnie, and whatever adventures he had known, he had reached this last place, where things became all past and no future.

We talked casually for a while. I told him about my drive west, and he told me about himself. His real name was Virgil, and he was indeed nicknamed after his birthplace in Oklahoma, where his dad had been a wildcatter. Most carnies, he told me, pick up nicknames. He had rented this room for five years, and I gathered that he had lived in a succession of rooming houses for a dozen years or so, ever since he and Minnie had divorced.

'As long as I was some kind of desperado, she thought it was exciting to be married to me,' he said. 'Soon as I tried to retire, she got bored.' He shrugged. 'You know how women are.'

'Yeah,' I said. 'So, like I said on the phone, I'm looking for Blue McMahan.'

'I know,' he said, appearing to lose interest in the conversation. 'We can talk about Blue, sure 'nough. But I'm gettin' hungry. You hungry?'

'I could eat.'

'Why don't we go get somethin' to eat? And talk while we eat?'

He was angling for a free meal, and I had no objection. A reporter hardly ever gets something for nothing. Information can come with a price, but often it's not expressed in dollars. Sometimes it's as simple as giving undivided attention to someone who's not used to being taken seriously. Reporters learn the arts of flattery and malarkey and use them shamelessly. If that fails, then sometimes you pull out your wallet, usually for a meal or a drink. Measured against the tabloids that shell out big money for exclusives, this wouldn't even register on the ethical scale. Go ask H.L. Mencken; he'll tell you.

We got in my car, and Tulsa steered me downtown. 'You like ribs?' he asked. 'We can get some good ribs at the Rendezvous.' He had exchanged his PJ top for a shirt and slipped on a pair of shoes, but the overall effect hadn't changed much. Already my car was taking on the mixed scent of beer and tobacco.

I knew the Rendezvous from my college days. As soon as we got a table and ordered, I realized my mistake. The place was packed as always, the noise level was deafening, and I knew we'd have no meaningful conversation until dinner was over. So I waited until Tulsa had his fill of dry-rub pork ribs.

'Beale Street's just over thataway,' he said as we exited the alley onto Second Street. 'One of my favorite bars –'

'Maybe some other time,' I said. 'Let's find a place where we can talk.' I guided him over to the lobby of the nearby Peabody Hotel. The ornate, high-ceilinged space was busy but not excessively noisy, and we found comfortable chairs not far from the centerpiece fountain.

He pulled a half pint out of his pocket. 'You want a drink?' he asked.

'No, thanks. Listen, Tulsa, I drove a long way to talk to you. We've had dinner, and now I'm in a talking mood.'

'Well, go ahead.' He nipped quickly at the half pint, looked around, and pocketed it again. Spending a few hours with him had not made me warm to his company. He seemed full of bullshit and resentment, a man life had not treated particularly well. It was not going to be easy to pry anything useful out of him.

'I told you on the phone why I'm looking for Blue,' I said. 'He's in trouble. Have you seen him?'

'Maybe I have.' He tried to put on a sly look and failed.

'That *maybe* doesn't sound very good,' I told him. 'It says you're not ready to be straight with me.'

'What's in it for me?' he asked.

'Aha. If I offered you money, would you tell me?'

'I just might.' The look this time was smug, which was more his speed.

'If I told you that I could get you arrested, would that make you more friendly?' I made a show of pulling out my cell phone, and I flipped it open.

He stared at it for a second. 'What does that mean?'

'I told you someone tried to kill Blue. I didn't tell you he's wanted for questioning about his own wife's murder. Whether you admit it or not, I think you called Faye McMahan not long before she was killed, to let her know Blue was on his way. Maybe you did it as a favor to him. Maybe it was a warning to her, maybe it was a threat. Whatever it was, we're talking about the murder of the mother of one of the governors of this fine state. And the Tennessee Bureau of Investigation, once they know about your connection with all of this, will scoop you up, Tulsa.'

'I didn't have nothin' to do with that.' He looked surly and defensive. I knew he hadn't invited me to Memphis out of charity but out of greed. Now he was no doubt telling himself he'd overreached. But would he be scared enough to tell me what he knew, or just enough to make me go away?

'Maybe you didn't, but they can make life very difficult for you. You used to be a carny. Did you also run cons with Blue? Anything in your past you don't want them to know about?' I flipped the phone closed with a snap, then flipped it open again. The screen glowed with a sinister light. His eyes were on it.

'Hell,' he said finally with a good-old-boy grin. 'Ain't no need for that. You go ahead and ask me. I'll tell you.'

I decided to start off easy. 'When did you see him last?'

'Oh, less 'n a week ago. He'd been staying in the room next door to me.'

That surprised me. I hadn't realized I was so close.

'How long was he there?'

'Maybe a couple of months. He needed a place to stay, and I got him into the rooming house. He was using a different name.'

'Was this around the time people thought he had drowned?'

'I guess it was,' he mumbled.

My questions continued, and so did his answers, although they were maddeningly fragmented. His sense of chronology, hampered by his drinking, was a mess, and he jumped from one time frame to another. I made him stop, go back, rephrase things. He became more and more impatient with me, but I didn't care. There was an important narrative here, and I was determined to dig it out of him.

After ten minutes, I noticed that he had drained his half pint. I reached over and put a friendly hand on his shoulder. 'What are you drinking?' I asked him. He turned the bottle so I could see the Jim Beam label. 'But I like Jack Daniels too,' he said.

The booze was slowing down his account, it was true, but it was also oiling his tongue, and I wanted him talking freely, not worrying about the consequences of what he told me. I went to the bar and got him a double Black Jack on the rocks, then brought it back and deposited it in front of him, along with a soft drink for myself. I needed to keep my wits.

He took a sip, nodded his approval, then lit a cigarette with a flourish and continued his lumbering tale.

Another twenty minutes later, I finally had it. It was complicated, like all of Blue's history, but it went something like this:

About two months earlier, there were brief mentions in the news of the drowning death of Blue McMahan, reprobate father of the state's former governor. Soon thereafter Blue showed up quietly on Tulsa's doorstep, invoking the tradition of carnival brotherhood and asking for a place to hide out for a while. He didn't tell Tulsa the reason – probably didn't trust him much. But one day Dewey Tackett, Blue's best friend, came to visit, and Tulsa eavesdropped while they talked. He gathered that what had sent Blue underground was something he learned during a phone conversation with his wife.

'He was talking to her regularly?' I asked.

'Yeah,' Tulsa said. 'He'd been out of touch for a long time, but he heard she was getting soft in the head, and he felt sorry for her. So he'd call her. But if one of those girls answered, he'd hang up. He was careful. Remember, he was—'

'Supposed to be dead. I know.'

Blue stayed quietly in the room next door for several weeks, going out frequently – sometimes for provisions or to make calls from a nearby pay phone, other times for undisclosed reasons. Tulsa, knowing Blue had always been a ladies' man, assumed he was meeting someone.

One night Blue took off for one of his secret nights out. Faye, he knew, was expecting him to call, and her dementia was making her increasingly agitated. He asked Tulsa to call her and say she would be hearing from Blue soon.

'I made a mistake,' he said gloomily. 'She asked me if he was ever coming to see her, and I said sure he was, real soon. I thought he'd be mad at me for lying to her, but I didn't see him till the next morning, and by that time it was all over the TV that somebody had killed Faye.'

Blue, Tulsa said, was devastated by the news. I couldn't see inside his head, of course, but it was not hard to imagine that he might feel enormous guilt over the death of the woman who had borne his son and then had to bear the indignity of years of abandonment. Knowing he was taking a chance on being spotted, he drove to Pilgrim's Rest to be present, even if only at a distance, for her burial.

'Funny thing about the way he reacted, though,' Tulsa said.

'How's that?'

'I told you he was hit hard by it, and that's the truth. But he acted like he wasn't a hundred percent surprised by it, you know?'

'By her death?'

'That's right. By her death.'

The drama wasn't nearly over. With Faye in the ground, Blue returned to Memphis badly shaken by Dewey Tackett's murder at the motel, a bloody act clearly meant for him. With his wife and his best friend both dead, Blue began to confide more in Tulsa. He also began drinking more, and one night in the midst of a rambling conversation, he handed Tulsa the biggest surprise of all.

'Him and Minnie,' Tulsa said, staring down at the last swirl of liquid in his glass.

'I beg your pardon?'

'He was spending time with Minnie.'

'Your ex-wife?'

He nodded, his face sour.

'Well, uh, after all ... I mean, the two of you were divorced.'

'I don't care. He should've told me.' His words were full of slurred, drunken resentment.

My head was reeling with this baroque story, and I complimented myself on sticking to soft drinks. 'Where was he going to see her?'

'I don't know for sure, but I think she was coming here to Memphis.'

'Where does she live?'

He gestured vaguely. 'Over in Blount County.'

He took a deep, ragged breath. 'That peckerwood's had girlfriends in three states, so how was I supposed to know he was getting together with Minnie without telling me? Friends don't do that. All the time he was hiding out here, the son of a bitch. Soon as he told me, I kicked his ass out. Told him I didn't care if we were friends or not, I'd turn him in if he wasn't packed and gone the next day. And he was.'

I called a mental time-out, leaned back into the soft cushions of the overstuffed chair, and looked up at the lofty ceiling. Only a few obvious questions remained.

'Do you have Minnie's address?'

'Uh-uh. Just a phone number. But I don't use it.'

'Did Blue go to her?'

'Who the hell knows?'

The drive back was mostly silent. My passenger stank of booze and bad breath, and I was eager to drop him off, but it turned out he still had one story to tell. As I swung onto Poplar, he began talking.

'I'm pretty good at figuring people out,' he said, waving his cigarette dramatically. 'You work the carnival circuit, you get to be an expert. I can tell Blue was a big man to you when you was growing up. You prob'ly looked up to him, didn't you?'

'Maybe I did.' Just what I needed in my car, a shrink with a degree in carnival psychology.

'Well ...' His voice took on a smug tone. 'I can tell you a few things about him. Like that time in St. Louis.'

'So tell me about that time in St. Louis.'

'Glad to. Me and Minnie and Blue, we was working a long con out of the Gateway Hotel. All using phony names. Minnie was the roper, Blue was the inside man, I was the muscle if we ever needed it, which we never did, 'cause Blue handled things so slick.'

'I know,' I said. 'The mark never even knows he's been taken.'

'Well, usually. But this one time it went wrong. Real wrong. The mark, he turned out to be a little crazy. Rich guy, young, a kind of a playboy. Smarter than we thought. He wised up to what we were doing, and he got Minnie alone in his room and worked her over. Then he called us on the hotel phone and said he was blowing the whistle on the three of us, and his old man, who was a big wheel in air conditioning or something, was going to make sure we all got put away for a long time. Blue, he just hung up the phone, told me to pack everything, check us out, and meet him in the garage in a half an hour. So that's what I did.'

He paused. 'Blue showed up with Minnie, and we took off. She was hurt, but nothing permanent. We didn't stop till we got to Little Rock, where we was working out of those days. A few days later, it hit the papers.'

I waited. I had a bad feeling about what was coming.

'They found the playboy in the hotel freight elevator with his head bashed in,' he said. 'I never asked, and Blue never told. But I knew.'

NINETEEN

My alarm went off at six the next morning. By six-thirty, I had gotten some coffee from the hotel's breakfast buffet and carried my laptop into a room off the lobby called the Business Center, complete with wireless internet service.

Any information I had from Tulsa Jenkins was automatically filed under the label *Needs Confirming*. So I plugged the phone number he gave me into my favorite people-finder website and came up with a name and address in a place called Bigger's Cove, which was indeed in Blount County. The name wasn't Minnie, it was Mrs. Lurleen Magnuson, but that didn't bother me too much. A little more exploring turned up the information that Mrs. Magnuson's husband, Harold, owner of two auto dealerships in Knoxville, had departed this world three years ago.

By nine I was back on old reliable Interstate 40, headed for Nashville once again. Tennessee, as any first-year geography student knows, is a rough parallelogram, shaped the way a shoe box would look if you stepped gently on it and it started to collapse to one side. The bad news for me on this bright autumn day was that I was coming from the extreme southwest corner of the shoe box and heading for the extreme southeast – not quite the farthest I could go within the state, but far enough.

This time I didn't pause in Nashville but plowed through, staying on I-40. Once the capital was behind me, I pulled off the freeway for lunch at one of those chain restaurants that specialize in Southern comfort food. While I waited for my order,

I considered calling Lurleen Magnuson but decided against it. If she was sheltering Blue, a call would only scare him off.

My scrambled eggs, biscuits, and gravy arrived, and I ate hungrily. If you want to work up a real appetite, I thought, try chasing a will-o'-the-wisp across the length of Tennessee. Then, just as the waitress was refilling my coffee cup, my cell phone rang. I didn't recognize the number displayed on the screen.

'Hey, Little Bit.'

'Blue!' A dozen questions fought for space in my mind, but all I could think to say was, 'Where the hell are you?'

'Now, don't you worry about that. I'm just calling to check up on you, see how you're doing.'

Don't alert him, I told myself. If he suspects you're on his tail, he'll bolt again.

'I'm doing fine,' I said, 'but I'm worried about you. A lot of people are.'

'Well, they don't need to be. Where are you right now?'

I thought hard. Did he know?

'I'm, uh, I'm at Wilkes Cottage. I moved in with my dad a few days ago.'

'Uh-huh. That's good.' He paused. 'Been wanting to say I'm sorry I had to leave you so quick that night—'

'It's all right,' I said, surprised at the emotion in my voice. Apologies of any kind from Blue were rare, and I felt suddenly protective of him. 'I don't blame you. I know somebody meant to kill you. I don't know why, but that's not the most important thing right now. We just need for you to come back.'

'I can take care of myself. Always could. You know that.' His voice sounded hoarse.

'Dammit, Blue—'

'And this number I'm calling from won't do you any good.'

'Sure,' I said. 'You're using one of those disposable cell phones. Very smart. For somebody who hasn't done anything, you sure behave like one of the most-wanted, you know that?'

'Listen,' he said, ignoring my sarcasm. 'I want you to do me a favor.'

I didn't hesitate. 'All right.'

'I want you to call Clara Tackett, Dewey's wife. I've heard she's taken it real hard since he was killed. I can't exactly call her 'cause she'd think she was talking to a ghost.' He started to chuckle, but it quickly turned into a cough that went on for several seconds. 'Would you give her a call? Just to say hello?'

'Sure I will.'

'She's in Knoxville.' I heard a rustle of paper, and he gave me the phone number.

You won't believe this, Blue, I said to him silently, but I'll be passing right through Knoxville in a few hours, on my way to where I hope you are. 'Okay if I call her in the next day or so?' I asked.

'That's fine.' He paused, and I hoped the muted background noise in the restaurant was not making its way through to his end of the phone. 'So tell me true: Anybody think I killed Faye?'

'I don't think so,' I said. *Except maybe your son.* 'At the most, they want to talk to you about Dewey and the motel. You could put everybody's mind to rest by not acting so goddam suspiciously and just coming back to Pilgrim's Rest.'

'Maybe someday,' he said vaguely. 'Thanks for calling Clara. You take care of yourself now, you hear?'

'Wait. One more thing.' I felt him on the verge of hanging up, and I desperately tried to arrange my thoughts. 'You remember Callie Darnell, don't you?'

A long pause, then: 'Uh-huh.'

'She's dead. Years ago. Murdered, it looks like. Someone buried her down below the falls, and her bones just turned up there.'

He said nothing, and I kept talking. I had to get it all out. 'Everybody thought the spot where they found her was a soldier's grave, but you knew better, and you mentioned it to Faye. It's been driving me crazy ever since. You know something about Callie's death, and Faye's too. And you've been hiding, acting like—'

Out on the interstate off-ramp, the driver of an eighteen-wheeler hit his air brakes. There is no sound quite like that, and it carried clearly into the restaurant. And into the mouthpiece of my phone.

'Where did you say you were?' he asked quietly.

'Blue—'

'You're a sneaky one, Little Bit,' he said. His tone was not sarcastic, just tired. An instant later, the line went dead.

I cursed – under my breath, I thought, but an entire family at the next table looked my way.

There was nothing to do but keep going, and so I did. After less than an hour, 40 took me over and through the irregularly shaped highlands of the Cumberland Plateau, then descended to the fabled Tennessee Valley. This had been one of the poorest regions in the country until F.D.R. – a god to many in my parents' generation – and his New Deal built dams, tamed the Tennessee River, and strung electrical lines that lit up the whole valley and much of Appalachia.

It's one of the quirks of Tennessee geography that in the course of a day you can drive from the raw flatlands of the old Mississippi Delta cotton country to the immensity of the Great Smoky Mountains, thousands of feet up. They're part of the Appalachian chain, which seems to go on forever, and they were part of the barrier that kept the American colonists in the coastal settlements until a hardy few ventured across the mountains and into what was to become Kentucky and Tennessee. Those were Scots-Irish, mostly, and they cleared the trees and fought the Indians and eventually farmed the land. They were my ancestors, and Stuart McMahan's, and Sis Lawlor's and Pike Darnell's. Looking at the formidable bulk of those mountains, I felt for the first time in years a sense of place, of kinship, of belonging. In Chicago I had been a smart guy, a striver, finally a failure. Here I felt like part of a tribe. Would the feeling last?

It was late afternoon when I finally reached Bigger's Cove. The Smokies loomed almost overhead, the last barrier before North Carolina. I was glad I wasn't going any farther, because the radio weather man had reported that it was snowing lightly up on Clingman's Dome, at the crest of the mountains.

The lowering sun behind me lit up the Smokies in their full blaze of autumn. It was if the Great Painter, torn between colors, had swiped his brush across his palette and flung all of it at the hillsides, speckling everything differently. I saw orange-red sugar maple at the lower elevations. Higher up were yellow birch and the speckled red-green of red maple. Scattered in among them were red oak and the rose-colored leaves of the sweet gum. At the highest elevations, almost lost in the mist, were the deep greens of spruce and fir.

And the 'smoke.' Rain falls heavy on these mountains, and they got their name from the peculiar way in which the mist will swirl in columns of what look like smoke, as if the mountains were a series of chimneys used to vent steam from deep within the earth. As if Satan himself were blowing smoke rings.

Bigger's Cove, Tennessee, population 516. It took me only ten minutes and one stop for directions to find Lurleen Magnuson's house. It was a handsome place on a quiet hillside road just outside town. The house was like a log cabin writ large and fancy, with stained and varnished beams, a peaked roof, and the overall look of a ski lodge. A brand new Ford Expedition sat in the driveway, and the smoky hills were a lovely backdrop in the fading daylight.

When I stepped out of the car, I saw my breath and shivered slightly. Lights were on inside the house. I had just started for the front door when I noticed that it was open, and I heard a voice.

'Are you Randall? Come on in before you catch cold.'

I went up the steps, and there she stood in the doorway. I knew her right away, despite the passage of decades, from the wedding snapshot. She was one of those women who don't change much, and in the case of the attractive ones, that's a blessing.

When I got up close, she scrutinized me. 'I guess it's you, so I won't have to ask for any ID.'

'Yes, ma'am.'

'If you don't call me ma'am any more, you can come in.' She had a throaty, self-assured voice, the kind sometimes described as tobacco-cured, and a brash manner that I somehow liked.

She opened the door wider, and I stepped into a large room with a beamed and vaulted ceiling that continued the alpine look. Indian rugs hung on the walls, and the furniture looked solid and comfortable. Upstairs, a loft led to other rooms. A fire crackled in the stone fireplace.

She noticed something in my face. 'You're trying to figure it out,' she said.

'What's that?'

'How I got from there to here.' She gestured for me to take a seat in the fireplace area. 'If you're nice, maybe I'll tell you. Can I get you something?' She headed back to an open kitchen. 'Hot cider? Or something stiffer?'

'Cider sounds good.'

She brought two mugs, each with a stick of cinnamon floating in it, took a seat, and lit up a menthol filter-tip. Then she spent a long time looking at me. I returned the favor. I put her at somewhere between Blue's age and mine, and I compared her with the girl in the wedding photo. She had put on weight, but it looked well distributed. The lines on her face were not excessive, and the streaks of gray in her black hair looked so attractive I guessed that they had been applied. She wore a loose-fitting, heavy-knit sweater with a high neck, well-fitting black pants and suede loafers. She also wore more jewelry than your typical housewife. A little flashy, I concluded, but a nice, well-tended package.

She had caught me looking. 'Like my outfit?' she asked, shaking a heavy bracelet. 'This is dressy for me. I usually go around in jeans. But it's poker night, me and some friends, and I like to get all dolled up for that.'

'Girls' or boys' poker?'

'Boys, mostly.'

The image fit. No sewing circle or book group for her, I thought. Instead, poker night with the boys, and she just might have the best stories to tell, too.

'When's the game?'

'They'll start showing up in about half an hour,' she said. 'We've got some time to talk.'

'Fine.'

'He's not here, you know,' she said abruptly, stirring her cider.

'I didn't think he would be,' I said. 'But if I asked to take a look around, would you let me?'

'Sure.'

I weighed her answer. Was that just the carny talking, showing me the right hand while hoping I'd pick the left? I made a quick decision.

'Then I won't bother,' I said. 'It's been a long drive. Two days of long driving, in fact. I spent last evening with Tulsa.'

Her eyebrows went up just a smidgen, but otherwise her expression didn't change. 'Blue said you might start in Memphis,' she said with a shrug.

'What else did he say?'

'That you'd probably be coming here too. "Randall's smart," he said. "And stubborn. So if he shows up, don't waste time trying to fool him. Go ahead and talk to him."'

'Really?' After several hours of Tulsa Jenkins' evasions, I wasn't sure I was ready for honesty.

'Ask me,' she said.

'All right. Do you know where he went?'

'Nope. He left a few hours ago, after talking to you. He said it'd be better if I didn't know—'

'Right,' I said. 'Better if you didn't know where he went. Sometimes I wonder if he's ever really confided in anyone his whole life.'

''Course he hasn't, Sugar,' she said with a tolerant smile. 'Blue just hands out little pieces of himself to people. You need to be satisfied with the piece he gives you.'

She was right. Faye certainly hadn't gotten all of him. I had gotten more than most people, more even than Sonny. Maybe I should have been grateful.

'Tulsa told me he thought you and Blue were seeing each other, that you were coming to Memphis for visits.'

She cradled her cider cup in both hands, studying it, and spoke without looking up. 'I went twice. First time was to pass him some money. I'd been his banker for years—'

'I'm sorry?'

'He doesn't trust banks. Every now and then, he'd send me some money to hold for him. I'd invest it in something safe and just hang onto it. Then, while he was in Memphis, he asked me for a chunk of it, so I drove there. It was good to see him again, but I didn't like the way he looked. He was afraid of something, I could tell. And tired.'

'You said you went there twice.'

She nodded. 'Second time was just to see him. He needed company. Look …' She paused to light up another filter tip.

'Every man I've been with, I was faithful. That includes Harold, my late husband, and even Tulsa, with all his problems. But I'm between men now, and by God, I'll behave any way I want to. If I want to spend time with a skinny, good-for-nothing—' She stopped and shook her head, as if to say *How do I explain?*

'I know,' I said. 'Blue likes the ladies, and they like him.'

'That's it,' she said. 'End of story.'

'He didn't tell you why he's been hiding out?'

'No, and I didn't ask. I learned that on the midway a long time ago. Every carny's got his own history, usually with something bad in it, and if he wants to keep it private, you don't pry.'

'I hope you don't mind my saying this,' I began, 'but I have trouble imagining you with Tulsa.'

She gave me a slight, appraising smile, as if deciding how much to tell me. Then she took a big drag and let out a cloud of mentholated smoke. 'I'm not going to bad-mouth him,' she said. 'Just say we were right for each other for a while, back when we lived on the road and went looking for thrills. One day I woke up, looked in the mirror and saw the first line on my face, and I knew that part of it was over. I divorced him and moved to Knoxville, got a job, enrolled in night school. Accounting. I wanted to be a CPA. Harold was one of the guest lecturers. He was a widower, and we started dating. Next thing I knew, I was Mrs. Harold Magnuson, and we built this place here.'

'You started over,' I said with some wonder. 'I always admire people who can do that.'

'Sugar, you just do it. Believe me, if things ever get bad enough with Life Number One, you'll move on, trust me.'

I silently wondered if the incident in the Gateway Hotel in St. Louis had anything to do with her decision. It wouldn't have surprised me.

I felt tired of chasing the will-o'-the-wisp named Blue and wished I could spend the whole evening with this ex-con artiste, the darling of the carnival circuit.

Outside, the light had gone. I tried to stifle a yawn, but it got away from me.

'You're tired,' she said.

'Tired of driving,' I said. 'I'm also tired of chasing your old friend.'

'Then why are you chasing him?'

'Because I believe someone wants to kill him, and he doesn't have the sense to know the difference between his friends and his enemies.'

I expected to surprise her, but she surprised me instead. Her eyes narrowed, her mouth tightened, and she nodded her head slowly. She may not have known that a killer was after Blue, but the news did not shock her. She had worked and traveled with Blue McMahan in his prime, and she knew that he sometimes walked in dark places. This Minnie is a tough one, I thought.

'Then you should find him,' she said quietly. 'Before those other folks do. You're the one to do it, too.'

'What do you mean?'

'Why do you suppose he told me to go ahead and talk to you? This old boy who hardly ever opens up to anybody?'

'Well ...'

''Cause he likes you. Not enough to let you find him, you understand. But he likes you.'

'I'm sure he likes a lot of people. Tulsa told me he's got girl-friends in three states.'

That elicited a throaty laugh. 'Sure he does. But he likes you in a different way. Back when him and Tulsa and me, we were running games, he'd sometimes talk about you and about his kid. I could tell both of you were special to him.'

'He talked about Sonny?' That surprised me. As much as I enjoyed Blue's company as a boy, I was aware that Sonny could have used some of it too.

'You bet he did,' she said forcefully. 'And most of all while he was here just now. Don't you think any father'd be proud of a son who made governor?'

'I suppose.' Sonny had been Blue's son for a long time with little to show for it except embarrassment. I was glad to hear Blue was proud of him. Too bad the son could never be proud of the father.

We heard a car pull up outside. 'First of the suckers – I mean the poker players,' she said.

'I guess I should go.' I got up, still stiff from my drive. As used-up as I was, I would have appreciated the offer of a bed for the night, but it looked like that was not to be.

She saw me out to my car, pausing on the way to introduce me to her friend, a prosperous-looking gent who, it turned out, was a banker in a nearby town.

As we stood at my car, I felt the chill of the mountains descend on me, and I wondered if I would ever catch up with this man. For the first time, I came close to hating him for putting me through all this.

'I don't think he's well,' she said abruptly. 'He'd never admit it. You know how he is about other people's sympathy. But he looks worn-out.'

I recalled the sound of his coughing on the phone.

'You're wondering where to go next,' she said with a trace of sympathy. 'Wish I could help. The only thing ...'

'What?'

'Well, just before he left, we were standing right here next to his car, talking about the old times, and he said something about how he's running out of carnival friends and maybe the oldest friends are the best ones.'

'So who's his oldest friend?'

'Sugar, he didn't say. He just asked me where the nearest liquor store was, and then he hit the road.'

'What kind of a car is he driving?'

She looked at me for the longest time. 'He'd kill me for this, but I don't care. I've got a right to decide what's best for him, don't I? He's driving a beat-up old Ford pickup, white under all the dirt. I didn't get a look at the plates.' She patted me lightly on the arm. 'If you find him, look after him. It's time somebody did.'

Another car pulled up, and she waved to the driver. 'Hope you brought lots of money,' she shouted.

She leaned over and gave me a quick kiss. 'You drive careful, now.'

I headed back into what passed for downtown Bigger's Cove. The only motel was full up, packed with tourists who were about to plunge into the Smokies for the annual fall colors tour. By then I was so tired it didn't matter where I slept, so I found a quiet stretch of road, pulled well off onto the shoulder, and climbed into the back seat. I had the windows down a little, and the crisp smells of the season were like a sachet on my pillow. Within minutes I was asleep.

The ringing of my cell phone awakened me. The darkness was almost absolute, so I couldn't see the time. The phone was up on the dashboard, and it took me a few seconds of scrambling, and muttered cursing, before I could retrieve it.

'Randall? It's Charlene Singletary. I've been leaving messages for you. Where are you?'

'I'm, uh ... I'm in the Smokies. I left my phone in the car for a while, so ... Why? What is it?'

'Your father.' I could hear the tension in her voice, her effort to keep it under control. 'He's been hurt.'

TWENTY

Pilgrim's Rest was a good hundred and fifty miles away, according to my sleepy-eyed look at the map, and I don't remember much of the drive back. Two-lane back roads, darkness, cold night air sifting in through the window I'd cracked open to help myself stay awake. I thought about stopping for coffee, but my stomach was so gripped with tension over the news about my father, coffee would go down like battery acid.

Somewhere along the way, my thoughts strayed briefly to Blue. He had won our game. The shifty old con man hadn't wanted to be found, and I hadn't found him. If he didn't want my help, let him take care of himself. I wished him luck and hoped he had found a safe place to hide from whoever was after him. I had an image of him sitting with that 'oldest friend,' whoever he was, swapping stories about carnival life or the big con as he faded into the sunset.

As I neared Pilgrim's Rest, I found myself drifting off, and I turned the radio on good and loud to keep me awake. I fiddled with the dial, scanning past the usual assortment of sermons and country-pop tunes that all sounded stamped out of the same song-making machinery. They reminded me why, over the years, I had fallen out of love with country music, the sound of my forebears.

Then, just a few miles outside town, I heard a woman's voice, raw and not pretty but straight and true, singing the words to what must have been an old story about a girl, a lover, and a broken heart. The recording was not very good – shallow and scratchy. It sounded like homemade music, but it came from a faraway place in my mind, and I found myself effortlessly awake and listening.

After a minute or so, though, I lost the signal, and try as I might, I couldn't get it back.

It was almost two in the morning when I reached the clinic outside Pilgrim's Rest. Several cars were parked outside, including Chief Chitwood's cruiser.

The front desk was unoccupied. Down the hall corridor I spotted Charlene and the chief sitting against the wall. I hurried to them, and the expressions on their faces told me I must look like hell.

'Where is he?'

Charlene got up and lightly touched my arm. 'Come in and see him,' she said. We walked down the corridor a few paces, and she parted the curtain on one of the emergency cubicles.

If I thought I looked like hell, my father raised it to another level. His mouth hung open slackly, all color was drained from his face, and his breaths came noisily. An oxygen tube was in his nose, another tube fed liquid into his left arm, and his right arm was heavily bandaged from wrist to elbow.

Mrs. Mullins, in a plain dress and what looked like my father's parka, sat rigidly in the corner of the small enclosure. We exchanged nods.

'They think he's going to be all right,' Chitwood said, 'but it was tense for a while. The doctor stitched him up and watched him real close. For a while, she thought your dad could be having a heart attack, which would have made things a lot more complicated.'

I turned to Chitwood. 'Did somebody try—'

'It doesn't look that way,' he said carefully. 'We'll know more in the morning, but I don't think this was any kind of assault. More like a bad accident.'

I looked at him in disbelief, memories of Faye McMahan and Dewey Tackett still vivid. A brisk young woman stuck her head past the curtain, looked us over with a smile, and walked on.

'The night resident,' Charlene said. 'She got a motorcycle

accident in here about an hour ago, with a couple of kids racked up pretty bad, so she's busy right now. But we had a good talk with her earlier, and she says we shouldn't worry.'

I touched my father's forehead. 'Why's he unconscious?' I asked.

She gave him a sedative,' she said. 'He was all wound up, having trouble breathing, losing blood. He wasn't able to talk much ...' She stopped, staring at me. 'What's wrong?'

I was leaning against the wall, rubbing my eyes. 'I'm sorry,' I said, trying to grin. 'It's just ... I don't know. All the way here tonight, I was in the twilight zone, thinking he could be dying or dead ...'

Charlene came over and touched me on the shoulder. 'He's going to be all right,' she said forcefully. 'I'm glad you came, and I know he is too.'

Leaving Mrs. Mullins to watch him, we stepped back into the hallway and took seats in uncomfortable plastic chairs where, piece by piece, they filled me in.

It began with a noise outside the offices of the *Call* just after dusk, when most of the stores were closed and the town square was quiet. A lone reporter, working late. My father slumped against the door, bleeding from a gash in his arm. A puddle of blood under him on the sidewalk, a trail of it leading across the street. My father mumbling, 'I hurt myself,' then gasping in pain. Ambulance summoned, and Charlene called at home by her reporter.

By the time she and Jerry Chitwood showed up at the clinic, the doctor was placing the last of many stitches in his right arm. What happened? My father was incoherent, he had lost a lot of blood, and the doctor, fearing complications, began running tests. Charlene called Mrs. Mullins and began trying to reach me, leaving messages while I was enjoying the hospitality of Lurleen Magnuson.

Meanwhile, Chitwood's deputy had followed the trail of blood across the street. It led along the walkway to the front steps of the library. A few drops speckled the steps, and the trail ended at the locked door.

I hurt myself. The knot that had sat heavy in my stomach ever since Bigger's Cove eased somewhat at those words. Bad enough, I thought, but at least not an attempt on his life.

My sleep-deprived mind raced through what they had told me. 'Whatever it was, I'd bet it happened in the Historical Society,' I said, pulling out my phone. I dialed up information and got a home number for Olen Stringer. He didn't answer the ring, so I left a message. 'It's Randall Wilkes,' I said tersely. 'My father was injured last night, and I think it happened where you work. Do you know anything about it? Call me.' I left my number.

'Chief,' Charlene said, 'doesn't your office have keys to all the public buildings in town? Including the library?'

He nodded. 'In fact, I've asked one of my deputies to meet me there with the keys in just a few minutes.' He got up with obvious effort, looking wrung out himself.

'I'll go with you.' I no longer felt sleepy. What had been exhaustion was being replaced by something that resembled anger. I just didn't know where to direct it yet.

'I'll wait here till you come back,' Charlene said.

'Why don't you go home?' I said to her. 'You really don't have to—'

'I told you I think a lot of your father,' she said, with just a hint of impatience. 'He's special, and he's important to this town.'

'Well, thank you,' I said.

I looked in on the patient and told Mrs. Mullins about my plans. 'I'll be here,' she said quietly.

The chief and I rode in near-silence over to the town square. The place looked eerie at night with all buildings darkened and the only illumination coming from widely spaced streetlights. We walked up the pathway past the Confederate soldiers' marker to the front door of the library building where a deputy, a young man in his early twenties, was waiting with the keys. A moment later we were inside, turning on lights.

'Over here.' The deputy had a flashlight, and he played it over the floor. Small, ruby-red drops led in an irregular trail across the entryway floor toward the flight of steps. We followed them, one drop at a time, and soon we stood in front of the door to the

Historical Society. The deputy clicked his way through the keys until he found it, then unlocked the door. We stepped inside and flicked on the lights.

Everything looked normal at first. Then I saw it. 'Look,' I said, pointing to the tabletop display in the center of the room. We approached it. The display was as before, but the glass case protecting it was smashed. Most of the top pane was gone, leaving an irregular, jagged hole. The little buildings and greenery were littered with shards of broken glass. It was if the sky had fallen in on the Cumberland Memorial Park and Civil War Study Center, sending its tiny inhabitants fleeing.

'No blood on the floor,' the deputy said. 'No glass either.'

'Here's why,' Chitwood answered from a far corner of the room, where he pointed to a wastebasket, broom, mop and pail. 'Looks like somebody cleaned up.'

'Damn, I want to talk to this Stringer,' I said.

'I'll talk to him,' the chief said. 'Don't go off half-cocked. Remember what your dad said about hurting himself. Just look after him.'

He was right. The deputy dropped me off at the clinic, where I finally persuaded Charlene to go home. Mrs. Mullins would not be moved, however, so we decided we would both sit with him until the clinic's day shift arrived, then see if he would have to stay longer or could be taken home.

I saw Charlene to her car. 'You were away for a while,' she said. 'The Smokies?'

'And other places,' I said with a yawn. 'The grand tour of Tennessee. And a wild-goose chase too. I'll tell you about it sometime when I'm more awake.'

'All right.'

'Thank you for looking out for him.'

She inclined her head with a smile of acknowledgment.

'You know, I'm jealous of the old guy,' I said.

'Why's that?'

'Well, I've been hearing from everybody how the ladies have always been attracted to Blue McMahan. But seeing the way you and Mrs. Mullins are looking after my dad, I'm beginning to believe the same thing about him. Who would have thought scholarly, unassuming Forrest Wilkes, Ph.D., was some kind of a babe magnet?'

She laughed, and once again I enjoyed the sound. 'Maybe it runs in the family,' she said.

I looked at her in astonishment. 'Charlene, are you flirting with me?'

She immediately looked so embarrassed that I felt sorry for her. 'It's all right,' I said, reaching awkwardly for her arm. 'It's all right.'

Damn, I thought as I watched her car pull away. *That really went well.*

At nine the day-shift doctor came in, looked my father over, and pronounced him fit to travel. He was awake and rational, although subdued and not inclined toward much conversation. Mrs. Mullins and I checked out a collapsible wheelchair from the clinic and took him home. By ten-thirty we had him ensconced in his bed with the curtains drawn. He dropped quickly off to sleep.

Although she looked bone-tired, I saw that she was reluctant to leave him for her own bed. 'Would you like to stay in here with him?' I asked her. 'I think he'd appreciate it. And you'll know as soon as he wakes up.'

She looked grateful. 'Yes, sir,' she said. 'I think I'll just do that.'

Out of what had become habit, I checked the doors and windows, then went to my own room, where I pulled off my shoes, fell into bed, and slept.

Far-off kitchen sounds awakened me. I saw it was after two in the afternoon. I had only slept about five hours, but I felt refreshed. A shower, a shave, and clean clothes made me feel better. Downstairs, I found Mrs. Mullins pulling some fresh-baked cornbread out of the oven. 'I figured somebody would be gettin' hungry about now,' she said.

'You're a mind reader,' I said. 'How's my dad?'

'He's awake and hungry,' she said as she sliced up the corn-bread. 'I was just goin' to take him a tray.' On the big kitchen table sat a bed tray with sliced ham and a tall glass of iced tea. To it she added two slices of cornbread and a small plate of butter.

'Do you mind if I take it up to him?' I asked.

'No, sir, not at all,' she said with a smile. 'Here.' Making room on the tray, she added a separate plate and glass for me. 'Careful goin' up the stairs, especially that place at the top where the carpet has a bump.'

My father looked terrible. He was the same ghastly-looking specter who had seemed near death at the clinic, only now he was awake. I didn't comment on his appearance but set up the tray for him, plumped his pillows, and pulled up a chair by the bed for myself.

As we ate, we made small talk. It was awkward to try to eat with his left hand, he said. I asked him how he felt, and he said a little better. His arm hurt, but the pain pills were helping. I told him he was lucky to be alive, and he just nodded, chewing thoughtfully.

'Mrs Mullins is very good to you, isn't she?' The words were out of my mouth before I knew it. Just days earlier, I had felt resentment and sarcasm about this near-comical relationship. Now I felt only gratitude to her.

'Yes, she is,' he said. 'She's a very special person. I was hoping you'd like her.'

'I'm just hoping she likes me.'

'You've no need to worry about that.'

'Dad ...' Again, I surprised myself. How long, I wondered, had it been since I'd called him that?

'Dad, what happened to you last night?'

'Oh ...' He gestured with his fork. 'Just something stupid. I need to be more careful.'

'But what happened, exactly? Jerry Chitwood's wondering, and so am I.'

When he didn't answer right away, I pressed on. 'We found the broken glass in the Historical Society. The chief is going to have a talk with Olen Stringer. Is there anything we should know?'

He just looked at me, and there was such naked pain in that look, I reached over and touched his hand. I could feel the veins and sinews in it, and it was cool to the touch, like Faye McMahan's foot on that awful night. I was worried for him and had no idea why.

'There's something eating at you,' I said. 'Whatever it is, you shouldn't have to deal with it all by yourself. Tell me what it is. Please.'

I waited. Downstairs I could hear the vacuum cleaner going.

'All right,' he said finally, letting out a deep breath. 'I need to tell someone. It's going to come out, and who better than you to hear it first? But you need to promise me that you'll let me decide when it's time to tell others. Can you keep a secret? Or is that the wrong question to ask a newspaperman?'

It was the first joke he'd attempted in our conversation, and I was grateful for it. 'I'll keep this one as long as you want me to,' I said. 'Unless there's some kind of threat to your safety, in which case all bets are off.'

'Fair enough.' He gazed out the window for a long time at the pale yellow riot of leaves in our side yard. Then, without looking at me, he started talking. He talked for fifteen minutes or so, and after the first minute I realized the import of what he was saying and wished I had my reporter's notebook on my lap. But I dared not interrupt him.

'I went over there last night to confront him,' he said, nearing the end of his narrative. 'He didn't deny any of it. He couldn't, I'd done my homework too well. Not that I could prove it, you know. It's not the sort of thing that would hold up in court, but I knew and he knew. He just looked at me, blinking. And I wanted to hit him. I couldn't, of course. He's younger and stronger, and it would have been a very unequal contest. So I just marched over to the display case and raised my hand and brought it down. I wanted to destroy it. Not the idea of it, which was still worthwhile. But this particular ... *thing*, which he had made possible and which was tainted from the beginning with his lie.

228

'So …' He smiled grimly. 'So I broke the glass, my little symbolic gesture. I knew I was bleeding, but I didn't know how badly. I remember walking across the grass toward the only light I saw on the square. And just as I got there, I became very dizzy, and I had to sit down right there in the doorway.'

He lay back and closed his eyes. The reporter in me wouldn't let it rest there, however. I asked him a quick half-dozen questions, all of which he answered in his careful, scholarly way, eyes still shut. Then it was finished. I had everything.

'Thank you for telling me,' I said. I got up and took his tray. 'Would you like anything else?'

'No, thanks. I think I'll rest for a while.'

I was almost out the door when I heard him say, 'If you're in need of reading material, there's something in the cubbyhole you might find interesting.'

I took the tray downstairs and ran water over the dishes. Then I went up to my room and lay down on the bed, which I noticed Mrs. Mullins had straightened in my absence. My mind was not just racing, it was in the red zone. The story he'd told me was fantastic, but it had the weight of my father's integrity behind it, his scrupulousness and attention to detail. Some of it was based on facts, some of it was supposition, but it added up to a convincing narrative. If he believed it, I believed it.

He had suspected something for weeks. One day he began making phone calls. Because of his Civil War research, he had connections not only in the scholarly community but also in the National Park Service, which administers the battlefields. His calls led him eventually to a man named Tom Tillman, superintendent at the Shiloh National Military Park, where Olen Stringer had once been assigned. My father and Tillman knew and respected each other, and the man was willing to talk about what he knew and what he suspected. All this allowed my father to put together first a notion, then a theory, and finally a conclusion.

As I went over the story, I found it playing out in my mind like a film, full of drama and skullduggery. I saw Sonny, newly out of office, full of plans to develop the Cumberland Plateau.

There was money to be made, no question, but some of his goals were less mercenary. He learned of my father's dream of a Civil War study center and approached him, offering to help make it a reality, knowing that such a project could make his own name shine in Tennessee politics again. I saw him touring the state's most famous battlefields and museums, looking for ideas. At his side was Lem Coldsmith, his friend, banker, and cheerleader.

They visited Shiloh, drove along its green, sun-dappled vistas, walked to the monuments, the graves of thousands of those who had worn the blue and the gray. Honored by a visit from the ex-governor, Tillman assigned him an eager and knowledge-able guide, a park ranger named Stringer. On the tour, Stringer showed the ex-governor and his friend the burial sites, many of them holding hundreds of bodies in mass graves. They told him of their plans for the center, and he was impressed. Sensing that it could be great, he wanted to be a part of it.

A few days later, Lem Coldsmith returned alone for a private talk with Stringer. There was only one problem with their chosen site for the center, he told Stringer. It was far from any known battlefield. Of course, there was that local legend about the Burning, but there was no physical evidence to support it. If only we could turn up something, he said. I can't tell you how important that would be to the town, to the state. I'm sure the Governor would be very grateful. At some point in the quiet conversation, the subject of money doubtless came up.

Meanwhile, the superintendent, a competent and conscien-tious man, had been concerned about night-time theft at the park. He suspected that Stringer was helping thieves locate and dig up valuable artifacts, and sell them on the black market. Before Tillman could prove anything, however, Stringer resigned from the National Park Service. He had plans for the private sector.

Months went by, and one day some kind of vehicle – a van, maybe a truck – carrying the skeletal remains of two Confederate soldiers, along with a battered belt buckle, made the journey from Shiloh to a farm outside Pilgrim's Rest. The skeletons had been carefully selected to make sure neither bore the marks of bullet or blade. At some time and place, the bones had been exposed to fire, enough to leave some of them scorched, then lightly washed. At the farm late one night, the remains were re-interred, only to be dug up later, with full flourishes, by Olen Stringer.

The Burning was no longer just a legend. In far-off Nashville, designers and landscapers began drawing up plans for a new park at the foot of Damnation Falls.

Was Sonny behind all this? Or just his devious money man? It was entirely conceivable, I knew, for an unscrupulous aide to carry out all kinds of shenanigans while protecting his boss by keeping him in ignorance. What was it they said the President always needed? Plausible deniability. How about it, Sonny? I wondered, with echoes of Watergate in my mind. What did you know, and when did you know it?

I was tired but not sleepy. Surrendering to the idea of being totally off schedule for a while, I got up. The door to my father's room was partly open, enough that I saw him and Mrs. Mullins sleeping. She was fully dressed and lying atop the covers. I took care not to disturb them. Some day, I thought, I'll have to find out her first name.

I took my cell phone down to the kitchen, where I called Lita Ray. She was angry with me for running off on my private quest, and she became more angry when I wouldn't give the reason for my disappearance.

'You said we were in this together,' she said, sulking. 'Now you're shutting me out.'

'I'm sorry,' I said. 'Did you make that list I asked you to?'

'The guys she dated? No, I didn't,' she said. 'I was twelve or thirteen. I don't remember names.'

It was hard for me to believe she couldn't remember anyone her big sister had gone out with. I decided she was being difficult. 'All right. Never mind.' I sighed. 'I'll talk to you later.'

Remembering my promise to Blue, I dug out the number he'd given me for Clara Tackett, Dewey's widow. A moment later I was talking to her. She spoke in a small, sad voice, and I understood what Blue had meant about the effect of her husband's death. I told her a white lie about how well I'd known him, and I said I was sorry for her loss. There was not much to say after that, and we hung up.

Suddenly hungry again, I made a sandwich and poured a glass of milk and carried them into my father's study. The musty smells of paper and old bindings felt immensely comforting to me. 'I'm glad to be home,' I heard a voice say, and recognized it with some surprise as my own.

I took a seat at his big roll-top desk. As before, it was nearly buried in books, magazines, news clippings, and manuscript pages. I saw that he was well along in the fourth volume of his Civil War history, *Wilderness to Appomattox*. The cork board was mounted on the wall as before, but the spot once occupied by the artist's drawing of the study center was now empty. Shreds of paper clung to the thumbtacks where my father had ripped the drawing down.

As I ate, I recalled something he'd said to me upstairs, something about the cubbyhole. The desk was a mass of cubbyholes large and small, but one in particular held memories for me. Sometimes my father, knowing that I loved poking around in his study, would leave things for me to read, usually things he had clipped from a newspaper or magazine.

My cubbyhole was the one on the far right. What was that he had said upstairs? *If you're in need of reading material ...*

I pulled it out. It looked like a letter, several pages long, on very old paper, and it was inside an acid-free plastic envelope sealed with tape. I broke the seal and looked it over. Three pages, handwritten in faded ink, the writing strangely familiar. Turning to the last page, I looked for a signature and saw none. But I knew the writing. The letter was from Mary Hightower. Turning back to the first page, I began to read.

TWENTY-ONE

The letter was dated January 19th, 1902. *My Dearest Sally*, it began:

Your last letter reached me today and sent me direct to the writing table. It is bitter cold here, and writing by the fire warms me inside and out. At this advanced age, where I seem to have outlasted most of those near and dear to me, I treasure our long connection over the years. This winter has been hard, and I've not been well, and I begin to think – somber thought – that I may never travel far from Pilgrim's Rest ever again. Thus the importance of your words on paper to me, dear sister.

The last time I wrote, I was full of news about our little town and my small life. Today I want to speak of only one thing, your reference to 'the cloud that has hung over your town since the war.' I feel it is time to talk of it.

By now, most know the story, or hints of it – how the people of Pilgrim's Rest, stirred by the passions of that awful war, murdered more than twenty young men of the Confederacy. Our town's leaders, knowing the power of the story, spread it far and wide. Every pro-Union sympathizer in eastern Tennessee drew courage from our example, hearing how ordinary citizens could, in a moment of crisis, join the war and fight to preserve this country. People traveled here to see the blackened remnants of the barn where those soldiers took refuge. For a time, all those who lived here – my friends, my neighbors, my husband – were considered heroes.

Then the war ended, passions cooled, and the story subsided to a whisper. But it persisted. Today, with most of the participants now

233

dead, who is to say whether it is true or not?

Now, writing to you, I want to say to the cloud over our town, 'Shoo! Go away!'

Oh, Sally, no soldiers died that long-ago night!

There, I've said it.

As you may know – even though I have never spoken of it – I was there. The scene was one of pandemonium. The crowd ringed the barn, torches held high. There is something terrifying about torchlight when it illuminates hatred on the human face. Some of those present, like myself, were frozen in silence, afraid to speak up. But most raged in earnest, and I had no doubt that those unfortunates inside the barn were about to breathe their last.

Then we heard the voice of Preacher John. The crowd parted, and there he was, borne on the strong back of his grandson, who had carried him all the way from the town. John by then was old, his legs shriveled by disease, his hearing nearly gone. His pastoral duties had long since been taken over by another. The grandson let him gently to the ground and supported him while he spoke. His voice was still strong, and it carried me back to sermons I had heard him preach when I was a young girl. And I, who am now old, remember his words of that night and thrill to them.

'They are God's creatures!' he shouted. 'Who among you, even in a time of war, would kill one of God's creatures who was not harming you?

'Let the war be fought,' he cried. 'The young must fight and die on distant battlefields, and each of these boys may yet be called to that reckoning. But there will be no killing here tonight. If any man touch fire to this wood, I will strike him down myself.'

And they shrank back. Sally, you should have seen it. That old man, bent and crippled, moved them by sheer force of his will and his goodness.

He had his grandson open the barn door, and he called them out – just boys, most of them, tired and hungry and frightened. And John asked if any would donate money to the soldiers so they could buy food on their way. A few reluctantly came forward – reluctantly, I say, for John's words had banked the fires of their hatred but not quelled them.

Then John gave the soldiers his blessing, and the young men, overwhelmed with gratitude, thanked God and our mercifulness. Just before they departed, our mayor – a man adept in the ways of politics – conferred with them. He asked them not to tell the story of their encounter with the people of Pilgrim's Rest, reasoning that it would only stir up enmity against us. Although our state was part of the Confederacy, all of the highlands, you recall, were for the Union in those divided days, and he did not want us known for an act of mercy toward the secessionists. The soldiers, to a man, swore to keep the secret.

They left, and one by one the crowd headed back up toward town. Soon most of the torchlight was gone, and my husband and I stood there in the dark. He, who had called for their deaths, was still angry and confused. But I was at peace. As I stood there, I imagined I felt a little spray of mist from the falls, like the balm of everlasting love.

I still feel what we did was right, but our community was torn by it. Preacher John, no doubt afflicted by the strains of that night, died soon thereafter. And before long the town's leaders, my husband among them, decided to spread the story of blood and fire that came to define Pilgrim's Rest. Someone burned the old barn to the ground. Shamed by the mercy they had shown, our townspeople chose to describe themselves – all of us – as avengers upholding the sanctity of the Union. And the few among us who felt otherwise were cowed into silence.

Until now. With my husband long dead, I want to speak up now. To cleanse my town. Can mere words lift a dark cloud and blow it away? I can try.

Oh, the cold. And the fire dying. Do you ever—

And there it ended. Just like that. No signature. Nothing. Had Mary Hightower gotten up to feed the fire, to boil water for tea, intending to come back to her letter? Had she died while writing it? I'd never know. Unfinished, it was never mailed. Sally had never seen it.

And the cloud hung over the town still.

I carried my half-eaten sandwich and unfinished glass of milk out to the kitchen, then went upstairs to my father's room. Mrs.

Mullins had left, and he lay in the bed with his eyes closed, his bandaged arm resting on his chest. I started to back out of the doorway, but he opened his eyes and said, 'Come on in. I'm just resting.'

I took a seat by the bed. 'How are you feeling?'

'A little better. The doctor tells me I should be able to attend the groundbreaking tomorrow.'

'Where's Mrs. Mullins?'

'I believe she's out shopping.'

'Has she been checking the doors and windows every night?'

'Yes.'

He noted the look on my face. 'Did you read it?'

I nodded. 'Where did it turn up?'

'In the same bunch of estate papers that held her journal. Only I didn't know it was there for a while.'

'When did you know?'

My question hung over the room like ... well, like the cloud over the town. *What did you know, Father, and when did you know it?*

'About a week ago.'

'And that started you asking questions about Olen Stringer?'

'Of course. At first I thought he was simply the luckiest amateur around. When I found the letter, I began to suspect that he might be a good deal more than that.'

'What are you going to do with the letter?'

He regarded me for a long time. 'What do you think I should do with it?'

I started to give him the easy answer, the scholar's answer: It's an important bit of history, so it should be brought out into the daylight, not hidden in a cubbyhole somewhere. But I didn't say anything, for I knew it was complicated. There was the legend, which had grown to the size and heft of a fact. And the so-called fact was the shaky foundation on which rested the Cumberland Memorial Park and Civil War Study Center, which my father surely wanted to see built.

Pilgrim's Rest had a bloody past, so the story went. And the tourists came, and the investors followed. Would anyone be interested in a place where they *almost* burned up a barnful of soldiers? Probably not.

'If the town has to rewrite its history—'

'What will happen to the study center?' he finished for me. 'That's up to the politicians and the investors, I suppose,' he said. 'I just write books.'

All he had to do, I knew, was leave the letter in the cubbyhole. Keep Mary Hightower's secret, and Olen Stringer's, and hope that Sonny, with or without his friend the furniture salesman, found enough money to raise the buildings. And the dream shared by Sonny and my father would take shape.

It was a seductive dream. Sonny must have seduced him with it, and I suspected that when the soldiers' bodies were first found, the Historian had decided to help the dream come true by scrapping his longtime skepticism about the Burning and writing the pamphlet that gave plausibility to the legend. He didn't rewrite history, he just bent it a little.

Now I was sure he was tempted to keep the secret of the letter, all for the sake of the dream. And knowing this – after all the disdain he'd shown for my ethical lapses – made me feel, suddenly, immensely superior to him.

Then, just as suddenly, the feeling went away, replaced by sadness. I wanted him to have what he wanted, without having to sell out to get it.

As I left him, he was looking out the window. 'What's Mrs. Mullins' first name?' I asked him.

'Ruth.'

'That's a nice name.'

'She'll be glad to hear you think so.'

I headed down the hall toward my room but was interrupted by a knocking at the front door. Not a polite, neighbor-come-calling knock, the louder kind, more like a demand. Halfway down the stairs, I thought I could make out a familiar figure through the leaded-glass panes of the door. When I opened it, there she stood in her familiar greasy white coveralls, blonde ponytail flicked over one shoulder. There was no friendliness in her look.

'Good afternoon,' I said.

'I think Blue McMahan didn't drown,' she said. 'He's still alive.'

I stared at her, trying to frame an answer. I guess I shouldn't have been surprised. She was smart, and she wanted Callie's murderer like a puppy wants its favorite bone. How long did I think it would take before she –

'You shithead.'

'What?'

'You knew. Didn't you? You ought to see your face.' Her voice began rising. 'You can't fool me. Why didn't you tell me?'

'Don't yell, all right?' I gently took her arm and led her out onto the porch. 'My dad is upstairs, and he's hurt.'

We leaned back on the railing, side by side. 'It's a police thing,' I said. 'Jerry Chitwood wants it kept quiet.'

She started up again, as if she hadn't heard me, her voice lower now but still urgent. 'If he's alive, and he's hiding, there's a good chance he killed his wife—'

'That's crazy. I know Blue. He didn't kill Faye.' *At least I hope he didn't.*

'Then why's he hiding?'

'It's simple,' I said. 'He's hiding because somebody wants him dead.'

'Who?'

I looked out toward the side yard where the first of the dead leaves were beginning to carpet the lawn in russet and yellow. Then I inhaled all the crisp scents of fall down to the bottom of my lungs, like a smoker after a long time without cigarettes. Chicago never smelled like this.

'Probably the same person who killed Faye. Listen, Lita Ray—' I turned to face her, and she obligingly looked up at me, her expression still without trust. 'I think it might be the same person who killed Callie all those years ago. Blue knows something, and it's made him worth more dead than alive to somebody.'

'Then why doesn't he just—'

'Go to the police?' I laughed softly. 'I'd love to know the answer to that. But I think it has to do with his ornery personality. He hates police like the plague. He hates anybody in authority. He's the most self-reliant person I've ever known.'

'So he can tell us who killed Callie?'

'That's my theory. Don't hold me to it. But until a better one comes along—'

'Then let's find him.'

'I've tried,' I almost shouted. 'Those two days I was away? I chased his skinny ass all over Tennessee, and he stayed ahead of me every step of the way. I've lost him for now, but if there's a way to pick up the trail, I will.'

I glanced at her and saw her expression soften. I really liked her at that moment. She hadn't much education, she'd had a horrendous upbringing, but she carried something inside her that made her stand straight. I'd seen it in a lot of country people – a sense of honor that had nothing to do with book learning or possessions. Lita Ray Darnell, I decided, would be a good person to have in your corner – and with that arsenal on her wall at home, a bad one to go up against.

At that angle, with the afternoon light slanting across her face, she looked downright beautiful, if a bit scrawny. Add a few pounds to her, and the resemblance to Callie would be striking.

'How did you figure it out?' I asked. 'About Blue?'

'It was Vern,' she said, shaking her head as if still finding it hard to believe. 'He started telling me today about a man who came to visit Daddy a while ago. He doesn't really know Blue McMahan, or remember him, but I do. He described him down to the last detail. His dark suit. His long face. The way he talked. It sounded crazy to me, but I just knew it was him.'

'What did he come to see your father about?'

'Vern didn't know. They just talked for a while, and then the man left.'

I thought it over. It didn't make much sense, but then where Blue was concerned, nothing did.

She still looked concerned. 'Something wrong?' I asked.

'Naw,' she said. 'It's just … Vern wants to spend the night in Daddy's room tonight. He's never done that before. He says

Daddy wants to talk to him.'

'Nothing wrong with that, is there?'

'I guess not. He says he'll sleep on the floor. Vern can sleep anywhere. I just wonder what Daddy ...' Her voice trailed off. Then she abruptly changed the subject. 'You said your dad was hurt. What happened?'

'Just an accident. He's getting better. Says he'll be in shape for the big groundbreaking tomorrow.'

'Oh, that's right,' she said, pushing off the railing and starting down the steps. 'Big day.'

'So what do you think of all this to-do?' I asked her.

'If it brings in more business to the garage, I'm all for it.'

After dinner I called Chief Chitwood to report on my odyssey around our scenic state.

'How's your dad?' he asked.

'I think he's going to be fine after a little rest,' I said. Then, remembering something from the previous night: 'Did you have that talk with Olen Stringer?'

'Yep. He said your dad was walking around the exhibits, he heard a crash, and when he came out, there was some broken glass and your dad was gone. He cleaned up, turned out the lights, and went home.'

'Well, it's a neat story,' I said.

'Has your father added anything to it?'

Let it rest for now, I told myself. 'Not really. He said it was an accident, and I'm satisfied with that. But I called to tell you about Blue. I chased him for two days. He heard me coming, and he split for parts unknown. Now I believe he's holed up somewhere with an old friend. If he's smart, he'll never poke his nose up into the sunlight again.'

'I suppose.'

'Chief, you've known him for a long time. Did he ever have a best friend around here?'

'You're talking about a long time ago,' Chitwood said. 'I saw him with you more than anybody else. When he was in town, I mean.'

'Well, he's not with me now, so that's no help. Anybody else?'

Chitwood was silent for a moment. 'With Blue, it was usually the ladies,' he said. 'I used to think there was one in particular, but I never knew who.'

'Would it have been Callie Darnell?'

'Nope, not as far as I knew. Sorry I'm no help. Wait a minute: I'm the police. You're supposed to be helping me.'

'I know, Chief, I'm doing my best. Anything from the TBI?'

'No, Randall. They're still running their investigation on Faye, but right now all of us are a lot more concerned with security for the ceremony tomorrow.'

'Oh, sure. I understand. I'd better let you get back to it, then.'

'All right. You have a good evening, hear?'

Up in my room, I cracked the window to let in a little of the night's chill, and I burrowed deep under the covers and went to sleep. Somewhere in the night, I found myself driving across Tennessee with Lita Ray at my side. Her white coveralls were clean and pressed, and she carried a hunting rifle across her knee. 'Careful with that,' I said. 'It's not loaded,' she replied, but I knew she was lying. In the backseat rode Callie, who was humming an old tune. I couldn't bear to look at her in the rear-view mirror.

Every time we passed a hitchhiker, I slowed to see if he wore a Rotary button in his lapel. Up ahead was the bridge above Damnation Falls, where Sonny waited for me. I stopped the car, knowing there was something else at the bridge that I did not want to see.

Sitting there, I looked past Lita Ray out into a field and saw Pike Darnell and his demented son seated on chairs facing each other, hands clasped. Vern's head was bowed, and his father's lips moved, but I didn't think he was praying.

TWENTY-TWO

It was noontime, and more than two hundred of us sat on folding chairs lined up neatly before a brightly decorated speaker's platform. We were in Farmer Burch's former cornfield, the corn stalks gone and the ground plowed, where a special-events company summoned all the way from Chattanooga had laid out a half-acre or so of bright green artificial turf to mimic the future lawn of the Cumberland Memorial Park and Civil War Study Center.

The speaker's platform was swathed in red, white, and blue bunting, alternating the Stars and Stripes with the Confederate battle flag. A curious pairing, I thought, but then there was nothing quite like the proposed study center either, so why not?

Behind the lectern up on the platform sat all the notables involved. In the front row were Sonny and Tish and the mayor of Pilgrim's Rest, who was also the town druggist, a man I remembered from high school. Nearby sat Olen Stringer, natty in his Historical Society khakis; the local Baptist minister, who had said words over Faye; and my father. He and Stringer, I noted, sat at opposite ends of the row.

In the back row sat the town council, along with Lem Coldsmith and the other officers of the Outerbridge Group.

It was a little like a Fourth of July picnic, but on a grander scale. The high school band, positioned to the right of the platform, was playing patriotic numbers interspersed with the kind of school fight songs usually played at ball games. I guessed that their repertoire of Civil War-era music was limited. We had just been treated to a drill team consisting of students wearing Confederate uniforms and carrying musket replicas.

Behind the crowd sat a paramedics' van, and not far away a catering firm, also from Chattanooga, had set up giant grills that were beginning to give off the irresistible odors of barbecued ribs and chicken.

And right in front of the speaker's platform a shiny, stainless-steel shovel stood propped against an ornamental stand, ready to turn the first official hunk of dirt.

Serving as a backdrop, against an autumn sky of the deepest blue, was Damnation Falls, its waters falling in slow motion, silent against all the bustle, noise, and music of the big event.

Gathered to record all this – because in the information age, nothing really happens today unless it's recorded – were TV camera crews from stations in Chattanooga and Nashville. Some of the big-city papers had sent reporters and photographers.

Charlene and I sat near the front just off the center aisle. She was busy scanning the crowd and jotting occasional lines in her notebook. The Monday edition of the *Cumberland Call* was going to cover this thing like the morning dew.

A few rows back on the opposite side of the aisle, I spotted Lita Ray, nicely dressed for a change in jacket, sweater and slacks, sitting with Pearl, the waitress from Ida's. On the other side of the crowd I saw Jerry Chitwood, belly straining at his jacket, conferring with the young deputy who had gone with us to the Historical Society. It was only the night before last, but it seemed a long time ago.

My eyes returned to the falls, framed at the top of the bluff in all the colors of autumn, almost as if fire and water could exist there side by side. I had learned some important things from Mary Hightower's unfinished letter. One was the location of the barn. It was here, all right, here in this field. Olen Stringer's hunch had been right. That crumbling stone foundation was the place. How did I know? Mary's clues were subtle, but I noticed two: one was that she referred to the townspeople heading 'back up toward the town.' They must have been down here below the bluff. The other was that she imagined feeling the mist from the falls, which would have been visible from the spot where the barn once stood.

Without knowing it, whoever killed Callie had picked a spot ripe with history. How was he to know that within twenty years shovels would begin tearing up the ground, and the earth would give her up?

How about it, buddy? I thought. Are you still around here somewhere? Am I getting close to you? My gaze swept over the notables and came to rest on Sonny, broad-shouldered and resplendent in a well-tailored dark suit. I'd known him since we were children. I remembered how he had tried to keep me busy with his book and how gruff he'd been when I told him I was sniffing after Callie's killer. And I was ashamed to admit that I couldn't strike him off the list of suspects.

The band wrapped things up with a flourish and the crowd, many of them parents, clapped and hooted approval. Up to the lectern stepped the mayor, whose main job was to introduce Stuart McMahan, Pilgrim's Rest's favorite son. Moving to the microphone, Sonny got a warm welcome. This wasn't his big speech, he said with a grin. He would subject us to that ordeal in a few minutes. Right now he wanted to introduce a man who was uniquely qualified to give us a historical perspective on the meaning of today's event – teacher, Pulitzer Prize-winning historian, and longtime resident of this town, Dr. Forrest Wilkes.

Looking pale, his right arm held in a sling, my father walked almost delicately to the lectern carrying a few sheets of paper. He placed the papers in front of him, looked at them for a while, then, with some difficulty, folded them and put them into his side jacket pocket. He looked out over the crowd gravely.

'This is a great thing we have planned for this place,' he said in measured tones, his amplified classroom voice carrying clearly over the field. 'The institution that will rise here will celebrate knowledge and the search for it, and it will acknowledge the importance of the greatest conflict ever fought on the soil of this nation. The war that raged through Tennessee and many other states tore at the fabric of our country and almost ripped it apart. But the country held. The Cumberland Memorial Park and Civil War Study Center, among other things, will celebrate the strength of the nation that held together without breaking all those years ago.

'It will also celebrate the truth, for history – to which I have devoted my life – is nothing more than a search for the truth. For some time, those of us who live here have believed that soldiers died here on this spot during the Civil War. Such an event, we thought, helped secure a place for us in the history of that war. I contributed to that belief by writing an essay describing the event. It was, I now regret to say, an event that never took place.'

The crowd began to stir and whisper. *Here it comes*, I thought.

'The search for truth is an imperfect thing, for we who conduct it are imperfect,' he went on. 'It is only recently that documentary evidence has emerged to cast serious doubt on that example of Pilgrim's Rest folklore known as the Burning.'

The whispers grew to mutters. I glanced at Sonny, who was watching my father with an intent and focused expression, alert as a bird dog to a movement in the bushes. He must have known at that moment that Forrest Wilkes was unveiling a surprise for him, but he gave nothing away.

'And we need to address the subject of the soldiers found here on this spot and buried on our town square,' he said. 'More evidence has emerged to suggest beyond any doubt that those unfortunate young men did not die here in this field in the year 1863, but at the battle of Shiloh a year earlier.'

'What the hell?' came clearly from one of the rows behind me. Olen Stringer sat absolutely still, his eyes on his lap.

'How they wound up here is a proper subject for investigation – for another time. Even more pressing, though, is this: After their awful deaths and their journeys since then, these two young men deserve to rest,' my father said. 'But if history is to be served, they must go on one more journey, this time back to the place where they fell. They deserve it, and we owe it to them.'

He stopped, looking exhausted, and I thought he was finished. But he was gathering strength for his last words.

'I hope these buildings rise here and that they become a great center of study,' he said. 'But they must be founded on the truth, not on a lie. And the truth is this: That act of violence that many of us thought defined us as a town never occurred. In its place a great act of kindness took place, showing that human mercy can take root and flourish even amid war. Maybe that is an even better foundation on which to build.'

He left the lectern and, walking unsteadily, returned to his seat. I can't recall ever admiring him as much as I did at that moment. The audience sat stunned by his words, and no one thought to applaud until Sonny, his alert expression now faded into something more somber, began clapping politely. Then the crowd joined in, but uncertainly, and the sound quickly died.

'Thank you, Dr. Wilkes,' he said, taking my father's place at the microphone. Then, loosening his jacket, he swept his arms wide and took in all the crowd and the setting. 'Isn't this a beautiful day?' It was a practiced applause line, and the crowd responded politely.

'I've been dreaming of this day for a long time,' he announced, and his expression began to loosen up a bit as the practiced public speaker took over. 'Back when I was governor, I began thinking of what I could do for the town that raised me, for the state that nurtured me ...' And he was off and running.

This guy is a politician down to his bones, I thought. My father's speech had no doubt rocked him back on his heels, and his way of dealing with it was to act as if it had not happened. Sonny was going to orchestrate this event no matter what curves might be thrown at him. And he was going to do it in his usual masterful way.

I had enormous respect for his political skills. But a measure of contempt for the man.

I settled back, only half listening, as Sonny took us through the planning and development of the center, the fund-raising, the search for talent to staff it. Since he made no mention of my father, I guessed that the invitation to be director of the center had suddenly been withdrawn.

At somewhere around the midpoint of his speech, when the crowd was laughing appreciatively at one of his self-denigrating jokes, I heard something behind me. It was a kind of ripple through the crowd, a combination of muttering and movement. Curious, I turned around, as several of us were doing, and saw Vern Darnell coming down the center aisle.

He was dressed as I had seen him that night at Possum's, in a neatly pressed denim shirt and jeans. His face suggested the look of a child wrestling with a particularly challenging puzzle. As he passed me, I saw the reason for the crowd's reaction. His right hand hung down at his side, and it held a gun.

A chill passed over me, and I blinked to clear my vision, to verify what I'd seen. I remember clutching at Charlene.

At that moment, several things happened at once. I heard Lita Ray's high-pitched '*Vern!*' and saw her lunging down the aisle after him. But she was too far away to stop him.

Up on the platform, Sonny saw him coming, and his expression went from puzzlement to wide-eyed shock as he spotted the handgun.

Vern's arm came up, and he began shooting.

I shouted something, grabbed Charlene, and thrust her down between the rows of seats with all my strength. She yelled in pain.

Vern squeezed off one, two, three ... I lost count. I saw Sonny duck behind the lectern, saw wood chips fly, heard a woman scream from somewhere up there. Tish.

Violent movement all over the stage as people flung themselves in all directions, toppling chairs. I saw the young deputy, his face a cartoon of fright, pull his gun and extend it in Vern's direction. But the barrel wavered, and he didn't fire.

Then, from off to the side, a figure appeared on the stage, its arm also extended. It was Kenneth Lively. He began firing down on Vern, a withering barrage of semi-automatic rounds, a deafening fusillade. Vern's body jumped and twitched as each slug hit him. Then he collapsed, as if a puppeteer had cut his strings.

Lita Ray, her voice tuned to an animalistic screech, flung herself on her brother's bloodied back.

And it was over.

But not really. The horror now began to sink in.

The crowd – mob, really – surged in all directions, voices raised in weeping or cries of alarm. Parents screamed for their children. Jerry Chitwood hollered commands to both his deputies, and I saw that all three men had their weapons out, barrels up, as they looked around frantically for more threats.

Charlene fought her way up from the ground past my protective arms. She needed to get to work. 'Who was hit?' she demanded.

'Vern Darnell is shot to pieces,' I said, as we made our way through the crowd and a jumble of chairs toward the stage. 'I don't know about the rest.'

We passed Lita Ray, prostrate over her brother's body. Sounds came from her but no words. Chitwood knelt by her and yanked the gun from Vern's hand. It was a large-caliber revolver with a stainless-steel finish, and I thought I recognized it as one of the weapons that had hung on Lita Ray's living room wall. I remembered her disdainful words: *Everybody knows my brothers got no business with guns.*

Atop the platform, I saw Kenneth Lively bend over and place his now-empty weapon on the planks, then step away from it and wait for the police. A few feet away, Sonny stood up from behind the shield of the lectern, shook himself like a man coming out of the night sweats, and looked around. 'Where's—'

Then he saw the little knot of people gathered around the spot where his wife had been sitting.

'Tish!' He clawed past them, flinging the mayor to one side. I caught sight of her lying face-up, her skirt twisted, her left leg bloody above the knee. 'We need a doctor up here!' I turned toward the paramedics' van and saw two blue-shirted men carrying bags and headed this way at a run.

There was more. I heard a commotion behind the platform. Charlene and I hurried around to the back, where some of the dignitaries had jumped or fallen along with some of their chairs. Two of the town councilmen knelt beside a body. As we moved nearer, I recognized Lem Coldsmith flat on his back, looking up at the deep blue sky. He had apparently taken one of the big slugs in his throat, and his entire neck was a raw and bloody mess. As I stood over him, I looked down at his eyes. They saw nothing.

My father stood nearby, looking dazed. 'Are you all right?' I called out to him. He managed a weak smile. Just then Mrs. Mullins came over and quietly took his arm. 'Can you take him home?' I asked. She nodded.

'Jesus,' I said under my breath, turning to Charlene, but she didn't hear me. She was on her cell phone, talking urgently. After a moment, she lowered the phone and looked at me.

'You want in on this?' she asked. 'I need all the help I can get.'

It took me a second to understand. I was being asked to transition from shell-shocked civilian to working journalist.

'You name it,' I said.

'Here.' She handed me the phone. 'We're putting out an extra tonight. I'll start gathering the main story' – she pulled out her notebook again – 'You do the color piece. You're on with Teddy Brown, who's my new city editor, and he'll take it from you. He's just out of school, and he's never handled anything like this, but he catches on fast.'

'Teddy? This is Randall Wilkes. I'll be feeding you color. Have you ever done rewrite?'

'No, sir.'

'You don't have to call me sir. Where I come from, reporters are young and eager, and rewrite men are grizzled and cranky. I haven't had time to take notes, so I'm just going to tell you what I see. It'll be spotty, but you'll weave it into what they like to call a seamless narrative. All right?'

'Yes, sir.'

'All right.' I climbed the stairs up to the platform, found a corner away from people, and looked around. 'The gunman, Vern Darnell, lay face-down in a kind of crouching position, his entire upper back and torso bloodied,' I said, trying not to speak too fast. I heard him begin typing immediately. 'His sister, Lita Ray Darnell, lay draped over his body, crying ...' At that moment, Jerry Chitwood pulled her to her feet, gently but firmly. I added that detail to my narrative.

'Get her out of here, dammit!' Sonny yelled at the two paramedics, who now had a stretcher and were easing Tish onto it. He followed them as they carried her down the stairs and headed toward the ambulance.

'Former Governor McMahan tended to his wife, Leticia, who was apparently wounded in the leg by a stray shot. As the only non-fatality, she was the first casualty to be carried away from the scene. Behind the speaker's platform lay the body of Lem Coldsmith, one of the investors in the Civil War center, who was hit by another stray shot, this one fatal.

'I'm going to back up now,' I said to Teddy.

'All right.' I could hear his fingers flying over the keyboard.

'In seconds, the scene shifted from one of celebration to one of shock and horror,' I said. 'Vern Darnell walked down the center aisle in the middle of the former governor's speech, and it registered with some in the crowd that he was carrying a pistol. As he opened fire, his sister came running up behind him, calling out, but she was too late—'

'Who was he shooting at?' Teddy asked. 'Could you tell?'

I hesitated. Good question. 'His shots appeared to be aimed at McMahan. At least one of the slugs struck the speaker's lectern. Others apparently went wild.'

'Can you give me more of the scene?' he asked. 'More of the overall scene?'

'Teddy, you're my kind of rewrite man. Hang on.' And a few seconds later I was giving him all of it – the look of the sky and the waterfall, the sound of the high school band, the smell of barbecue grilling. Then the bark of gunfire, the screams, the metallic sound of toppling chairs. I looked around as I spoke, at the scene of carnage. I knew that before long the human side of me would be worried about Tish, would ponder the meaning of the two deaths, if meaning was there to be found. And, most important, would seek to learn what had propelled Vern Darnell – good-natured, simple-minded Vern Darnell – on his grisly mission. I already had an idea.

But for now, the newspaperman in me was simply happy to be back at work.

TWENTY-THREE

I followed Charlene to the *Call* newsroom and stayed as she put together the extra edition. At her request, I edited her main story and Teddy Brown's color piece, smoothing out a line here, squirting in a fresh detail there. When the four-page extra was mostly pasted up under the banner headline *2 Killed in Shootout at Civic Event*, I left. I hadn't expected to ever have another taste of this ink-stained business again, and I was grateful for this one.

I drove straight to the clinic, where a small army of people and vehicles had gathered. The media, it seemed, had been alerted and had converged once again on our town. If anything, this was even bigger than the murder of the mother of an ex-governor. Elbowing past a scrum of TV and print reporters at the door, I found more inside, then came up against a barrier of stony-faced state troopers blocking access to the emergency rooms.

But I caught the eye of Jerry Chitwood down the hall, heard him say, 'He's the Governor's friend,' and was allowed through. The first enclosure I passed held two gurneys, each bearing a zipped-up body bag.

All the activity was focused on the next enclosure. Just outside stood Allard Timms of the Tennessee Bureau of Investigation, deep in conversation with Chitwood. Standing quietly nearby was Kenneth Lively. Inside I spotted Sonny looming over both of the clinic's doctors. Tish lay in the bed, her face pale and sweaty under one of those silly-looking surgical caps.

Sonny looked up, saw me, motioned me in. I gripped his shoulder, then moved to the other side of the bed, where I took Tish's hand, careful not to disturb the IV stuck in her arm.

She recognized me and smiled, but her look was vague, and I knew she was on something. 'Oh, Randall,' she whispered. 'I'll never be able to wear shorts again.'

I looked down and saw a dressing just above the knee. Her entire thigh was bruised and swollen.

'Sure you will,' I said. 'You'll be one of those mysterious ladies with a mysterious scar, like in the spy movies.' I was babbling, but she seemed to appreciate it.

'You're sweet,' she said in a vague voice. Then: 'For just a second, I was sure Sonny was dead. Thank God for Kenneth.'

'Yes,' I said. 'Well, that's what cops are trained to do, isn't it?'

'But he never shot anybody before. I asked him once. Never in all those years. Isn't that funny?' Her eyes lost focus under a surge of painkiller.

Sonny summoned me around to him. 'Bullet plowed all the way up her thigh and chipped the hip bone,' he said in a kind of growl. 'We're going to put her in the ambulance and move her to a real hospital right now. I know the chief of surgery at Parkridge in Chattanooga. He's standing by.'

I had a sudden thought. 'Didn't you say Lem Coldsmith flew here the other day? Where's his plane?'

He nodded, and his face brightened as he got my meaning.

'It's a helicopter, and it's parked about a mile from here.' He called Kenneth Lively in. 'Get hold of Lem's 'copter pilot, and tell him to warm up. He's flying my wife to a hospital. And I'm going along.' Lively pulled out his phone and began punching numbers.

Allard Timms had overheard and stepped in from the hallway. 'Your man'll have to stay, Governor. You understand.'

Sonny nodded. Although Lively's action was what the cops would call a righteous shooting, he no longer carried a badge. There would be questions and paperwork and some kind of inquiry.

During my drive to the clinic, as I went through the awkward

253

transition from working journalist to concerned citizen, thoughts had been taking shape in my head. I needed to put them into words before Sonny got away.

'Can I talk to you before you leave?' I asked him. 'And the chief and Mr. Timms too.' He looked at Tish and back at me, and I could feel his impatience to get going. 'It's important,' I said.

A minute later we had assembled in a small office belonging to one of the doctors. Sonny sat behind the desk, the rest of us stood.

'Do you have any ideas why Vern Darnell went after the Governor?' I asked the two lawmen.

Timms spoke for the two of them. 'Not yet,' he said tersely. 'We've got men out—'

'Let me just tell you a couple of things I've learned, and then I'll get out of your way,' I said. 'First, I'm pretty sure the gun he used came from his sister Lita Ray's place. She's got a small arsenal on her living room wall. Where is she, by the way?'

'Down the hall,' Chitwood said. 'I've got a deputy watching her. She's all worked up. Are you saying she might have—'

'No, I don't think she had anything to do with this. For that, I think you need to have a talk with her father.'

'Pike?' Chitwood looked surprised. I liked him, and I considered him a decent man, but I was beginning to think he was missing signals.

'Yes, sir.' I turned to Timms. 'He's staying at one of those assisted-living places outside town called Restful Acres. Pike Darnell is crazy and full of hate, and I personally think he may have killed his own daughter twenty years ago—'

In response to Chitwood's expression of surprise, I added, 'He molested her when she was a girl, and she hated him for it. Lita Ray knows about it. She can tell you.'

I caught a wary look from Sonny. I'm sure he was wondering if his connection with Callie would have to come out. I wanted to reassure him, but I couldn't. I simply didn't know what could stay hidden and what could not.

'I don't know what ideas he put into his son's head,' I went on, 'but I know that Vern spent the night in his room last night so his father could talk to him. You might want to look him up.'

Timms nodded, making notes in a small notebook.

'There's a character named Briggs who's staying there. Says he's a lumberjack on disability. I think he's running some kind of medical scam, but that's irrelevant right now. He may have overheard something between Vern and his father, so ...'

'I'll have a word with him,' Timms said. He looked up from his notebook. 'I hear you've been chasing Blue McMahan.'

'That's right.'

'And?'

'I haven't found him.'

'The chief here tells me you've got a theory about all this.'

'Well ... yes. It's a little complicated.' I paused for a second, pulling it all together. 'Because of something Faye McMahan told me before she was killed, I think Blue either knows who killed Callie Darnell or has a pretty good idea. Since then, it looks like someone's been trying to kill off Blue and most of his relatives—'

'Why?' Sonny broke in, and I turned to him. His face was full of hurt and rage. 'Why kill my mother? Why try to kill me and Leticia today? How does that make any sense?'

'One reason could be that Pike just hates your entire family, but that seems a little farfetched,' I said. 'I've been working on the notion that the killer was trying to draw Blue out into the open. When Faye was killed, it brought Blue back to Pilgrim's Rest for her funeral, and it almost got him sliced open in a motel room. He went on the run again, and today Vern tried to kill you. As for Leticia, I think she just took a bullet meant for you. The idea was to bring Blue up to the surface again.'

'Well, that makes no sense at all,' Sonny said heatedly. 'Vern Darnell just committed suicide today. He must have known it would come to that.'

'He was simple-minded, Sonny,' I said as gently as I could. 'Maybe he knew, and maybe he didn't.'

'You're saying his father might have sent him to do that,'

Timms said. 'Do you think he sent him to kill Mrs. McMahan too, and her husband at the motel?'

'I don't know,' I said. 'It's a theory. One thing I do know, though: Pike Darnell is a sick, sorry human being. I'm not a policeman, but I sure think you should have a talk with him.'

Timms nodded, closed his notebook, and left the room. I let out a deep breath, staring at Sonny as he stared back. I believed what I'd just told them about Pike Darnell. I believed that Blue was the intended target all along. But deep down, there was still room for a sliver of doubt. I felt the sliver working at my innards, pricking them, telling me not to be too hasty, to look not just at the father but also at the son.

Could Sonny have been the target all along? I wondered. Were all the other killings just a way of clearing the path to him? And if he were the target, was it because of something he knew – or something he had done?

Sonny and I held each other's gaze, and I knew each of us was trying to read the other's thoughts. As the doctor stuck his head in, I blinked first. 'We're ready to move your wife, Governor.'

'All right.' Sonny heaved himself out of the chair and punched my shoulder lightly as he went by. 'See you.'

'I don't think Blue ever killed anybody,' I said.

He stopped, shrugged, and went on.

And then I remembered Tulsa Jenkins' story about St. Louis.

I walked toward the front desk until I spotted Lita Ray in one of the intake rooms. She was sitting on the examination couch, ankles crossed, swinging her legs like a kid. But it was not a kid's expression she wore. She was chewing gum at double-time, and her eyes darted around the room like those of a trapped animal.

The young deputy stood watch nearby, eyes on the floor. He seemed to wear his shame like a soldier's heavy backpack, and I remembered the way his gun hand had wavered when he pointed it at Vern. I wanted to reassure him, say to him that no man knows if he's capable of killing until the moment arrives. But I didn't want to make it worse by speaking.

'Hi,' I said to Lita Ray.

'Hi,' she answered around the gum. I noticed that she wore her Grand Ole Opry jacket, the front flecked with her brother's blood.

'I'm sorry,' I said. 'I'm very sorry about Vern. I don't think he's to blame.'

She gave me a quick look from under lowered brows, then looked away. 'There's a hole in his head,' she said with no inflection. 'I could see inside there.'

'Are you all right?' Stupid question, I thought.

Five or six slow nods in time with the chewing.

'Lita Ray, do you know what your father said to Vern last night?'

She shook her head.

'But you can guess, can't you? I think Pike sent his son out on a mission to kill Sonny, like some kind of suicide bomber. He can't have loved him very much if he did that.'

The deputy shuffled his feet. Lita Ray made no response, just kept chewing as if she needed gum for fuel.

'I've just told Jerry Chitwood and the Governor what I think, so I might as well tell you too,' I said, 'I think your father killed Callie. I think she hated him for what he did to her, and maybe she threatened to turn him in, and he killed her. And I think Blue McMahan found out about it somehow – maybe just recently – and Pike's been trying to find him and kill him ever since. And when Blue went into hiding, Pike sent Vern out to kill enough of Blue's relatives to smoke him out.'

She looked up at me, her brow furrowed in thought. 'So how would Daddy handle Blue now, with Vern dead?'

'I don't know. Maybe he'd send you out to do it.'

That got the first laugh out of her, a low, soft one.

'All right, I'm kidding. I honestly don't know. Your father's crazy, all right? All he does is hate. He's responsible for a lot of death and sorrow. The police are going to be asking you about him, and anything you can—'

'Darnells take care of their own business,' she muttered. 'We don't need the police.'

'What the hell does that mean?'

But before I could get any more out of her, Allard Timms stuck his head in and demanded some time with her. I left, feeling uneasy.

I passed Kenneth Lively in the hallway, leaning against the wall, head down. His posture reminded me of the deputy's, and for a moment I was struck by their similarities. The deputy had been unable to kill and was shamed. Lively had killed and was ... what? Shamed? Proud? Never having killed anyone, I had no idea what was going on in his mind. One thing, though: when he saved Sonny's life, he wiped out all our schoolyard enmity. I walked over to him.

'Thank you,' I said. 'I'm glad you were there.'

He just nodded without looking up.

I moved on. As I passed the cubicle with the body bags, I saw Jerry Chitwood standing over one. I stepped inside the enclosure. The bag had been unzipped a few inches, enough to reveal Vern's face. The grisliness was hidden; there were no marks or blood visible. The eyes were closed, and the face looked thoughtful and serene, even intelligent.

'He's about forty years old,' Chitwood said. 'Did you know that?'

'I probably did, but I forgot,' I said. 'He acted a lot younger.'

'Once when he was nineteen or twenty, I caught him and some other boys with some fruit they'd stolen off a roadside stand,' Chitwood said. 'It wasn't much, and the farmer who ran the stand was the understanding sort, so I gave 'em a lecture and sent 'em home. I found out later that Vern went back to the farmer and said since he couldn't return the fruit, he'd be glad to work off the price. And he did, for the next two weekends.'

'Doesn't sound like somebody who'd slice you up with a gut hook, does he?'

'No.'

'Somebody fucked with his head, chief. Go see his father.'

'I will.'

'You know, Lita Ray told me her brothers had no business

with guns. She was right. I think she's the only sane one in the family. If that other brother, the one in prison, is anything like his father—'

Chitwood was looking at me strangely. 'What's wrong?' I asked.

'Nothing,' he said. 'I was just thinking about the other brother. Wingo'

'What about him?'

'Well, I haven't seen him in a coon's age – and probably won't ever see him again, and that suits me just fine – but I can tell you he's the spittin' image of his old man, that's all.'

'Just what we need in this world,' I said. 'Another Pike Darnell. If somebody had put the father away years ago, like they did the son, we'd have been spared a lot.'

Looking like he had something on his mind, the chief zipped up the bag. 'Got to get back to work.'

At home, I found my father and Mrs. Mullins having a quiet supper at the kitchen table. She offered me a bowl of soup and a pulled pork sandwich. Realizing that I was in equal parts exhausted and famished, I accepted gratefully.

My father looked like a man on the edge of collapse. 'Why don't you get to bed early?' I suggested.

'I think I will,' he said. 'It's been quite a day, hasn't it?'

I told him about my visit to the clinic. 'Does this mean it's over?' he asked. 'All the fear?'

'I think so,' I said slowly. 'Or at least it will be when they put Pike Darnell away someplace where he can't spread any more of his poison.'

Then I remembered the rest of the day's events, particularly my father's words as he addressed the crowd below the falls.

'Don't let me get too sticky here,' I said, 'but I want you to know I'm very proud of you. For what you said. It took a lot of courage.'

He brushed the thought away lightly with his bandaged hand. 'I just told the truth,' he said simply. 'It was one of those times when only the truth would do.'

'So, uh ...' I didn't quite know how to ask it. 'Is the center—'

'Is it dead? It just might be. I suppose we won't know for a while. It's out of our hands now. We have to let the politicians and the money managers decide.'

'Lem Coldsmith was the prime money manager on this project.'

He nodded. 'I know, and now that he's gone it may be that none of those buildings will rise on that beautiful spot. And with so much blood staining that piece of ground, maybe it's all for the best.' He chuckled. 'You know I've been teaching a few classes at your alma mater, and I've learned a new expression from my students: "It is what it is." That seems very apropos here.'

'What about Olen Stringer?' I asked, remembering that he had never returned my phone call.

'I don't know, and I don't care right now,' my father said with an elaborate yawn. 'I hear he's already left town. I say good riddance. If the law wants to go after him, I'll certainly help, but I've a more important concern.'

'The dead soldiers?'

He nodded. 'The dead soldiers. Getting them home.'

We all turned in early that night. But before we did, I went around the house checking doors and windows. My paranoia, I knew, was probably due to the stress of the day.

But it didn't feel over.

I tossed for a long time, slept uneasily, and awoke before first light to listen to the breeze move magnolia leaves against my window screen in a gentle scraping motion, like skeletal fingers begging for my attention.

My mind was racing like Lita Ray's Mustang V-8. I remembered the sight of Faye dead and Blue resurrected. I remembered sitting on the sloping porch of the moonshiner's cabin with Blue all those years ago, listening to the sound of Uncle Tim Tyrell's storyteller voice. I thought about Blue hitting the road just ahead of me at Bigger's Cove but stopping at a liquor store on his way out of town.

I thought about other things – details, mostly – things that had made little sense to me at the time, but were beginning to make sense now.

Abruptly I threw off the covers, got out of bed, and got dressed as quickly as I could. I thought I knew where I could find Blue.

TWENTY-FOUR

I passed the house as quietly as I could – although it's hard to come in on little cat feet when you're driving on gravel – then found a narrow turnoff where I parked the car, a few dozen yards off the road so it would be harder to spot. From there I walked back to the house. I had a flashlight in my pocket but didn't want to use it until it was necessary.

All looked quiet. It was that moment of dawn when things just begin to separate themselves from the dark, a beautiful time and a lonely one, but a good time to be out and about if you want to surprise someone. A light rain had fallen during the night, and the ground and dead leaves underfoot were soft enough not to advertise my passing.

I saw no vehicles in the dirt driveway or the yard. The warped floorboards of the porch creaked as I approached the front door, but no one stirred or called out. The door was unlocked, a fact that stunned me until I remembered that I was in the country, where most people are honest. I went inside and looked around the small house, which didn't take long. Then I went outside and looked around the back.

I should have felt antsy, but for some reason I found myself blessed with limitless patience that gray, misty morning. So I just had a seat on the front porch rocker and waited, rocking and thinking, as the day took shape.

After roughly an hour of my newfound patience, I heard somebody coming up the road. A Dodge pickup pulled into the driveway, and Sis Lawlor got out.

She looked mildly surprised to see me. 'Hello, hon,' she said.
'Hello, Sis.'

She carried a tall grocery bag stuffed with what looked like clothing and set it down by the front door, then took a seat in the rocker next to me. 'You come all the way out here to see me this early?'

'Yes, ma'am. I came to ask you a few things, if you don't mind.'

'Not at all.'

'I took the liberty of going inside and looking around,' I said. 'I know it's not polite, but ...' I shrugged.

'Uh-huh?'

'I saw a bunch of bread crumbs and a jar of mustard and some wax paper on the kitchen counter,' I began. 'What with all that, plus the ham in the fridge with most of the meat sliced off, looks to me like you've been putting together quite a picnic.'

She laughed lightly. 'Well, you'd be right there, I suppose.'

'I had a look at your spring house,' I went on. 'It's a real relic from the old days, isn't it? You'd told me it was covered with poison ivy and cobwebs, but I couldn't find any back there. Just a neat little place made of stone with a freshly swept floor. I wonder if you wanted to keep me out of there because you were getting it ready for a visitor. And ... oh, yeah. There's a Ford truck parked behind your house, and I don't think it's yours.'

I glanced sideways. Her expression had gone somber, and she was waiting for what she suspected must be coming.

'I remembered a lot of things this morning. You know how your mind just drifts when you first wake up, and sometimes you're able to make connections you didn't even see before. I remembered us talking about how Blue McMahan used to chase all the ladies, and not long before that, Walter Howard had told me that there was a time when you were one of the great beauties of this county.'

'Well, that was very kind of him,' she said, sounding as if she took no pleasure in the compliment.

'And the sound of your voice when you talked about how women were drawn to him. "There was a time ..." you said, and you didn't finish the thought, but you didn't really have to. Just a few days ago I was chasing Blue all over the state of Tennessee, and I never caught up with him. The last person to see him told me he took off like a scared jackrabbit, headed for points unknown, but she said he took the trouble to stop at a liquor store on his way out. I noticed an unopened bottle of Southern Comfort in the cabinet over your sink. It's not the one I brought you.'

'Randall, you're a smart young man,' she said, shaking her head.

'Did you put him up in the spring house?'

'Yep. Until we decided it wasn't a good enough hiding place.'

'Are those his clothes?' I asked, looking over at the paper bag.

'Uh-huh,' she said with a nod. 'I'm washing 'em for him.' She pronounced it *warshing*, a word that took me back years.

'And you took him food.'

'Sure I did. He likes my sandwiches. My potato salad too.'

'Are you going to tell me where he is?'

'Oh, shoot.' She shook her head in what looked like a mixture of stubbornness and frustration. 'There's people after him.'

'Not any more, Sis.' I leaned toward her and spoke urgently. 'Pike Darnell and his son Vern were after him, but it's over. You heard about what happened below the falls yesterday?'

'Uh-huh.'

'Well, what does Blue have to say about it?'

'I haven't had a chance to tell him yet. He's sick.'

'What?' I remembered the sound of his coughing on the phone. 'How bad is it?'

'It's not good. But he won't let me—'

'Now listen,' I said, putting my hand on her arm. 'He needs a doctor, and if he's worried about his safety, we'll get the police—'

'No police,' she said.

'You don't want him to die, do you?'

She drew herself up in her chair. For just a second, behind the old woman with the rugged features, I glimpsed one of the great beauties of the county. ''Course I don't. And I'm not gonna let him.'

'Then take me to see him.'

We got in my car, and I followed her directions. I noted with some surprise that she was directing me through the town and out to the Colony. It was broad daylight when I pulled up in front of the old hotel out on the bluff. Over the veranda, the hand-carved wooden sign saying *Redemption House* had partially slipped its moorings and was dangling from a single hook.

'Better park around back, hon,' Sis said to me.

I did so and pulled into the grassy area shielded by the two rear wings of the hotel, where my car would be all but invisible. She led me to one of the back doors, where she and Blue had gained entry. The door was unlocked, but I saw no sign that it had been forced.

'Neat job, Sis,' I said admiringly.

'That was him,' she replied. 'Even when he ain't feeling good, he—'

'I know,' I said. 'He still remembers all his old tricks.'

I followed her down a dark corridor and into the kitchen, where I tried to turn on the lights but failed. 'Electricity's off,' she said, 'but we don't want to attract attention anyway, so I brought candles.'

I pulled out my flashlight and turned it on so we could cross the kitchen.

'I tried to put him into one of the rooms,' she went on, 'but he felt closed in. So I brought him a mattress, and we set him up in here.' She indicated for me to go through the big swinging doors that led to the dining room.

It was hard to see in there at first, with the tall windows shuttered, but a ray of pale light shone down from a small skylight, its glass panes encrusted with years of grime. I switched on my flashlight and quickly found Blue lying on a mattress in front of the dead fireplace, eyes closed. When he heard me approach, he opened his eyes.

'Hello, Little Bit.'

265

'Don't give me that Little Bit stuff. I'm bigger than you are.'

'Hello, there, Randall. Don't shine that in my eyes, okay?'

I turned off the flashlight and found that I could see fairly well. The dining room was as big as I remembered, and it looked even larger now that the long communal tables and chairs had all been folded up and stacked against one wall. The high, peaked ceiling had rough beams running across it.

'I'm mad as hell at you,' I said to Blue.

He just nodded. He badly needed a shave and was covered with several blankets that Sis had apparently fetched for him. His arms lay atop the covers, and he appeared to be wearing a brand new pair of pajamas. His dark suit and tie hung on the back of a nearby chair.

An array of unlit candles on saucers were lined up alongside his bed like little white soldiers, and a few chairs had been set up nearby, holding jugs of water and several plastic containers that apparently contained food. I also spotted an open fifth of bourbon.

'She's been taking good care of me, ain't she?' he said. 'She's somethin'.' He began coughing, a heavy, rasping sound that shook his skinny frame.

'Do you know what's wrong with him?' I asked her.

'I'm just tired,' he said.

'Will you let her answer?' I turned to Sis.

'He's got no fever,' she said. 'But he's undernourished and worn out. That cough worries me, 'cause it might be the beginning of pneumonia, so he could use a doctor. But if you asked me – and I've doctored a lot of folks – I'd say he's too tough to die anytime soon.'

'Why didn't you just keep him at home?'

'I wanted to, but he said it was too dangerous for me. So we decided on this place.'

I pulled a chair over to the mattress. 'All right, listen,' I said. 'I think you've been running from Pike Darnell and his son—'

His face took on a familiar look – wary, guarded, giving nothing away.

'—whether you admit it or not. And I know it has something

to do with Cassie Darnell's death. Listen carefully. Yesterday Vern Darnell tried to kill Sonny. He wound up shooting Leticia instead—' Blue's face registered shock, and he tried to sit up. I pushed him back and was surprised at how frail, how insubstantial he felt.

'But he didn't kill her, just hurt her pretty bad. He did kill someone else, a bystander. Then Vern was shot to pieces by Sonny's bodyguard. It was bloody and it was awful. We want to make sure that Pike Darnell doesn't send anybody out to kill ever again.'

He was listening hard. In all the years I'd known him, I'd coveted his attention. At this moment I had it as never before.

'Sonny's all right?' he asked finally, lying back on the mattress. 'And Leticia will be all right?'

'I think so.'

'Would you pass me that jug of water?'

I handed it to him. He drank greedily, spilling some of it down his front, then lay back. Sis was right. Whether seriously ill or not, he was clearly exhausted. Years of living on your own, followed by months of running and hiding out, can do that, I guessed.

'I want to get you to a doctor,' I said. 'And Jerry Chitwood wants to have a long talk with you, not to mention the Tennessee Bureau of Investigation.' Another wary look from him. 'Don't worry, I don't think you're actually wanted for anything except questioning – which, considering your history, is some kind of a miracle. But ...' I found myself struggling for words, because I had some harsh things to say to him. Along with a carefully constructed lie.

'But I think I finally figured out why we've had such a rash of killings around here. It was all to get you to come out of hiding, wasn't it? And if you follow that logic, then there's no getting around it, Blue: Five people are dead because of you.'

He held up a hand as if to stop me. 'No, just listen.' I ticked them off on my fingers. 'Faye. Your wife, who raised your son when you weren't around, which was most of the time. A decent young girl named Opal Hicks. Dewey, your best friend, who had the bad luck to look a little like you. Vern Darnell, who was basically a good man but who was someplace else when they handed out the brains. And Lem Coldsmith, a man you may never have heard of, but don't be surprised if he gets a longer obituary in the *Tennessean* than all the others. I always looked up to you, Blue. I always wanted you to think well of me, but I need to say this: You've got some of their blood on your hands.'

Now it was time for the lie. 'And we don't know if it's over yet. Pike Darnell is behind all this, and the police are going to take a hard look at him. But who knows if they can pin it on him? Could be he's got enough sneakiness left in that diseased mind of his to try again, to find somebody else to do his killing for him. This could keep going, Blue, and next time you could lose your son. Or Sis here. You don't want that to happen. It's time you told them what you know. Make it stop.'

I sat back in the chair and took a breath. It was a neat little lie. I didn't believe for a second that Pike Darnell was still a threat, not with his killing instrument gone, but I had to convince Blue that he could still lose people close to him.

He didn't answer, and I wasn't sure I had swayed him. But I saw enough hesitation in his face to make me think I had some leverage. It was like doing an interview. I had inserted the crowbar, and now I had to pry the stone out of the wall. All I needed was more leverage.

I stood up and went over to Sis. 'You know I'm right,' I said, and I was gratified to see her nod. 'He needs a doctor, and he needs to talk to the police.'

'Did you mean that, about somebody coming after the Governor? Or me?'

'No. But I want him to believe that. Will you talk to him? I know you're important to him, and maybe he'll listen to you.'

She went over, sat in the chair, and leaned over him, taking one of his hands in both of hers. They huddled that way for a long time, and I heard her speaking softly, as if she were telling him an old story. Midway through, she paused to shake a cigarette out of a pack and light it for him. 'Now don't you burn down the place,' I heard her say. Then she resumed talking in that soft voice.

My cell phone rang, and I flipped it open. 'Randall?' It was Lita Ray.

'Who's that?' Blue asked distractedly.

'Nobody important,' I said with my hand over the mouth-piece.

'What did you say?' Lita Ray asked.

'Nothing. Uh ... how are you?'

'How do you think I am?' she said with her characteristic twang, and I heard what might have been a tiny touch of humor in it. I recalled the first time I saw her over at Ida's lunch counter, when she was funny and brisk and sassy, and I liked her a little right then. Lately she'd had more tragedy than any one mortal deserved, but I had a feeling she'd come through this all right. She could turn out to be the toughest Darnell of them all, I thought.

'I've seen my favorite brother shot down like a dog, I've been grilled by cops, local and state,' she went on, 'and I've learned that my sainted daddy is an even worse human being than I used to think. On the whole, I'm not doing too well. But I didn't call you to complain.'

I waited. She seemed to be gathering her courage for something.

'It's like this,' she said. 'We're going to be burying Vern on Monday. At the church cemetery, over near Burning Bush Baptist, the one where Mrs. McMahan belonged. It won't be a big deal, and I really don't know how many people will turn up, considering ...' She let the thought trail off.

'But I know Vern liked you. He said he did. And so I thought I'd invite you. Will you come?'

I didn't want to. But I didn't have the heart to tell her flat-out.

'I'll sure try, Lita Ray. Thank you for asking.'

'Good.' She sounded relieved to have it over.

'Has Allard Timms gone out to see your dad yet?'

'I think so. He said he was going. He asked me to come along, and I said I just plain didn't want to. The way I'm feeling, I don't need to ever look my daddy in the face ever again.'

'I understand.'

'How about you? I suppose you're still looking for Blue McMahan, huh?'

'Actually, I found him. I'm with him right now.'

'You're kidding me! Well, I wish I could be more excited about that, but I'm afraid it's too late.' She sounded tired and dispirited. 'I guess I just don't care anymore. Where is he?'

'He's, uh … he's someplace safe. I don't want to get specific until I get him in the hands of the police. Then we can all relax.'

'I'm almost ready,' she said. 'I'll be ready to relax soon, I hope. Real soon.'

We hung up. When Sis saw that I had finished talking, she came over. 'I talked to him,' she said quietly. 'I poured it on. He's so tired of running, I think he's almost ready to just give it up, talk to the police, do whatever he needs to do.'

'But?'

'Well, you know how stubborn he is. Once he's got something fixed in his mind, you can't budge him. He says before anything else happens, he wants to talk to his son.'

I pulled out my phone. 'That shouldn't be—'

'No,' she said. 'He wants to see him here.'

'What?' I was not happy to hear that. 'Is this some kind of game he's playing? Is he just waiting to get his strength back so he can pull his jackrabbit routine on us again?'

'I don't think so. I've had him with me for two days now, and I've never seen a body so wrung out. He's not planning anything. He's acting like a man who doesn't have a lot of time left.'

'You said you didn't think he was going to die anytime soon.'

She ignored that. 'You know why he came here.'

I thought back to my talk with Lurleen Magnuson. 'Because he's run out of friends?'

She nodded, looking immensely sad. 'I think he's run out of everything. If he wants to see his son, then he should.'

I sighed and flipped open my phone. She put a hand on my arm. 'Just one more thing,' she said, her voice even lower. 'Don't tell him where his father is. You can meet him and bring him here, can't you?'

'I suppose … but I don't get it.'

'He's still afraid of something.'

'Of what?' I was quickly running out of patience with Blue McMahan.

'He won't tell me, but you know he's not a man who scares easy. And he's scared.'

'Well, he's just being paranoid.'

'Maybe,' she said. 'But would you bet his life on it?'

'Oh, hell. All right.' I punched in Sonny's cell phone number and was answered by a grunting sound on the other end.

'It's Randall. I apologize if I'm interrupting anything.'

'You're not. We got Tish settled into a room, with doctors and nurses dancing attendance. Every now and then it helps to be an ex-governor. Anyway, I'm sitting in the lounge having a big iced lemonade. I've been back to refill it twice. Getting shot at dries out your throat, did you know that?' His voice cracked as he spoke, and I could only guess at the strain he'd been under. He's tired, his father's tired … The whole world felt tired to me.

'How is she?'

'She's pretty amazing, considering,' he said, pride in his voice. 'She's hurting, but she doesn't complain. She makes jokes. I think one of her doctors is in love with her. She's talking about going to see one of those Hollywood plastic surgeons and shopping in Beverly Hills while she recuperates.'

'I'm glad it wasn't worse. Say hi for me.'

'I will.'

'Sonny … I'm sorry to spring this on you, but I need to tell you that I found Blue. I'm with him right now.'

'Uh-huh?' His tone instantly became guarded.

'He wants to see you.'

'Uh-huh … Well, he should be having a sit-down with Jerry Chitwood right about now. I'm pretty busy.'

'I know that. I wouldn't be calling you if I didn't think this was important. All the time he's been on the run, he knew Pike

Darnell wanted him dead. It makes sense now. He must have known that Pike killed his own daughter—'

'You know this?' It didn't sound like a friendly question.

'No. It's just how I've put things together. But it makes sense. It explains why a half-wit like Vern, who didn't appear to hate anybody, would try to kill you.'

'All right,' he said brusquely. 'But why does he need to see me?'

'I'm not sure. You're the only relative he's got left. He may just want to unload everything on you before he has to talk to the police. If that's so … well, you know he's told a lot of lies in his life. If he's finally ready to tell the truth, I'd sure want to hear it.'

I could hear him breathing. It was clear that he didn't want to see his father. Why would he? Sonny owed the old man nothing.

I needed to do more to persuade him. 'He's sick,' I said. 'I don't know how sick, but he might have a touch of pneumonia. He won't even see a doctor until you come first.'

'Well, shit. I sure hope he's glad to have you for a cheering section.' More breathing. Then finally: 'Okay. But I can't get away till tonight. I want to spend the day with Tish, make sure she's all right. Then I'll hitch a ride out of here after dinner, see him for a while, and make it back here later tonight. Ken's still there and can't drive me. Maybe I can get a state trooper …'

That set off an alarm bell in my head. I knew how skittish Blue would be around police, and I knew I had to set up the connections carefully.

'Fine, but one more thing,' I said. 'I need to meet you in town and drive you to him. All right?'

He cussed about that for a few seconds, then said he'd meet me at the town square at eight and hung up without a goodbye.

I went over to Blue and Sis. 'He's coming, but he can't make it until tonight. He's worried about Tish.'

''Course he is,' Blue said. 'That's fine. I'll just wait.' He had a far-off look in his eyes. I wondered if he was thinking about what he would say to his son after all their years apart.

'You two get out of here,' he said abruptly, pulling himself up into a sitting position with his back against the rough stone of the fireplace.

'Uh, I don't think we should.'

'You're making me nervous,' he said, and I heard some of the old vigor in his voice. He struck a match and began lighting candles. 'I got everything I need here. Deck of cards, bottle of Jim Beam, plenty to eat. Go on, get out. I'll see you tonight.'

I looked at Sis, and she made a what-can-you-do? face. 'We might as well,' she said.

'I'm a little worried about security here, since we can't lock the door behind us.'

Blue fished around in his blankets and came up with a gun. It looked like a .22 revolver. 'She gave me this.'

'It was Will's,' Sis said apologetically. 'He used it for varmints that got in the garden and for plinkin' at tin cans.'

'Nobody's gonna bother me,' Blue said. 'Go on. Git.'

I drove Sis back to her place, where she planned to begin doing Blue's laundry. 'You don't need to come tonight,' I told her. 'Maybe we can go out there together tomorrow morning.'

She leaned on her front doorframe and grinned a weary grin. 'He's a handful, ain't he? It's hard to be a friend of Blue McMahan.'

'Just like it's hard to tell the truth?'

She nodded. 'But both of 'em are worth it.'

TWENTY-FIVE

It was still just mid-morning, but I felt as if I'd been going most of the day. As I hit the outskirts of town, I passed a strip mall, saw signs advertising food, and felt my empty stomach respond.

The mall was the town's concession to modernity, something that made it look like anyplace else in America. Everything there was part of a chain – an auto supply place, a nail salon, a hair-cutter's, a pet supply store, and three fast-food joints – pizza, roast beef, and ice cream. I pulled in at the roast beef place, went in, and ordered a sandwich and a Dr Pepper. I sat at a window table and ate, watching the cars go by and wondering: If I pulled a Rip Van Winkle, slept for the next twenty years the way I'd stayed away for the past twenty, and then came back, would all of Pilgrim's Rest look like this? Or would there still be a peaceful town square with quirky, one-of-a-kind stores and shops under the shade trees? One thing I did know: The soldiers who lay beneath that bronze marker would certainly have departed for a more fitting place. My father wouldn't rest until they were.

As I finished my sandwich, my eyes wandered over to the ice cream shop. It was the Big Scoop where Junie Willets worked when she wasn't at school. Today was Saturday. And this was the main reason I'd picked this mall for lunch.

I walked over and spotted her through the plate glass before I reached the door. Even with the frilly apron and the paper cap with the Big Scoop logo, I recognized the girl in the photo I'd found stuck in the mirror frame in Faye McMahan's bedroom, the one showing Faye with her two young care-givers.

I went through the door and stepped up to the counter. 'Hi, Junie. I'm Randall Wilkes.'

'Oh. Hi.' She was a pretty brunette with a soft voice and a sweet smile.

'Do you have a minute?' I looked around. The place was not very busy.

'Sure.' She called out to someone in the back. 'Harold! Taking a short break, okay?'

We took a seat in one of the booths. The two other girls behind the counter looked our way and giggled.

'Are they going to gossip about us?' I asked.

'Sure,' she said, twirling a stray lock of hair around her finger. 'That's all we've got to do around here. They're harmless.'

'Junie, I know your mother doesn't think much of me, and I appreciate you talking to me. I'll try not to bother you for long.'

'If it's for Mrs. McMahan and Opal, I don't mind,' she said. 'Do the police know—'

'I can't talk for the police, but after what happened yesterday, I imagine everybody's got Vern Darnell on their list. It shouldn't be long before they can prove it.'

'Well, all right, then,' she said. 'It's just sad. Vern used to come in here. He always got the peach-flavored.'

'I think there's an explanation for what he did,' I said, but I didn't want to linger on the subject. 'You know, when I phoned you that time, talking to you seemed a lot more urgent. Now it's more a matter of just tying up loose ends, but I do have a few questions, if you don't mind.'

'Will this be in the paper? You're some kind of a reporter, right?'

'I'm not really a reporter any more, and no, it won't be in the paper.'

'Okay, then.' She flashed a bright smile, the kind that broke high school boys' hearts.

'Did Mrs. McMahan get many phone calls?'

'Uh-huh, she did. She liked to talk on the phone. She'd talk to the ladies in her prayer group. One of 'em was Opal's mom. And her son would call pretty regularly, and sometimes the Governor's wife. They all talked a lot.'

'How about visitors?'

'Hardly any, at least when I was there.' She paused. 'Do strangers count?'

'How do you mean?'

'Just ... Well, one evening when I was with her, this guy comes by and says he's looking for work. You know, odd jobs?'

'Uh-huh. Was that unusual?'

'Just a little. It was after dark, and you don't see that many strangers just walking around the Colony, you know?'

'You remember anything about him?'

'Uh-huh.' She grinned. 'He had a smart mouth.'

For a moment, I wondered if that had been Blue, running one of his games. 'What did he look like?'

'Oh ... older.'

'Older like me, or a lot older?'

Another grin. 'Like you. He was taller'n you and kind of handsome. Polite and everything, but he looked a little rough. I told him we didn't need anybody, so after a while he left.'

I reflected on that. Had Faye's killer stopped by one evening to case the house and have a polite chat with one of the girls? Possible. The man didn't sound old enough to be Blue, so who was it? The description could fit Briggs, the ex-lumberjack who was renting a room near Pike Darnell at the rest home, but that was a bit of a stretch. If he was laid off with a disability, he wouldn't likely be looking for odd jobs.

'Junie, you could tell Mrs. McMahan's mind was slipping, couldn't you?'

She hesitated. 'Yes, sir. Me and Opal would talk about it. We felt so sorry for her. Sometimes she'd be bright and sharp, and other times she'd be just ... you know, she'd forget things, she'd imagine things. That's why she needed me and Opal to look after her.'

'What kind of things would she imagine?'

'Well ...' She looked uneasy.

'It's all right,' I said. 'You're not being unkind to her. I have a feeling she'd want you to talk to me.' True or not? I didn't know. But it felt right.

'She'd talk about her husband. You know, the man who died a few months ago? And she'd say things like, "I need to talk to him." She'd be real impatient, like, "He's so unreliable. He said he'd be coming to see me, and I'm still waiting."'

'That sounds like her,' I said.

'And, uh ...' She pursed her lips, looking reluctant to go on.

'Yes?'

'Well, it sounds crazy—' She stopped, embarrassed. 'I don't mean to call her crazy. It's just that a few times, not long before she died, she got to talking about somebody being killed. Some girl. And it was all mixed up. But she said her husband knew what happened, and she'd get all panicky talking about it. Opal said she thought Mrs. McMahan was saying her husband killed somebody. But I heard it different – that he was there or he saw it or something like that. It was just ... you know, she'd get so frantic, we'd have to hold her until she calmed down.'

'Did you ever mention this to anyone else?'

'No, sir. She begged us not to tell anybody. Said her husband could die on account of it—'

She had that right, I thought.

'—and since he was already dead and all, we thought it was just her mind acting up. So we didn't say anything to anybody.'

'Thanks, Junie.' I got up. 'I really appreciate this. I'm glad you were there to take care of her when she ...' I trailed off as a stray memory plucked at my mind.

'Just remembered one other thing. On Faye's calendar in the kitchen, I noticed one day when Opal was sick, and it looked like you were going to get somebody to fill in.'

'Oh, right. I remember. I had to call around. I finally got Lita Ray Darnell to come over. She's Opal's cousin.'

'I didn't know that, but it makes sense,' I said. 'I saw her sitting with Opal's family at Faye's funeral.'

'Uh-huh. Well, I knew she was busy at the garage, but she said she wouldn't mind doing it, because Opal was her favorite cousin. She's nice.'

'I think so too,' I said. 'She's the only good Darnell left.'

A long, hot bath and maybe a nap at Wilkes Cottage sounded good, so I aimed the car in that direction. As I drove through town, though, I saw the police station up ahead and spotted the chief's cruiser parked out front. On impulse, I turned and pulled up alongside it.

Inside, Chitwood looked up from his desk as I knocked on his open office door. 'Randall.' He seemed even gloomier and more preoccupied than usual.

'Am I interrupting?'

'Not really,' he said in a voice that suggested otherwise. 'What can I do you for?' It was an old country locution, one I'd grown up hearing, and it made me grin.

'I'm on my way home,' I said, aware as I spoke how gradually I'd come to think of my father's place as home. 'Just thought I'd stop by and see if there's any news.'

He didn't answer right away. His eyes dropped back to the papers he'd been studying on his desk. Finally he said, 'Allard Timms and his boys have been going over Vern Darnell's place top to bottom, looking for anything that would help. He says he probably won't get out to talk to Vern's father until later today, but it's next on his list. I spoke to the Governor about an hour ago, and he said his wife is doing all right, considering.'

Sonny apparently hadn't mentioned his upcoming visit, and I was not about to break the news. The chief would have plenty of time to be mad at me for taking so long to tell him Blue was in town.

'Did they look into where Vern got his gun?'

'Uh-huh. It was like you said, one of Lita Ray's. They all used to belong to her daddy. Vern had a key to her place, she said, and he must have just gone in and took it. She's a mess over this. I hope it doesn't start her drinking again.'

'So do I. Chief ... remember that night out at the Hunting

Lodge, when she was busting up the place? You mentioned that she'd always been able to hold her liquor.'

'Well, I thought so.' He chuckled. 'I've seen her come out of Possum's with a crowd after some heavy drinking, and she'd be the only one not about to fall over.'

I thought about that for a moment and was about to phrase another question when I noticed the look on his face. He was once again studying the papers in front of him, and he looked grim. 'Something wrong?'

He nodded, holding up what looked like a faxed document. 'This. It's about Wingo Darnell.'

'The brother? What about him?'

'He's out,' Chitwood said succinctly. 'Been out of prison for six months, and I never knew a thing about it.'

'What?'

'And I wouldn't know about it today if I hadn't started asking around.' He chewed on his lower lip and lit a cigarette while he emptied his overflowing ashtray into a wastebasket. 'He was doing twenty to life for murder. It was a bad murder, over drugs, with what they call aggravating circumstances. But he got an appeal, the conviction was tossed out on a technicality, and they weren't able to retry him because all the low-life witnesses have faded away. Dead, disappeared, whatever. He's been out on the street since April.'

'Where is he?'

'Nobody knows. He lived in Atlanta before he was sent up, and he may still be there. Maybe I'm getting all worked up over nothing, but considering what's been going on with his family lately, it bothers me knowing he's out there somewhere.'

'Me too. Have you got a picture of him?'

'Nope, but I've asked Atlanta PD for his booking photo. I remember him, though. Big as the side of a house – two-forty, two-fifty pounds easy – full beard, usually wore coveralls. Always traveled with a gun or two in his pickup. Whenever he'd get in a fight, we'd have to call out the whole department ...' He shook his head. 'A bad man. I'm sure prison hasn't made him any better.'

279

Our eyes met, and we both had the same thought.

At Wilkes Cottage I finally got that bath and that nap, and they made me feel better. In the late afternoon I got up, went downstairs, and found Mrs. Mullins in the kitchen. She was happy to fix me an early supper, and I ate it with her at the kitchen table. She made quiet but good company.

I cleared my throat. 'Uh, I suppose you were raised around guns, like most people in this town,' I said.

'Yes, sir,' she said. 'I had three brothers and a daddy that hunted.'

'My father doesn't like guns, and that's fine,' I said. 'But I just want to mention something. There's a shotgun in the closet of my room. A 20-gauge. It has two shells in the magazine and another in the chamber, with the safety on. It's basically ready to fire. I'm guessing you'd know how to use it – if you had to, I mean.'

She nodded. I was glad she didn't ask any questions.

I found my father in his office, and he invited me in. I noticed the extra edition of the *Call* lying on his desk, with its uncharacteristically large banner headline, and picked it up.

'She did a fine job on that,' my father said.

'I agree.'

'She gave you a byline.'

'Hmm?' Then I saw it, over the color story on page one: *By Randall Wilkes, Special to The Call.*

'Well, thank you, ma'am,' I said under my breath. To him I added, 'I wasn't sure I'd ever get one of these again.'

'Let's hope it's not the last.' He shuffled some papers busily. 'You know, I was always proud of you,' he said, looking down at them. 'I just wanted you to do your best.'

'I know,' I said. After standing there awkwardly for a few seconds, I went to get my jacket. My father looked up as I passed the door to his office. 'Going out?' he asked.

'I think I'm going to do a good deed,' I said.

'Well, I'm glad.'

'I may be late,' I said. 'Would you make sure Mrs. Mullins checks the doors and windows tonight?'

This time he seemed on the verge of a question, but he just nodded. 'Good night,' he said.

As a boy, I'd always loved the town square at night. When I'd stay up late with Sonny or other friends and we'd cruise through town, the square looked very different at that hour, no parked cars or people, just darkened buildings. It made me feel very adult to drift through that late-night world.

I revisited the feeling as I sat parked in the Toyota in front of the library and Historical Society. The air was moist with coming rain, and each streetlight wore a faint corona of mist. It was lovely, and it made me nostalgic for a time that once had been, or maybe never had been.

To pass the time, I switched to battery and turned on the radio, twirling the dial past the usual staccato of news bulletins, strident disk jockey's voices, and generic music. A little rock, some oldies, yet another preacher, and a snatch of country that sounded as if it had been recorded in a Hollywood sound studio, complete with strings and backup chorus.

Then I found it again, that sound that had surprised me during my sleepy drive back from the Smokies. Not the same song, not the same singer. A male voice this time, rough and untrained, singing in what they sometimes call the 'high lonesome sound,' about a man who leaves his home and best gal for the big city and comes to regret it. The music sounded at once plain and pure, and it came with the surface scratches of what might have been an old 78 rpm record.

I wondered where this sound was coming from, so I waited. The scratchy music came to an end, and a deep, sleepy male voice said, 'Sammy Farrell singing *Where I Come From* on the Oriole label, from 1933. This is WMO, old-time music for the folks around Pilgrim's Rest. I'm Marvin Owens, and this is coming to you straight from my garage. We're only on a few hours at a time, whenever I feel like broadcasting, but when we are, we're worth a listen. Let me take a minute now to tell you about Horton's Hardware, the friendly store in Pilgrim's Rest, where you can ...'

I saw headlights in my rear-view and shut off the battery. It was the big black GMC, and it pulled into the spot next to mine. Behind the tinted windows I could just make out Sonny in the passenger seat and Kenneth Lively at the wheel.

I got out, and Sonny rolled down his window. 'We meet again,' he said. 'Let's do this, all right? You can ride with us.'

I hesitated briefly. It didn't matter, I supposed, who did the driving as long as I gave the directions. But I was surprised to see Lively, and it must have showed.

'Ken met me at the city limits,' Sonny said as he got out and climbed into the back seat, beckoning for me to join him. 'I'm always more comfortable having him with me, 'specially driving around to mysterious places at night.'

'All right, Sonny, but he doesn't go inside. If he does, it'll throw a crimp in things. I know Blue.'

'I'm sure you do,' he said with just the right touch of sarcasm. 'Okay, he stays outside. Now get in. It's cold, and I want to get back to my wife as soon as I can.'

I climbed in, nodding at Lively, and he nodded back over his shoulder. At this rate, we'd be fast friends sometime around the next Olympics.

It didn't take long to get out of town. As the houses thinned out, I heard Lively say, 'Fire up ahead,' and we saw a big pile of burning leaves in a front yard, giving off that wonderful scorched smell that had always said autumn to me. The figure of a man was darting around, beating at tendrils of fire that threatened to spread from the leaves through his yard.

'Poor son of a bitch,' Sonny said. 'All he wants to do is clean up his yard, and next thing he knows, something's out of control.' As we left the fire behind us, he commented, 'I suppose we should've stopped. He might've voted for me.'

Soon we were rolling along that darkened stretch of highway that led to the Colony. 'Any sign of our friend?' Sonny asked his driver.

'Nope,' Lively answered. 'I've been looking. He must have turned off.'

'False alarm, huh? You've been a cop too long.' In response

to my quizzical look, he said to me, 'Ken thought we might've been followed, starting around the time the trooper handed me over to him. I kid him about being Mr. Security, but I like the way he watches out for me. Makes me feel important, and you know how I enjoy that.'

'How long since you've seen Blue?' I asked Sonny.

'Damn. Probably not more than once in the last ... oh, ten years or so. He wasn't there for my inauguration, but he did show up one day about a year later. Just walked in, told my secretary who he was, and I came out. There he was, in that godawful undertaker's suit of his, looking a little scruffy but not seeming to care.'

'What was he doing there?'

'He said he'd just stopped by to tell me he was proud of me. We sat there in the outer office for a while, I got him some coffee and gave him one of those ballpoint pens with the governor's seal on it. After a while he figured out I wasn't going to invite him back to my office, and he left.'

'Maybe he *was* proud of you,' I ventured. *Funny thing,* I thought, *this must be the night to hear about pride between fathers and sons.*

'Yeah, and maybe I could have used some of that a lot sooner,' Sonny said, closing the subject.

Just a few minutes later we reached the hotel. I directed Lively to park in the protected area between the wings of the building, and I led them to the back door.

'Like we agreed ...' I began.

'Ken, you stay out here,' Sonny told him. 'Don't let anybody interrupt us. I'll try not to take too long.'

The door, inexplicably, was locked, so I banged on it. After a minute, it was opened, and there stood Blue, looking ghostly in the light from the candle he held.

'I was feeling better, so I got up and bolted this thing,' he said to me. He stared at Sonny, squinting in the feeble light. 'Well. Hello, son.'

'Hey, there,' Sonny said, and they shook hands soberly, like lawyers at a contract signing. Blue led us through the kitchen.

When he pushed through the double doors into the dining room, I saw that he had lit every candle. They sat on the floor in a rough semicircle around the mattress by the fireplace, making his bed look a little like a funeral bier.

Blue stood stiffly by the mattress. He had put on his suit over the pajamas. Chairs were nearby, and he indicated that we should sit. 'I'm still a little wobbly, so hope you don't mind if I …' He eased himself down onto the mattress.

'Drink?' he asked, pointing to the bottle.

'No, thanks,' Sonny said. 'I won't be able to stay long. I need to get back to my wife.'

'Sure.' He put the bottle down. 'Thanks for coming.'

'You wanted to tell me something?'

'Uh-huh.' Blue clasped his arms around his skinny knees and began a slight, gentle rocking motion. He closed his eyes, and his face went through changes, and I could see that he was in some kind of pain. I had the uncomfortable feeling that I was eavesdropping on something intensely personal.

'You want me to leave?' I asked.

'No,' Blue said. 'I want to tell you both something.'

He was getting no encouragement from Sonny, so I spoke up again. 'What is it, Blue?'

He reached for the bottle and took a long pull at it.

'I want to tell you how Callie Darnell died.'

TWENTY-SIX

He began talking in a soft rasp of a voice, his vocal cords worn down by years of drink, tobacco, and assorted other indulgences. Blue was a master storyteller, but this was not one of the old Jack tales, full of high spirits and heroic cunning. It was just revisited pain, and he told it haltingly and badly. The journalist in me would want to smooth over the rough spots, step back a few paces, and tell it something like this:

He saw her, and liked her. She was a sun-tanned, sweet-smelling magnet for men, all fun and good times, and he was the dark traveler who'd done crimes and made a life of separating people from their money. The attraction was immediate. But both knew it was just a fling – young girl, older man – that would end whenever he got in his beat-up car and drove out of town.

So, one evening, he drove them down to the place below the falls. He'd brought a bottle, and things were nice and relaxed. Cigarettes, bourbon, soft music from the radio, the roar of the falls, and lots of what they used to call necking, which led to the inevitable conclusion. Both of them liked sex, treated it as something casual and fun. In that respect, if no other, they were a good match.

It became late, and one by one the other cars began pulling out from under the trees by the lake. They got to talking, and after a while she had emptied the bottle, and she talked more. She had an almost unerring radar when it came to men, and she must have felt it was safe to confide in him – especially since his time in Pilgrim's Rest was coming to an end, and he would soon be on the road again. So she told him two things she had not told anyone else, even her sister.

She was pregnant. And Sonny was the father.

He was surprised but not shocked. From what he had seen on this visit, his boy was edging into young manhood, he was vital and good-looking, and he definitely liked the girls. A lot of them. He began calculating what to do about the pregnancy. This girl was smart and experienced. She shouldn't be much of a problem if he offered to steer her to a doctor. He had some money put back, and he knew Faye had some. He was watchful about his money, but after all, this was a family problem, and although often absent, he was the nominal head of the family.

So he began his smooth talk, his gentle persuasion, only to get a new surprise.

She was going to marry the boy.

Had she told him about the pregnancy? he asked her. Yes, she had. She had seen the look of uncertainty cross his seventeen-year-old face. Naturally he was fearful of such a life-changing thing. But she was older, she knew how to handle him. She knew she could bring him around and that they could be happy together.

Why? he had to ask her. Why marry him? You've known a few men – he had to be careful here, careful not to antagonize her. But it's true, he went on. You've know a few men. Why this boy?

Because he's going to be somebody, she said with conviction. I don't know who or what, but he's special. They were strange words coming from Callie Darnell, who took men as just a diversion, and he listened.

Because the father knew it was true. Even at the usual distance he maintained from his family, he knew his son was one of a kind, someone destined to lead, not follow. A big businessman, maybe, or a politician. A career that allowed him to use this talent of his, this ability to attract people to him and make them want to follow him. His son would be the first in his family to go to college. Forrest Wilkes, the scholar, father of the boy's best friend, had seen this spark in him and was helping him get his education.

Some fathers feel resentment when their sons surpass them. He would not. He wanted his son to go out and conquer.

And he knew with absolute certainty that the boy could not do it with this woman. She would stunt his growth, hold him back. This marriage isn't going to happen, he thought. I'm not much of a father to him, but I won't let her get in his way.

What was he going to do? Vague thoughts began to form. He'd buy her off, if that's what it took. He'd do it in a gentlemanly way, so that she'd feel no insult. And his son would be free to go out and make his mark in the—

She was getting out of the car.

After their lovemaking, she hadn't bothered to dress. Drunker now than he had guessed, and naked, she was weaving through the trees in an unsteady dance, arms widespread, chanting in a soft, singsong voice, 'I'm going to marry him. I'm going to have his baby.' Over and over.

He looked around. Were any cars still parked nearby? It was too dark to see. She was getting farther away from him, and it seemed that her voice was more distinct now. It sounded as if she was having a conversation with herself. If she got any louder, she could be heard over the sound of the falls. He had to stop her, bring her back to the car, calm her down.

He darted through the trees, a little too drunk himself, and lunged for her, got an arm around her. 'Hush,' he said to her. 'You hush now.'

But she would not hush. She read his intent, knew he wanted to keep her silent. She fought him, raising her voice to a yell. 'I'm going to marry Sonny McMahan! I'm going to have his—'

His strong forearm came up under her chin, cut off her wind and her voice. He began dragging her back to the car, keeping up the pressure on her neck so she couldn't yell out the secret any more. All the way back he dragged her over the uneven ground, almost stumbling over rocks and roots. Her hands gripped his arm, trying to loosen it, but her own weight helped keep the pressure where he wanted it.

Somewhere on the way back, her hands went slack.

At the car he found her limp and unresisting. He bundled her into the seat and got in next to her, intending to talk some sense into her.

He found her dead, her windpipe crushed, her tongue slightly protruding from her mouth, her face a deep red, almost purple.

For a long time he sat with her. Did he think about that time in the hotel room in St. Louis? Maybe. When next he looked at his watch, it was well past two, and he'd come to a decision. He touched

*her cheek lightly and said, 'I'm sorry, girl.' Then he popped the trunk
and pulled out a shovel he always kept there. He slung her over his
shoulder and carried her about fifty yards to the edge of a cornfield.
He dug until he was too tired to go on, and he buried her between
two rows.*

*Back at the car, he found her familiar locket on the car seat, its
clasp broken. He bundled it up with her clothes and shoes, weighted
the bundle with a large rock, and threw it into the center of the lake.
Then he had a smoke and tried to calm down, telling himself again
that it had been necessary. Not for him, but for his son and yes, for
his wife. He didn't feel particularly noble. To him if felt more like the
payment of an old debt.*

*Most fathers give their sons a life by raising them. He hadn't stuck
around for those chores. So he'd given his son a life by ending the life
of another.*

Blue finished his story. He lay back, eyes closed, looking in the
fluttering candlelight like a corpse at a wake.

Sonny, who'd been utterly silent throughout, got up and,
shoulders slumped, walked across the large room to stand at
one of the tall, shuttered windows. I sat by Blue's side for a
while, still absorbing the story. I was too stunned to hate him.

I eventually found the energy to ask him. 'Why now?'

He didn't answer, but I thought I already knew. 'You're tired,
aren't you? Tired of running, tired of all this.'

He nodded almost imperceptibly. 'I don't care about the *police*,' he said, 'but I thought it was time Sonny knew. Now he's
got to decide what to do.' A sound that might have been a soft
chuckle came from his throat. 'He'll prob'ly hate me for dumping this on him.'

For that and a few other things, I thought.

Finally I got up and joined Sonny. He stood facing the window, panting softly like a racehorse cooling off. There in the
dark, away from the candlelight, he was barely visible.

I was about to speak when he interrupted. 'I gave it to her,' he
said. 'The locket.'

You didn't spend much on it, did you? I almost said it aloud.

'For a while there I thought you might have done something to Callie,' I told him. 'I'm sorry for thinking that, even for a second. I should have known you better.'

'Okay.'

'I was even more sure that her daddy killed her. I don't think I'll be apologizing to him anytime soon.'

When he didn't respond, I knew the question I had to ask. 'She told you? About being pregnant?'

'Yeah. But she didn't say anything about getting married. Not that I remember, anyway. I thought she'd just take care of it. I thought she'd know what to do. Next thing I knew, she was … gone.'

'Would you have married her?'

Deeper breaths now. He sounded like a man who couldn't get enough air. 'I don't know. Hell. All right, no. I wouldn't have. Okay?'

'Well, he sure spared you that, didn't he?'

Sonny turned to me then, his face contorted. 'He *killed* her.'

'I know he did, although maybe they'd call it manslaughter. But he did kill her. For you.'

'What are you doing? Putting this on me? Fuck you, my old friend. You can't put this on me. I would've found some way to handle this—'

'Finding her a doctor, you mean? Maybe that would have worked. And maybe it would have come back to bite you in the ass just before election time. I know you always said Faye put you in the governor's office. Well, could be Blue did too.'

'Whose side are you on?' It came out almost hatefully.

'I'm not sure. Everybody's, I suppose. Journalists aren't supposed to take sides, remember?'

'You got kicked out of that club, remember?'

'I haven't forgotten. What do you want to do now? About him?'

He thought. 'Turn him in. He needs to tell this to the police.'

'Right. He said he'd talk to them. Knowing him, I'm not sure exactly how truthful he's going to be. And whatever we tell them is hearsay.'

'I know what hearsay is. I'm the one here with the law degree, thank you.' He thought some more, and I could hear his knuckles pop as he clenched and unclenched his big fists. 'God damn. I could almost kill him myself when I think about what he set off. If Pike Darnell had just gone after him, it would've been some kind of justice. But my mother ...' He sounded close to tears.

'I know. There aren't any heroes in this story, Sonny. It's time we handed all this over to Jerry Chitwood. Blue owes a debt for what he did, and it's not our job to say what that is. Let's not forget a doctor should look at him, too. I just want to ask him a couple of things first.'

I went to Blue and leaned over him. 'Hey,' I said. He opened his eyes.

'You must've mailed her sister that postcard from Memphis, huh?'

He nodded. 'Callie showed me once how she liked to sign her name.'

'How did you know they were after you?'

'Faye,' he said. 'The night I ... the night it happened, I felt pretty wrecked. Stopped in to see Faye on my way out of town, woke her up. And I guess I told her – without really giving her chapter and verse, you know – but I was drunk and wound up and talked too much. And she was smart. This was a long time before she got sick, and she was real sharp, could put two and two together. She knew what I did, and she kept my secret all those years, even when I treated her bad. She was that kind of woman, that Faye.'

Did it ever occur to you, I was tempted to say, that she might have kept it for Sonny's sake, too?

I remembered her raving the night she was killed. *That's not a soldier's grave*, she had said about Callie's resting place. *Blue told me.* The old secret had festered within her for years and now, with senility setting in, it would no longer stay hidden. It would, in fact, get her killed.

'And then she got sick,' I prompted him.

'And her mind started going. In and out. One night a few months ago she called me in Memphis, all hysterical. Said she'd given away the secret, didn't mean to, but it happened while she was having one of her spells. She cried and said she was sorry.'

'She told Lita Ray, didn't she?'

'That's right. You're pretty smart too. Take after your daddy. Yep, she told Lita Ray. And I knew the Darnells'd be coming after me. So I went for a swim in the mighty Mississip' and didn't come up.'

'Lita Ray could've let the cat out of the bag without thinking, and her father could've—'

'No,' he said in a wheeze. 'She thought about it, all right. She's a Darnell. They're all alike.'

I got up, pulled out my cell phone, and dialed the chief's number as I rejoined Sonny. He answered almost immediately, sounding rushed. 'Chitwood.'

'Chief, it's Randall Wilkes.'

'Randall, I'm a little—' Static interrupted him.

'What? I can't hear you. Listen, I found Blue McMahan. I'm with him now. Can you hear me?'

More static. Then: 'This is not a good time. Pike Darnell's been killed. I'm at the home.'

'*What?*'

'Timms found him. He was sliced open. Just like Dewey Tackett.' The static was now a low hiss, and I could hear a commotion in the background, voices, a woman sobbing. I snuck a look at my phone and was dismayed to see the battery was near death. Don't quit on me now, I said to it silently.

'Did you talk to the man named Briggs?'

'He's gone. Nobody knows where.'

'Chief ...' I fought to keep my voice under control. 'I'm about to lose reception here. Did you ever get that photo of Wingo Darnell?'

'I did, yeah.'

'On the booking sheet, were there any tattoos?'

'Uh, yeah.' More low-level static as he paused to think. If I could have reached through the phone line, I would have shaken him.

'One on the back of the neck, and one on each bicep.'

'Listen!' I fairly shouted it. 'Briggs is Wingo Darnell. He's had a lot of years to lose about fifty pounds and a beard. He wants to get even with anybody who ever hurt Callie. He killed his father, and he's coming after Blue McMahan. You need to send a deputy out to the old hotel on the bluff right away.'

'I can't hear—' The line went dead.

'Shit.' I turned to Sonny. 'Give me your phone.'

'I left it in the car, in my satchel. What did he just tell you?'

'Come on.' I pulled out my flashlight and started for the door. As we crossed the kitchen, I tried to describe what I'd heard.

'What was that about a deputy?' Sonny asked, bumping heavily into a countertop. 'Nobody knows we're here.'

'That car you thought might be tailing you – how do you know he really turned off?'

That shut him up for a moment. 'Is Ken armed?' I asked as we reached the locked door.

'He wouldn't be much good to me otherwise.'

'Fine. We need to get him in here with us and call for some protection. If I'm wrong, and Wingo's headed for parts un-known, then we can all have a good laugh.'

We unbolted the door that led to the grassy enclosure. Cool air sifted in, along with the smell of rain. It was a gentle rain, not at all like the apocalyptic storm that accompanied Faye's murder. I'd always loved a gentle rain. But not tonight.

My flashlight showed the way as we walked to the big sport-utility. Just before we reached it, we saw the shape of a man on the hood. It was Kenneth Lively. He lay on his back.

There was no blood, but his head was twisted at an impossible angle, so that he appeared to be looking through the windshield. I couldn't see his face and didn't want to.

'Oh, my God.' Sonny reached out a hand, let it drop. 'Ken.'

I killed the flashlight and looked around wildly. Wingo had been here just moments earlier. Where was he now?

Sonny reached for the man's ravaged neck and felt fruitlessly for a pulse. Not knowing how to avoid it, I stepped forward and patted down the torso and pants pockets. No car keys. Empty holster. I reached in through the open driver's-side window and fumbled for the ignition. It was bare of keys. I almost stumbled over something on the ground by the car. 'Is that your satchel?' He picked it up and quickly went through it. 'Phone's gone.'

My senses were wired, waiting for a gunshot or a knife-wielding figure to burst out of the darkness. Nothing came.

'The whole building's dark,' I muttered. 'He didn't know exactly where we were. Inside, I mean.' I looked around, squinting at the building's wings, each with two stories and rows of windows. 'Maybe what he did ...' Taking a chance, I turned the flashlight on again and quickly swept the two wings. At the far end of the southern wing, I saw it. A broken window on the second floor.

'He's up there,' I said. 'Come on.' Sonny and I swapped looks, and I knew each was thinking the same thing: If we make a break for it, we can get away, get to a phone, at least save ourselves.

The moment passed, and we both nodded. 'Come on,' I said again, and we made it quickly to the back door. Once inside, we bolted it.

'He may not know where we are yet,' I whispered as we made our way back to the dining room. 'He's going through the rooms on both floors. Eventually he'll make it to the front and the reception area. We need to be ready.'

'How the hell ...'

'Blue!' I called out. He lay there as before, eyes closed. He cradled the nearly empty bottle on his chest. The candles were growing short, but they still illuminated our side of the room. 'Where's the gun?'

'What?' He seemed to be coming out of a nap.

'Sis' gun. Where is it?'

'Oh ...' He fumbled among the blankets and brought out the .22 revolver. I broke it open and found the cylinder loaded with six shells. All right, I thought. Better than nothing. I silently thanked Will Lawlor, a man I'd never known, who bought this pistol for plinking at tin cans and keeping varmints out of his garden. I hoped it would be effective against something a little larger.

Talking fast, I filled Blue in on our predicament. He took it calmly. 'All right, then.' He worked himself up to a sitting position and began looking around the room, assessing the layout.

'Looks to me like we're sittin' ducks here,' he said, indicating the candles. He was right. But the thought of waiting in the dark for an assassin to strike was equally terrifying. We talked briefly and came to a compromise: two candles in each of the four corners of the room. While Blue extinguished the extras, Sonny and I distributed the rest, and soon the room was cast in a kind of low twilight, lit by the undernourished moons in each corner.

There were no locks on the doors that led to either the kitchen or the reception room on the adjacent wall. We piled up several of the long, heavy folding tables in front of the door to the kitchen, leaving our phantom adversary only one way to get at us. We, and our small-caliber weapon, would be ready for him.

Then we reassembled by the cold, soot-smelling fireplace. It held the husk of a charred log and an oversize set of well-used fireplace tools, including a brush with few bristles left. We kept our eyes trained on the door across the room and were careful to speak in low voices. Blue sat with his back to the dirty bricks, Sonny and I on each side. He had known that a Darnell or two were after him, Blue told us, he just wasn't sure which ones.

'I remember this Wingo. He's the worst of them all,' he said without emotion. 'Ice cold, that old boy. At least his daddy believes in God. Wingo believes in hurting people.'

I could think of no response to that. I tried to focus on the face of the man I'd met a few days earlier, the one who called himself Briggs. At the time, I gave him a quick once-over and thought I had his number – likable, shallow, a little bit of a con artist, a flirt around women. Now I knew I'd looked in the face of evil and not even recognized it. Now I was seriously afraid of him.

I found myself muttering. 'What?' Sonny said.

'Just thinking out loud. When he's in a hurry, he breaks necks. When he wants to linger, to take pleasure in it, he slices people open.'

'Thank you for sharing that.'

We talked aimlessly for a while to keep the tension level down. 'This remind you of anything?' Blue asked.

'No, what?'

'That time we went 'coon hunting.'

'Oh. Right.' It came back to me then, one of the few times the three of us had done anything together. Sonny and I were fifteen, Blue was in town, and Faye was visiting her folks in McMinnville. Since she considered Blue a bad influence, she usually forbade her son to spend much time with his father, but this time he was free.

Blue professed astonishment to hear that we had never gone 'coon hunting – one of those rites of passage for Southern boys. Sonny and I knew that raccoon meat was not particularly tasty and that 'coon hunting was a fairly sedentary pursuit, since the dogs did most of the work. But Blue was persistent. He was no hunter himself, but he knew the hunters who lived around our town, and soon he had us fixed up with a couple of dour-looking backwoodsmen who owned a brace of 'coon hounds.

The five of us went out late one fall evening and spent the whole night sitting around a fire listening to the dogs chase raccoon scents through the woods. They never found one, but we had a good time nonetheless, listening to the hunters' stories about past hunts and being allowed to nip at the bottle passed around by the adults. We came out of the experience feeling a little more grown-up.

'I remember that,' Sonny said. 'The next morning, you took off.'

'I suppose I did,' Blue responded. A pause, then, 'You know, I'm the only one he's really after.'

'Uh-huh?'

'You two could go, leave me the gun, hike over to one of the houses, I bet they're less'n five minutes away. Call our old friend Jerry Chitwood. What do you say?'

I started to respond but Sonny cut in. 'You mean that?' I heard astonishment in his voice. He might have been speaking to an absolute stranger.

'Sure. I'm used to taking care of myself.'

'Well, now we're taking care of you,' Sonny said, with gruffness this time, but something else as well. It may have been the sound of a son talking to his father.

The room grew cold. Blue began shivering, and Sonny rearranged the blankets around him. I strained my ears but heard nothing unusual. The light fall of rain on the roof, our own breathing.

'I've been thinking about Vern ...' Sonny began.

'Me too,' I said. 'It wasn't the old man who sent him out to kill, it was Wingo. Hiding out in that house, under everybody's noses. I'm guessing he didn't even tell his father who he was, figuring the old man was too far gone to know him. Just waited there, whispering his poison to Vern, until he figured he had his shot at Blue. Then he'd kill the old man too. Anyone who ever hurt Callie had to die.'

'How did he find Blue?'

'I don't know. Maybe he found him when I did. Maybe he knew I had the best chance to smoke him out, and he just kept an eye on me. That must have been Wingo who broke into Longstaff House when Tish was here, and I'd bet he was trying to get a clue on Blue's whereabouts.'

'Give me the gun,' Sonny said abruptly.

'Why?'

'I was always a better shot.'

'Who says?'

'All right. Then give it to me for another reason.'

'Which is?'

'Faye. And Ken. And the bullet that came for me and tore up my wife's leg instead. The thing is, I'm just readier to kill somebody tonight than you are.'

He had me there. 'All right.' I passed it to him, and he got up slowly.

'Oh, man, it's been a long day.' He stretched his arms out, then walked over to one of the shuttered windows. 'I think I can hear the rain,' he said.

I heard it too, the light pattering of raindrops on glass. Beyond the beams overhead, the high ceiling was lost in shadow. It had been years since I'd seen the room in full daylight, with the shutters off and the light coming through the skylight.

As Sonny walked back toward us, I heard a small sound from overhead. Not loud, just the scrape of metal against metal. The skylight. I looked up toward it but couldn't make out anything in the dark.

Another sound, this one louder. Sonny heard it too. He stood in the center of the room, directly under it, tilting his head back to see what it was.

'Look out!' I yelled.

Too late. I heard the slam of the skylight door, saw a figure plummet downward from the ceiling. It landed on Sonny, and both collapsed loudly onto the floor with the crack of limbs hitting wood. Sonny cried out in pain, and I heard the gun hit the floor.

And I heard a bellow, halfway between human and animal. Not of pain, but of rage. It was Wingo Darnell, who had dropped out of the sky on this rainy night to kill us all.

TWENTY-SEVEN

Sonny, with his bulk and muscle, surged on top of the other man, only to be thrown off as if by a pile driver. As he landed a few feet away, the breath driven out of him, I saw a glint of metal in Wingo's right hand.

Without looking, I reached behind me and grabbed the first handle I found amid the fireplace tools. It was the shovel, and I jumped toward the dark figure, swinging it back and forth, to give Sonny a chance to get to his feet. He did so, limping slightly. I heard him grab one of the folding chairs, and then he came at the other man from a different angle, holding the chair by its curved back and also swinging it from side to side. We must have been a sight, two men with makeshift weapons who knew little about violence, facing one who reveled in it. Out of the corner of my eye I saw Blue standing with his back to the fireplace. 'Stay there!' I yelled.

Our enemy scrambled off the floor and into a crouch. I saw no sign of the smooth-talking small-timer named Briggs. Wingo Darnell wore camouflage shirt and pants, a dark wool knit cap, gloves and boots. His face had been blackened, the way hunters and night fighters mask their light skin. His eyes picked up the candlelight, and they were those of a predator.

'I want the old man,' he said his voice sour with hate.

Sonny, already slightly out of breath from swinging the chair, replied, 'You can't have him.'

Wingo came for me first. He feinted at my face with the knife, and when I raised the shovel to block him, he came in under it, sweeping across my midsection with a backhanded motion. I felt the blade strike me, and I knew it had opened me up all the way back to my spine. In an instant, I would be pouring my guts out onto the floor …

I staggered back, knees buckling, as I realized I was still intact. My belt had stopped the blade.

He saw my confusion and fear. 'You're easy,' he said, and came at me again.

With a deep-throated shout, Sonny charged him from the side – not swinging the chair, but using it as a battering ram. Its four legs caught Wingo in the stomach and chest and drove him away from me.

'Come on!' Sonny yelled. I followed him, swinging the shovel high and then downward with all my weight behind it. Wingo saw it coming and threw up his free arm, taking the flat of the shovel easily with a layer of muscle. As I raised my near-useless weapon, he aimed the knife point at my belly and lunged. I couldn't get out of the way …

He slipped. On the gun. It twisted his leg to the side, and he grunted and went down on one knee. As he did, his knife arm swept sideways at me again, and this time, I felt it bite at my shin, as if an ice cube had touched me there.

Before either of us could react, the knife struck again – a jab this time, straight into Sonny's thigh. He shouted and cursed in pain.

Then Sonny swung his chair, and I heard it connect with Wingo's head, an unmistakable sharp crack. The man sank to both knees, shaking his head violently to clear it, hands still high, that ugly knife still a threat.

Sonny and I were both hurt, but we couldn't stop. He changed his grip on the chair, holding it now by two of the legs, and – heedless of the knife – brought it down on the man on the floor. It struck Wingo's bowed shoulders, bringing him lower. The knife hand drooped.

'You killed my mother, you son of a bitch from hell,' Sonny said between gasps. 'I'm going to—'

He didn't get the chance. A scrawny figure in black shoved

its way between us, holding the empty bourbon bottle aloft. It came down on Wingo's head with a shattering crash, spraying us with glass shards. In an instant, Blue launched himself onto the man's bowed back from behind, riding him, left arm around Wingo's neck, right hand high in the air, holding the neck of the bottle.

Down it came, with what waning strength Blue had left. He drove the jagged end into the side of Wingo's neck once, then again. Then, fumbling, he shifted the bottle neck in his hand so that the sharp end was nearest his thumb. And from underneath, he drove it up into the man's throat. The sounds that followed were new to me. They went on for a minute that seemed like an hour.

Then it was over. Blue rolled off the body, slipped in the blood, and eased himself to the floor, where he lay on his back, breathing like a man with very little life left in him. Sonny and I sat nearby, heads on our knees, panting.

I don't know how much time passed. 'I think I'm gonna be sick,' I heard Sonny say.

'Me, too,' I said. 'But you first.'

Limping heavily now, he made his way over to one of the tall windows and vomited there. He came back, wiping his mouth. 'Sonofabitch,' he said softly. Then he said it again.

My left foot felt warm. When I examined it, I found that the sock was sticky with blood from the wound on my shin. The blade had gone through flesh and muscle.

'How's your leg?' I asked Sonny.

'Hurts like hell,' he said. 'He stuck me, and I think it went in pretty far. But it's just a puncture wound. I'll live. We'll all live, by God.'

I found the gun and put it in my pants pocket. We helped Blue over to the mattress and sat by him. He was weak as a newborn. But I was beginning to think he was indestructible.

'Sorry I can't offer you boys a drink,' he said. Then, in a surprising gesture, he reached over and touched Sonny lightly on the arm. 'Thank y'all for coming back for me.'

Sonny, head down, just nodded.

'Remember that 'coon hunt?' Blue said. 'Something tells me we'll remember this night longer.'

I couldn't help laughing at that. Half-crazed as I was, I was ready to laugh at anything. I looked at Sonny, to pull him into the joke, but he sat absolutely still, staring past me. I followed his gaze.

There in the far doorway stood Lita Ray Darnell.

The candlelight in the two corners showed me that she was dressed like her brother, her face blackened. She held the double-barreled 12-gauge shotgun I remembered seeing on her wall, and I could make out some kind of a handgun stuck into her belt. I had no doubt that the twin chambers of the shotgun were loaded and that the hammers were cocked. And that some of us were about to die.

'Stand up,' she said.

Sonny and I stood slowly. Blue struggled to his feet, taking even longer.

'Get away from him,' she said.

I did, moving a few feet toward the center of the room. I had my reasons. I knew her focus was on Blue, not on me.

Sonny did not move. He stood about three feet from Blue.

'Get away,' she said to him.

'Not going to,' he said, his voice deep and rich with all the authority of a man who once had run all of Tennessee.

I half-turned my right side away from her. She had heard no shots and had no way of knowing about the gun. I eased it out of my pocket, then let my arm hang at my side.

She looked over at the body on the floor, crumpled amid the glass. In the half light, the pools and spots of blood shone like ink.

'You killed him,' she said with no emotion. A pause, then: 'He said I might have to do this.'

A thought began to grow. 'You called him here, didn't you?' I was working it out as I spoke. 'You're the one. You're behind all this.'

She didn't bother to look in my direction.

'You sure had me fooled. Acting like that Briggs guy was

301

bothering you. Making sure you got a DNA test when you must've already known she was dead and who killed her.' As I talked breathlessly, other instances of her lying came to mind, and I felt an odd respect for her ability at pure play-acting. 'Making up the story about Blue visiting your daddy. Pretending to be drunk out of your mind that night at the Hunting Lodge when all you wanted to do was get close to me, find out what I knew about Blue.'

Keep talking, I told myself. As long as we're talking, she's not shooting.

'But I can't believe you sent Vern—'

'No!' She turned to me then, keeping the gun trained on the others. 'I didn't know he was going to get Vern to do that. I never would have let him. But then it was too late.'

I started to say something reassuring, to tell her that I understood, but Blue broke in.

'Hey, there, girl.' Even with his weakened voice, he sounded almost like the Blue of old. 'I know you been looking for me. I'm truly sorry about your sister—'

I was waiting for an exchange of insults, for hatred spewed across the room, for anything except what happened.

Lita Ray brought the shotgun up fast, snapped it into position just below eye level like a hunter whose quarry had just bolted from the underbrush. In the same instant that I realized she was about to fire, I raised the revolver for a desperation shot – no time to aim. In the same instant, I glimpsed Sonny lunging toward Blue, trying to throw himself in front of him.

He was too late.

The shotgun boomed, its recoil kicking her shoulder back.

At that distance – ten yards or so – a 12-gauge loaded with just about anything will fire a tight pattern. Sonny took only a few buckshot in the shoulder, but it was enough to turn him sideways.

The core of the pattern struck Blue full in the chest, knocking him backward against the fireplace, where he sank onto the floor.

Within a split second I had fired off a shot at her. It was one-handed instead of two, it was jerky instead of smooth. It was also lucky. The little .22 slug hit her in the left shoulder. It wouldn't have done much damage to a large man, but she was smaller, and she fell back, hit the wall, and slumped to the floor.

I walked toward her, having the presence of mind now to shift to the two-handed grip I'd been taught during a trip to the Chicago PD firing range. I heard Sonny groaning, but could not take my eyes off her, for two reasons. She was watching me. And she still held the shotgun.

'Don't do anything, Lita Ray.' I heard the pleading in my voice.

Smoke from the 12-gauge blast hung in the air. Her left arm lay on the floor at her side, apparently useless. Twisting her face with the effort, she began raising the barrel with her right.

'Don't.'

It swung slowly in my direction.

'Please.'

It was on me. Her lips moved soundlessly.

I ducked and fired at her head. My aim was good.

The shotgun barrel, looking like the mouth of Hell, erupted light and noise at me, and I felt the Devil's wind riffle my hair.

My knees hit the floor, just as the shotgun fell to the side with a clatter I could barely hear. My ears rang.

Lita Ray lay dead, a neat hole just above her right eye. The air smelled of burnt gunpowder.

I leaned over, and this time I was truly sick.

I found Sonny sitting by his father's body, just looking at him. Blue's chest was caved in, and I saw that he still gripped the bloody bottleneck in his right hand. His eyes looked up at the ceiling with no apparent interest.

I helped Sonny up, and slowly we made our way out through the kitchen and the back door. It felt as if we'd spent two days in that place, but it was still the middle of the night. He had two wounds to tend, I had one, and we must have looked almost comical the way we tried to help each other walk.

'Nearest house?' he asked. I had positioned him to my right,

303

because my left ear was still ringing like Quasimodo's bell tower.

'That way, I think,' squinting for the sight of lights amid the trees. We tried not to look at Kenneth Lively's body, which lay still draped across the hood of the SUV.

The light rain continued, but now it was more like a heavy mist. I looked up at the gray-black sky, opened my mouth wide, and drank in what I could. It felt cool. It tasted like a benediction.

'She said something to you,' Sonny commented. 'What was it?'

'I couldn't hear. She could have been just cussing me. It would be like her. But ...'

'Yeah?'

'I don't know. She might have been saying *Darnells take care of their own business*.'

EPILOGUE

Here we are at the end of the story. Way back at the beginning, I promised to tell you the truth. So was it true? Well, truth is a ball of mercury that, try as you might, you can't pluck up with your fingertips. And here's one of journalism's dirty little secrets, maybe the central one: Objective truth is impossible.

But human truth – truth as one person knows it – is within reach. That's what I tried to deliver, and I think the result is pretty good, if a little untidy. Journalists like to tie their stories up neatly, but often they find they must leave that to the historians. Life at close range is too messy.

The Cumberland Memorial Park and Civil War Study Center is one of our untidy loose ends. With Lem Coldsmith gone, most of the funding disappeared. And the public's support collapsed after the two soldiers' bodies were transferred, with all the respect due them, back to the place where they had fallen. The center will not rise on that beautiful piece of land below the falls.

Another loose end is Olen Stringer, but Forrest Wilkes, who is not a vindictive man, simply wants to forget him. That was made clear to me just the other day when I visited my father's new workplace, located not far from Wilkes Cottage.

Bowed but not broken by the collapse of his and Sonny's dream, he had quickly gone to work enlisting support for a much more modest project. Under the auspices of the University of Tennessee, money was raised to buy and renovate one of the Colony's shabbier and more neglected homes. Some rooms will be sleeping quarters for needy scholars, others will be used for seminars, still others for a library. It will be known simply as the Tennessee Civil War Study Center. No park, no theater, no splendid location. But it will be a place of learning, and Forrest Wilkes will be its director.

The latest and most violent events touched off what people like to call a media feeding frenzy in our little town, but after a while it died down, as these things always do. There was no way to prove the reason behind all the killings, so a convenient story took shape – that the Darnell clan had nourished a long-running hatred for the McMahans, one that eventually boiled over. Feuds are a part of our tradition here in the mountains, so that story had the ring of truth. It will have to do.

As the last leaves fell, the season became a time of funerals here. I went to Vern's because I'd been invited. And I attended Lita Ray's, even though I wasn't invited. I felt a faint, lingering affection for her and believed that whatever she had turned out to be was, in some twisted way, the work of her father, the man who birthed most of the evil in the story I've been telling you.

And, of course, I was there along with Sonny and Tish when they lowered Blue into the ground. A lot of the town's old-timers were there too, including Sis Lawlor. Faye, we discovered, had set aside a spot for him right next to hers. *Roam all you like, you rake and rambling boy*, she seemed to be saying. *Someday you'll lie alongside me.*

Sonny, it turned out, never hired anyone to replace me as ghost-writer of his memoir. Not long ago he asked me to take another crack at it, promising I could do a warts-and-all biography and even put my name on it. The country's ready for a politician who tells the truth, he said. This could be our ticket back. Yours and mine.

I'll always like Sonny. And the country may indeed be ready for the truth. But I'm not sure he is.

I told him I'd think about it.

What I didn't tell him was that I already had a job, because he would have laughed at it. A couple of weeks earlier, Charlene had asked me if I would like to work at the *Call*.

I thought you didn't need any reporters, I said.

This is not a reporter's job, she said. To be honest with you, I don't think you should be working as a reporter. This is a copy editor's job.

Oh, I said.

I had nothing against copy editors. I spent several months as one, early in my career, before I got locked irrevocably into the reporter's life. But it was sedentary, some would say dull. It wasn't about digging into people's lives or butting heads with politicians. It was about grammar and punctuation and syntax and accuracy. About addresses and the spelling of names, dates of births and deaths. All right, it was dull.

But it was journalism.

I'll do it, I said to her.

And now, after a few weeks, I'm getting to like it. I'm still a reporter at heart, but I enjoy going over stories to make sure they're accurate. To make sure they're true. Every now and then, one of the young reporters will drop by the copy desk and ask me what it was like to work in Chicago, and I'll tell stories about the *Examiner*. About covering a big murder story on the North Side and then matching Mike Royko drink for drink at the late, lamented O'Rourke's Pub. Telling those stories, I'll feel a bit old. But valuable. And still part of one of this planet's craziest and most necessary professions.

I know what you're thinking: After what I've done, is this the beginning of some kind of redemption? Will Randall Wilkes, the columnist who fell from grace, ever find his way back to the keyboard?

Who knows? Go ask H.L. Mencken.

Sometimes they'll question me about that night at the old hotel. And at that point I'll have to beg off, because it's still too early. The memories are too fresh, the nightmares still too frequent.

I awoke from one of them just the other night, sweating, breathing like a marathoner. Charlene reached over and touched me lightly on the shoulder and said, It's all right. Try to go back to sleep.

It *was* all right. And I did.

I still haven't seen her poke a fire, though …

Another night, when I couldn't sleep, I got up and walked through Charlene's house, checking doors and windows out of habit, listening to the gentle snoring coming from her grandfather's room. I settled in on the living room sofa and switched on the radio for company. To my surprise, it was tuned to WMO, and someone was playing a fast bluegrass fiddle tune, the notes coming out as clear and sparkling as the water cascading down a waterfall.

On impulse, I picked up the phone, dialed information, and a minute later I had the sole proprietor of WMO on the line.

'How are you, my friend?' he asked in a sleepy drawl.

'Just fine,' I said. 'Do you take requests?'

'I sure do. I'd rather take a request than just bore people by playing my favorites every night.'

'Do you have *Wildwood Flower*?'

'Oh, my Lord, yes. I've got, I think, three different versions of that one.'

'They usually play it fast, but do you have one that's slower? And just instrumental?'

'My friend, I think I've got just what you want. Who do I send this pretty song out to?'

I was ready with my answer.

'Play it for Callie,' I said.

available from
THE ORION PUBLISHING GROUP

☐ **Red Sky Lament** £6.99
EDWARD WRIGHT
978-0-7528-7819-5

☐ **Clea's Moon** £6.99
EDWARD WRIGHT
978-0-7528-7688-7

☐ **The Silver Face** £6.99
EDWARD WRIGHT
978-0-7528-6451-8

☐ **Damnation Falls** £6.99
EDWARD WRIGHT
978-0-7528-8184-3

All Orion/Phoenix titles are available at your local bookshop or from the following address:

Mail Order Department
Littlehampton Book Services
FREEPOST BR535
Worthing, West Sussex, BN13 3BR
telephone 01903 828503, *facsimile* 01903 828802
e-mail MailOrders@lbsltd.co.uk
(Please ensure that you include full postal address details)

Payment can be made either by credit/debit card (Visa, Mastercard, Access and Switch accepted) or by sending a £ Sterling cheque or postal order made payable to *Littlehampton Book Services.*
DO NOT SEND CASH OR CURRENCY

Please add the following to cover postage and packing

UK and BFPO:
£1.50 for the first book, and 50p for each additional book to a maximum of £3.50

Overseas and Eire:
£2.50 for the first book plus £1.00 for the second book and 50p for each additional book ordered

---

BLOCK CAPITALS PLEASE

name of cardholder ....

address of cardholder ....

delivery address
(*if different from cardholder*)

....

....

....

postcode ....

postcode ....

☐ I enclose my remittance for £ ....

☐ please debit my Mastercard/Visa/Access/Switch (delete as appropriate)

card number

expiry date   Switch issue no.

signature ....

prices and availability are subject to change without notice